CAPTURING THE QUEEN

DAMAGED HEROES: BOOK TWO

SARAH ANDRE

For more information regarding subsidiary rights, please contact the Publisher:

BEACH READS
11923 NE Sumner St, Ste 320134
Portland, OR 97250

Edited by Anya Kagan, Touchstone Editing
Cover Design by Christa Holland, Paper and Sage

Print ISBN: 978-1-946310-00-2
Digital ISBN: 9781946310019

To John, Dave, and Margaret.
After three novels, I think my readers are beginning to clue in
that my stories center around the deep love-hate complexities
of sibling relationships. This is not a reflection on you. Or you.
But maybe you... Have we started again?

1

Sean Quinn thrust a final time, grunting as nirvana flooded through him. His sated relief lasted mere seconds before morphing into such repulsive self-loathing it threatened to drop him. The diminutive brunette in his arms had saved him from utter humiliation back at the bar. It'd be really great if he could remember her name.

Shame drove him to kiss her damp neck and murmur an incoherent endearment. She panted heavily, eyes closed, head lolling against the graffiti-covered brick wall. The May breeze stirred her bangs and intensified the stench from the dumpster they stood behind. Rotting garbage mingled with her stale-cigarette breath and perfume that smelled like dying Stargazer lilies. The olfactory overload twitched his nostrils and sent down frantic flight messages from his brain. He loosened his grip on her thigh and slipped out of her, compulsively straightening her short skirt even though her panties were still clumped around her ankle.

The woman opened eyes the color of wet leather. They were devoid of emotion or animation or any sense of hope. Her smeared makeup and half-shadowed face reminded him of the disjointed Picasso he was restoring at work. Even though this had been her invitation and they'd both gotten off, it was pretty clear he hadn't done her self-esteem any favors.

"Gotta cig?"

Sean shook his head. Belatedly, he glanced around the dimly lit alley, then snapped off the condom and tossed it into the overflowing dumpster. A few minutes ago a crowded Wrigley Field could've watched—that was how much he'd needed to get his rocks off. He tucked himself back into his underwear and zipped his jeans.

God, he was scum. He never did shit like this. Why had he let Gretch get inside his head tonight? The expression she'd flashed from across the dance floor had reopened every adolescent wound he'd suffered at the hands of popular high school girls. Geeks like him would never get the homecoming queen. How many times did he have to humiliate himself before he got the message and stamped out the hope?

"You live around here?" the brunette asked.

Again, Sean shook his head.

Her laugh was more of an exhale, puffing from her nose. Maybe it was a sneer. "Not much of a talker, are you?"

"Guess not," he offered, instead of the instinctive shrug.

She'd made no attempt to reach for her panties. As he stooped for them, she kicked them aside. "Don't bother. They're filthy."

There was no accusation in her tone, but it reminded him again of how he'd ripped them down and plowed into her with the grace of a bull. How he'd pumped and pumped with barely restrained rage, staring at her full mouth because if he closed his eyes he'd see someone entirely different. Someone who'd used bolt cutters to slash through his carefully fabricated armor.

He'd give his Maria Callas aria collection to travel back to the moment he'd overheard Gretchen Allen tell their boss her Saturday night plans. Then he'd bitch-slap the hope out of his earlier self and stay home to finish *Crime and Punishment*. Most of the time he understood his place in society. Tonight's lesson? Casual wall sex with a stranger was soul-wrecking.

Sean stepped back a pace and shoved his hands in his pockets. The least he could do was offer to buy this woman another drink, but that meant going back inside Teenie's Martinis. Chancing another encounter with Gretch, who'd clearly hooked up with the metrosexual shithead she'd been obscenely grinding against. Sean blinked the image away, drained and desolate.

"Has anyone told you that you look exactly like Adrien Brody?"

Yep. Lots. He didn't consider it a compliment. "I gotta run," he said.

"Right. Early day tomorrow?" She smoothed her wall-snarled hair without looking at him.

"Something like that." He shifted his weight. The serenity of his tiny apartment called like a siren as he navigated the jagged rocks of after-sex banter. "Can I... pay for a taxi?" He didn't want to order an Uber—didn't want to know her address.

She glanced at the dented steel back door of the bar, as if the answer lay there, then her lips flattened. "Yeah. All right."

They walked in sync, but worlds apart toward Erie Street—her in high heels and no underwear, him shouldering epic self-disgust and the creepy-crawly need to wash. What the hell was her *name*?

The sounds of downtown Chicago on a Saturday

night grew louder. A horn honking, a shouted profanity, two women squealing with laughter...

Luck was with him at the curb, and he hailed a passing cab almost immediately. As he flipped open his wallet, she slid in and muttered an address to the driver. Sean shoved two twenties at him through the open front passenger window.

"Hey," she said softly, reaching to close her door. "What's your name again?"

Oh good. "Sean."

"Sean what?"

He paused. This was the time to say "Quinn," right? Then ask her name? Fatigue washed over him. "Does it matter?"

The driver cleared his throat. She ignored him and grinned at Sean, the smile never reaching the world-weariness in her eyes. "I guess not."

"Goodnight." Sean knocked on the roof twice and stepped back, watching until the taillights faded. He glanced back at the giant, neon-blue martini glass. Should he go back in? Make sure Gretch was okay? *Right. Like she needs protecting.* Like he hadn't learned his lesson with her a million times before.

Sean turned and trudged toward the Franklin El station. A screech of tires peeled around a corner behind him. He swiveled, blinded briefly by a flash of brights. A shiny black Suburban with illegally tinted windows crossed into the opposite lane and aimed straight for him. He lunged behind a lamppost just as the car jumped the curb and screeched to a halt, feet away.

The passenger door kicked open, and a suit got out. Crew cut. Bulge of a holstered gun, left side. Mirrored shades. At midnight. The stereotype almost made Sean laugh, but there was nothing funny about the FBI pinpointing his exact location. Or contacting him this late.

"Get in." Although respectful, Crew Cut's voice had the calmness of someone used to being obeyed. Feared.

"You've got the wrong guy."

The rear window whirred down, and Sean glanced back. *Son of a bitch!* Sure explained the dickhead vehicular dramatics. "I resigned, remember?" Sean snarled. "You applauded."

"Obey the nice man, Nancy. Get the fuck in."

AMID THE BODY-THUMPING TECHNO BEAT, Gretchen Allen squeezed through the crowd toward her housemate, her gaze flitting left and right. Of utmost importance was maintaining a cool and confident expression. She nodded to acquaintances, acknowledged the overt looks from men and the flashes of jealousy from women, but barely saw them.

Where is he? What a weird freaking night. To have encountered Sean "the Enigma" Quinn *here* of all places. He didn't do bars. Didn't even sit in the break room with the rest of them during lunch. Yet, not ten minutes ago, he'd stood at the edge of the dance floor, looking aloof and oh so hot... She couldn't have embarrassed herself more, gaping at him like a half-wit. Christ in a cradle!

Gretch craned her neck the other way, hunting for the stiffly out-of-place coworker in black jeans and a white button-down, instead of his usual slacker-wear. They were barely passing acquaintances, but she'd give her right arm to figure out what made him tick. Tonight she had home field advantage—maybe in this loud, boisterous atmosphere she wouldn't feel so stupid talking to a guy who was *soooo* cerebral that her only defense was to pelt him with snark.

No sign of him. *Damn it.* Maybe it had been a mirage...or someone who resembled him, because come on! Sean at a nightclub?

Gretch reached her housemate's side, unable to continue the blitheness of her façade. For some reason the night now stretched monotonously before her.

"Uh oh. That's your order-an-Uber-Dwayne-I-ain't-driving-you-home face." Her housemate boomed the good-natured, thoroughly incorrect observation, ignoring the stares his foghorn voice and massive bulk generated.

"I haven't decided," she called back. "You wanna cast a vote?" They both turned toward the jam-packed bar, and she tried to view her LVR app date, Brandon, through her housemate's eyes. Tall, blond, fit... Without a doubt the hottest guy here. A great dancer. And best of all, she'd only caught genuine male interest—nothing predatory or freaky about him.

"Doable," she declared flatly, turning back to Dwayne. She clasped his shoulder and eased off a stiletto, wiggling her pinched toes. If only she could snap her fingers and be home, curled up on the sofa, laughing at one of Dwayne's porn-style critiques of a romcom hero.

"On the pro side—" Dwayne tapped his chin with an index finger, "I like the whole Norse Viking thing he's got going on. Very delicious. But massive points off for the incessant need to flash his cash at every available opportunity. Trés bourgeois."

Brandon was at that very moment stripping off bills, grinning at the bartender's quip amid the teeming throng clamoring for drinks. *Even, white teeth. Lovely smile.* She could get through this.

Her date du jour clutched two martini glasses and searched over the heads of the crowd, spotting her immediately. She smiled at the compliment. He smiled back and jerked his chin.

Dwayne imitated a game show buzzer. "And massive deductions for that entitled-white-male expression. Big yuck."

"Oh, shut up," Gretch said through her laughter. "You'd do him in a second."

"But we're voting on whether he's good enough for you, your highness."

Brandon strode unhesitatingly through the crowd, his innate assurance seeming to part the masses before him. Okay, a little arrogant, but a man with a healthy sense of self-worth helped feed the perpetual black hole inside her. She was beautiful and desirable enough to capture a guy like this. Her stomach roiled, but ignoring the reaction was second nature, and Gretch increased the flirt in her smile as Brandon closed the final yards.

"Final verdict," Dwayne said in her ear. "I stood next to him in the urinal. I vote: oh hell yes."

So be it. Gretch squeezed back into the narrow stiletto. "My best friend from childhood, Dwayne Collins," she introduced. "Brandon Myers. He's in banking too." As expected, the men launched into a quick six degrees of separation to find commonalities. Gretch sipped her martini. It tasted like battery acid, and she grimaced.

"...hedge fund portfolio manager," Brandon ended.

"I'm on the other end of the spectrum," Dwayne boomed. "I cull your clients for signs of money laundering. Hang the rich!" His belly laugh jiggled his chins. More people paused and glanced their way.

Gretch smiled at Brandon, who did not look amused. *Hmm.* Getting along with her childhood bestie wasn't a make-or-break factor, but it was definitely a canary in a coal mine. Maybe this was a mistake...

Brandon turned to her. "Let's head out."

Her spine stiffened at the curt command. Sign number two. No one ordered her around. *Was* this a mistake? Why was her antenna so fucked up tonight? Behind him, Dwayne made silly googly eyes at her date. Gretch relaxed. Everything was fine. Her evening had just been thrown for a loop, was all. "I haven't finished this drink." She sipped the battery acid again, partly so Brandon understood that she held all the control, but mostly for courage.

With the ruthless cruelty of a Disney stepmother, she ignored the inner protests and slipped her hand in his. This was the price she paid. And she was prepared to pay it over and over until she finally filled the gaping pit others called a soul.

Sean climbed into the Suburban and slammed the door. "Has hell frozen over?"

"Don't flatter yourself," his oldest brother said. "I'm not happy to be working with you either."

"Glad we agree for once. Have your Men in Black drive me home."

Jace Quinn, suited like the assholes in front, nodded to the driver watching in the rearview mirror. The Suburban bumped off the curb and smoothly ran a red light, the glow washing Jace's tense profile in soft rose hues. "I need you to identify something." His tone was low. Not because of the goons in front. Because he was embarrassed to ask for help.

Sean was the youngest of five Black Irish boys from the South Side. His older brothers, aged a year apart, had dominated their rough neighborhood growing up. They were collectively responsible for the state football championship trophies the high school still proudly displayed, and each had signed up for multiple tours of duty in Iraq and Afghanistan.

And then there was Sean. Seven years younger than

the Pack. Uninterested in team sports. Skeptical of the patriotic dogma masking the blundering greed for oil that had given rise to Al-Qaeda and ISIS. But his worst faults in the Quinn family's eyes? His archaeology and fine arts degrees. Conserving and restoring art for a living. Devouring opera and classical literature in his downtime.

Yeah, it was all fun and games bashing baby brother's sissy lifestyle until they needed his expertise. Sean thumbed the road behind him. "I live in the opposite direction."

"I'm not fucking around here, Sean." Jace inhaled like he was about to go off on a rant, then glanced at the men in front and exhaled, jaw tight. "We think another avenue opened up and artifacts are being smuggled in through O'Hare. I just need you to authenticate something so we can begin tracing it to ISIL operations."

"Newsflash: you and I were a disaster working in the same organization."

"Knock off the histrionics. You quit because I made you look bad."

Because you took all the credit for work I did. Sean shook his head mutely, staring ahead.

"Besides, the contract anthropologist works normal hours. I want to tag this smuggler tonight, red-handed."

Ah, yes. No human on earth was more dangerous than Jason Robert Quinn with something to prove. That explained this mini kidnapping. Jace, a former SEAL, was still incensed at being hired at the bottom of the FBI operations hierarchy. In a nod to Lady Irony, special agents were required to have a college degree. Given Jace's military expertise, the Chicago field office was piloting a new associate program, fast-tracking vets like Jace into SA positions while they attended night school, but at the moment Jace was still humping along as a lowly special agent *associate*.

Both the driver and Crew Cut stayed silent. If either of them were in charge, they'd have done the talking, which meant this late-night espionage trip was Jace's idea and probably not even sanctioned by the FBI. "Shouldn't you three have a special agent supervising you?"

His brother cuffed him, which wasn't uncommon. Crew Cut chuckled a nasty sound. Sean rubbed his head, hardly registering the blow as much as the double sting to his pride. First: he hated his baby brother role. He was twenty-nine and a magna cum laude, for fuck's sake, and yet here he was, speeding toward O'Hare against his will. And second: he hated his need to matter in some tiny way to his superhero brother. Despite protesting, he was going along with this mission with all the starch of a wet noodle. Why not admit it? He was intrigued to use his intellect to assist the FBI again, and treacherous baby brother puffed with pride at being chosen for the ride-along.

"What's the situation?" he asked quietly.

Jace reached into a briefcase at his feet and withdrew a thick manila file. "We received a tip from the subcontracting company that supplies O'Hare's janitors and baggage handlers. They believe one of the nightshift custodians is smuggling in small items stowed beneath seats. My men are interrogating him at the TSA office right now, but he's one big 'I don't know.' Which is where you come in."

The file landed on Sean's lap. He turned on the overhead and leafed through the pages slowly. The top report confirmed what most Americans already knew: ISIS, or ISIL, as the government referred to them, smuggled Syrian and Iraqi antiquities to the West in an ongoing effort to pay for weapons and recruiting. Whereas ISIS had previously contracted with diggers and levied a twenty percent tax on their sales, the report showed an alarming new trend: they'd assumed a corporate-like control over all aspects of the digs, equipment, dealers, and middlemen. Even more disturbing, the group had become experts on the values of certain relics and targeted those biblical sites for excavation.

"This item you want me to inspect," Sean said, scanning pictures of previously captured contraband, "do you know the country of origin?"

"No, but the plane arrived this evening from Frankfurt."

Sean checked his watch. Most of O'Hare would be dead quiet. The nightshift custodians were probably sparser and less supervised, and undoubtedly could take a lot longer cleaning cabins than their dayshift counterparts. "Conflict antiquities headed for the West are usually smuggled through Turkey or Lebanon," he said.

"We know. Now we need to know value, origin, and whether the piece has ever had any legitimate paperwork."

"Provenance," Sean corrected, leafing through more pictures of mosaic tiles, clay jars, and jewelry the FBI now possessed. He closed the file and watched the night speed by. Intrigue pumped a second wind into him. A potentially priceless artifact... Quite a different ending to what had been a disastrous evening. "Did you trace me through my cell phone?"

"When I didn't find you tucked in your bed on a Saturday night? Yes."

Thank God the Suburban hadn't arrived five minutes earlier.

"Why were you out barhopping? You don't even drink." Oddly enough, Jace looked like he was interested in the answer.

"I wasn't barhopping." *I'd finally gotten up the courage to ask out a coworker. Until I saw the look on her face.*

Jace arched a brow. "Trolling to get laid?"

A snort from Crew Cut in front. Sean handed the file back without answering. A right cross, left hook combo would instantly dislocate both their jaws. Sean visualized the exact degree of torso twist, the power of his delivery, the crack of bones. He had a shelf jam-packed with martial arts and kickboxing awards; he could pull this off. But then Mom's birthday dinner at the Quinn house next week would be a bitch. Not to mention being arrested on federal felony assault charges.

"ETA five minutes," the driver said.

Sean breathed in slowly, centering his chi. "How long will this take?"

"Dunno."

"Ballpark it, Jace," he snapped. "I have a shitload of work in the morning."

"It's Sunday, stupid."

"The billionaire waiting for his art doesn't care."

His brother folded his arms, his expression falsely sympathetic. "Aw, cleaning paintings for a living. Sure sucks to be you."

If only Jace possessed the skill of properly motivating people. One microscopic gesture of appreciation would go so much further than being a Quinn bully. Sean stared out the window, rapidly tap-tapping the side of his thumb on his thigh.

"Fuck you, too," his brother murmured.

Sean grinned without looking over. So the former SEAL, decorated war veteran, dickhead of a brother still remembered Morse code. Long ago, that shared skill had changed their relationship. One of the few times Sean had captured his hero brother's respect. Emphasis on *long ago.*

THE TWO-WAY MIRROR provided a perfect view of the stark and brightly lit observation room. The plaque on the door read *Federal Inspection Station Holding Cell.* Inside, a task force from TSA, FBI, ICE, and CPD ringed the perimeter, each in a threatening arms-crossed, legs-spread stance. Jace sat across from the custodian, barking out questions that were answered in broken-English, but stubbornly repetitive "I don't knows."

On the other side of the mirror Sean fisted his hands in his pockets, awaiting the arrival of the smuggled item. Evidently it had been taken through a TSA screening machine to make sure it wasn't a bomb. Which was sharp foresight, given the plane had landed after a ten-hour overseas flight and the passengers were long gone. Sean glanced at his watch. Almost one. He had to be at work at eight. The epically humiliating evening at Teenie's Martinis seemed like days ago, although the woman's perfume had transferred onto him, so the essence of his remorse filled his every breath. *My kingdom for a shower.*

He leaned against the small conference table and wearily tuned back in to the interrogation, which was going nowhere. What had been established was that the man, Ahmet Asuman, was a green card immigrant from Turkey. He'd worked as a third-shift custodian for four years and had a clean employee record. He didn't know who'd taped the item to the bottom of seat 23A, he didn't know anyone in Germany, and he didn't know what was in the package. He'd found it when his vacuum bumped a hard object. It sounded legit to Sean, but Jace leaned over the table, getting all up in Asuman's face.

"If we pull security tape for every day you've worked, will we see you holding other packages that your *vacuum* has bumped?"

"I don't know."

"It's a yes or no question, Mr. Asuman. Have you found items before?"

Sweat sheened Asuman's forehead. His black eyes were wide and wild as he cast about the room for his answer. "Maybe. One, two times?"

"What did you do with the packages?"

The custodian scanned the formidable task force surrounding him and swallowed convulsively. "Threw them out."

"The security tapes will show that?"

"No. At home I throw them out."

Jace nodded affably, like he'd expected this answer. Sean stiffened at the casual body language. You had to know Jace to recognize nothing about him was affable right now.

"When were these one or two times?" Jace asked.

"I don't know."

Jace pointed to a TSA official. "Start pulling security tapes and have them sent to my office." He also nodded at Crew Cut, who walked out with the officer. Sean grinned despite himself at Jace's gravitas. If only Asuman or the officials in there realized this interrogation was being conducted by the FBI's version of a grunt.

Seconds later, Sean's door opened and a TSA officer walked in with a package wrapped in brown parcel paper and thick string. Strands of duct tape dangled from the sides. "No trace of explosives. Couldn't distinguish what it was in the x-ray. To be honest, it looks like junk."

The gloved guard placed it on the table and Sean knocked on the mirror. When Jace got out of his chair several officers clustered toward the door, too. Sean pulled disposable latex gloves from a wall dispenser box, snapped them on, and took a seat, not bothering to look up as the group trooped in. His brother sank into the seat next to him and handed over a sizeable Swiss Army knife.

Sean snipped the strings, heart beating faster at the possibilities within. He gently unwrapped the package and pulled away the padded cotton. His breath stilled. "It's...it's a cuneiform tablet."

Jace twitched impatiently. "Speak English."

Sean pointed at the wedge shapes etched in the ancient clay. "These are some of the earliest forms of writing that archeologists have found." He rummaged through his recollection. "The text could be Akkadian."

"What does it say?"

Sean shook his head. "I'm only slightly familiar with Mesopotamian anthropology. It could be a letter or an inventory list... Maybe part of a diary." He studied the beautiful piece. "I can't tell you its value, either."

"Okay. The bureau can scour eBay and art auction sites for similar items."

Using both hands, Sean gently picked up the tablet, as heavy as a dictionary. Underneath, littering the cotton wrapping, were grains of sand. "Freshly plucked from its ancient home," he murmured. "If I had to hazard a guess, this came from the biblical city of Mari. In Syria. There's incredible looting going on in that region, and they're known for having thousands of tablets on all aspects of their lives." He glanced up at Jace hovering beside him. "And if I'm right, then we're looking at around three thousand BC."

A couple of officials whistled under their breaths. Sean rewrapped the cotton around the plundered artifact, his adrenalin waning. Watching the news clip of ISIS decimating the Temple of Bel in Palmyra, a biblical site so precious to all cultures, he'd wanted to weep. Such powerlessness in the face of mass desecration. Which was worse: ripping an ancient culture from the ground both as psychological warfare and to buy weapons, or bombing the site to smithereens because it was pagan to fundamentalist Islamic beliefs?

Sean refolded the brown wrapping. "Sorry I can't tell you more."

His brother clapped his shoulder and squeezed, a gesture so unfamiliar that Sean flinched. Jace let go like he'd been burned. "No worries, little brother."

"Get the FBI to rehire me," Sean blurted. "I'll consult on this smuggling operation." In the silence that followed, he prayed for the ground to swallow him up. Seriously, could he sound more like a five-year-old wanting to join the big boys? *Pick me, Jace, pick me.* Memories of that particular plea rose to the surface. The agony when it never happened. Sean tried to channel his earlier reluctance for getting into the Suburban. It was so much safer not caring what you meant to other people. But that dignified guy had been replaced by a pathetic spectacle burning for a crumb of Jace's respect.

His brother stood, the deliberation on his face crystal clear: his visceral need to solve complex cases and impress the brass warring with working alongside a brother whose oddities baffled him. "How else could you help?"

Sean motioned to Asuman, slumped dejectedly in his chair. "Whoever he's selling the tablet to will have a lot more artifacts. I can go in as a buyer."

"Too dangerous."

"I'm a fourth-degree black belt."

Jace picked up the package. "Yeah, I can see handing Mom that bit of logic when the bad guys show up with AK-47s."

Sean shot up, tipping his chair. The police officer behind him jumped aside. "Sorry." Sean snatched the chair and shoved it under the table. Why couldn't he just shut up? These guys were getting the full spectacle of the pathetic Quinn family dynamics. Up next: whining and clinging to Jace's leg. Yeah. It'd happened. Chicago's Air and Water Show, age eight. Sean still hadn't gotten over the humiliation.

He straightened his shoulders and reached deep for a reasonable tone. "You'll need someone who knows the worth of the pieces. The lingo. The condition. I can consult through an earpiece if you don't want me near the dealer." He closed with motivation too enticing for Jace to ignore: "You know my expertise will make you look good. And I could potentially help disrupt a terrorist supply chain." *Pick me, Jace.*

His brother exhaled loudly. "Fine." He didn't look over. "I'll pull some strings. Don't fuck this up." He nodded to the driver. "Take him home."

3

"How long will you tolerate his beatings before you to take a stand?" Gretch's frustrated tone barely walked the edge of compassion. Yes, it was totally over the line. Even Zamira, sitting in the next cubicle, raised her eyebrows. Gretch nodded her understanding of the inappropriate comment, but damn it! She was action-oriented. You have a problem? Solve it! Encouraging victims filled with so much fear they remained paralyzed both tested and inspired her.

This caller, Eve Last-Name-Unknown, was her kryptonite. For two months the smart, well-spoken woman had called regularly, and Gretch had quickly bonded with her. Weeks of applying all her training: empathetic listening, providing resources, encouragement... Even offering her own cell number as a catalyst had failed. The woman remained stubbornly stuck in her clogged sewer of a marriage.

"I apologize," Gretch said into the headset, although the latest story of the bastard's abuse ignited a visceral need to shriek and throw the device. "I have no right to speak to you that way."

"It's okay," Eve said softly. "This isn't who he is. Really. If only his job wasn't so stressful."

Gretch opened her mouth, but a snarky retort hovered too close. She let silence slide her skepticism across the open line. In the background of Eve's home, cartoon hijinks and giggles erupted. Eve had mentioned two daughters before. So far the husband had kept his hands off them, but how long before his abuse lashed out further?

Zamira leaned over Gretch's shoulder and tapped the first item on the crimson Chicago Abuse Hotline poster stapled to the cubicle. *Do not become emotionally involved with the caller.* Gretch had broken that rule by week two.

"Get a grip," Zamira mouthed, gently wrestling Gretch's empty coffee mug from her clenched fingers. Gretch nodded. To be of any benefit, she had to step back from the edge.

"Is he home now?" she asked Eve, smoothing the caller intake sheet on the clipboard beside her. *Abuser on premises? Emergency assistance requested?*

"He's at work."

"Do you need me to call nine-one-one or get a volunteer to take you to the ER?"

"I've got ice packs on my bruises, I'll be fine." Eve sighed. "I just needed to hear your voice. Talking to you makes me feel sane."

Gretch stopped ticking items off the sheet. "You *are* sane," she said, emphasizing each word with the energy of her old personal training job. "His anger may be directed at you, but you *know* this is not about you. You're a good person. You have the right to be loved and be happy. You also have incredible strength and courage—"

"Oh, come on, Gretch. If I were any of those things, he wouldn't get so angry with me." Eve's voice wavered on the last word.

Gretch stared at the poster's rules. No magic words there to get Eve to see the light. "Only you have the power to change your world and get out from under this, Eve. We can brainstorm steps right now."

Zamira set down Gretch's refilled mug, the coffee a perfect shade of creamy brown. Cinnamon dotted the swirling top and filled the air with homey comfort. Gretch inhaled deeply and closed her eyes. As much as these calls ate away at her faith in basic human decency, her Sunday shifts with Zamira were among her favorite hours all week. Gretch grinned over and touched her fingertips to her chin, withdrawing them a few inches— the ASL sign for *thank you*. During slow shifts, Zamira taught her the elegant language of the deaf culture, and it was so damn cool.

"I have to go," Eve said, and the grin slid off Gretch's face.

"Wait—"

"I'm grateful for your time, Gretch. I'll be okay because he really does love me. Last week, he left some flowers from the garden and a note saying he was sorry."

The rote sentences came as no surprise, but guilt still squeezed Gretch's heart. Except for the one time she'd convinced Eve to start a plan, each call ended with this tone of resignation. As always, Gretch reiterated her assurance of support, but when the line disconnected, she slid the headset off with a frustrated grunt.

"One day she'll be ready," Zamira said in her rich, soothing voice. Her fingers shaped each word gracefully as she spoke.

Gretch recognized the signs for *one* and *day*. She also knew a few swear words, which she signed back. "Give me five minutes with that husband," she retorted, jaw stiff.

"Unwise. That man has no problem hitting a woman."

Another call came through, and Zamira reached for her headset, placing it carefully over her elegant peach hijab. "Your shift ended ten minutes ago. Go enjoy your Sunday."

Gretch made no move to leave, although she straightened the cubicle for the next volunteer, Sandra, who was chronically late. No way would Gretch leave Zamira alone. What if another call came in? No one deserved to be put on hold when it took every ounce of courage to place the call in the first place.

Gretch scrubbed her fingers through her hair, both to release frustration and fluff up her headset hairdo. *Enjoy your Sunday.* Knowing Eve would face that bastard when *his* shift ended?

Gretch sipped her coffee. Her day was officially wrecked. She should just go home and do laundry. No, Dwayne was visiting his family; being alone when she was this frustrated wasn't a good idea. Maybe head to the gym and lift weights until her muscles shrieked as loudly as the thoughts in her head? Too many men. She couldn't deal with the entire gender at the moment. She needed a place that renewed her faith in couples in love. A walk through Lincoln Park? Watch the world go by at D'Angelo's Café? It had received top reviews in last Sunday's *Tribune* for romantic ambiance. Granted, it was across the city, but the afternoon loomed, lonely and empty.

On the corner of the desk, her muted phone screen lit with an incoming text. Brandon.

You left too soon. Let's meet up so I can repay the (.gif of fireworks bursting.)

A shudder rolled through her. She typed a cryptic blow-off. Men were not on the agenda today. At all.

Even in the blinding afternoon sun, Sean recognized Gretch's willowy figure and spiky platinum hair like he would a Bernini masterpiece or the first strands of La Boheme's *Che Gelida Manina* aria. His heart beat so erratically that if EKG leads had been stuck to his torso, an ambulance would be screaming in the distance. The sudden hush couldn't be his imagination. He glanced around and yep—the other patrons were as drawn to her as if an asteroid streaked toward the peaceful café.

Gretch jaywalked across the wide street, her long-legged stride and confident poise a smoke-and-mirrors trick hiding her prickly temperament. Okay, that wasn't accurate. She defined bold majesty, like some mythological warrior goddess. She took what she wanted, said what was on her mind, and didn't suffer gawking fools. He'd fallen hard for her fearlessness, her determination to live life on her terms, but he'd quickly learned to worship her from afar. Any verbal encounter meant matching her acerbic wit to the point of a WWE smackdown. He'd reigned as champion until last night, across the bar's dance floor. He hadn't been able to shut down the pathetic pining fast enough.

Sean set down his tea cup before the tremor in his fingers outed him further. *Pull it together!*

So he'd fucked up last night. The bar scene was her turf, and being the best restorer at Moore and Morrow was his. But here—this café? It was the perfect place to finally show her he was dateable. *Hi, have a seat. Can I buy you a coffee?* How hard was that? What if they had a great conversation? Found lots in common? Sean steadied his erratic breathing, as if facing down a martial arts opponent.

She headed closer, her eyes locking on to the last

empty wrought-iron table just as a couple carrying a loaded tray nabbed the seats. Sean grinned at the haughty displeasure flashing across her face.

Those *Queen of Fucking Everything* expressions. Last year he'd impulsively bought a tin of peppermints with that phrase emblazoned across the lid, but it still lay at the bottom of his knapsack because she was so out of his league. Today? This was serendipitous. *Hi, have a seat. Can I buy you a coffee?*

At ten feet away, her gaze landed on him. Her stride stalled. His introverted instinct was to pretend he didn't see her, but one did not *not* notice Gretch. Sean forced his hand into an indifferent wave.

She scanned the populated tables once more and halted at his. The perfect spring day morphed into air so oppressive he had to breathe through his mouth. His heart thudded like a conga drum. *Here goes.* "Hi—"

"You do realize you're taking up an entire table for four."

The invitation died on his lips. His sarcastic alter ego awoke like Godzilla. "Is this your charm-school way of asking to sit with me?"

"Hell no. I can't tolerate men today."

"I see." He ignored the insecure side of him that was paralyzed by her ire. She'd said *men*, so A: this wasn't about him; and B: she'd included him in the species subset. His brothers wouldn't have been that generous. Sean touched the knapsack at his feet. "Allow me to vacate, so that you, a single, can occupy the table for four."

She pursed her lips. Not like his logic had stumped her—more like she'd expected her brushoff to be met with laughter and a second, *cajoling* invitation to sit with him. His breath streamed out. *Oh shit.* Why couldn't he instinctively know how to act before everything became a social gaffe?

He sat back and kicked out the opposite chair with his foot. "Have a seat."

"How gallant." Gretch folded into it sideways, hooking a slim leg over the arm. He'd never seen her in jeans, and impossibly, they emphasized her coltish legs more than miniskirts. Her stilettos were a shiny Ferrari red and sharply tapered at the toe. She cocked her head and assessed him with eyes a unique blend of rosy brown and kobicha. In his spare time, he'd tried to re-create that exact shade with his paint palette, to no avail.

She seemed oblivious to the men around her, but their voracious glances emboldened him.

"They don't have wait service out here," he said without stuttering, drooling, or his voice cracking. "Can I get you a coffee? Pastry?" *A tin of mints that describes you perfectly?*

"No. Thank you." She tapped long, red nails on the table. "Any more caffeine and I'll turn into a comic book supervillain."

And this was where he got stuck. Should he cite stats on caffeine and its effects on the human body? He could expound for hours. What would guys like Jace do with that cute supervillain remark? *They'd say something cute and goofy back. Do it!*

"You, uh—smell like cayenne pepper." He chugged his decaffeinated tea. *Seriously, it'd be so great to choke and die on the spot.*

She arched a brow. "Why are you here?"

He glanced at his cup instead of replying.

"I mean, why aren't you cleaning the Wickham art? You told Hannah you'd finish this weekend."

"I worked all day. I'll wrap up tomorrow." He frowned

at the third degree. It wasn't like she was his boss. "Why are you here?" *So much for serendipity.*

Gretch nodded at the D'Angelo Café sign with royal indifference. "The grand opening was written up in the *Tribune*." She kicked her leg around and sat up. Her heel struck the pavement with a sharp click. "Why were you at Teenie's Martinis last night?"

He swallowed convulsively. Answer honestly or with protective snark? He placed the cup on the table, turning it in microscopic increments until the café logo faced him squarely. "I overheard you tell Hannah where you were going." He traced the logo with his thumbnail. "Thought I'd check it out. Buy you a drink."

"Then why didn't you?"

He paused. He'd braced for: *"I'd have to be awfully drunk to accept a drink from you."* What now? No way would he tell Gretch he'd lost his nerve, bumped into the other woman slinking his way out the back door, and succumbed to her lewd proposition. "Turns out I'm not into that scene." *Any of it.* But because Gretch hadn't battered him with the sentence he'd expected, he added, "So...would you have had a drink with me?"

She cocked her head and examined her nails instead of answering. Sean glanced at the patrons, the bustling square, the long shadows easing toward their table. Five cars slowed for the traffic light. He retraced the logo, his knee jiggling. He should've chosen snark, because whatever came out of her mouth next would wound deep. Her silence strained every muscle in him, stretching him like some medieval torture rack. Five more seconds and he'd beg for mercy.

"You're a nice guy," she said in that awful, kind tone his brothers' girlfriends used. He braced for The Adjectives. Weird. Strange. Peculiar... Gretch rested her arms halfway across the table, fingers splayed, still looking at them instead of him. "I was so sure I couldn't tolerate any man this afternoon without going ballistic, but you're...different."

Hope rose. Different wasn't bad! "Maybe we can—"

A faint smile appeared on her face, and his vocal cords seized. Hope swan-dived off Kilimanjaro, the free fall stealing his oxygen.

"You'd never survive me, Sean."

The nerd panicking within wholeheartedly believed her. The fourth-degree black belt took exception. "You hardly know me."

"I date a certain kind of guy for a certain kind of reason." She reached over and twisted his cup so the logo slanted at an unacceptable sixty-two-degree angle. Immediately his skin crawled with the need to right it, but she'd stuck her chin in her hand and waited, that faint smile still in place, like a cat watching a cornered mouse.

He folded his arms. "And what insurmountable feat does it take to be that guy?" His jiggling knee made the table quake.

Gretch laughed, and the throaty sound washed over him, almost capturing his attention from the cup that needed turning. Desperately.

"It'd take a miracle." She rose gracefully. "See you at work."

Sean multitasked dragging the cup into position, watching the smooth sway of her hips, and thinking up a miracle. She wouldn't tolerate chasing. It'd be smarter to ignore her for a day or two—act as if this encounter hadn't taken place. He inhaled until his lungs hurt. Amid the dominant aromas of coffee, gas fumes, and cigarette smoke, he could still catch her peppery scent.

His smile hurt his cheeks. She'd called him *different*. That was huge.

4

———

"My name is Sami Adyton," the distinguished elderly gentleman said, bowing over Gretch's outstretched hand instead of shaking it. "I have an appointment with Walter Morrow."

Gretch beamed at his gallantry and covertly assessed the two men flanking him. Both were steroid-massive and grim. The one on the right, staring at her with undisguised interest, held a carry-on suitcase horizontally. Interesting. The art restored at Moore and Morrow drew insanely wealthy clients, but no one had ever brought their projects in under bodyguard before. Or maybe Adyton felt safer with them around, given the cane in his right hand.

"He's expecting you, sir." Gretch gestured toward the open doors of the conference room. "Please have a seat in there."

She popped into Walter's office, but her boss was on the phone, looking cross as he scribbled notes in a file.

"I know it's critical," he barked. "I said I'd do it. Do you really need to lecture me on this, Joe?"

The navy suit was one of his best, a sure sign of the

importance of his upcoming presentation on why Adyton's art deserved Moore and Morrow's expertise. He glanced up, and she motioned to the conference room. "He's here," Walter said solemnly. "Okay." And hung up.

"Adyton brought two bodyguards."

No surprise flickered across Walter's face. Doubly interesting. What was in that suitcase?

Walter stood and straightened his already-straight crimson power tie. His nervous expression was so atypical that Gretch blurted, "You look fine. What are they bringing us?"

Walter picked up a thin file, clearly avoiding eye contact. "Don't you have payroll to attend to?"

Gretch frowned. "You know I'll have to write up the acquisition contract anyway."

He passed her without comment. He never acted like this. He never used that rude tone of voice. What was going on? She followed him out. "Should I bring coffee?"

He turned at the conference room entrance. "Payroll, Gretch."

The second the door clicked behind him, she marched into his office and scooped up his outgoing mail, scanning the papers littering his desk. An inventory list that had handwritten Arabic scrawled in the margins snagged her attention.

Adyton's name was typed in as seller, and Tomas Hussain was listed as buyer. There were twenty items on the list, and the total of a hundred thousand dollars circled at the bottom. Warehouse location on Knox. Gretch whistled as she crept from the office and hurried down to Hannah's. Her bestie would cough up why Walter was acting like they were accepting the Crown Jewels. Maybe they were—a hundred thousand dollars' worth.

"...hope to finish the Picasso shortly," Hannah said

into the phone. "We'll be ready to transport and rehang this final set at your convenience, sir." Her face was in flames, her shoulders hitched like a coat hanger was wedged in the back of her lab coat. Had she not named the artist, it still would've been obvious who the client was. "Yes... I meant to call you, Harrison. Sir." Hannah cringed.

Gretch took a seat, smiling her encouragement. How awkward to feel so intimidated by a client who'd probably be your father-in-law before year's end.

After a few more stilted comments, Hannah hung up and pantomimed blowing her brains out. "It never gets easier."

Neither did telling Hannah to grow a backbone with Harrison Wickham. "Does Walter know Arabic?"

Hannah's harried expression morphed into a blank look. "Not that I know of. Why?"

"He's meeting with a Sami Adyton," Gretch said. "I don't have a proposal started. What's the project?"

"Jeez, I can't recall." Hannah rubbed her forehead, clearly on mental overload managing staff and restoration projects, dealing with her sick great-aunt, and moving to a new condo with Devon, who spent most weeks back in New York cleaning up some corporate mess.

"It was in a suitcase, and the client brought two bodyguards."

"Wow." Hannah's brow knitted. "Nothing's ringing a bell."

"Are we supposed to get a huge project?" Gretch pressed. Surely Hannah—the co-owner—would know. She'd have to staff for it. "I saw a list on Walter's desk. Twenty artifacts worth a hundred thousand dollars." She held up Walter's outgoing mail as proof she was supposed to be hanging around his desk.

Her bestie shrugged in apology. "I'll speak to him as soon as he's through."

That was about the time Gretch would know, too. He'd need contracts drawn up. No doubt Sean would be chosen as the restoration tech. This was where his obsessive-compulsive tendencies became precious assets.

"Boss?" Sean said from behind.

Gretch started and twisted in her chair. See, the problem with Sean was he moved with the litheness of a panther. Not like he had a slight build or tiptoed. He just constantly appeared out of thin air, taking her by surprise.

As Hannah greeted him, Gretch frowned. He stood in the doorway making direct eye contact with Hannah as if Gretch weren't three feet away. As if they hadn't shared a café table yesterday, where he'd clearly indicated he wanted to be more than coworkers.

"You're late," she snapped. Not that she had the slightest administrative pull. Nor did she give a shit what time Sean strolled in. It was just an irrational need to keep stripping away the stoic, almost bored expression he always wore. Besides, it was only common courtesy for him to notice her.

His unreadable dark eyes shifted and swept over her camouflage-print minidress. The flare in his nostrils was barely perceptible—Hannah probably hadn't caught it— but confidence bloomed hot in Gretch's chest.

"Is it army-dress-up day?" he asked. His perpetually quizzical eyebrows rose a fraction higher. "Did I not get the memo again?"

Ugh! He was such an ass sometimes. Not one man riding the El this morning had taken his eyes off her, and vanity aside, she'd expected it. Ever since puberty, she'd been a magnet for the baser side of men. Except Sean. His M.O. was no reaction. Even yesterday, when she'd tossed his passive attempt to ask her out back in his face, he hadn't blinked. No disappointment, no surprise, nothing. Army-dress-up day! "If only you knew a sexy dress when you saw one."

He lifted a shoulder in a halfhearted shrug. "The mud color bleaches your skin. Now your choice of makeup has too much yellow tint."

"Sean," Hannah admonished, shooting Gretch a look of warning.

"Just explaining the logic behind the color wheel."

Gretch huffed out a breath. Of all the people to hand out fashion advice. But why escalate? The men on the El hadn't been looking at her skin tone, and Sean wasn't looking at her figure. His precision at eyeballing hues and blurting his opinion without regard to whether he insulted someone was legendary. Walter had stopped parading new clientele past their golden boy long ago.

"Was there something you wanted?" Hannah asked him in a gentler tone.

"Logistics of this week." He straightened and stuffed his fists in his pockets. "The Picasso will be done by the end of the day. If Dane can crate Wickham's collection, I'll start on the Art Institute's Etruscan mosaic."

"Walter's meeting with someone." Again the look of bafflement. It wasn't like Hannah not to know incoming and outgoing art pieces like a mother knows her children. "His new project might take priority."

Sean nodded. "Okay. Let me know." He knocked twice on the threshold, his annoying signal that he was done with the effort of being social.

Before he could step into the hall, Gretch called, "And you didn't submit your timecard Friday. If you want a paycheck, I better have it by ten."

He pivoted back. An expression so raw and primal crossed his face that her heart thunked to a stop, then thudded up again painfully. Who was *this* Sean? Before she even finished the thought, his standard sardonic grin reappeared. "Sir, yes, sir." He saluted then disappeared down the hall without a sound.

"Insufferable!" She stood and smoothed her darling dress. Why hadn't he shown her this side yesterday? She totally would have said...*maybe.*

"What's going on between you guys?" Hannah asked.

"Nothing." Gretch threw her an easy grin and headed for the door. "Absolutely nothing."

She glanced at the closed conference room door on her way back to her desk. Her phone dinged as she sat down, and she scanned Brandon's newest text. It marked her thirty-fourth wedding proposal, and was as short, cute, and empty as the rest. She knew what she was good at, and why his message was worded for her hand in marriage when she'd declined another evening with him. Men and their penises!

Gretch shut the cell phone in her desk drawer. She picked up the supply bill from NaraGoods as a faint ding came from the drawer. *Brandon... Give me a break. It was one—*

The company line rang, and she snatched the receiver, her cheerful receptionist greeting strained, just in case Brandon had somehow found out where she worked.

"Sean Quinn, please."

"I'm sorry, he can't be disturbed."

"He already *is* disturbed. Interrupting him won't compound that."

Gretch cocked her head in delight. "May I ask who's calling?"

"Jason Quinn. His brother."

"Brother?" she squeaked. Strangely, her brain flailed

with something witty to say. "I—I was so sure he was raised by bears." *Wow, that was crazy lame!*

"Close. Four brothers who are Bears fanatics."

"No sisters?"

"Much to my mother's dismay." His chuckle was low and lovely. A Quinn who could socialize.

"No wonder Sean can't relate to women," she purred.

"That has more to do with the four of us dressing him up in Mom's evening gowns."

"No!"

"No." The grin in Jason's voice was unmistakable. "But damn, I wish I'd thought of it before now."

Gretch jumped up and perched on the edge of her desk as if flirting in person. "*Please* tell me some dirt." Her voice came out breathy and silly. She frowned. She didn't do silly. And why would she want to know details about Sean, anyway?

Her lanky coworker took that exact moment to stroll in and drop his timecard on her desk. He didn't so much as glance at her sexy pose, her hem riding almost to her panty line. Seriously, it was like she wasn't even in the room. Without a second thought, she held out the phone. "Your brother."

Hell froze over, pigs flew, and hark, the herald angels sang! Sean's mask slipped, and a mess of emotions raced across his face. Gretch caught annoyance, curiosity, and joy before he grabbed the receiver and turned his back on her.

"Jace? I can't talk right now..." His shoulders stiffened. "Yes, I did say that, but not during work hours."

Gretch ate up the sight of him. The untidy dark brown hair, the slim build that was all lean sinew. She'd been a personal trainer long enough to know he had to be doing everything right. Healthy diet, just the right amount of high-impact aerobic activity mixed with perfectly proportioned strength training. If only his button-downs didn't always cover his ass! Even spiffed up Saturday night, his fitted shirt had remained untucked.

"No, I can't do that either," Sean muttered. His grasp on the phone turned his knuckles white. More silence and finally a sigh. "Okay. I'll meet you out front at noon."

She was *so* going to be hanging around the sidewalk at noon. One more opportunity to explore what made the Enigma tick. And she was dying to meet Jason—Jace.

"Yes, Jace, I get the urgency. I said I'd go."

Urgency? Gretch stood and gnawed on her lip. Sean never went anywhere. He holed up in whatever cubicle was equipped for that particular project's requirements, stuck earbuds in (probably disco), and went into a mental zone so deep she'd only experienced it once, competing in a triathlon. Was there a family crisis?

He grunted what must have been a goodbye, turned, and handed her the receiver without meeting her gaze. She intentionally let their fingers brush as she accepted the phone. Not one iota of a reaction from him. It had to be the family emergency. "Hope everything's all right," she said, cursing her high octave. "No one ever calls you."

Sean glanced over then, his usually soft brown eyes hard and cold. The sudden alpha-toughness stirred something deep. It was all she could do not to stagger into his arms. *Christ in a cradle, where had that alien feeling come from?*

"It's all good," he said. "Gotta get to work."

Wait. This guy had hemmed and hawed his way through asking her out not twenty-four hours ago, and now he was walking off like she was a potted plant in the corner? "Hannah wants you to work on that charity painting next," she blurted. "The one Harrison Wickham planned to donate to a senior center."

He spun back. It was a freaking high to see those

quirky eyebrows knot, watch his frown carve even sharper angles into his cheekbones. When he let his guard down and displayed emotions, Sean was really quite handsome. "That piece of shit? Why?"

"Turns out Harrison wants it after all. Skip the Etruscan mosaic; this is the newest priority." She nodded to make her lie more convincing. Goosebumps skittered along her skin. Why had she recklessly screwed with his projects? It wasn't sabotage so much as a test: here was a glimpse of the ugliness inside her. How would he deal?

She had yet to meet a man who got her, but somehow, stealthily, in these last two years of working together, Sean had shown he was different in almost every way. He didn't fawn over her, never reacted to situations where she knew exactly how other men would behave. His response to this practical joke would peg him one way or another. If he ended up so furious it ruined this budding *thing* they had, so be it. A part of her would be relieved.

Besides pressing his lips into a flat line and nodding curtly, Sean reined in any other emotions and loped back to the lab. Gretch studied his retreating form, her breath streaming unsteadily. Yes, she was a bitch, but this was a great plan to get over him.

Just as another client walked through the door, her cell phone erupted in a series of muffled dings.

5

———————

Sean rolled the kinks from his shoulders and stepped into the warm sunshine. "Fuuuuck," he muttered, stopping short. Jace was leaning nonchalantly against the black Suburban, laughing at something Gretch said. When he responded with his own quip, she coyly touched her earring and shifted her weight, thrusting her hip inches closer to him.

Cue the *Habanera* aria from Bizet's opera, because the maddeningly provocative Carmen had just sprung to life.

They made a great couple, damn it. Dual DNA lottery winners. Innate self-confidence. Both consuming and discarding lovers like oxygen... It made sense that they'd be drawn to each other like Bogart and Bacall. But cerebral observations did nothing to relieve the jealousy flickering through Sean like a live wire.

Moments remained before they'd notice him. He pushed aside the inner turmoil and stood motionless, hoarding images of Gretch to replay in the wee hours. Those long legs and the astounding figure poured into that obscenely short camouflage dress. The lovely way she tilted her head so it exposed the slender column of her neck. How she fluttered her fingers so gracefully while she spoke, almost like a translator for the deaf. Everything about Gretch was sexy elegance, the kind that torched a dangerous lust inside him. A lust so dark he'd fucked a stranger in an alley to slake his hunger for her. He winced as shame suppressed the inner inferno like firefighting foam.

Jace spotted him and jerked his chin in the universal get-over-here command—for a kid or a dog. Sean strolled over, peripherally engrossed with Gretch, inhaling her spicy perfume, but warily eyeing his brother. "I've only got an hour."

"I'll get you back in time, Nancy. Jump in."

Sean flushed and reached for the door handle. He hadn't been gifted with Jace's quick wit or cutting comebacks; he was a declawed cat born into a family of pit bulls. Arguing would only decrease his stature in Gretch's eyes.

"So, how 'bout I pick you up Sunday at six," Jace said smoothly.

Sean spun around. His brother ignored him, but Gretch looked right at him, almost like she waited for his reaction. He swallowed. There was nothing to react to— this was Jace, lifelong champion, former SEAL, now part of the FBI's International Ops Division. Even in Sean's earliest memories, all Jace had to do was glance at a woman and her clothes fell off.

Despite his brain's signal to get in the Suburban, Sean remained frozen at the Sunday-at-six significance. "You're busy," he stammered. "It's Mom's birthday." *The party I wanted to invite her to.*

His brother grinned at Gretch the way a child would at a new Happy Meal toy. "Mom'll love her," he murmured, and the truth hit Sean like a freight train. Mom would. She adored spunk, sass, and socially outgoing girlfriends. The kind her four elder sons dated. In college, Sean had brought his first girlfriend, an introverted lit major, home. It'd been the most uncomfortable evening in his long and tortured history of uncomfortable family evenings. He'd vowed never to put himself or another girlfriend through that again. A vow he'd have broken in a heartbeat if only he'd had the guts to ask Gretch out yesterday.

She smiled a message he couldn't decipher—probably pity—before shifting her gaze to Jace. "Sure." She fingered her earring again. "Sunday at six." Then she rattled off her phone number, and Jace was ready-Freddy with his smartphone.

Sean climbed into the back of the Suburban, his stomach in knots. If he hadn't begged his brother to help on this case, those two would never have met.

A woman with a honey-blond ponytail and wide cornflower-blue eyes twisted around in the front passenger seat and stretched out her hand. "Good to see you again, Sean."

"Oh hey, Margo. How's the new anthropologist working out?"

"Joe Taylor? Pissed not to be on this case, thanks for asking." Special Agent Margo Hathaway smiled. Planes could land in O'Hare guided only by that smile. When Sean had consulted on the occasional case, his obsessive disposition hadn't triggered sidelong looks from her like it had with other agents. And he'd appreciated how methodical she was in gathering facts and weighing all options.

"I'm only helping out this one time."

Her ponytail bobbed as she nodded. "And we appreciate it. We sure miss you around the office."

Sean jerked his head toward the sidewalk. "I couldn't stay."

"I know. It's a shame you two couldn't work together. Anyway, I'm your wife."

"Excuse me?"

Jace slid in beside him. "She's your undercover spouse." He shut the door and nodded to Crew Cut behind the wheel. "You remember Dirk from the airport?"

Sean managed a curt nod. As the car rolled forward, his brother handed over a credit card, business cards, and an authentic-looking Illinois license. "You're William and Jane Bixby."

Sean frowned between him and the smiling agent, still turned in her seat. Technically, Margo was Jace's superior, but the dynamic wasn't playing out here. Why would she let him assume the lead? And why this farfetched ruse? "I thought I was consulting on artifacts."

Even the way his brother shook his head was patronizing. "You're an interested buyer. She's your bodyguard, should anything go wrong."

Sean clenched his teeth. *Typical Jace espionage shit.* It was why Sean had resigned his infrequent consulting role a few months after they'd hired his brother. "What do you mean *wrong*?"

"Asuman gave up his buyer." Jace handed over a photograph of a fierce-looking bearded man. "Mohammed El Bashtan. Rents a booth in the Broadway Antique Market."

"I know BAM," Sean muttered. He'd bought his vintage sofa there.

"He sells Middle Eastern antiques, but according to Asuman, many of the pieces are conflict antiquities. We're tracking whether El Bashtan has extremist ties, but need more evidence. You're going in as a big spender." Jace handed over a worn wallet, ostentatiously bulging with bills. "I'll want this back untouched, but flash it around, talk your art-speak so he knows you're legit."

Sean frowned. It was noon on a Monday. "And the reason Joe Taylor isn't doing this?"

"He's staffed on another task force now."

Sean switched wallets, handing his to Jace. "Let's go back to the 'if anything goes wrong' part."

"Margo is just an added precaution. One of her blouse buttons is a video camera. Her job is to wander around his booth recording the inventory. No worries, baby brother, you're safe." Ah, there was Jace's earnest expression... Sean had years of tortured baby brother memories that all started with that innocent look from one of his brothers. Jace gestured wildly. "And you got your black belt at—what? Nine? Made the rest of us look like chumps? You can handle him."

The praise ratcheted up the tension in Sean's neck. Jace wasn't a guy to hand out compliments at his own expense. Before Sean could respond, his brother's attention was snagged by a buzzing text. Sean glanced at Special Agent Hathaway, still shooting him that sunny smile. As far as Sean could recollect, Margo didn't know baby brother, and any further protesting would solidify his sissy status to her too.

After a minute of silence, Jace murmured, "Besides, if anything went wrong, I'd never hear the end of it from Mom."

Aaaand sissy status achieved, right on cue. Sean stared out his window as the car slowed for a right turn. No doubt Sunday's party would include his older brother inadvertently outing him as even more of a social moron to Gretch, too.

And shit, it wasn't fair Jace hooked up with her so easily. What sort of norms did the über-beautiful work off? Did they instantly size each other up and know they could chance their hearts? Or was it all a game, just wall sex with a stranger and walking away without drowning in self-disgust?

Sean tried to rest his temple against the pane, but shifting in the seat caused the new wallet to protrude into him. He shifted back. The lump remained, like a heavy appendage had grown on his ass cheek. This undercover op was so not worth interrupting his day for. And his childish need for Jace's respect had cost him his dream girl.

"It's up ahead," Margo said, pointing to the vast building.

Sean straightened and wiped damp palms along his jeans. He could do this. In an hour he'd be back in the comfort of his cubicle. The only potential danger in his day was not finding the wit to out-snark Gretch. Or accidentally overhearing her infectious laugh. To get any work done, he'd long ago invested in quality earbuds and drowned himself in operas. Today was Mascagni's *Cavalleria rusticana*. He played the calming *Intermezzo* in his head, but it did nothing to slow the crescendo of his heart.

6

———

S ean tried to look like a lunchtime browser, but adrenalin pulsed like a caffeine dump, and the arm "Jane" linked hers in was as rigid as the rest of him. For the past ten minutes they'd meandered the antiques market, which mostly held midcentury-modern items, heavy on furniture, jewelry, and snobby-looking clerks.

What if El Bashan saw through the charade? What if the antiques dealer packed a concealed weapon? Or wore a suicide vest? *What kind of a stupid...?*

"What's it like working with my brother?" Sean blurted to shut down the thoughts.

"Probably the same as growing up with him." Margo laughed, completely at ease or else putting on a terrific front. "Arrogant, decisive... As you know, *I'm* the special agent, but it's hard to pull rank when he's on my team."

"Be careful. He'll take that inch and run all the way to Oklahoma."

Margo shrugged as if the warning were sour grapes from an envious brother. "He's in a new program where we provide a lot of slack and see what they do with it."

Enough to run their own investigation at midnight? "Where were you Saturday night?"

"The O'Hare interview sounded straightforward enough to send Jace and Dirk as the FBI task force representatives. And by all accounts—" she gestured to him, "—he made a good call bringing you back as a consultant." She grinned, eyes merry. "He's never experienced failure in any form, am I right?"

"Now multiply that three more times and you've got my older brothers." Sean tried grinning back, but his cheeks felt inflexible, like they were in a territorial dispute with his lips.

"No kidding? What do your other brothers do?"

Look up noble *in the dictionary.* "Jace is the oldest. Patrick is a lieutenant at Fire Station One Twenty-six on South Kingston. Gage and Dillon are still in Afghanistan. Both Special Forces."

"No one else works with art?"

That familiar defensiveness crept up Sean's spine. Already the easy rapport with Margo was taking a turn. "It's called conservation and restoration."

Margo slowed down, pulled out her phone, and texted, which seemed ruder than normal. He glanced away. A booth cluttered with Middle Eastern wares was on the right, and a portly man, who resembled the photograph in the file, was on the far side of the booth, speaking on his cell phone in a foreign language. *Oh yeah. I'm tracking down ISIS in the middle of a Chicago market.* Sean sucked in a breath.

"Oh, look, William," Margo exclaimed, pocketing the phone and dragging him to the booth's glass-partitioned case. Jewelry in bronze, turquoise, amber, and other semiprecious stones winked up at him. "Let's go in."

She marched fearlessly into the small, jam-packed space, but Sean stayed put, studying the setup. These artifacts were not Mesopotamian era. Nothing looked older than a couple of hundred years, which didn't rule them out from being conflict antiquities, but only provenances would prove or disprove that. At the end of his perusal, he met El Bashtan's gaze. The dealer's sentences became staccato, and the call quickly ended. Sean wandered over to an oak curio cabinet where Margo ogled hand mirrors, picture frames, and some feminine knickknacks Sean couldn't identify.

El Bashtan's pungent cologne, a citric base with heavy tobacco notes, marked his approach long before he stood behind them. "May I be of assistance?"

Sean turned, instinctively settling himself on the balls of his feet—a fight stance. The shopkeeper laced his fingers on the apex of his belly in a dainty manner. His eyes seemed friendly enough, but watchful. A man who missed very little. Sean swallowed dust.

Margo gestured to Sean with an indulgent smile. "My husband knows antiques. He's always searching for something unusual."

"I'm on the procurement committee for a small museum in Wisconsin," Sean said, surprised his voice sounded so matter-of-fact. He took out the thick wallet and withdrew a business card, ignoring the man's wide-eyed reaction to the wad of bills stacked inside. "My specialty is ancient Middle Eastern artifacts." The high-value smuggled artifacts would probably be in a more private location. "The items I'm interested in are much older than these. Do you know of any another shops in the area?" He stuffed the wallet back in his pocket.

Except for one raised eyebrow, El Bashtan regarded him without expression. Sean didn't blink, although surely the man could see the rapidly throbbing carotid in his neck.

What a colossal mistake, thinking he could handle an

undercover assignment! He was better suited back at headquarters, left alone to examine these items from the tape on Margo's blouse button. Even then, a lot would be guesswork. Archeology was synonymous with research and testing. He couldn't just look at that Egyptian necklace over there and immediately identify it as an ancient carnelian glass funereal collar, worn during the reign of Thutmose III in Dynasty 18. He doubted even a highly trained field archeologist could. But at least someone else wouldn't be *acting*. He could barely pull off being Sean Quinn, much less an undercover museum curator.

"What is it you are looking for, Mister…" El Bashtan eyed the business card at arm's length. "Bixby?"

Sean mentally flipped through the file he'd been given on the way to the airport, then rattled off confiscated relics. "Vessels, pottery, coins, statues, jewelry— around the time of the Bronze Age. Or perhaps Roman, Greek, and Byzantine periods. Naturally, each would need a well-documented provenance."

"Of course, of course." El Bashtan looked around his store as if he could magically open a drawer or cabinet and present such an item. Margo had gone back to wrapping up her slow circle of the booth, looking high and low with an enchanted expression. No doubt her film footage would be useless, filed away forever.

El Bashtan held up the fake business card again. "If I may take some information from you, I shall call my sources. I can get you museum-quality pieces. Nothing illegal, of course, nothing from *Daesh*." The highly derogatory Arabic term for ISIS again left Sean like a fish out of water. Would a small-town Wisconsin curator know that?

He nodded stiffly and followed the seller to a beat-up desk in the corner. El Bashtan asked more detailed questions about the relics Sean sought and jotted notes.

When asked about a budget, Sean made up a range from moderate to hinting at extravagant. Since there was an email address on the business card, he suggested sending photographs and prices. Let Jace and the new anthropologist, Joe Taylor, take it from there.

El Bashtan reiterated that he'd call his contact, and was robustly confident he could meet the museum's requirements. "And for the madam," he said as Margo sidled up. He flourished a small, exquisitely engraved wooden box. "This is from Kabul, my homeland." He showed it to Margo with a smile. "To thank you both for your kind visit today." After quickly wrapping and bagging it, he gave Sean his card. "We shall meet again, Mr. Bixby."

Doubtful. Sean nodded and followed Margo around the glass partition and back into the main hall. "Hurry, dear, we'll be late to pick up Alice." She tugged his arm.

Sean blinked over at her, and the warning glare she returned was strong enough to shut his mouth. They could talk in the Suburban.

Once outside, though, she tightened the grip on his arm and walked right by it. "Taxi!"

Sean pivoted and looked at the SUV. His ride back to work. His lunch hour was almost up. As the taxi pulled alongside, Margo whipped out her phone and rapidly typed a text, angling it so he could see the screen.

Received a box. GPS tracking or listening device? Initiate s.h. protocol.

"You getting in, ma'am?" the driver called through the passenger window.

"One minute."

Her phone dinged: *Roger that.*

"What's SH?" Sean asked.

Margo whipped open the cab door and held it for Sean. His mother would've had a stroke. "Get in." The tone and her stance caught him by surprise. Here was the special agent in charge of this case. Here was the authority she hadn't displayed in front of Jace, her lowly associate.

That observation took a back seat to the fact that Sean wasn't joining the bureau on any further adventures. "I'll get my own cab. I've got a ton of work." He added, "See you at home, Jane," in case the box was bugged.

"Folks?" the cab driver called impatiently.

"Get. In."

Sean shook his head, scanning the block for another taxi. She stepped into his personal space and snarled the command a third time. He blinked down into her fresh cheerleader face, screwed up in aggravation. If he had a dime for every time a woman looked at him like that...

He took a deep breath, prepared to politely decline again, when her subtle, all-American scent filled his nostrils. He couldn't help himself. "Dove soap?"

"Oh my God. What's *wrong* with you?" She pushed him into the cab, and just like that, Sean was kidnapped by the FBI—again.

7

Jace waited until his little brother shut the bathroom door of the safe house before turning to Margo. "He's—"

"I don't want to hear it." She held up a palm. The last time a woman stood before him with this rigid posture and appalled expression it had been Miss Gaston, the librarian he'd made a pass at in fifth grade. "We almost compromised our only lead. Take him back to work, and we'll wait until Taylor frees up."

This was such an overreaction to a box they'd known within minutes wasn't a GPS tracker, and it wasn't likely the tech currently taking it apart would find a bug. "You've worked with Sean, Margo. He's way more brilliant than that hack who replaced him."

"He may be, Jace, but not in the field. His inability to prioritize through a potential emergency or follow orders put us in jeopardy."

"Margo—"

"He was fixated on the soap I use!" she shouted. Down the hall, the toilet flushed, and Margo flipped her wrist, signaling the end of the discussion.

"He's a methodical hand-washer. We have time." Jace used an overformal tone so the irony wouldn't seep through. "Let's just see what his take is on El Bashtan, and the stuff you taped."

Margo pursed her lips, and Jace stood unflinching beneath her blistering gaze. Why was he sticking up for his odd, indefensible brother? Because he'd never served under a woman, and he was man enough to admit it chafed to the point of insubordination. Every time he got away with *his* course of action over hers, it was a small win. It was why he'd grabbed his little brother and headed to O'Hare when the tip first came in, rather than waking up Special Agent Hathaway for permission.

It was also a testament to how badly Sean had shaken her up out there on the street. Margo's fatal flaw was collecting opinions and ruminating on a perfect plan instead of acting on gut instinct. One day all that fact-finding and fairness would be as detrimental as Sean's olfactory fixation. As expected, she glanced at Dirk to gauge his point of view.

Without missing a beat, Dirk said, "He was real helpful during the O'Hare interview. I agree with Jace, ma'am. Sean isn't in the field now."

Jace exhaled, the tension in his neck easing. *Blood brothers.* Funny how simpatico Jace and Dirk were. So much more than Jace and Sean would ever be.

Margo fingered the button on her blouse, her gaze dragging from the closed bathroom door to the dining room table where a tech worked on the wooden box. Resignation spread over her features. "All right," she said. "But that's it. We're done using your brother as a consultant. Again." She sighed. "I guess we should grab lunch while we're at it." She nodded at Jace. "Go see what's stocked in the fridge."

He bristled. He'd gladly endured being a grunt for the

honor of becoming a SEAL, but special agent associate was as low as he'd go in the FBI. A special agent associate making sandwiches for the team? Not happening. "Hope there are MREs in there," he said lightly. "That's the extent of my skill in the kitchen." Naturally, the FBI wouldn't stock Meals Ready to Eat for informants and operatives.

The door down the hall opened, and Sean loped toward them. Jace kept a careful eye on Margo's dubious expression. If she repeated her order, he'd have to comply, but making a team lunch in front of his little brother... Jesus. His humiliation would be complete. He gave a half-shrug and cranked up his grin. "Or we can send for takeout?"

"You're telling me you can field-strip an M240 blind but can't slap together a turkey sandwich?" The enamored agent impressed enough by Jace's medaled career to allow him to overstep authority was long gone. And to be fair, he deserved it; he'd assumed the lead each time she slogged through her weighing-all-the-facts approach. His defiance wasn't only because of her gender. He damn well deserved to be a special agent. Or her boss: a supervisory special agent.

Sean sidled up to them, sniffing the remnants of the soap he'd used on his hands. Thankfully, Margo didn't see it on account she was still giving Jace the stink eye.

"I can't be held responsible if I use spackle instead of mayo," Jace joked, avoiding eye contact with Sean at all costs. By the time each son hit middle school, their mother had been big on assigning chores, like whipping up a complete dinner for seven and having it ready promptly when Pop came home. Sweat trickled down Jace's back. This point was so not worth the energy, but he was invested now, and backing down was not an option.

Margo glanced at Sean, and it was like a light bulb went off. Her frown disappeared as she disconnected the surveillance part of the button and handed it to Dirk. "Take Sean and get started. We'll have lunch on the table in ten."

We? What kind of IED had he just stepped on? She turned back to Jace, brow arched. "I've heard you'll take an inch and run all the way to Oklahoma." She jerked her head toward the kitchen. "Guess today's field lesson is the identification, applied research, and effective use of mayonnaise. And just in case you haven't picked up on subtle intonation—" she pointed to her mouth, "—this is my condescending voice."

Jace spread his hands. "Margo—"

"And yes, this is going in your evaluation." She spun around and marched into the kitchen, and he followed with one thought swirling through his head.

Special Agent Hathaway, you just declared war.

GRETCH CHIRPED out her standard phone greeting without losing laser focus on inputting payroll.

"It's me," Sean said in a muffled monotone, like he was covering his mouth. "I don't know when I'll get back."

Her focus imploded, and self-annoyance transferred to her voice. "Uh-oh. Notify the press! The Quinn brothers are loose in the city."

"Tell Hannah I'll finish my eight hours, no matter how long I have to stay."

Gretch paused, frowning. She'd pitched a softball for him to hit out of the park with one of his cutting comebacks. It was definitely not like him to ignore it. "Everything okay?"

A moment of silence. "A typical afternoon with my brother."

None of this sounded right, and worry niggled her gut. Whatever caused his bad mood, the last thing he needed was to stay late for a practical joke she'd played on him. "Listen. About that charity painting—"

"Talk at ya later."

Gretch stared at the receiver and unlit phone console. "Talk at me *later*?" she muttered. He didn't say shit like that, either.

Hannah walked in with a manila envelope and placed it in the pile for the mailman. "Why do you look like you don't know how to hang up a phone?"

Gretch slowly hung up. What the heck could she call what she and Sean had going on? It certainly wasn't chemistry. But she also didn't want to get him into trouble. With the practical joke or by tattling on him for ditching work. "Just spaced for a second." Her phone let off another muted ding. Then another in rapid succession.

Hannah grinned. "Let me guess. Some hottie just asked you to marry him?"

"Yeah, but this guy thinks 'no' is negotiable. It's getting annoying." Although maybe it was Sean with a message he couldn't say over the phone. *Seriously! What a weird conversation.* Gretch whipped out her phone and checked her texts. Nope, all Brandon.

You might want to rethink that answer, sweetie.

Meet me at TMs @ 8

Text me that you received this message!

"What the hell?" she muttered.

Hannah rounded the desk and read the messages over Gretch's shoulder. "Jeez. I thought you said it was a fun night."

"It was." No more or less than her usual LVR app

hookup. He came off a bit physical when she tried to leave his apartment, but still cloyingly sweet. She glanced up at Hannah. "Do these sound intimidating to you?"

Hannah bit her lip. Such a glass-half-full friend, never wanting to think ill of anyone, even after all she'd been through with the freakishly screwed-up Wickham family last October. "Does he know where you live? Or work?"

Gretch shook her head. "I lie when they ask direct questions, and only give out my cell number when I think it's safe. *And* if I want to see them again." Which she had at the time. "But this..."

"Can he track your phone's location?"

"I don't think so." Gretch blinked. "Unless he can hack." A shiver rippled through her.

"Turn it off just to be safe." Hannah sat on the edge of the desk. "I'd make Dev take you home, but he's in Manhattan until Wednesday." She bit the side of her thumb, frowning at the phone screen. "I'll ask Sean to take you."

"No—"

"At least to the El station."

"I can take care of myself."

The haunted look on Hannah's face stopped Gretch cold. Hannah never spoke of it, but the horror she'd lived through at the Wickham house still clearly affected her. "It won't hurt for Sean to at least walk you to the station," she said softly. "He has a black belt in karate."

A huge puzzle piece clunked into place. The lithe body, the silent way Sean appeared. He was nerdy, but not in the classic sense. Something about him had always been different—enticing, challenging. It made sense now, and was so freaking hot. She could totally imagine him spinning a one-eighty, landing in a crouch. Striking, dropkicking... A rare spark of molten desire shivered through her. "*Black* belt?"

Hannah nodded and stood. "That's why he didn't make the office Christmas party. He was teaching a self-defense course after work."

The yummy lava feeling dried right up. That was so *not* the reason. He was a hermit who couldn't be bothered to socialize, even with people he worked alongside day after day.

Gretch picked up the NaraGoods invoice, and only then realized she still had the payroll software up. "I'll ask him later."

"You're totally blowing me off. Go ask him now or I will." It was so rare for Hannah to boss her around that Gretch blinked, wide-eyed. Hannah must've taken it wrong, because she shrugged and began walking toward the lab. Where she would not find Sean working.

"I'll go!" Gretch jumped from her seat. "I'll ask him."

Her friend stood aside, arms crossed, and Gretch had no choice but to make her way to the empty cubicle and bend over like she was talking to someone. The Picasso lay on his large white counter. Beside it, in a precise row from large to small, were tools and cleaning supplies. Except for a capped water bottle with dregs left and earbuds connected to a mini MP3 player, both placed at exact angles, there was nothing of Sean's personality— not pinned to the walls or taped on the computer moni- tor. *Typical.*

Hannah still stood in the reception entrance, so Gretch gave her a nod and enthusiastic thumbs-up. After a hesitant return nod, her bestie walked in the opposite direction. Without a thought, Gretch sat on the wheeled stool and reached for the music device. If this was disco, she was *so* going to rag on him when he came back. She plugged in an earbud and pushed "on."

A string of violins held a note, filled with sweetness and longing. Her breath stilled. Sticking in the other bud, she closed her eyes. More string instruments followed, building the yearning, then an entire orchestra carried the melody, pulsing the harmony through every cell.

Wave after wave of goosebumps swept up her arms as the music built and crested. The dying notes reverted to the softly weeping violins. On the final note, Gretch swallowed the lump in her throat, then turned off the player with trembling fingers. A feeling she couldn't place overwhelmed her. Love? Regret? She wasn't familiar enough with either to recognize what pulled at her insides. But without a doubt, that was the most beautiful song on this earth.

"Who knew?" she whispered, not knowing if she meant the existence of such a heavenly piece of music or the emotional depth of Sean. The main line ringing in the reception area snapped out of her daze. Christ, what if Sean came back and found her here, lounging on his stool and wearing his buds? She tossed them on the counter and sprang out of the cubicle, smacking right into Dane, the new guy. He stuttered a "hello," clearly surprised to see her there, but was still too new to remark on her popping up like the gopher from *Caddyshack*.

"Is, uh, Sean around?" he asked. "I have a question about the wet bath."

"He went on an errand. Go ask Hannah." Gretch hurried around him to her desk. The poignant music replayed in her head, the swelling sensation in her throat choking her. Like she needed these violins wrenching her heart all afternoon. She sat clumsily and eased off her high heels. Onscreen, her cursor blinked steadily on *payroll hours worked*. The NaraGoods invoice lay unpaid. Her phone screen was littered with messages from Brandon, each more obscene and aggressive than the last. *Shit.* She looked around the office, chewing off her lipstick. He truly hadn't been this unbalanced Saturday night. She could spot those freaks a mile away.

The guy could text all he wanted; she wasn't going to feed into this. She turned the phone off, like she should have when Hannah had suggested it. When she picked up Sean's timecard, her hand still trembled. It was because of the music. Shits like Brandon didn't scare her.

Walter's door opened, and okay, she jumped. "I have some acquisition contracts," he said briskly, laying files on her desk. "This is a priority."

Finally. The contents of the suitcase. Gretch could barely maintain the disinterested smile until he closed himself back in his office. She snatched the top file and rifled through. "Holy Christ in a cradle." A damaged Quran whose pages were all gold leaf. Worth three-point-five mil. This must have been what was in the suitcase.

She set aside the file and opened the second one. Inside was the inventory list she'd seen on his desk, but retyped. The revised copy had no Arabic scribbled in the margins, and the total at the bottom was not circled, nor did it add up to a hundred thousand dollars. It had been changed to sixty million.

8

———

Sean returned just before three, stiff with the need to let loose on a punching bag. Or his brother's face. What a shitty, worthless afternoon.

While a technician had scrutinized the wooden box, Sean had pointed out artifacts he recognized on the video file. Margo and Jace made turkey sandwiches for the group, then Jace loudly announced Sean's veganism and produced a small salad with sardonic flourish. Although Margo studied Jace with something close to disgust, when she glanced Sean's way, her expression mirrored that of most women who spent time around him in his four brothers' presence: curiosity and pity.

Sean shouldn't care. He'd never apologized for his sorry existence among his testosterone-overloaded brothers and had no intentions of starting now, but that kindhearted glance sure got old. And Margo hadn't known he was a freak until Jace had once again messed everything up.

In the end, the bugging–tracking device was just a simple, exquisitely carved box from Afghanistan, now ruined. Sean had insisted on collecting the remnants to restore it, then suffered the indignity of their smirks and eye rolls.

By the time he walked into the quiet, temperature- and humidity-controlled interior that smelled of turpentine, paints—and Gretch—he was fed up with the FBI and anything to do with black market smuggling.

Fortunately, Gretch was on the phone. "Oh, Mr. Adyton, you're such a flirt," she said. Though she snapped her fingers to get Sean's attention—seriously, had that ever worked on a guy?—he headed straight for the sanctuary of his lab. Turning in, he stopped short. His stool, his MP3 player, and his earbuds were all askew. He pinched the bridge of his nose, eyeing the Picasso and tools. Untouched. Who'd been in here, rearranging his private property? He ground his teeth as he rolled the stool back into the proper position and gathered up his music. Thrusting in his buds, he pushed play, and Turiddu sang his first tenor note. Sean's jaw sagged. The perp had messed with the MP3! Listened to the entirety of Sean's favorite piece. Before the FBI fiasco, he'd purposely stopped the opera in that exact place so he could look forward to coming back to the *Intermezzo*.

"Sonofabitch!" He ripped out the buds and strode to the wet bath area. Dane, goggled, was bent over the container where distilled water solution was loosening the backing on a van Eyck.

"Hey, man," Sean said, coming to a halt. "Were you in my cubicle?"

Dane glanced up. "I looked for you, but Hannah answered my question."

Sean studied the Plexiglas partition that separated the wet bath area from the other restorer, Anna. He frowned. Should he ask her? People claimed he overreacted to others touching his things, but they were *his*. And his privacy was his. And today his dignity had taken a beating too. He cranked his neck until he heard a pop. *Fuck it.* He had too much work to finish. "Thanks." Sean double-knocked on the partition and spun on his heel.

"Gretch was leaving when I got there, if that means anything," Dane called.

Sean threw another rough "thanks" over his shoulder, although the hairs on his neck pricked. *Gretch?* How often did she snoop through his stuff? He'd never noticed it before, and he could easily identify even a half-centimeter shift of his possessions.

He slumped on the stool and glanced at his book bag under the desk. That hadn't moved. He rifled through it and shoved half a protein bar in his mouth. He might look like a bitty-side-salad dweeb, but his metabolism burned like the sun. His low glucose level was probably feeding this seething irritation.

"I covered for you."

He swiveled on the wheels.

Gretch rested an arm along the top of his cubicle, half her hourglass curves still hidden behind the gray polyester-blend siding. "Walter and Hannah have no clue you ditched work."

His mouth was too stuffed to form words, so he leisurely kept chewing. She got off on men stumbling over themselves for her—flattering her, opening doors, no doubt carrying her groceries...and responding instantly.

If Jace crammed half a protein bar into his mouth, he'd give her a goofy grin, point a finger at his cheek, and chew faster. God forbid she should be kept waiting for Sean's blathering gratitude at not telling the bosses he'd been late. *Well, fuck that.*

"You chew weird," she remarked, and then he did speed up before she could pick him apart further. There were enough abnormal things about him without adding chewing to the freaking list.

He swallowed the half-eaten bolus, which was so large he swallowed a second time to clear his esophagus. Given the Heimlich maneuver or Gretch's manicure, he'd be on the losing end of that decision. When the bulk of the protein bar safely passed his airway, Sean leaned an elbow behind him on the counter. It touched his MP3 player. "Why were you listening to my music?"

A rosy flush bloomed under her makeup. *Crazy* strange. Gretch didn't get embarrassed. "I came to give you a message, but when you weren't here, naturally I had to check and see if you listened to disco."

"Naturally." He poured contempt into the word and stared into her lying brown eyes. "However, there was no message. You knew I wasn't here—you saw me leave with my brother."

She blushed harder. It reminded him of Hannah. "What was that?" she asked abruptly, nodding to his player.

Her interest was uncharted territory. What was she setting him up for now? "A one-act opera composed by Pietro Muscagni in eighteen ninety-nine."

"An opera? I didn't hear any screeching voices."

She was a cool drink of water, he'd give her that. Sean unwrapped the other half of his bar. "You heard the *intermezzo*. The opera's equivalent to an intermission. It's usually instrumental."

"It was ethereal."

He grunted, because again, he'd anticipated ridicule. And her description was apt. Who knew she could discern a magnificent *intermezzo* piece?

"Maybe, if it ever comes to town..." She splayed the back of her hand, studying her fingernails.

The ghost of the thick bolus stuck in his throat. Was

she going to ask him out? Through buzzing ears, he faintly heard, "...you'll give me a heads-up."

He nodded like a yanked marionette. Sure. Give her the heads-up so she could ask Jace out, or that preppie shit from Saturday night. "Gotta work," he said, but she stayed there, hypnotized by her nails. What was with her today? She hated being dismissed. At this point she should be halfway back to her desk, tossing a caustic remark over her shoulder.

"I was wondering if...after work you could...uh..." She cleared her throat, the flush now bright red. He didn't speak. Didn't move. She was going to ask him out after all. He stared hard at her mouth, willing the words to come. *Go to dinner with me? Catch a movie? Play the whole opera?*

She frowned at him like his face was saying something entirely different. Was he scowling? He tried to rearrange his features, but Gretch's glossy lips formed a perfect arc of displeasure. "Oh, never mind. You're such an oddball."

Long after the judgmental *clip-clip* of her high heels faded, he stared at the spot where she'd stood. What had he done wrong?

HOURS LATER, Sean rolled up his earbuds and tucked them into the smallest compartment of his drawer organizer. He stood and stretched his lats, appreciating the finished Picasso for a moment. This was why he'd gotten into the career. It was like the soot of the fire had never blackened this exquisite painting.

He carefully packaged the canvas and placed it in the finished cubbyhole, then carried back the piece-of-crap painting no longer slotted for a senior center. It was heavier than the Picasso and yellowed with age, although even that resembled a static saffron shade. Sean squinted at the sprawled signature on the canvas. Salvatore. *Never heard of him.* Tomorrow would be a bitch—there'd be no sense of accomplishment intricately restoring something to the same ugly state.

He logged into his computer, his stomach growling fiercely for more than the protein bar and the leftover quinoa he'd found in the break room refrigerator hours ago. Paging down to the bottom of the listed Wickham art, he checked the Picasso as completed, tallied the total hours, and emailed it to Walter. Sean made a mental note to hurry through the piece of shit tomorrow. Even restored, it wasn't worth a dime, and Harrison Wickham wouldn't appreciate a large restoration bill.

He skimmed the few emails in his inbox, mostly office memos from Hannah. One of her subject lines—*Thank You*—brought him up short, and he clicked it open.

I'm never sure where you and Gretch stand with each other, but I appreciate you agreeing to see her home tonight. If she mentioned just walking her to the El station, ignore her. Someone's given her the creeps enough for her to swallow her pride and ask you for help. She needs it ALL the way to her front doorstep.

Have to use email, since she's expecting me to say this in person and is guarding your hallway like a samurai warrior.

Thanks again, see you tomorrow. –H

The grumbling in his stomach turned to roiling as he glanced at his watch. A quarter to nine. *Shit.* Gretch had been gathering the courage to ask for his help, and because he couldn't pull off a normal expression, she'd put herself in a potentially dangerous situation.

He concentrated on the moment out front today when Jace had been grinning, thumbs already typing her name. Gretch had arched her neck, touched her earring and said... *555—* Sean screwed his eyes shut... *3014.*

He snapped out of his trance and punched the numbers into the company phone, his heart pounding like a bass drum. *Please let her be home safe.* Nothing would sound better right now than some sarcastic comment about his audacity to call her this late. To call her at all.

But it didn't even ring. The call went straight to voicemail.

9
————

N*ine o'clock. Who would call so late?* Gretch snatched the landline before Dwayne awoke from his snoring sprawl on the faux-velvet sofa. She glanced at the caller ID and murmured a greeting as she slipped into the kitchen.

"Oh my God," Hannah exclaimed. "You're all right."

"Why wouldn't I be?"

"You didn't ask Sean to walk you home."

Gretch winced at the accusing tone. "I was your personal trainer for six years, Hannah. I'm strong enough to defend myself."

"In a minidress and stilettos? What if that creep had been lurking nearby?" Hannah sounded so worried that guilt wormed into Gretch's defenses.

"I told you I never give out my real last name or address to new pickups," she replied. "I lie about where I work on my alias's social media pages, *and* I left during rush hour while it was still bright daylight."

The silence on the line lasted long enough for her to hear her own words. She winced.

"Honestly, Gretch, that's a bit sick."

You have no idea. She inserted a carefree laugh. "Girl's gotta have some excitement in her life."

"Well, it's come around to bite you in the ass."

Gretch stiffened. "Has it? Because I'm home safe."

Hannah made a sound, half sigh, half exasperation. "I'm sorry. It's none of my business."

"No, I'm sorry." Gretch rested her forehead on the wall by the phone mount. "I appreciate your concern, sweetie, but I'm in total control." *Always.*

Hannah's second sigh mixed disagreement with surrender. "Okay. Let me call Sean. He's still at the office, worried sick."

Gretch jerked upright, a tingle of alarm zipping through her. "Sean?"

"When you gave me the thumbs-up, I emailed him my thanks. He just got around to reading it, and your cell phone isn't on."

Of course her phone wasn't on. She didn't want to field sicko texts from Brandon. "The battery's dead," she lied. She just had to ignore her phone for a few days until Brandon moved on. Problem solved.

"Listen," Hannah said, "the self-defense course Sean teaches? You're going to find out when it is and go."

Sean wearing the black belt of a martial arts master? All buff and in command? Giving combat demonstrations and instructing *her*? Oh, hell no! "Says who?" she demanded.

"Says your boss. You lied to me during work hours."

Gretch rolled her eyes. "Giving you the thumbs-up is not *telling* a lie. I'm not doing anything that involves Sean."

"And when I call him back, I'm giving him your address," Hannah said, as if Gretch hadn't spoken. "He'll be on your doorstep at eight to escort you to work." She hung up while Gretch was halfway through shrieking a profanity.

Dwayne grunted awake in the next room. "Another mouse?" he called out gruffly.

"No." Gretch peered around just in case, then slunk back into the living room. Should she update him on what a creep Brandon had turned out to be? No. Just one more friend who'd freak out unnecessarily. "Hannah," Gretch said, replacing the phone in its charger cradle. "Treating me like a goddamn child."

Dwayne sat up with the prolonged groan people with weak core muscles emitted. "It's about time someone treated you like a child," he mumbled. "You constantly act like one."

Gretch grabbed the remote and shut off the TV. She hadn't *had* a childhood—literally didn't know what "acting like a child" meant. She slumped into the club chair adjacent to the sofa. "I don't need people bossing me around or protecting me, damn it."

Dwayne cocked his head. "I'd give anything to have that confidence."

Confidence. Sean in white pajamas and a black belt. Gretch hugged a throw pillow. She had to get out of going to that class, period. And the humiliation of Sean—*Sean!*—escorting her tomorrow. Maybe she'd get up super early and give him the slip. When he showed up, Dwayne could tell him she'd already gone in to work. She plumped the pillow with her fist and threw it aside.

No. Hannah would never forgive her.

SEAN PRESSED THE ALLEN/COLLINS buzzer outside the apartment building, then jammed his clammy hands in his windbreaker and rotated on the step. The aromas of coffee, bacon, and Dolgo crabapple blossoms permeated the cool morning. Sheathed newspapers lay scattered around his feet in a disorganized mess. He nudged one with his toe until it was perpendicular to the step, started in on the next one, then whistled out a breath. *Calm the fuck down. This isn't a date.* He tore his eyes from the disorder and glanced around.

Gretch's refurbished neighborhood was in a good location, close enough to downtown but still holding a quiet, suburban feel. Spring buds bloomed along the boulevard. Down at the corner, a blue awning boasted a mom-and-pop grocery store.

After what seemed like a pointedly rude delay, the outer door opened with a faint squeak, and he braced himself for Gretch's caustic greeting. An obese African-American stood with a hand on his hip, looking him up and down in that clichéd effeminate way. Irish Spring and a dense knockoff cologne overpowered the air. Sean swallowed his cough.

"Please tell me I didn't haul my fat ass all the way down here so you can hand me a religious pamphlet."

This was her housemate? The call button did say Allen/Collins. "I—uh—I'm here for Gretch?" Why had he said it like a question? He cleared his throat. "She's expecting me." Hopefully. What if Hannah hadn't notified her?

The man's brows rose to comical height. "She's never brought a man home before." He studied Sean again, lips pursed. "And you sure don't fit her type."

Right back at you. Sean shifted his weight. "I'm a colleague. Sean Quinn? I'm taking her to work?" For the love of God, why was he saying everything like he disbelieved it himself?

"Oh." Collins' face cleared. "Well, come on up."

"I'll wait here."

A slow smile spread, and black eyes twinkled. "Naw. This'll be fun. I'm Dwayne Collins, her long-suffering housemate." They shook hands, and Collins held the door wider.

Sean slid by and hesitated in the small foyer. Collins pointed to a tiny, ancient elevator with a sliding grate. There was no way that thing would hold them both. "I'll take the stairs," Sean said. "What apartment?"

"Five A."

He nodded and bolted up the steps two at a time. At the turn he spotted Collins still in the foyer watching with that peculiar smile. Like, given the eager sprint up the stairs, the man didn't believe Sean was just a coworker. But it wasn't eagerness. It was basic physics: burning off nervous energy.

Sean turned the corner and bolted up flight after flight until he was on the right floor. By the grinding squeal, the elevator was still ascending, and Sean waited politely, heart trip-hammering. He glanced at the brass 5A. Such an ordinary white door with a metal peephole and black-soled scuff marks at the bottom. Probably made by someone with their arms full of grocery bags. Someone impatient. Goosebumps raised the hairs along his arm to stiff attention.

She was in there. Maybe it was his imagination, or the heightened sense that always happened around Gretch, but her peppery perfume was unmistakable from here.

Collins squeezed out of the elevator and lifted an eyebrow. "Damn. You're not even out of breath."

Sean shrugged. The climb actually felt good. He rolled his shoulders and followed Collins into the apartment. Yep. Mingling with her housemate's robust scents were Gretch's perfume, hyacinth soap, oatmeal, cinnamon, and coffee.

"Your Ladyship," Collins called. "Your princely escort has arrived."

Sean sucked in a breath. "Uh…"

"I hope you left him in the foyer," came a muffled reply amid the rapid *click-click* of heels. A door opened at the end of the narrow hallway and there she was, in an azure silk blouse and black miniskirt that squeezed her without mercy. Sean's heart thumped painfully behind his Adam's apple.

"Oh," she said with a shaky inhale, glancing at Collins. "You didn't." She waved haphazardly, like shooing a fly. "Get yourself a cup of coffee, Sean, I'll be right there." The door slammed shut.

Collins' smile was as shiny as a toothpaste commercial. "Well, well, well."

"We're not dating," Sean said so fast it sounded like one word.

"Yes, I see that, darling. And I'll raise you a: *not yet.*" Collins cocked his head. "What do you take in your coffee?"

"I—I'll just wait outside."

"Don't be a fool. This is our chance to dish on the queen. Believe me, she's in there shitting bricks, and I want to know why."

So did Sean. And he liked the way Collins referred to her in royal terms.

Sean followed him into the kitchen, but something about this reminded him of the few awkward dates he'd experienced as a teenager. What to talk about while he waited? What to do with his hands? He folded his arms. No. As his brothers enjoyed pointing out, now he looked like he was pouting. He stuck his hands in his pockets. Yeah, that worked. He leaned against the counter, confidence growing. "What do you do?" he asked, almost high-fiving himself at how causally that came out.

"Banking. Customer due diligence."

Finance, sports, legalese, and the mechanical workings of engines. Sean never had a response to these subjects. He nodded thoughtfully.

"So." Collins prolonged the word as he poured coffee into a mug stenciled with *She Who Must Be Obeyed* in garnet and gold. "How long have you two known each other?"

"Couple years. Ever since I began working for Moore and Morrow. How about you two?" It wasn't curiosity as much as Sean instinctively redirected any subject away from himself. Hell, the details of his life bored even him.

"Oh, honey, I've known her since the fourth grade." Collins handed him the steaming mug. "Her mama chased a man here from California. I'll never forget the sight of that little girl showin' up in class. Little blond pigtails and a don't-fuck-with-me expression—teacher had no idea she was coming either."

"What was she like as a kid?" Sean sipped the coffee, which blistered his lips, but it was better than gawking at the surprising gossip.

"The same ice queen she is now, only on a miniature scale."

"How do you live with that?" Maybe he could pick up some tips.

Collins snorted. "That act is like the tippy-top of the iceberg." He flicked a hand. "There are channels and floes and thousand-foot waterfalls underneath all that snippy PMS shit."

Right. Sean rubbed the back of his neck, squinting. "Channels and flows and waterfalls of what?"

Collins laughed, belly and chins shaking with mirth. "I like you, Sean Quinn. I'm beginning to understand the door slam."

"No, seriously." Sean's heart beat way faster than after

the five-floor sprint. He was standing at the precipice of a huge secret. "Tell me what she's like underneath."

Collin sobered and shifted his weight, wincing. "She's incredibly protective of the suffering and downtrodden." He gestured with his mug. "Take me, for instance. I was bullied and beaten every day of my childhood, and you should've seen how fierce she'd get. Like this little girl had an invisible Wonder Woman costume." He waved his other hand toward the window. "Now she volunteers at a women's shelter Wednesdays, and a crisis line on Sundays. Spends every Thanksgiving and Christmas working a soup kitchen—first one there, last one to leave. And before she buys groceries, she stops by Mrs. Ferguson's next door to see what she needs. The poor dear has macular degeneration and is legally blind."

Sean nodded because speech was beyond him. For sure this wasn't Gretch-from-the-office. Although she *had* recruited the office staff to support Hannah at her apartment eviction meeting last October. That had been damn decent.

Collins air-toasted him. "And she'd kill me if she knew I told you all that."

As if on cue, a door opened and Gretch's assertive footsteps drew close. Sean thanked Collins for the coffee, pouring the rest down the drain. He'd have rinsed the mug out, except the man was beside him in an instant, reaching for it.

"Don't keep her waiting over something stupid like that," Collins warned Sean under his breath.

Sean's universe righted itself. Yes, *that* was the Gretch he knew.

He nodded his thanks and met her in the hall, masking any hint of how her nearness and that spicy scent wrecked him. "Ready?" he asked, opening the front door. She wiggled her fingers at her housemate and sailed on by without responding.

Collins grinned in undisguised glee. *Glad someone's enjoying this.* The man held out an open tin of cinnamon mints. "Here. Just in case you get lucky."

Sean took one. "By lucky, I assume you mean I spontaneously drop dead and the medical examiner appreciates my fresh breath?"

Collins chuckled. "Or lucky as in: you man up, handsome." The door shut in Sean's flaming face. He inhaled unsteadily and turned. Gretch stood by the open elevator, and he headed for it like it was a guillotine. Not because he feared the ancient contraption. Because of how close they'd have to stand together, and how long it would take for that damn thing to descend.

10

———

See, this was what happened when everyone got hysterical over her business. Twice on the way to the El station, Gretch spied a tall, handsome blond who looked exactly like Brandon. Both times it turned out to not be him, but by the time she pushed aboard the train in front of Sean, her stomach was a tight vise of nausea. *Fuck Brandon.* She knew how to stick up for herself, and she was done cowering. She'd have turned her phone back on as a symbol of her bravado, but the mash of commuters made moving impossible. In fact, the only space left was pressed tightly against the front of Sean.

Their glued bodies swayed to the rhythmic push-pull of the train. His book bag was wedged between his slightly spread legs. Their proximity meant it was between hers, too.

Her heels brought her nearly to his height, but she focused on his freshly shaved, sharp chin, instead of those brooding eyes. His clasp on the bar positioned his right bicep a millimeter from her boob. With each sway, the lemony-fresh laundry scent of his shirt enveloped her.

She stood rigid with tension, unable to ignore the hardness of him. *All* down his front. A part of her was disappointed; he'd always seemed above the average male's pervasive lust, what with the classical literature, his finesse at work...the music that had brought her to tears yesterday.

The other part of her reveled in her seductive power. He may have control over those emotionless expressions, but he couldn't hide this. And as long as she stayed in control of a guy, everything was fine. What would *it* be like with Sean?

The train lurched, throwing the standing commuters off balance, and Sean's free arm snatched her about the waist, steadying her. The embrace fused their pelvises tighter. She froze at the exact instant his jaw clamped in horrified acknowledgement, and they careened apart like two opposing magnets. Gretch apologized over her shoulder to whomever she'd body-slammed, and bit her lip. Seconds later the train screeched to a rapid halt, and with a *whoosh*, the doors opened. Masses shuffled and bumped past them.

"Oh shit," Sean breathed, squinting over her shoulder. She struggled to turn, but he clasped her again. "Don't!"

The doors hissed closed, and the abrupt acceleration pitched her into him. His steely embrace didn't drop. Exhilaration and claustrophobia warred within her. Unless she initiated it, being clutched this tightly by men —unable to move—made her want to shriek. And yet this was Sean. Harmless, oddball Sean, whose arms she once in a while fantasized being wrapped in. Here was her wish. *Relax already!*

He lowered his forehead so their noses almost

touched. His lips were right *there*. She sucked in a breath. "What are you doing?"

"Hiding behind your spiky hair."

See, the problem with Sean was: you never knew whether he had this incredibly dry sense of humor or he just thoughtlessly insulted others. His grip tightened, and, as she was still distracted by the meaning of his comment, her muscles subtly relaxed against his.

"One-two-three, go," he muttered.

"What?"

With fluid grace, he executed a tight twirl around the book bag, so his back was to the commuters he'd just faced. Her heart skipped a beat. The authoritative manner, the elegance of the move—it was right out of her childhood daydreams, before life went so horribly wrong. She'd pretend to be a princess in a red ball gown being swept into a swirling waltz. Once in a very rare while, that fantasy still came to her in dreams—spinning giddily in the arms of a man whose touch didn't repulse her. The sophisticated man had no face. He wore a tux and was really, really good, like the male dancers on that reality TV show. But this was Sean. Half nerd, half hermit. If he was adept at ballroom dancing, she'd die of laughter. Or swoon.

She found herself relaxing fully, the bulge pressing her pelvis not as unpleasant as men's erections usually were. The train rocked them to and fro. In her head, she swayed and twirled in her satin gown, and finally found the courage to glance into Sean's espresso eyes. They weren't on her. He didn't even seem aware of her or their erotic locomotive body rhythm. Instead, he studied the blocks they rocketed past, his usually tilted eyebrows knotted, his jaw taut.

"Sean?"

"We're getting off at the next stop."

She snapped out of her girlie crush. "Maybe you are, but I'm not walking the rest of the way in these heels."

He turned from the window and stared at her in that fathomless way, like he was strip-searching her mind. Ordinarily it was incredibly annoying, but this time she felt paralyzed by his gaze—the slow way his dusky black lashes lowered, the steel band of his embrace...

"I don't need your protection, Sean," she said curtly, but her breathy voice ruined it. "I'm just humoring Hannah. For today only."

The brakes squealed as they approached the next station, and lurching momentum plastered them tighter. His hypnotic eyes darkened, focusing on her mouth. *Christ in a cradle, he's going to kiss me!* Her pulse stampeded, and her lips parted on instinct.

He pressed his mouth gently to hers, the kiss achingly slow and measured. His lips were warm, the pressure light, like he was giving of himself instead of taking from her. He tasted of coffee and cinnamon and something pleasantly male.

The train jolted to a stop, and their lips bumped apart with a clumsy smacking sound. He raised his head, his face mirroring her bewilderment. The doors hissed open. He formed a syllable, no doubt to say sorry—it had been a mistake. She didn't want to hear anything out of that mouth. It would ruin the perfection of his kiss.

"I thought you wanted to get off," she snapped, nudging his book bag with her toe. "Let's go."

As they cut through the mass of bodies, she was pretty sure he muttered, "When do you ever do what I want?" She glared at him, but he was looking over his shoulder.

Gretch descended onto the platform and spun around, primed to rip into him and demand an Uber. Again his focus was elsewhere, his face pale. She followed his gaze. Amid the noise of the crowd hurrying around them, a bearded man with heavy eyebrows waved from an adjacent door as he stepped down too. "Mr. Bixby!" He appeared to be looking at Sean, and Sean seemed to think so too.

"He's not talking to you, hon," she said in a voice reserved for five-year-olds. She linked arms and pulled. "I'll pay for an—"

"I thought that was you," the man said, hurrying over. "Although I confess a bit of surprise..." He gazed at Gretch, and let the sentence hang. *What the hell?* By the dread on Sean's face, he was unmistakably in trouble. Because of the kiss? Because Sean was linking arms with her? Was it any of this man's business?

Sean cleared his throat and gestured to her. "This is—"

"His wife," Gretch blurted indignantly. The man's mouth dropped open.

"No," Sean spat out. "She's not." He unhooked his arm like he was shaking her off.

She stood breathless from the sting to her heart. The commuter noise around her faded to a dull hum as she blinked at Sean. The least cruel man she'd ever met. He ignored her as he shook the man's hand.

"Did you get my email?" the man asked, scrutinizing Sean's face intently from under those bushy brows.

"I...uh...I haven't had a chance to respond."

"Then it was fortuitous we met here." The man spread his arm to encompass the platform. "The gentleman I wanted you to meet is just down the block."

"I can't." Sean glanced around wildly. He swept a hand through his chronically messy hair. "I have an appointment," he said. "Maybe another time, Mr. El Bashtan."

"We're perfectly free," Gretch said through her teeth.

Sean's slanted brows added to the helplessness and horror he threw her way. What was he involved in that made him this squirrely? She gave him her infamous death glare before smiling over at El Bashtan. "May I come too?"

"No!"

Fucking Sean! Gretch ignored him as she oozed as much sexual innuendo into her smile as possible. "I won't be any trouble," she purred to El Bashtan. It took so little to sway men. She could do this. Screw Sean for having this side life he was so obviously trying to hide. She'd finally figure him out. She increased the wattage and squeezed the bearded man's forearm, recognizing the second he faltered. Her ego swelled in triumph.

"As you wish, miss."

"Missus," she said, with a withering side-glance at her coworker. She fluttered her hand. "Please lead the way, Mr. El Bashtan."

11

We are so fucked!

Perspiration glued Sean's shirt to his back as they set off down the block. El Bashtan chatted courteously with Gretch, but his steady frown proved he was guarded and unamused. *Two Mrs. Bixbys, Jesus Christ.*

Sean fell a step behind, fingering his phone in his windbreaker. How could he alert Jace to this disaster without further implicating himself—and now Gretch—as frauds? If El Bashtan had sent the email invitation to William Bixby, it'd gone to the FBI task force. Maybe the address they were heading toward was included.

A block and a half from the El, they turned on to a side street, which housed small shops and a bakery that wafted cinnamon-sugar and warm yeast scents. No cars or pedestrians were visible this early, and most of the display windows were still dark. On any other day, it would've been a street Sean deliberately cut down to reach a destination with a minimum of crowds. Today it meant no witnesses and no help. There was no way he'd walk Gretch any further into this danger.

Still in plain sight of the busier main street, Sean stopped and retrieved the cell phone. "I'm letting our other appointment know we're running late," he called, and the two halted patiently. He pressed Jace's cell number and sucked in a breath.

It was answered on the first ring. "Can't talk—in a meeting." Jace hung up.

Because El Bashtan and Gretch stood several feet away, Sean conversed with no one, apologizing for the delay and promising to send the file right over. Gretch's eyebrows knotted. Good. She was catching on. Art restorers had no files on their phones to send anywhere.

Sean pressed the Share My Location option, which sent Jace an instant map of his cell phone's position, then texted: *sos*. Pocketing the phone, he joined the other two, and, as a final warning to Gretch, forced his lips into a wide, cheerful smile. Life wasn't amusing. He rarely smiled. Just as he hoped, Gretch's eyes flickered in alarm.

"All set," he said to El Bashtan. "Although I'd prefer if I saw your artifacts alone."

"Nonsense," Gretch blurted in a high voice. The sly triumph from the train platform had vanished. "You're not going anywhere by yourself...*dear*."

"Please, please." El Bashtan ushered them toward a shop on the other side of the bakery. "It's just this way."

As Sean stepped off the curb, Gretch slipped her hand in his. Not knowing what else to do, he squeezed it. Their kiss had been a spontaneous fluke. The erotic rhythm of the train oscillating their bodies back and forth had done such a number on his nerves and cock that when he'd spotted El Bashtan studying him, Sean had thrown caution to the wind. If he was going to die today, he was going down with his ultimate wish fulfilled: a simple kiss from Gretch.

Her supple lips and spearmint taste had been his

undoing. Even in the midst of this disaster, all he craved was to do it again, somewhere safe. And for much, much longer. As it was, something had transformed between them, because holding her hand felt right, even though they were approaching a place that might very well support ISIS. No doubt the shop owner had a concealed carry permit. Sean's martial arts training would've provided solace had Gretch not been around for this debacle.

The shop's interior was dark. A white sign hung on the glass door with "closed" in blood red. The bright red of a fresh wound, not the dark, coagulated kind. Sean shook the thought from his head.

El Bashtan dug a small ring of keys out of his pocket and unlocked the three locks lining the steel. He reached in, flicked on the lights, and held the door for them. Sean swallowed thickly as he followed Gretch inside. The place smelled of mold, and dust swirled in the dim overhead light, leaving most of the store in an ominous shadow. The portion of the store that was visible looked like it had been decorated by a hoarder; little aisle space remained due to cluttered merchandise stacked everywhere.

"Please look around," El Bashtan said. "My colleague will be here shortly."

Why would he still want to present his wares? Surely he was suspicious. Sean needed a backup plan fast. First up: a layout of the store. Hopefully an exit at the other end would lead to an alley, or even better—a busy street. He pushed Gretch in front of him. They shuffled down the first aisle, avoiding the messy arrangement of antique tables, writing desks, sofas, and cupboards. Large manila tags with prices listed in bold black marker dangled off the furniture. Smaller white tags dotted accessories, lamps, grimy books with torn bindings, and dinnerware that littered the surfaces. At a glance, the antique shop looked more like a Goodwill store. The clutter strung Sean out more than the danger they faced. The floating dust twitched his sinuses. This was literally his vision of Hell. How could this owner have third-millennium BC relics?

The aisle abruptly ended, like a maze, and they cautiously made their way down an adjacent path to the back of the store. There was no exit. Mirrors in various stages of warped disrepair hung on the entire back wall. Gretch made eye contact in the closest and said through stiff lips, "Where exactly are we, and why?"

What to tell her? This was an FBI undercover investigation gone horribly wrong? One he'd begged to be on? Or that it began as a typical exploit in Jace's constant pursuit to be the best? He'd been an SAA for three months but still needed to stand out like he needed his next breath. *Hey, why not catch an ISIS accomplice without going through proper, red-tape agency procedures, like waiting for the team anthropologist to wrap up another case?*

Conscious of the mirrors and El Bashtan by the entrance on his phone, Sean picked up a glass ashtray and studied it closely, so his head was lowered. "I met him yesterday and asked about an artifact."

"Why is he calling you Bixby?"

Sean shrugged. "Because I rarely give anyone my real name."

Gretch scoffed, but in a testament to what a freak she must think he was, she didn't press the lie. Her lips tightened, and she drilled him with her annoyed-princess stare. "Are we in danger?"

He placed the ashtray back in its exact position and turned to her. "Yes." He never thought he'd miss her haughty expression, but the flash of fear replacing it speared through him.

"Why?" she whispered.

"This man we're supposed to meet. He may have ties to ISIS."

Gretch's breath hitched. "Call nine-one-one."

"And say what? We're in a junk store and haven't met the owner, but he may be dangerous? Running a shop like this?" He gestured at the wares.

She glanced around the clutter, then at El Bashtan, who was nodding and still talking. Her fingers tangled together. "What are we going to do?"

Her voice sounded childlike, and he ached to hold her close again. Instead he turned slowly, like he was taking in this hoarder's paradise.

There was a wooden door in the far back corner. No doubt the owner's office. Surely there was a back exit through there, or a window in a bathroom they could climb out of. He glanced at his dark phone screen. Jace clearly hadn't gotten the text; there was no cavalry coming. He had to protect Gretch. "Let's just leave. He knows I had another appointment, and his colleague isn't here. We'll tell him I'll come back another time."

Gretch's expression cleared and, after a few seconds, she nodded. "Okay. And if he gives us any guff, you do your karate chop thing."

"Deal." He hid his surprise. How did she know about his martial arts?

They slowly made their way back through the aisle-maze as El Bashtan stuck his phone in his pocket and smiled. "The best of news. My colleague is on his way."

"I'm afraid we can't wait," Sean said, plastering on a regretful smile. "I'll call you and set up another time."

"No, no. He is just down the street."

Sean's gut clenched. They had to get out of here. "Thank you for your time, Mr. El Bashtan." He brushed by the man, adding, "This is an interesting store."

"Mr. Bixby. The items you search for are not on display. He will be right here."

Sean reached for the doorknob, but movement in his peripheral vision froze him. El Bashtan had shifted into the aisle, blocking Gretch. She stilled behind the hefty man, her dark-chocolate eyes wide and pleading.

Do your karate chop thing. Inwardly Sean sighed and gathered himself at his center, where his warrior waited, coiled like a deadly serpent. "Mr. El Bashtan, she needs to get by."

As he stepped toward El Bashtan, the door behind Sean opened. He pivoted back. A gray-haired man holding a four-pronged cane hobbled in, his onyx eyes merry with welcome. He looked past Sean, and a smile broadened his face. "Good morning. Isn't this a surprise?"

"Mr. Adyton," Gretch exclaimed.

Sean frowned between the shop owner and Gretch, who squeezed past to clasp Adyton's hand and peck his cheek. "I didn't get to say goodbye yesterday," she said in her flirt-mode voice.

"Gretch?" Sean murmured.

"Mr. Adyton is one of our clients," she said, beaming. "You'll probably be his restorer."

Sean nodded, but a sick taste entered his mouth. Jace's undercover investigation had just detonated. Now both these men knew he wasn't Professor Bixby from Wisconsin who collected relics. And they knew where he and Gretch worked, potentially putting all of Moore and Morrow at risk. This fiasco could not have a more doomed conclusion if it had been named Operation Titanic. Their only saving grace was that Adyton didn't know his silly Bixby act was an FBI-led task force op.

Tires screeched, and Sean spun back. A black Suburban rocked to a stop at the curb.

12

G retch recognized the FBI Suburban the exact moment Sean dashed out of the shop. Light bulbs went off, and chills raced down her spine. Whatever Jace and Sean had been up to yesterday was tied to this store. And this impromptu excursion, that had clearly freaked Sean out right from the El station, wasn't something trivial he'd been investigating in his spare time. They really had been in danger. Did this have to do with the mysterious inventory list and massive price change?

The heavily tinted windows and Sean's back blocked whomever it was he spoke to through the cracked front passenger window, but his stance was as rigid as it been on Saturday night across Teenie's dance floor.

Both older men watched the scene, then glanced at each other. Their look fueled her misgivings.

El Bashtan turned his beady stare toward her. "Mr. Bixby is quite an unusual fellow."

He was, and no doubt the men were as startled at Sean's abrupt exit as she was, but the bearded man's remark flared the defender in her. It was one thing for her to think or even say that to Sean's face, but uttered by a stranger, it was as offensive as if the man had just insulted her. "Actually, he's insanely brilliant."

Adyton clasped the cane in both hands and leaned his weight on it heavily. "May I ask what brought you both in today?"

Her answer would make or break whatever Sean had set into place yesterday. Whatever had made him just rush out of the store. Gretch scanned the dusty merchandise. Adyton sold cheap shit, but he also possessed a gold-leaf Quran that required bodyguards. Maybe he was in the business of renovating and reselling high-end art somewhere else. She went on gut instinct. "Part of our client service is to gather potential buyers interested in the art we restore," she said. "Did Walter not mention that yesterday?"

The old man shook his head, his eyes steady and searching on hers. It suddenly seemed airless in here. Any word could trip her up. She nodded to Sean, given she had no clue what Bixby's first name was. "We were on our way to an appointment when we met Mr. El Bashtan. That's the other party's car; they must be anxious to meet with us."

Wait, now the men would want to meet with Jace!

"Not on your beautiful piece," she added hastily. "We offer the service to clients with fully restored artifacts. Perhaps that's why Walter didn't mention it yet." Was she blathering? Perspiration beaded her upper lip.

The bearded man held up a hand, the universal sign to stop. "You said he was your husband—"

Sean's rude rejection on the platform made so much sense now. She struck a pose, showing off her best assets. "Oh please, Mr. El Bashtan. Look at me. How can you think I was serious?" She fought to keep her flirtatious smile from faltering. "It's an ongoing joke at the office." An office she was going to have to quickly warn if they received a call checking on whether a Bixby worked there.

"So the other woman *is* his wife."

Her heart skipped a beat, and this time the smile faltered. Did he have a girlfriend? Maybe someone in the FBI? "Probably. I don't know him well enough," she admitted.

El Bashtan blinked, the slow deliberateness resembling a crocodile. "And he indicated his search was on behalf of a museum in Wisconsin."

Christ in a cradle. "We don't want to jeopardize our clients' privacy, so we tend to work with aliases when researching the buying and selling portion of our trade." Did that make sense?

The men exchanged a second glance chock-full of doubt. Her lungs refused to work properly. Had she just helped Jace and Sean or made things worse?

Outside, Sean stepped back, nodding. The window rolled up, and he strode to the store, poker-faced. Part of her went weak with relief, while another emptied more sweat out her pores. Now came the really tricky part. Making sure whatever came out of his mouth jibed with all the lies she'd just spouted. "Here he comes now." She needed the men's focus turned toward Sean, so she could warn him with everything but words.

Sean opened the door, and Gretch transferred all her panic into her expression. "Was that the buyer we were supposed to meet this morning?" she brayed, nodding urgently.

Sean blinked a few times. For once, his expressionlessness was a godsend. "Yes." His posture remained rigid, his eyes riveted to hers.

"That's what I thought. Well, Mr. Adyton, it was nice to see you again, and I'll have Walter explain the details of our additional service. Mr. El Bashtan..." She swept by them, ready to shove Sean backward out the door, but he pivoted aside and pushed it open for her.

"Gentlemen," he said, and then they were outside in the cool, sweet morning air. Safe.

Sean settled a palm on the small of her back and steered her toward the Suburban. As he reached for the door handle, he cleared his throat roughly. "Whatever went down in there, you have my eternal gratitude."

"How about next time we just stay on the El?" Her knees shook, making it hard not to fall into the SUV on her wobbly heels. Climbing in, she greeted Jace, in the passenger seat, who introduced the female agent driver. Gretch only caught her first name, Margo. The last name was drowned out by Sean shutting her door and Gretch's skittering heart still pulsing in her ears.

He hurried around and got in the other side. When the Suburban lurched forward, Gretch rested her head against the leather and exhaled a long sigh. Now that she was out of danger, she rode the adrenalin rush. When had she ever felt the exhilaration of the hunt without the dread of the expected aftermath? Maybe she'd missed her calling as an undercover cop or CIA spy.

"What happened in there?" Jace demanded. He'd turned almost fully in the passenger seat so he had a clear view of both of them. The affable guy from yesterday had morphed into an intense agent in full interrogation mode.

Gretch glanced at Sean, beseeching his understanding. Either she'd helped him or wrecked everything. "I told them Moore and Morrow also recruits interested buyers for art we restore, and that we'd been on our way to such an appointment. That we do it anonymously, which is why Bixby, here, said he was from Wisconsin."

Sean's eyebrows rose comically high. A faint grin appeared. She turned her attention to Jace. "I said you were the buyers. That you'd detoured to meet us."

"That's actually brilliant under the circumstances," Margo said quietly. She studied Gretch in the rearview with interest. "You've got a knack for this."

A warmth spread through Gretch. By no means did she lack intelligence, but it never occurred to her to pursue a lofty goal like working for the Bureau. Generally, she ruined career starts because of the mess she made socializing with the men there. Hostess, pharma rep, personal trainer... Eventually she'd be avoiding so many disastrous encounters it was easier to pick up and start anew in a completely different field. And what would life be like if she was actually *challenged*? She'd totally nail the FBI physical qualifications—

"Sean said you knew the owner of the shop," Jace interrupted in that energetic agent tone, ignoring his partner's compliment. Gretch told them about Adyton, the Quran in the suitcase, the bodyguards, and her presumption that there was another shop with high-end art. She was about to add the inventory list priced at sixty million, but that might get Walter in trouble. She'd ask him about it later.

Jace began typing on his phone.

Margo braked for a light and turned to Jace. "Let's interview Walter. Get a background check going on Ad—"

"Already started." Jace kept texting.

"Check for warehouses or other shops under his name."

"Texted Dirk to investigate that angle."

"His bank—"

"Next on the list." The clipped tone shut down whatever Margo intended to say next. She cut her eyes front and glared at the red light.

"You can track his bank transfers, right?" Sean asked, oblivious to the tense dynamic between the two agents. "See if he's sending funds to known ISIS accounts?"

A muscle spasmed along Jace's jaw. Gretch braced herself.

"Just submit your resignation again, Sean," he said without looking up. "Effective immediately."

Sean snorted. "How about you look up the details of my contract?" He jabbed a finger at his brother. "My agreement with the FBI was to *consult*. I don't know covert operations. Or what to do when I suddenly have two wives."

"I'm sorry we put you in that position, Sean," Margo said. Another puzzle piece fell into place. Margo had been a part of yesterday's adventure too. Gretch huffed out a breath as a band inside her chest eased. Sean kept glowering at his older brother. The sullen pull of his lips had all the marks of an inferiority complex, which was rich coming from an opera–Shakespeare buff. But his inner agony sparked her sympathy.

"In my opinion," she said, "they had no idea the FBI was outside their shop. We haven't tainted your investigation."

Jace snorted. "Oh, they knew. Art collectors don't come screaming up to an obscure store first thing in the morning—"

"We don't know what they know," Margo interrupted in a tight voice. "The investigation could be compromised, or Gretch just strengthened Sean's role in continuing with this case. We need to pull back and evaluate the state of our op before proceeding."

The muscle in Jace's jaw popped again. He scrolled

through his phone with a mutinous expression, and if anything, Margo's words seemed to make Sean feel worse. He slumped back. "Look, we've inadvertently involved Gretch. They know where she works. If they realize any of what she said was a lie, you need to provide her some kind of protection."

"*Me*?" she exclaimed. How had this suddenly become her problem? Sean arriving at her doorstep got her into this mess in the first place... "Worry about the fact that, if anything, they know you're a fraud. I'll be fine."

"If you were *fine*," he retorted, "we'd have arrived at Moore and Morrow separately. Maybe you should vet your pickups more carefully, princess."

Jace glanced up from his phone. "Pickups?"

Gretch ignored him, sneering at his younger brother. "I asked you what was wrong on the train. Maybe if you opened your mouth once in a while, instead of communicating in one-word grunts, I could've figured out how to ditch El Bashtan instead of begging to join in the fun."

Sean shook his head like he was tired of explaining something to a child. "The point is, Jace, we have priceless art in that lab. I'd hate to see the place firebombed."

Gretch rolled her eyes. "Would you lighten up? Adyton—"

"Both of you, shut it," Jace said quietly. He was reading his phone screen, that same muscle clenching along his jaw. After a minute, he looked up at Margo. "Adyton is on our smuggling watch list. His shop listed a gold-leaf Quran on eBay yesterday. Five hundred years old. Asking price four mil. Condition is 'fragile, being refurbished at Chicago's finest restoration firm.' Six-week bid date. We can track the product, the sale, and wherever he transfers the proceeds."

The Suburban turned the final corner. "So in the

end," Gretch said, arching her brow, "our blundering adventure *did* help your case."

Sean stiffened, like he didn't appreciate her coming to his defense. Jace didn't answer. In the rearview, Margo gave her an appraising look. "Under the circumstances, you both handled yourselves well. We'll get through this hiccup." She nodded to Sean. "Just carry on about your business, and keep all of this confidential."

As the car rolled to a stop outside Moore and Morrow, Jace stuffed his phone into his breast pocket and hopped out.

Sean yanked on his own door handle, pinning Gretch with an icy glare. "It isn't necessary to defend me to Jace. I can speak up for myself."

"Yeah, I've noticed. In fact, I wish you'd shut up once in a while." *Fucking Quinn brothers.* Ignoring Margo's quiet laugh and the hand Sean held out, Gretch stepped from the vehicle and made a show of adjusting and smoothing her skirt. Jace was by the office door, waiting for them. He'd put on his sunglasses, which made reading his expression difficult, but he held himself as stiffly as Sean. When she reached his side, Jace murmured, "What was that about pickups?"

She batted the comment aside with a wave of her hand, Sean's words still chapping her ass. "Pay no attention. Your brother's acting like Chicken Little." She ignored Sean's grunted profanity as they trooped into the reception area.

Hannah stood at Gretch's desk, the phone to her ear. When she saw them, her worried features smoothed out. "I was frantic," she said, hanging up. "Where have you two—" She stopped as Margo and Jace appeared.

"Jason Quinn, FBI, ma'am," Jace said, flipping open a wallet. "This is Special Agent Margo Hathaway."

Margo displayed her badge with less Hollywood pomp. "We'd like to speak to the owner."

A myriad of emotions raced across Hannah's face, predominantly shock and alarm. Like she needed to be dealing with this, when she was so worried about Devon and his company. Before Gretch could assure her their presence had nothing to do with Moore and Morrow, Hannah turned to her. "Is this about Brandon stalking you?"

And there it was. The stupid topic she'd have gladly kept from either Quinn brother until her dying day.

"Stalking?" Jace muttered from behind. She didn't turn, just shook her head and motioned Hannah away from her desk.

"This is one of the owners, Hannah Moore. This is Sean's brother," she said, diffusing the mystique of an agent marching in with his tough-guy attitude. Hannah glanced in disbelief between the two men, no doubt because they looked nothing alike. As if reading her mind, Sean glowered and dropped his eyes to the carpet.

"They have some questions about the Quran Mr. Adyton brought in yesterday."

If anything, Hannah looked more flustered as she ushered Jace and Margo into the conference room and asked Sean to go get Walter and the project.

"I'll get him," Gretch said hastily, thumbing his office right behind her. She may as well pre-explain her lying about additional services. Walter would not take kindly to any of it. He lived by devout Christian rules and the reputation of Moore and Morrow, both of which she'd played fast and loose with this morning. Luckily, she answered all calls and would know if Adyton checked on her explanations.

She turned and stopped short. Sean had moved with the speed of light and now leaned against the wall near

Walter's office, arms folded, lips pressed in censure. Strange how she couldn't recall the enchantment his mouth had conjured an hour ago.

"Chicken Little?" he bit out.

"My social life is none of your damn business."

A smirk appeared, feeding her ire. "It's enough of my damn business that I hoofed it all the way to your side of town this morning. It's enough of my damn business that Hannah requested you take my martial arts class this eve—"

"So much for your eternal gratitude! Let me be perfectly clear, Sean: I don't need you to bodyguard me, and I have no intention of taking your class. Ever."

"Really?" he replied, the word dripping with false friendliness. "'Cause Hannah made it sound like an order."

Gretch folded her arms. "She would never assume that kind of authority over me, and you know it."

"Let's go ask her, then." Sean gestured at the conference room. "After you."

Gretch struggled to keep the panic off her face. Hannah would totally side with Sean. Even if she didn't, having this dumb discussion in front of Jace and Margo wasn't worth accepting Sean's dare. "Fine," she sputtered, "email me the details. But don't expect me to be all Suzie Sunshine with your other students."

He shrugged, back to the poker face that ratcheted every nerve in her body. "I doubt they'll care." He knocked twice on the threshold. "See ya tonight."

She glared at his loping retreat until he vanished into his cubicle. She'd ace his goddamn class tonight.

Still fuming, she opened Walter's door. He was on the phone and stopped mid-sentence, frowning. "We have a situation," she began, but he held up a hand.

"I'll be out there in a second, Gretchen."

She made her way back to her desk, snatched her phone out of her purse, and turned it back on. Twenty-three texts. One from Zamira about next Sunday's shift at the hotline, the rest from Brandon. She read each dispassionately. This was a guy who got his jollies being a pest. There were no clues that he'd been stalking her around town. She sighed and muted the device. Best just to ignore him.

13

———

The tall, gray-haired, gray-suited man who placed the Quran on the small conference table had to be the other owner. Jace scrolled through the pictures of the eBay offering as introductions were made, and after shaking Walter's hand with a quick one-two pump, Jace nodded to Margo, who'd bogarted the seat at the head of the table. "Appears to be the same Quran."

"I'm unclear why you're here," Walter said, sitting across from him. "Is there a problem with this artifact?"

Jace drilled him with a lethal stare. "Have you dealt with Adyton or anyone from the Days of Olde shop before?"

Walter shook his head, the cooperative mood on his face stalling as his own unanswered question hovered in the air.

"It's an ongoing investigation, sir," Margo said, blinding him with her cheerful smile. "Not something we can comment on, but your company is not our focus. We just have a couple of questions about the piece."

Jace stiffened as she basically overrode the authority he was establishing. Even worse, Margo went into interrogations with a cheerleader's sunniness, the tinge to her questions almost apologetic. *Sorry to bother you folks, just a couple of questions.* Her approach was even too nice for the good cop-bad cop routine. This was the FBI, damn it! But in the end, she was the special agent, and he was the lowly putz "learning" on the job. She pulled a legal pad out of her briefcase and clicked her pen. "How did Adyton receive your name?"

"A referral."

"We'll require that name," Jace interrupted, pulling up the FBI's Terrorist Screening Database.

Walter and Hannah traded worried looks.

"We're only fact-finding at the moment," Margo said gently.

Walter fingered his collar and straightened his tie. Each fidget detonated another particle of Jace's patience. He intensified his stare. "Sir?"

"Saleh Talal. He lives in Park Ridge. We've completed extensive work for him."

Jace typed in the name. No hits. He glanced at Margo and shook his head.

"What type of work are you doing for Adyton?" she asked.

Walter's brow puckered. "Restoring the artifact. It's what we do."

"Does your company check incoming art against any databases of stolen items?"

"That's not the kind of clientele we have," Hannah blurted, blushing the same crimson as the executive chairs in here. "These are millionaires and billionaires."

Jace nodded. "Please answer the question."

"Of course not." Walter yanked his collar again. "We build our relationships on mutual trust and our excellent service." Sweat glistened on his forehead. "Are you implying this Quran is stolen?"

"Not at all," Margo said. "But if it were, do you have a system in place to identify it?"

"Only if they asked us to verify their certificate of authenticity. It's a service we offer right from the initial consultation. Gretch handles all provenance research."

Margo flashed her perky smile. High school cheers ricocheted around Jace's head. *Kick it, punt it, run it down.* "Are you doing that research for Adyton?" she asked sweetly. *Stop that frown, it's a touchdown!*

"No." Walter glanced at his watch. "I doubt we can help you further."

"Actually, you can." Margo clasped her hands and rested them on the pad. "I'd like to ask Gretch a couple of questions about her provenance research."

TODAY WAS QUINTESSENTIALLY a *Tristan and Isolde* day. Sean selected the tragic love triangle by Wagner, an opera so heavy and dramatic it initially had a reputation for killing off singers and conductors due to the exertion. He went straight to the third act, where the hero begs for relief from the torment of his love.

Next he set up his workstation, collecting the tools and chemicals the project would require, then arranged them by frequency of use, and finally sub-grouped them by size. Each step in his routine relaxed him further. Finally, he grabbed the ugly charity painting and paused. Maybe it was this morning's adrenalin versus the exhaustion of last night, but the canvas was too heavy. Whoever transferred this from the Wickham mansion last October should've picked up on the unusual weight back then. Sean closed his eyes. Who'd handled the painting? *Oh yeah. Robbie, the intern. Mystery solved.* He rotated the frame and traced the seam attached to the back of the canvas. *Jesus.*

He ripped out his earbuds and internally dialed Hannah. "When you're done with my brother, can you take a look at something?"

"I'm free," she said. "Jason left, and Margo is meeting with Gretch."

"Why?"

"She's interested in how we authenticate provenances. Be right there."

Now that the music wasn't blaring, the office buzzed with distracting noise. Like Gretch touring Margo through the break room and explaining the eccentricities of the ancient coffee maker.

Within a minute, Hannah stood at the entrance to his cubicle. "Oh my gosh," she cried. "What are you doing?"

Her words jolted him from his chair. "I was about to clean—"

"You know this isn't a priority, Sean. We're under crazy deadlines."

Sean frowned at her. *What the hell?* Hannah never raised her voice, never confronted anyone. Besides, Gretch had been emphatic...

Gretch. His jaw clamped. This was her idea of a practical joke? Goddamn it! What if he'd spent days cleaning this POS?

"Sorry, Hannah," he said in a stilted tone to cover his fury. "I really spaced it." Now it was her turn to frown, but he'd learned long ago how unintelligent it was to tattle. He fingered the second seam under the ugly canvas. What was under here? "It's just—I think this is hiding another painting."

Margo murmured something, and Gretch's peal of laughter sounded like fingernails on a chalkboard. He gritted his teeth. All he wanted was revenge. Cold, humiliating payback that would knock Gretch off her fucking throne.

"Mr. Wickham doesn't want it back," Hannah said. By her tight lips, her attention was still on his idiocy and the potential loss of billable hours. "If we follow his wishes then technically we can strip the outer canvas off, clean it, reframe it, and still donate it. But not *now*."

"Got it."

She reached over and felt the seam's bump. The dawning interest on her face mirrored the curiosity inside him. "What do you think is under here?"

Sean shook his head. "How about if I finish this off the clock?"

"All right. Keep me posted."

"IT's like solving a mystery," Gretch said, logging onto the computer in the conference room, then sliding the monitor between her and Margo. "You start with the current purchase and trace who owned the art all the way back to when it was created. Hopefully the piece already comes with an original certificate of authenticity, a COA, also known as a provenance."

Margo began jotting notes on her pad, raptly watching the monitor. "I imagine there are lots of problems, given wartime looting or poor recordkeeping."

"Yeah, it happens more than you know. It's like searching for your ancestors...one church fire and generations of people's lives are suddenly much more difficult to prove. Here's what I'm working on now."

Gretch opened a manila file with her current project's documentation, receipt of sale, and the owner's basic research that came with the provenance. "This is a Viviard." She pulled out a photograph of a still life in filtered sunlight. "First, I authenticate his signature and the date of completion. See? Eighteen ninety-one." She displayed close-up photos.

"The present owner bought this painting on eBay. Here's his receipt. The prior owner, who put it up for auction, is the nephew and heir of a deceased woman who owned it. Here's a copy of the painting among her insured assets.

"And based on this customs receipt, the woman bought it in Paris in nineteen sixty-five. See—here's the shop's name. My job now is to find out when and where *they* acquired it, and so on, back to Viviard's decision to sell sometime after he'd painted it."

She grabbed her coffee mug. "So far I have the inventory lists for the Parisian shop as far back as nineteen fifty-three. I use a translation app on my phone. You just hover over the word, and it translates."

"How easy is it to forge any of this?" Margo pointed to the shop inventory listed by the year. "Could the whole thing be a bogus paper trail?"

"Sure. And it's way too easy to forge a COA. Another service we offer is forensic analysis. If this was painted last month and someone forged Viviard's signature and declared it painted in eighteen ninety-one, we can test the age of the paint and the canvas. Or compare the minutiae of his painting style, or his signature with his other works. Right now we farm that part of our service out, but one day Walter wants to have a branch here."

Margo sat back and tapped her pen on the pad. "So smugglers dealing with ancient artifacts know forensic testing will prove the correct age, but to get someone to fork over thousands or millions, provenances will have to be forged."

Gretch nodded. "There's no question in my mind that's being done."

"The gold-leaf Quran. Would you be able to trace the piece from Adyton and his eBay listing to where it came from before?"

"I wouldn't get far without his permission. But anyone bidding on it should be able to request and receive the provenance. If the seller says no or that he'll only provide it to the winning bidder, that's a huge red flag."

"Can we trace it through stolen inventory lists?"

"It'll take forever." Gretch produced her laminated Stolen Art Alert cheat sheet. Four cultural watchdog sites were listed, sponsored by INTERPOL and UNESCO. "Even searching for a gold-leaf Quran would be a needle in a haystack."

"We'll initiate a computer search on keywords. *Gold leaf* should narrow it down."

Gretch shook her head. "That's what I mean. The haystack is millions of archive numbers, very few descriptions. You can't believe how many museums and libraries in the Middle East have been looted."

"We have the manpower to try." Margo frowned and tapped her pen on her pad. "Perhaps a two-pronged approach. Gather intelligence on the forgers who are creating the fake provenances to scam these ignorant art collectors."

Gretch laughed. "Don't let the rich hear you calling them ignorant."

"But it's true, right? They get enough documentation to establish provenance and fork over millions."

Gretch nodded. The way Margo spoke to her on a colleague level was cool. "I've heard somewhere that forty percent of the art world is probably made up of forgeries. A provenance and the trust of a reputable dealer are all the wealthy clients have, unless they go through the expense of forensic testing."

Margo reached for her phone. "I'll initiate a warrant

to begin the forensic test on the Quran so we know exactly what we're dealing with."

"Can you do that if it's privately owned?"

She nodded without ceasing the rapid typing. "If there's suspicion that the profits pay for weapons or recruiting lone wolves, we'll have no problem under the PATRIOT Act."

Kicking ass and taking names. The nervous energy from this morning's success gripped Gretch again. "I've already established a rapport with Mr. Adyton. I can see if he'd answer questions on the provenance."

Margo shook her head. "We'll do that from our end, but thanks for all this information." She shook Gretch's hand. "I meant what I said in the car. You've got a knack for this."

After she left, Gretch tapped her fingernails on the ceramic mug, staring at the Paris inventory list. The FBI. That would be such a cool career. She brought up Adyton's Quran on eBay. How great would it be to use her research skills to authenticate him as a legitimate art dealer or out him as a smuggler? That would really knock Margo's socks off. Just place a bid for the Quran and request verification of the provenance. After that, it only took one thread to unravel deception.

14

The karate studio's tinkling chimes announced Gretch's late arrival. "Sonofabitch," she whispered, horror flashing through her. Had less advertising covered the broad windows, she'd have seen the trap before bursting in like this. She pressed against the door to slip back out, but Sean, in black-belted pajamas, swiveled from modeling a stance and grinned broadly. Any other time she'd have melted at how it lit his face. But not here, with five little boys staring wide-eyed at her.

"Welcome. Stand next to Phillip, please." Sean pointed to the smallest boy at the end of the line, who sported a mop of bright red hair and a watch way too big for his wrist. When she remained stationary, Sean's brows lifted. His challenge glinted openly.

Damn it. Damn *him*! She'd lose face either way, although arriving at work tomorrow as a yellow-bellied coward was worse than whatever humiliation he planned tonight. She released her grip on the door handle and set her shoulders.

"Class, meet our guest, Miss Gretchen Allen," Sean

said, his calm instructor voice contradicting the confrontational expression the boys couldn't see.

The boys immediately broke their imitation stances and bowed as one.

"As a special surprise for our guest, we'll switch from practicing katas to learning judo throw-downs."

Of course. Gretch closed her eyes as a chorus of cheers went up around the dojo. *Sonofabitch.* Jaw clenched, she tossed her purse under the front desk, kicked off her flip-flops, and shrugged out of her oversized sweatshirt. *Let's get this shit over with.* She spun around and stepped onto the cool mat, her posture regal and rigid.

Sean's gaze swept over her black knit tank and snug yoga pants. The long, slow appraisal wasn't anything she'd witnessed from him before, as if this hottie ninja had bound and gagged the restoration geek. Her courage stalled. This was going to be a bloodbath of humiliation. How would she get through the hour? Or look him in the eye tomorrow?

Like you always do. Shut up and rule the situation. She marched toward Phillip, who opened his mouth to speak, but closed it after a glance from Sean. Gretch winked at the little boy and stood in line, dredging up her über-cool bar-scene composure.

"This is an over-the-shoulder toss you can use when your opponent comes at you from behind." Sean spoke to the boys, like he was no longer aware Gretch was in the room. "We'll break it into components and then practice. First—I need a volunteer to help demonstrate." Every boy's hand waved frantically.

"Pick me, Sensei," Phillip pleaded, on tiptoes. Gretch pursed her lips and studied her manicure.

"How about if we choose our guest?" Amid the groans of disappointment, Sean called her name. He backed up to the middle of the mat and crooked his finger. He was so fucking predictable!

"You're so lucky," Phillip whined.

"That's not the word I'd use," she murmured, and headed out to center stage.

She faced Sean dourly, and he gazed back like he was waiting. For what? Her to chicken out? She shrugged. "Let's do this."

"You have to bow to Sensei," Phillip stage-whispered. "You were supposed to before you stepped on the mat too."

"Oh, dear God," she muttered, and although Sean didn't repeat his broad grin, a predatory gleam entered his eyes. She clenched her teeth and bowed at the waist.

"Very good." Sean walked behind her. "This is one of the self-defense moves that will counter an opponent doing this." He slid his arm around her clavicle and tightened his grip, gluing her backside to the front of him with much more authority than anything he'd done on the train this morning. The body heat coming through his pajamas was like being plastered to a furnace. The pressure on her lungs was uncomfortable, but damn if she'd utter a peep.

"We've talked about breaking this hold by raising your arms and dropping to the ground, right?" His commanding voice buzzed in her ear. "But a second method is a throw-down, also known as a takedown or tossing your opponent. Gretch, why don't you demonstrate?"

Amid the snickers and calls of "do it!" she summoned regal mockery. "You want *me* to toss *you*?"

"Isn't it on your bucket list?" His tone was low and amused, and his breath stirred her hair. He adjusted his hold tighter. There was no way she could inhale, much less escape. His limbs molded against hers too closely—she couldn't get purchase to back-kick him in the balls.

Fury and embarrassment morphed into determination. She was a toned, fit ex-personal trainer. He had no idea how strong she was. She gripped the arm that held her prisoner, snapped forward at the waist, and used all her might and muscle to flip him over her shoulder. He bent effortlessly with her, until they were in a porn-style, downward-dog yoga pose. The boys erupted into giggles.

"Any day now, Miss Allen," he said loudly, for their benefit.

"Why don't you go—"

"Don't you swear in my dojo, Gretch," he murmured. The steely tone and intimacy of their position awoke something within. A ferocious hunger for something. She tightened her grip on his forearm to hold back the shiver.

With humiliating ease, he hauled her back to the original stance. "As you can see, class, it's not as easy as it looks on TV."

Sean spun in a blur until he stood before her, then manhandled her arm until it was wrapped around his throat. He still smelled of lemons, and now fresh sweat. Gretch inhaled unsteadily. Technically, she was in a position of power, the perpetrator. The controller. Why did she feel so helplessly feminine? To counteract the silliness fluttering through her insides, she flexed her bicep, but the firm grip he had on her arm gave him comfortable room to breathe and speak.

"The trick," he continued, "is to create a fulcrum and lever. Step forward with your right foot and shift your weight—like so." His demonstration raised her on tiptoes, plastering her fully along his backside. Butterflies shimmered low in her belly. "This allows you to use the person's momentum to follow through. Like this."

A subtle twist tossed her into the air. She landed with

a graceless *whoof* on the mat. He knelt beside her inelegant sprawl. "And then," he said in a voice meant only for her, "it's lights out." The look in his eyes oozed pure confidence and smoking-hot promise.

Gretch gaped at him. Her limbs quivered like jelly, much worse than when she'd crossed marathon finish lines. She couldn't summon anger if she tried. All she wanted to do was drown in that scorching gaze.

Sean's expression shuttered. "You okay?"

She nodded, and he helped her up like the wretched rag doll she was. "Excuse me," he said formally, and wandered about adjusting grips and instructing the boys, completely unaffected by that spark of sizzling chemistry.

Partnerless and enthralled, Gretch tracked every move of this *other* Sean. Who knew the temperamental introvert was good with kids? Or could transform into a commanding warrior? Did he even realize how freaking sexy he was right now?

Back turned, he bent beside two boys. The cotton *gi* strained, providing what those loose jeans and button-downs never could: a clear view of his tight ass. She stared at the muscled orbs outlined in the uniform. Too soon he straightened. Now his well-defined shoulders and slim hips captivated her. Her pulse flowed thickly as she fantasized about being alone with him on the mat. Dropping to her knees before him. Easing down those white pajamas...

She pressed her lips and spun around. What kind of rabbit hole had she fallen into? He didn't belong anywhere near the black void inside her. He'd gotten his giggles. The lesson had never been meant for her. Besides, she'd already demonstrated how ineffective she'd be if Brandon ever caught her from behind.

In five long strides, she was at the desk.

"A warrior never retreats," Sean said, his nearness and

quiet authority making her jump. How the hell did he move so *silently*?

"I'm not a warrior, and I'm not retreating," she snapped. "I need to get home." She picked up her sweatshirt and purse. "You made your point to the little boys. Glad I could help." She rummaged for her unlimited El pass.

"Turns out that ugly Wickham painting is *not* on the priority list."

She stilled. On any other man, she'd have sworn the soft tone was filled with humor. She glanced at his hard mouth and swallowed. Nope. No humor there at all. He rested an ass cheek on the desk and folded his arms. She'd never noticed those sinewy biceps before either—

"On the bright side," he added, "I get to add Hannah to the list of people who think I'm short a couple million brain cells."

"It was a joke. I started to tell you yesterday, but you were so focused on the adventure with your brother."

He shrugged loosely, the tilting eyebrows and shuttered expression transforming him back into the guy she worked with and didn't understand at all. "No harm done. Hannah set me straight."

She nodded, despising the heat blistering her cheeks. He was supposed to be *angry* so she could grasp the memory of his ugly fury every time she felt this weird attraction. But no. His stoic reaction reversed the prank and reinforced her immaturity. What a miserable fucking night.

She shoved into her flip-flops. "See you tomorrow."

"The class is almost over." He stood tall and commanding in front of her. "Let me take you home."

"I'm done with your bodyguard services, thank you very much."

"But Brandon is still out there, right? Still stalking you?"

Her breath caught at his concern. "He's not stalking me."

"Don't parse words with me, Gretch. You won't win that either."

She glared in sullen defeat. Behind him, shrieking boys were flying in the air unsupervised. She jerked her chin. "You need to get back."

Without turning, Sean clapped his hands twice. The boys immediately plopped into cross-legged formation, as motionless as Stonehenge. Gretch's mouth sagged open. Sean refolded his arms, his gaze direct and unblinking. "It's the blond guy from Teenie's, right?"

The swirling lights of the dance floor flooded back. Sean's aloof expression. How quickly he'd disappeared. She stiffened. "In the future, if you see me out in public, just ignore me."

One of his comical eyebrows lifted further. "I can ignore you about as much as the sun in a desert, Gretch." Just as her insides began to melt in a gooey, sticky mess, he added, "Did it ever occur to you that eventually you'd hook up with someone clinically deranged?"

Her breath yelped out in a half-sneer. "There are some lessons you are *so* not qualified to teach me." She yanked the purse strap up to her shoulder. With the speed of a cobra, he snagged her wrist, and the purse swung wildly in the air. Her heart sprinted off rhythm. A timeless moment passed, filled with unspoken challenges. A clock ticking somewhere to her left chipped away at the fathomless stillness in the studio.

Sean blinked first. "I apologize," he said, a muscle twitching along his jaw. "Your dates are none of my business."

She wrenched away. "You can say that again." Great,

now she sounded about as old as the boys sitting so miraculously silent. "See you tomorrow." She burst out the front door.

The May evening had chilled in the past half-hour, and goosebumps dotted her skin, but fury kept her powerwalking the blocks to the El platform without donning her sweatshirt. *Clinically deranged. The son of a bitch!* Who was he to regulate who she went out with?

Gretch paused, eyeing the men around her for a tall, handsome blond. When she spotted none, she seethed some more at Sean's interference. And his stoic response to her punking him with that stupid charity painting. There was no chemistry here. No future. No fairytale of waltzing in a red gown in those sturdy arms. Sean was an introvert who lived inside his head. All that hoity-toity knowledge and emotional depth... Dating him would be like hopscotching through a minefield blindfolded. Eventually she'd end up in shards and fragments. *No, thank you.*

Besides. She preferred men like his brother, anyway.

Once on the train, she slumped into a seat. As the city lights whipped past, she checked the eBay bid for Adyton's Quran, ruminated over Eve's struggle with her abusive husband, and even practiced the new signs Zamira had taught her, but her treacherous mind continued to loop back to Sean's iron embrace tonight. The quiet authority and primal gleam in those dark brown eyes when he'd knelt beside her gasping body.

And then—it's lights out. Jesus. When he was that other guy, Sean was pure sex on a stick. In little white pajamas. She had to avoid *that* guy at all costs.

15

A fter staring at the ceiling for hours, obsessing over every detail of his dojo encounter with Gretch, Sean fell asleep just before his alarm rang.

He hurriedly dressed and ate, unrested and in full self-recrimination mode. Why hadn't he just gotten up and gone to work in the wee hours? He could have started on that mysterious Wickham painting, which had seeped into his thoughts little by little until it was a dull nag. Now, during regular work hours, he'd have to give the Etruscan mosaic his full attention.

He strode into the Moore and Morrow break room for a well-needed cup of coffee and stopped short. Margo, in a blue suit that did nothing to hide her gun holster, sat at the round table with Hannah. "There you are," she chirped. "You don't answer your phone."

"No." He cast about for something more grown-up than *I don't like to talk to people.* "Not when I don't know the incoming phone number."

She smiled sweetly. "Well, good news. Adyton sent an email to Bixby yesterday afternoon; he'd like to meet you again. We've studied the op from all angles and think this is legit. Hannah said it was okay for you to take a few hours off."

Sean headed for the coffee pot before his no-fucking-way expression outed him. "You heard Jace loud and clear. I can't handle covert ops."

"First of all, Jace is an associate; he does not give the orders. Second, we need to find out the extent and location of Adyton's artifacts. Looks like you and Gretch did a good enough job fooling him as Bixby that he doesn't suspect FBI involvement, or he would've pulled the project yesterday. He's interested in the potential buyers Moore and Morrow can bring to the table."

Hannah gasped. "Moore and Morrow?"

"Gretch told him you refer buyers and sellers to each other."

"Sweet baby Jesus, Walter's going to hit the roof."

"I don't trust Adyton," Sean declared, pouring the coffee without turning around. "He knows Gretch and I work *here*. Why the cat-and-mouse email instead of calling Moore and Morrow?"

"He still thinks you're Bixby. Seems reasonable he'd use Bixby's email."

"And maybe he did call here," Hannah said. "When Gretch gets in, she can listen to the messages. I'm not familiar with how to work her console."

Sean glanced at his watch and frowned. Gretch was sixty-six minutes late. Punctuality was as important to her as the right shade of lipstick. The early hour wasn't a factor either; as a trainer, her appointments had begun at five in the morning. In fact, her exuberant energy was obnoxious as hell to an insomniac like him.

He stirred his coffee and turned to the women. "Did she have another appointment this morning?" When Hannah shrugged and shook her head, every muscle in his body stilled. How could her best-friend-slash-boss not know Gretch's habits and schedule?

"She's never late, Hannah." His clipped words were marred by his jaw, which refused to unlock. "She has a stalker out there and ISIS sympathizers who may or may not be playing us. No doubt they all know where she works."

Alarm washed over his boss's features. She dug out her phone and pressed the screen a few times. On speakerphone, Gretch's exuberant voicemail message began. Hannah disconnected. "Maybe her phone's still off." She darted a glance at Margo. "She didn't know if this guy could trace her GPS by the phone number."

"He could reverse-look-up the phone number for her address in two seconds."

"Shit," Sean breathed. He should never have let her walk out of the dojo last night.

Hannah pressed her screen again. "I'll call her house."

This time the phone was picked up, and Dwayne boomed out a greeting. "Gretch left at her usual time." His voice echoed around the break room. "She hasn't arrived yet?"

Sean plunked his mug on the counter and bolted to the reception desk. No black purse under the table, and although her perfume permeated the space, it was not fresh. He toured the labs and cubicles, heading last to his —the farthest from his coworkers'. He'd give anything to see her spinning on his stool, messing with his shit.

His cubicle was empty. He struggled to regulate his breathing as he hurried back up front. Margo paced the reception area, phone glued to her ear. "—could be a coincidence, but just reporting it in..."

Hannah was knocking on Walter's door. She slipped inside as Dane wandered in from the street.

No, he hadn't encountered Gretch from the El station to here.

Walter followed Hannah out, mouth tight. "We need to do something," he said pointedly to Margo. She quickly signed off and pocketed her phone.

"What I suggest is you call her roommate again and get a description of what she's wearing. And someone figure out how to work the phone console so we can listen to messages."

Sean lunged for Gretch's ergonomic chair and began rifling through drawers until he found the manual. He flipped to the index while Walter gazed over his shoulder. Together they figured out the surprisingly complicated message retrieval system. The digital screen lit up and indicated five messages. Sean hit *play*.

Two clients with questions about their projects, one price inquiry, and a hang-up. Sean scrubbed a palm across his mouth as Walter hit the arrow key for the final message.

"This is Joseph Adyton. Please return my call as soon as possible." The old man rattled off his number.

Walter pressed a button to retrieve the details on the screen. "He called an hour ago." Sean shut off the device as Hannah picked up the phone with shaking fingers. Her face was ashen.

"Put him on speaker," Margo ordered. "Everyone remain silent."

Anna walked in at that moment and was immediately shushed before she could open her mouth. She stood, eyebrows knit, clutching the diagonal strap of her satchel bag.

"Days of Olde, Joseph Adyton speaking."

"This is Hannah Moore of Moore and Morrow Restoration returning your call," Hannah said, her quivering voice ending like a question.

"Oh yes. Thank you for calling me back," the man said, his voice a cheerful contrast. "I had a question about the billing and completion date we'd agreed on."

Silence blanketed the office as everyone gazed at each other in confusion.

"Hello?" Adyton said.

"Yes," Hannah blurted out. "That would be handled by Walter. Let me see if he's in." She placed the call on hold and turned to Margo. "Should I ask him if he's seen Gretch this morning?"

"If this was a kidnap," Margo answered gently, "he'd list his demands. Not discuss how much he owes you."

Anna gasped and slapped a hand over her mouth. Walter turned wordlessly into his office and shut the door to take the call.

Something inside Sean threatened to burst. Maybe it was epic self-hatred. "We have to do something." No way could he stand around with his thumb up his ass another second. He'd seen enough TV shows. He pointed to Hannah. "Email us all a picture we can show people on the streets—"

Margo held up a hand, a faint smile on her face. "That's not efficient. You all go about your daily business, and we'll start a search."

"How?" Sean ignored Hannah's frown at his belligerent tone.

"We'll get a search warrant for her cell phone records and track the stalker-date. We'll figure out which corporate and transportation security cameras she passes on her way to work and pull those. If anyone did approach her, we'll study her body language. And, if someone actually abducted her in broad daylight, hopefully we'll have a clear digital image of the perp to work with."

Sean controlled the adrenalin overdrive with a deep breath. "So you're officially opening a case?"

Margo began texting. "We'll assume control on the basis that it may coincide with our blood artifact investigation." She looked up with a grim smile. "Unfortunately, it means you're working alongside your brother until we find her."

Sean shrugged and headed back to his cubicle. He'd gladly live in the same *room* with Jace if it meant finding Gretch unharmed.

"Blood artifact?" Dane murmured as Sean walked past.

He paused to answer patiently. "Relics smuggled into the U.S. The profit is used to recruit lone wolves and buy weapons."

Sean turned into his private sanctuary. He rearranged his neat rows of supplies into neater rows beside the damaged Etruscan mosaic. The routine and orderliness were dual tranquilizers. There was nothing more he could do to find Gretch. Obsessing or hanging around his colleagues would only exacerbate the pressure building within. As it was, the spiked endorphins would make the intricate cleaning a huge challenge. Maybe Vivaldi's *Concerto for Strings and Bass* would help.

Shrieks erupted down the hall. Sean popped off his stool and squinted at the crowd still clustered in the reception area. Jace had arrived, cocky, handsome, and grinning. Standing by his side was Gretch, stupefyingly gorgeous. Safe.

Sean forced out a harsh exhale, relief rendering his legs weak. His shoulders remained stiff, aching from the stress and recent sleepless nights. Gretch glanced around at the outbursts with a confused half-smile, then swiveled, locking eyes with him.

He hated that she meant so much to him. Hated how helpless he was over this attraction. He meant nothing to her. With everything in his power, he'd make sure she never knew how this hour had taken years off his life.

He managed a curt nod and reclaimed his stool, reaching for the cotton-tipped swab. She was here. She was unharmed. His brother, the hero, had saved the day again. No need to rush over there and gawk like the rest of them. He had a shitload of work to do.

16

"You're okay!"

"We were so worried!"

"What happened?"

Were her colleagues squealing at someone else...? Gretch glanced over her shoulder. *Nope. What the hell?* And why had Sean given her that angry look?

"Look who I found," Jace announced, like he'd rescued Gretch from a well. She blinked over at him. They'd met at the door to Moore and Morrow a second ago.

She smiled thinly. "Was I lost?"

Hannah hugged her hard. "Thank God," she whispered. Defensiveness straightened Gretch's spine. She'd be the first to admit she dazzled as the center of attention —when *she* had control over what that meant.

"When you didn't show up for work..." Hannah began just as Walter's door shot open. He stood in his threshold, gaping at Gretch like she was a two-headed alien. This was getting old.

"I'm an hour and a half late." Gretch emphasized each

word, eyeing her associates one by one. "I had an emergency."

"But you're never late." Walter said at the same time as Hannah blurted, "Why wouldn't you call?"

Her damn phone! "The...uh...battery died." By the expressions on their faces, everyone knew she was lying. Gretch homed in on Hannah, the only person who should've known why the cell phone was still on mute. "Will someone *please* tell me what's happened?"

"You were kidnapped."

Gretch spun around. Sean leaned in the threshold, arms crossed, observing her coolly, like he hadn't just made the most outrageous claim ever. He pointed to Margo. "She's pulling your texts so we can track down your stalker." He jerked his head at his brother. "And presumably he's collecting security tapes of any location you may have walked by. You can imagine our surprise, you wandering in here when you're the focus of an FBI investigation."

Her gaze darted back to Hannah, whose worried expression backed up Sean's words.

"Well." Any remaining words escaped her. Her privacy was now the office gossip. And yet they'd cared enough to be this overprotective...

"Where've you been?" her bestie asked softly.

"I, uh, got a call at home to help someone." She certainly didn't need to air the details in front of everyone. They had enough fodder for one day...or three years. She skittered a look from Jace to Margo to Hannah. "I'd be happy to discuss this in private."

Hannah motioned to her office, and Gretch took special care to breeze by Sean as if he didn't exist. Once inside, they all claimed a seat, except Walter, who stood near the closed door, arms folded.

"I'm so sorry," she blurted out. "It never occurred to me there'd be this kind of reaction."

"Why didn't you just call?" Hannah said. "We've been worried sick."

Gretch nodded to the phone on the desk. "Does anyone know how to retrieve messages around here?" A moment of silence acknowledged her point.

"Where were you?" Margo asked gently.

Gretch tugged the hem of her skirt. "I volunteer at an abuse hotline on Sundays. I don't know how long I've counseled this one woman to take the first step to leave." She knotted her fingers together, her frustration and worry for Eve as fresh as when the call came this morning. "Each time we've coordinated a plan, she refuses to leave at the last minute. I've given her all my numbers—told her to call anytime, and I'll come get her." Four concerned faces watched her carefully. "This morning she called my house just as I was walking out the door. I went straight to her place. I didn't want to give her enough time for second thoughts. But I was so focused on her, I didn't think about calling work or the fact that you guys might be worried. I mean, Anna's late all the time." She winced. She never ratted on anybody.

Jace leaned forward, forearms on his knees. "Is the woman safe?" His tone was so gentle that the high drama of the morning was finally too much to bear.

Gretch blinked back tears. Tears! "We got her," she whispered. "And her two girls. I took them to a shelter where I also volunteer, and came straight here."

"And no one followed you?" Margo asked. "The men from the Days of Olde shop? Your stalker boyfriend—"

"He's not my boyfriend," she said quickly. "And no. I saw no one suspicious."

"What about the woman's husband?"

Gretch shrugged and shook her head. "He wasn't

home when I got her out of there. I don't know his name or what he looks like. But she's told me before that he works long hours."

Walter scowled. "You're risking your life and don't know the woman's last name?"

"We give them the option of remaining anonymous, and *she* was risking her life."

"You take public transportation," Jace said. "How exactly did you get her *out*?"

Gretch paused and gauged his expression. Did he think she was lying? "I took an Uber." After a slight hesitation, he nodded. He could totally nail a poker-face contest—must be a Quinn thing. Which was not a compliment.

"The point is: I'm fine, and I'm sorry."

Hannah threw her a dubious look, but thankfully didn't press further. Instead she turned to Walter. "What happened with Adyton?"

"We got it squared away." His usually patient tone was absent. "We'll have to pull Sean off whatever project he's working on, though, and put him on this immediately."

Hannah nodded. "I'll go tell him. What's the projected completion time?"

"He'd like it in three weeks."

"That's impossible!"

"He was perfectly willing to give the Quran to another firm who said it was possible."

Margo and Jace traded grave looks. He bent over his phone. A few seconds later, he swore. "Adyton pulled the eBay Quran."

Under the conference table, Gretch gripped her knees. She'd placed a bid yesterday afternoon and requested the provenance. Had her interference ruined something? Had they somehow traced the dummy email account back to her? "Maybe," she stammered, "he wants to have the piece restored before he auctions it off."

Hannah nodded. "No doubt the damaged pictures were hurting the bids, but the fact is we can't do a good job in three weeks. In the long run, this will hurt our reputation."

"And I can't let you hand the project back. It'll shut down an easy lead." Margo turned to Jace. "Have we found any warehouses in his name?"

He shook his head. "We've searched for companies, real estate, and assets."

"Then start researching Adyton's bank for any SARs."

"I'll take Sean on the Adyton appointment—"

"Nope." Margo's voice was firm. "You're on research today."

A muscle spasmed along Jace's jaw. He nodded tightly and rose.

Gretch stood too. "If you'll excuse me," she said quickly, "I have a mountain of work."

No one spared her a glance. "What's a SAR?" Walter asked, paranoia lacing his voice.

"Banks are required to file suspicious activity reports on customers," Margo explained. "Any transactions that raise a red flag."

Jace held the door for Gretch. She flicked him a smile as she passed and hurried down the hall.

"Wait up." He was right on her heels. "Give me the deets on this stalker, and I'll—"

Damn it. "There *is* no stalker. This is not a thing! I went on one date, and he's pestering me to go out again, that's *all*." She rounded her desk.

Rather than be affronted by her response, Jace's warm blue eyes twinkled. "Guess you have quite an effect on a guy, huh?"

Finally—someone who egged on the flirt in her. "You

have no idea." The husky confidence in her voice spread through her. She lowered her lashes. "I tend to rock their worlds."

His lazy smile spread, slow and delicious. Clearly he knew its effect on women. "I'm looking forward to Sunday, Gretchen Allen."

"Uh huh," she breathed. She clasped her hands like a librarian. "Good luck with the SARs thing."

"Piece of cake."

The main door closed and the office resumed its tomblike silence. Gretch groaned and kneaded the throbbing headache in her temples. If she hadn't walked in on something out of a *CSI* episode, she'd have pleaded sick and taken the day off. Now she had to wait six more hours before she could get back to the shelter and check on Eve.

"I'LL NEED any SARs and backup you've accumulated on your customer, Joseph Adyton." Jace flashed his credentials and slapped the bench warrant on the obese banker's desk.

"Dwayne Collins, at your service." The man laboriously hoisted himself out of the chair. His handshake was limp, his palm clammy; both unforgivable first impressions. Jace had been drilled from childhood to clasp firmly, shake vigorously, and look the other person dead in the eye.

Collins had managed the eye contact all right, but more like how a man would size up a prime rib. Jace had nothing against gays, but he didn't appreciate this man's overt confidence in converting him.

"And I didn't catch your name," Collins said.

Jace stuffed the wallet in his breast coat. In his haste

to flip it shut before lingering eyes could read the epically embarrassing *Special Agent Associate* title, he'd botched the vague intro. "Jason Quinn."

"Quinn." Collins tilted his head. "I met a Quinn yesterday." He squinted. "Looks nothing like you—"

Not interested. "It's a common name, sir. The reports?"

"Oh, I have reports, Agent Quinn. Reports on top of reports. I'm days away from busting some pretty big names in the town."

Of course you are. "I'm here for Adyton at the moment, sir. Do you have evidence of money laundering?"

Collins pursed his lips. "Of course," he said in a resigned, sulky tone. "Took you guys long enough. If you institute laws forcing us to spy on our customers, the least you can do is read the red-flag reports."

"That's the Treasury Department, sir." Jace paused and regrouped. Something about the African-American man rubbed him wrong. Maybe it was the prissy self-importance—like he had the criminal world's financial tricks all figured out, if only someone would listen to him.

"I'll have my assistant send in the boxes. You may as well get comfortable." Collins perused him hungrily and nodded to the round table in the corner. "This'll take a while."

Still not interested. Jace clenched his jaw to keep the words in.

"Coffee?"

"No, thank you. What do you have on Adyton?"

"Appears he's using the typical white-collar techniques. Placement, layering, use of smurfs…"

Jace headed for a seat before the banker could read the confusion flashing across his face. He was a fucking SEAL. He knew covert reconnaissance, combat operations through massive cave complexes, extradition of U.S. hostages. What the fuck was a smurf?

The blah, blah, blah spewing from Collins' mouth was clearly important, but to have to admit ignorance in the face of the fat man's superiority complex... *Shit. Maybe fake it and see how much comes out in the files.*

The desk phone rang as Jace put his briefcase on the table.

"Put him through," Collins said. "And bring in the Adyton files."

Jace pulled out his laptop.

"Sure, I remember you—you're kind of hard to forget," Collins said loudly. "How did you find me?"

Jace rolled his eyes.

"Oh, I'm so flattered you remembered. Yes, that's right, I'm her housemate... What do you mean she hasn't texted back? Are you sure you have the right number?"

Jace abruptly headed out. The pretty assistant had ogled him while showing him into the office. Bet she'd explain these money-laundering terms so he'd sound like he knew his shit tomorrow, reporting the results back to the task force.

The banker's booming voice still carried out here. "Hell yes, come on over this evening. Of course I'll keep it a surprise."

17

Sean adjusted the SUV's passenger vent so the air conditioning flowed directly on him. Sweat covered his brow, and his heartbeat thumped loudly in his ears. Why the fuck had he agreed to this field-espionage crap? These microbursts of courage, this need to be a hero—it was going to get him killed. "I'm not going to wear a wire."

Margo laughed. "You watch too much TV." She glanced over at the next red light, her sky-blue eyes sparkling, then rummaged in the deep console between the seats. Out came an ordinary-looking pen. "Here. It's why we asked you to wear your lab coat. Just click it like this, and the mic turns on. Digital, voice activated, and records up to six hours."

He appraised the device. *Aw, hell, lighten up.* "Thanks, Q. Where's the Aston Martin?" Sean forced his lips to curve along with her laugh. He could act like a big sissy, or he could march into Adyton's shop and get this the hell over with. They were four blocks away. "Seriously. Any words of wisdom?"

"We're looking for any information on the size and

scope of his operations, locations of warehouses, merchandise within, and anyone he works alongside."

"Besides El Bashtan."

"Turns out El Bashtan is a middleman and a small fish. All indications are that Adyton is either the head of a substantial ring, or high up in the hierarchy. We've pulled his phone and email records and are investigating those leads. Jace is taking the financial angle, but anything you can gather in your Bixby role will be of great help."

He nodded. At two blocks away, she pulled over. "Walk the rest of the way, so they don't spot the car." She gave him her cell number and Bixby's wallet minus the wad of cash, then tucked in an earbud and asked his name to test the pen. "I'll be in the bakery next door," she said. "If you feel like you're in over your head, your safe word is *tangerine*."

Sean clenched his jaw to keep the word from flying out. It took very little to visualize the next family dinner, and Jace's entertaining story of how Sean compromised an international smuggling investigation caterwauling *tangerine*. He yanked the door handle. "I'll do my best."

"The Bureau thanks you for your help. You're very brave."

Funny, that was the last word he'd have chosen. He shut the door, knocked on the roof twice, and headed down the street, hands deep in his pockets. Scents wafted past. Garlicky gyros from the Greek restaurant across the street, exhaust as a city bus roared by, and sour urine on the homeless man asleep in a doorway.

The next block held stale beer and vomit from a bar that had thrown open its doors, and a discordant mix of perfumes from a group of women waiting at the crosswalk.

Breathing shallowly, Sean turned onto the quiet street from yesterday, where honey and cardamom dominated from the bakery next door to Days of Olde. "I'm here," he muttered, as he strode to the door.

He stepped into the dusty clutter, his OCD instantly rebelling. Two middle-aged women were perusing the far aisle, murmuring to each other as Adyton waited a respectful distance away. The ordinariness of the shoppers and shopkeeper eased some of the tension banding Sean's torso. He lifted his hand in greeting.

"Ah, Mr. Bixby," Adyton called. "My great-nephew Victor is in the office." The old man pointed to the lone door by the mirrors, now standing open. "Please go in and introduce yourself. I'll be right with you."

Sean picked his way to the office and entered another hazard zone. Stacks of papers littered the desk and floor. A filing cabinet with drawers stuffed-to-spilling stood in the corner, next to an empty watercooler on a wood stand. A brick house of a bodybuilder lounged near the desk, thumbing his phone screen. He sported a buzzcut and a goatee. The comforting bakery aromas were stronger in here, masking most of the underlying dust and old-man stink. The ovens must be right on the other side of the wall.

"Victor?"

The man glanced up, startled. "Wow. Some stealth moves there."

Try a lifetime of evading four brothers and a father in a crowded house. "Your great-uncle asked me to wait in here."

"Yeah." Victor motioned to a sturdy metal chair on the other side of the messy desk. "You deal in art?" His accent was pure American, his attire right out of a sporting goods store.

Sean claimed the chair and breathed through his mouth, because Victor had glazed himself in the woody sweetness of men's body wash. "Mostly art restoration," Sean answered. "You?"

Victor shrugged. "Dabble in a few things. Help the old man out if there's heavy lifting."

What questions to ask? "I'm assuming you have climate-controlled warehouses."

"Sure. State of the art."

Sean visualized Margo thumping her head with her palm. He needed intel fast before Adyton came in and grew suspicious. How to establish a connection? A question he'd asked himself since grade school. He shifted his weight. "I uh —I'm working on the gold-leaf Quran. Pretty sweet piece."

"Yeah. Just got that in a few days ago."

"Assyrian?" A wild guess, but given the brutal civil war, Syria was the highest probability. One side or the other was systematically stripping museums clean to pay for weapons."

Victor nodded. His phone whistled a tweet, and his attention was riveted to the device.

Adyton called out a goodbye. Too close—like over by the aisle with the ashtray. "So where are your warehouses?" Sean blurted.

"Couple blocks over."

"Are we going this afternoon?"

Victor tore his gaze from his phone, eyebrows knit at the flurry of dumb questions from a geek. Sean knew the expression well. "Dunno."

Time was up. Adyton shuffled into the office and shook Sean's hand. "Thank you for coming in today. I look forward to a mutually beneficial relationship." The accented greeting was marred by the scrutiny of his gaze.

"I should be at work on the Quran," Sean said lightly. "My deadline is suddenly tight."

The old man bowed his head once in acknowledgement. "It could not be helped. We received a substantial offer on condition of the date."

"Perhaps you could offer my name if they'd like to consult further. Three weeks to repair so much damage is a risk. Why pay so much money for a sloppy result?"

Adyton kept silent as he maneuvered to his desk. Victor's attention strayed from his cell phone long enough to see his great-uncle situated, before he refocused on the screen.

"I will pass the word along," Adyton said, leaning back in his chair with a wince of pain. "Tell me more about the service you offer matching buyers and sellers."

Why haul me down here to ask a question better suited for Walter over the phone? Unless Adyton hadn't believed Gretch. Alarm for her helped form the words. "Our consultation isn't formal enough to list on a brochure— it's merely word of mouth. We know the value of the piece and can trace the provenance so both buyer and seller trust they've received a fair price for an authentic artifact." It sounded so legitimate, Sean was surprised Walter didn't offer the service. "Is there an acquisition you're interested in selling?" *Get something useful for Margo.*

Adyton studied him long enough that Sean's pulse picked up a notch. Was he pressing too hard?

"I have a statuette of an ancient sun god," Adyton said at last, and spaced his hands about twenty inches apart. "Solid gold. It dates back to the second millennium BC." His eyes strayed to the doorway, like he expected company. Why? Sean strained for a sound out in the shop, but the only noise was another whistled tweet. "Victor," the old man admonished his great-nephew quietly.

"Is the statuette here?" Sean glanced around the

untidy office. He had to get more for Margo than this cat-and-mouse exchange. "I'd like to inspect it."

"We can arrange that for later this afternoon."

The certainty that the old man was playing him grew. "Mr. Adyton, I don't have the time to stop my restorations at every whim." He said the words sharply enough that Victor's thumbs froze and his attention swung fully to the conversation. Sean spared him a glance. The guy could unleash immense power with those overdeveloped muscles, but he wouldn't have a quick reaction time, which gave Sean the advantage if it came down to a fight. The thought emboldened him to re-address Adyton with the impatience of someone wasting his day. "Victor told me your warehouse is nearby. Take me to see the piece, or let me get back to work."

Sweat streamed freely down his back. He may have forced Adyton's hand, but he'd also dug himself in deeper. Everywhere his gaze landed, he spied a tanger-ine-colored object: a pair of bookends, a row of plastic binders, a plastic cup atop the watercooler. None could even remotely be mistaken for salmon, peach, or orange hues, either. Perfect examples of tangerine.

Adyton folded both hands on his desk and cocked his head. Sean met his gaze with the skill of a baby brother adept at hiding his panic from much more threatening, eagle-eyed stares. The airless office and heavy lab coat suffocated him, but his heart beat the dull thud of someone who'd drawn a line and was standing firm.

"Very well, Mr. Bixby." Adyton opened the top desk drawer and produced a key rimmed in red plastic. He wrote some numbers down on a slip of paper and handed both to Victor. "I shall say goodbye to you here. If you'd be so kind as to suggest one or two buyers who'd be inter-ested in the piece, we shall be on a path to a very prof-itable affiliation."

Sean nodded and swallowed. Victor fidgeted and shot his great-uncle a look. This had been too easy. It had to be a trap.

"If, however," Adyton continued, "this is not a legitimate service, I will not look kindly upon you or Miss Allen."

And there it was. In the age of information gathering, the one who'd just been threatened was Gretch. They knew her real name, knew where she worked, and in lying to protect Sean, she'd dug their association with this smuggling ring deeper. It was Gretch they'd go after, and she possessed no self-defense skills to speak of. With immense effort, Sean managed to shake the old man's hand without reacting to the warning.

Out in the fresh air, Sean sucked in a breath. Victor motioned to the right, and they quickly walked back to the busy street with the bar on the corner. Brakes screeched nearby. A horn blared, then a second one, the angry disharmony heightening Sean's unease.

Victor slowed, assessing whatever scene unfolded, but Sean took advantage of the distraction and dug for his phone. At any moment, this undercover op would go south. It wasn't pessimism—it was reality. And Gretch had no FBI protection, no safe word, and no idea of the danger she faced.

He called Margo. "Hello, Gretch," he said loudly when she answered. He plugged his ear as furious shouts were exchanged on the street. "I've been detained."

"Good work. I'm shadowing."

Sean glanced at Victor, who seemed to be bored of the altercation and had finally noticed him on the phone. Sean motioned a "go ahead" wave and they began walking again. "Start researching buyers interested in ancient sun god statuettes." He paused for effect. How could he convey his concern for Gretch? No way could she go home by herself tonight. "I know who might be interested—Margo. Is she in town?"

"I'm not following you, Sean." Margo had the same sharp tone as during the taxi debacle outside of BAM. He doubled his efforts to send the cryptic message.

"Terrific. What hotel is she staying at?" The strain in his voice made it an octave higher.

"I know you're trying to tell me something, but you need to be clearer."

"I said *what hotel*?" Sean repeated, firmer. "I hope it's in a safer neighborhood than last time." Victor studied him under knit brows. Sean mouthed, "Gunshots." It cleared the bodybuilder's suspicion, and he motioned to the left. They turned another corner, off the busy street. Rows of identical warehouses lined both sides as far as the eye could see. Sean needed to get his head in the game. He wasn't even paying attention to what street they'd turned down.

"Are you telling me Gretch should go to a hotel?" Margo asked in exasperation.

"Yes." Relief poured through him. "Yes. I'll speak to her as soon as I get back."

Sean entered the cool, dry unit with renewed confidence. It took Victor a minute to find the light switch, then he snapped them all on and the vast space illuminated in grid formation. Every cranny was stuffed with crates and cardboard boxes.

Victor pulled the slip of paper from his pocket and looked at the numbered aisles. He jerked his head. "This way." As they walked down the center aisle, Sean studied the spaces, counted the rows, and gauged the heights so he could re-create it as accurately as possible for Margo.

"How often do you get shipments?" he asked.

"Twice a week, sometimes more."

That was a hell of a lot of looting. "This is quite an

operation." There had to be four, five hundred separate containers stacked in here. Chills coated Sean's skin. All blood artifacts. Literally a stolen culture. And the profit paid for worldwide chaos and murder.

Victor halted and bent to retrieve a box beneath a bay. He pushed through a tangle of straw and lifted out the statuette. "Here she is."

"He," Sean corrected automatically, then caught the stiffening of the other man's shoulders and plastered on a grin. "Notice the absence of boobs." As expected, Victor immediately relaxed and laughed. Sean may not ever be a testosterone-laden alpha like his brothers, but he knew their lingo, their commonalities. And female body parts were a large obsession. "Mind if I take a picture?" At the hesitation on the man's face, Sean gave a one-shoulder shrug. "Time management, man. If I can see my source this afternoon, I'll be able to show her the artifact instead of trying to describe it."

"All right." Victor propped it on the straw, but Sean's synapses were finally firing creatively. "Hold it, so your hand gives a sense of scale."

"I don't want to be in the picture."

"You won't be. Straighten your arm out. A little further so the light shines off the gold. That's it." Sean snapped a picture of the statue in Victor's palm with a clear shot of the warehouse in the background. "Perfect." He held out his hand. "Do you mind?"

Victor passed it over, and Sean hefted the weight. Not that he had any proof without testing, but artifacts from this period were rarely made of solid gold. "Tell your great uncle this is gold leaf too. Probably covering bronze. He should not be pricing this as pure gold."

As expected, respect dawned on the bodybuilder's face. "You think your chick will still be interested?"

"Depends on the adjusted price. I'll be in touch." Sean pulled off a casual salute and strode away.

FIVE MINUTES BEFORE CLOSING, Hannah called Gretch into the conference room. She switched the phones to night message mode, lips pressed tight. Conference room meant this was not Hannah chatting like a bestie, updating her on Devon or what was happening with Devon's sister. This better not still be about the morning's fiasco. Anna had pestered her all day for details on why everyone thought she'd been kidnapped. Instead of his usual worshipful gawk, Dane had looked at her funny. And once Sean had returned, he'd never left his cubicle. The guy's bladder had to be the size of Lake Michigan.

Gretch shoved in her chair, glancing at the main door. All she wanted was get to the shelter. Eve had proven time and again that she would back away from a solid plan of action and return to the abuse. What if she was second-guessing the shelter right this minute? What if she'd already returned home?

Gretch marched stiffly into the conference room and greeted Walter, who was already seated, hands folded, expression grave. Butterflies pitched and dove in her stomach. She perched on the edge of a chair and smoothed her skirt.

"I'll get right to it," Hannah said, coming in and closing the door. "Margo called a few hours ago, and we agree with her recommendation."

Gretch braced herself.

"We strongly suggest you check into a hotel."

"And bill the company," Walter added, which was thoughtful, given he was the tight-fisted partner.

Nevertheless, Gretch folded her arms and exhaled

loudly. "I'm honestly not in any danger. Why won't anyone believe that?"

"Will you let me read all of Brandon's texts?" Hannah countered.

And let you glimpse my sick world? "I liked you better when you had no backbone." Underneath the rudeness was a compliment, and her bestie reached over, tugged one of Gretch's arms free, and squeezed her hand.

"Please do this for me. Or sleep at our new place. It'd be on the sofa; Devon's coming back late tonight, but I'll tell him—"

"I'd rather sleep on a park bench." Gretch fought a smile. "Not because of Dev. After ten minutes with your great-aunt, I want to hide her oxygen tank." There could be only one queen in this universe, and Aunt Milly was under the mistaken impression it was her. "Seriously, Hannah, I have a housemate whose size is intimidating to most."

"This was a strongly worded recommendation from Margo. Whatever happened with Sean today worried her enough to suggest it."

Gretch flushed. It was the damn eBay bid. Or the lies she'd spouted in the Days of Olde store. She'd tripped Sean up. God, what if he was in danger now because of her? Why hadn't he spoken to her when he'd returned? "Did Margo suggest a hotel for Sean too?"

"No. Luckily, they don't know his real name."

So she had only herself to blame for this banishment. Fuck it. If it would get her on her way to the shelter, it wasn't worth another second of debating. "Okay, fine."

"That's settled." Walter jerked his head toward the door. "Why don't you book a place, and I'll take you over." That was double sweet. Walter had evening mass every Wednesday at the Holy Name Cathedral, on North Wabash. In fact, if he didn't hoof it, he'd be late.

"I appreciate it, but it's my volunteer night at the shelter." *Finally.*

Hannah shook her head. "Margo doesn't recommend any extracurricular activities."

"Christ in a cradle—"

"Gretch," Walter interrupted, "I'm very uncomfortable with your language *and* this situation. For once, please do as we ask."

Gretch swallowed the urge to throw a verbal tantrum equivalent to blowtorching the freaking room. No way would she be a no-show at the shelter. "I've worked too hard to develop a relationship with this woman," she said tightly. "I'm not abandoning her for some vague danger. I'll say yes to the hotel *only* if I get to spend the evening at the shelter."

She eyed her two bosses. Hannah had her hands full with her great-aunt, who suffered from emphysema and was as stubborn as a toddler. Church was back on the table for Walter, and it was like holding a carrot out to a donkey.

"Go," she said to them in her trainer's bark. "I'll be fine."

Hannah shook her head, her fingers flying on her phone. Who else would she ask to help? "Oh no." Gretch made a grab for the phone, but Hannah swerved out of reach. A few seconds later, a ding rang through the room. She glanced at the screen and held up the phone triumphantly. "Sean will meet you by the front door."

"Forget it. I'll spring for an Uber."

Walter jangled the keys in his pocket. His mouth twisted in a weird way.

Gretch clenched her hands. Every minute she spent in Sean's presence was fraught with danger. *Tiptoeing into that minefield, blindfolded.*

Very little about him should be attractive, and yet the

more she uncovered bits of his personality he tried so hard to hide, the hotter he became. Oh, not LVR-app date hot; that was what was most disturbing. This kind of confusion never happened with the men who fed into her need to feel beautiful. It was the guy who saw her true skin tone under makeup instead of her skintight dress. That just wasn't right.

The least she could do was text Dwayne to meet them at the shelter with an overnight bag, so Sean didn't have to escort her to three places. Gretch sighed in frustration and defeat. This was all so unnecessary, but she did appreciate how her friends rallied when they thought she was in trouble. "Thank you both. I'd love to spend my evening with Sean." The sincerity in her words surprised her.

18

"**...A**nd what really pisses me off," Gretch continued, "is how no one has proof that I'm in any danger." See, the thing about Sean was she could be herself; argue like she'd wanted to with Hannah and Walter.

Sean fell back to let an oncoming pedestrian pass. "Sometimes a vague threat is just as menacing."

She snorted. "Name the vague threat."

"Okay." He halted in the middle of the sidewalk. "You say Brandon isn't stalking you."

"He's pestering me."

"When's the last time you turned on your phone?" Under her glare, his brows rose in wide-eyed innocence. "One day? Two? Is it a record since you've owned a smartphone?"

"Shut up, Sean." She snatched her phone and flashed the lit screen in his direction. No need to tell him she'd kept it on mute, or that Brandon had sent another flurry of rude texts today, even seemed to think meeting her again was imminent. There was no blond guy in the vicinity. She stuffed the phone back in her purse, her muscles tight with annoyance.

"Listening to instinct is the first step in self-defense," Sean said gently.

"If I listened to instinct, you wouldn't be the one walking me to the shelter."

His expression hardened. "Sometimes a simple 'thank you' goes a hell of a lot further, Gretch." Then he brushed on by, continuing that loping stride along the boulevard without her.

Seriously? She could think of ten snarky comebacks to that softball. Gretch raised her arms, beseeching the early evening sky. "Hold up," she said, hurrying to catch him. "I'm sorry. That was uncalled for and I am thankful. It's just—" She paused, searching for the right words. "Here's what my instinct says."

That stopped him. His eyes were warm and inter-ested, his body still, as if he were thoroughly engrossed in whatever was about to come out of her mouth.

"Margo wouldn't recommend a hotel for me because of Brandon." A wariness flickered, and he cut his gaze. It confirmed her suspicion. "What happened with Adyton?"

He shrugged. "I clarified the answers you gave him, his nephew took me to a warehouse a few blocks away, and I inspected an artifact. Hopefully Margo can track who owns the place, and what else is in there before I have to come up with a potential buyer. In the meantime, for whatever reason—" he gestured down his body, "—you've got me. I'm happy to do this."

"So this *is* because of the stuff I told Adyton and El Bashtan."

"No, it started before that. I consulted on a minor case last Saturday that's suddenly snowballed into a poten-tially massive international smuggling operation. And now you're involved. Adyton will find out we're lying soon enough, and he has *your* real name. A showdown of some sort is only a matter of time."

With an eighty-year-old man. She wasn't going to get caught up in this Chicken Little bullshit. She motioned for him to turn left. The shelter was the last house on the block. "If Margo was that worried, she'd stick me in a safe house or something."

"There's nothing concrete enough. No doubt Jace is pissed at Margo for assigning me, though. He'd have manufactured a crisis in a heartbeat to show off his combat skills."

"Can't be better than a kickass black belt."

"You haven't seen a former SEAL ambush that cyclist over there and conduct a search-and-seizure of the grocery bag for explosives. It's a sight to behold."

"More than flipping an unsuspecting student in front of a bunch of eight-year-olds?"

His laugh tripped up her heart. So rare. Such a marvelous, deep sound. She glanced over. His shaggy hair stirred in the evening breeze, and the residual smile transformed his face. When he looked like this, his quirky looks were as virile and handsome as any hottie's, only in a much more extraordinary way.

"The shelter is over there," Gretch said, her voice low and breathy. He shot her a startled glance. Did he think she was flirting? As conflicted as her feelings were, she had to shut down his hope. God help her if this guy, who was so adept at reading people, ever found out about the freak show thriving inside. She walked a tightrope between normal, office Gretch and the creature that trolled for one-night stands.

"Are you still going out with Jace this weekend?" he asked, the lightness in his voice at odds with his tight expression.

She couldn't have formed a more perfect question to

knock Sean's hope out of the ballpark. "Hell yes. Why wouldn't I?"

His silence was bloated with words. She hurt for him, but her survival was more important than his ego. It took half a minute before he muttered, "I'm pretty sure agents can't date anyone with a tertiary involvement in an investigation."

"Your brother doesn't have a problem with it."

"My brother never has a problem with anything that benefits him."

She bounded up the three steps and punched the code into the security keypad. "Maybe you should break the rules once in a while too," she said over her shoulder. "Women like bad boys." She reached for the door handle, but Sean's hand shot past hers and gripped it first. How annoying that his chivalry was the go-to characteristic she noticed now, instead of his epic geekiness.

Just then he handed her a gift from the gods: he peeped inside the open door. She almost howled at his furtive, nerdy expression. "Expecting vestal virgins?"

He flushed. "I'll be out here whenever you're ready to leave."

Great. Twice tonight; leave her zinger lying there like roadkill. She bit her lip to keep from blurting another apology. The only relationship they could have was trading barbs. Yeah, he was wasting his evening waiting around for her, but she hadn't asked him to, and she didn't need people controlling her life. With a stilted "thank you," she strode into the homey foyer. The soft snick of the door closing squeezed her heart.

She greeted Hank, the evening receptionist who doubled as a security guard, and signed in, trying to shake off this weird emotional state. Eve and her girls were the priority. By now they'd been here almost nine hours. Had they settled in okay?

She found Eve in the TV room with her daughters and two other residents, watching *The Big Bang Theory*. Everyone except Eve smiled along with the audience's laughter. When Gretch caught the woman's eye, Eve's shoulders slumped in relief. After murmuring something to her daughters, reassuring the younger one when the girl's face puckered, Eve walked into the hall.

"Hi," Gretch said quietly, and hugged the frail, exhausted-looking brunette. "Want to go somewhere quiet and talk?"

Eve nodded, her pressed lips white around the edges. Gretch motioned to the dining room that had places set for the upcoming dinner. From the kitchen beyond, mouthwatering aromas of marinara sauce and buttered garlic bread woke Gretch's stomach. Sean had to be hungry too. She'd make it up to him by buying him dinner before they got to the hotel. For now, this was all about Eve.

"I thought about your bravery all day," Gretch said as they sat down.

Eve promptly burst into tears. "Are you joking? I'm so scared... I can't do this."

Boxes of tissue were placed strategically in every room, so Gretch grabbed the dining room stash and plunked it in front of Eve. "The hardest part is already behind you. You've left him, and all three of you are safe. We'll help you every step of the way until you have a secure future."

"Those are just words." Eve cried into the tissue. "I have no job, no skills, no money. I'm choosing a future of homelessness."

Gretch grasped her new friend's hand, holding it firmly until the sobs were sniffles. "You've held in a lot today, haven't you?"

Eve nodded. Tears streaked her face. She blew her

nose. "I've had to—for the girls. Amy has barely left my side. They're too young to understand."

Gretch repeated the same assurances she'd uttered each time she'd spoken to Eve on the phone before this eventful day. The shelter's safety, their anonymity, the skills training offered here, therapy and resource counseling, room and board, legal advice, grooming and clothing supplies, a whole network of friends and supporters now and in the future... Gretch finally paused for breath. She probably sounded like a brochure at this point, but if one of the points was hammered home, maybe Eve wouldn't look back.

The sniffling turned to nodding and finally to a tremulous smile. "Thank you for all you've done. I...I would've taken so much more from him...until—" A fire came into her eyes. The abuse had changed, she'd told Gretch that morning. It was the catalyst for finally seeking escape. The bastard had turned his sick attention onto the girls. "I could kill him," Eve whispered. "You have no idea."

She didn't meet Gretch's gaze, which was perfectly fine. It gave Gretch the courage to squeeze her hand and say, "I do have an idea. It's why I've hounded you each time you called. The symptoms of sexual abuse start off small, but by the stuff you told me—him being so loving to the girls and so hateful to you, their withdrawal from their friends, the falling grades... It had all the signs." Each word rang with determination. "You made the right call. Your kids aren't safe anymore."

Eve's eyes searched hers. "It almost sounds like this happened to your daughters."

Sound dimmed. Gretch glanced away. It'd be so easy to shrug, to change the subject. This was her baggage, carefully packed, locked, and stored in the deepest recesses of her soul. But it'd taken so long to get Eve to see the light. Maybe if she shared her history, it would help Eve realize the peril of going back to him.

"I *was* the daughter." Gretch inhaled a shuddering breath. "And I begged for help, but my mother chose to believe their lies. In both of her marriages."

"Jesus." Eve's eyes widened. "What did you do?" she whispered.

Gretch pulled off a careless shrug. She yanked a tissue from the box and concentrated on shredding it. "Survived. Put a chair under the doorknob. Stayed with girlfriends as often as I could. Joined every sport to stay after school or compete on weekends..." She blinked rapidly. If she fucking cried, she would never forgive herself. "I, uh, got a basketball scholarship to Bradley University, in Peoria. Never went home again." Her long exhale relaxed her shoulders. She'd gotten through it. Her first acknowledgment ever. She blinked to dispel the dizziness.

Eve wiped her eyes, her earlier fragility gone. *Good.* Then revealing the horror was worth it. Anger was necessary to move on. It was what got Gretch out of bed, what had made her such a formidable trainer at Chicago's biggest gym until she'd gone through too many men there to show her face again. It was fury sitting on her shoulder every time she accepted another LVR app date to fill the void.

"I'd never have guessed," Eve murmured. "I mean, you're so cool and beautiful and in charge. How did you get over it?"

You don't. Gretch looked her in the eye. "You put one foot in front of the other until your past is far behind you."

"Do you ever speak to your mom?"

She nodded haltingly, rearranging the setting she sat at so the fork was vertical on the napkin. *Lord!* She was acting like Sean. "Yes, I've forgiven her. It took lots of therapy." God was going to strike her dead. She needed to steer the conversation away from her before she gagged on the lies. "They have great counselors here."

Eve immediately shook her head. "Oh no, my girls have had enough—"

"Wait." Gretch reached for her hand. Eve's skin was ice cold. "It's crucial for your daughters to talk to a professional about their encounters." The thought of lying on a couch discussing the details sent a wave of nausea through Gretch, but that was because she was an adult. Tina and Amy had their whole lives in front of them. So much recovery time. Years to heal and have healthy relationships before they ended up like her. "Your daughters are precious. Do everything you can for them."

"His job. He's very important. If this got out..."

"Your only focus is the girls. They need to feel confident about themselves and their bodies again. Your husband blew any chance to ever be near them, and if you need me to testify in court, I'll be there."

The grateful beam Eve threw her was a balm. It made lying about recovering from the abuse worth every word. Maybe Gretch would be a different person if she'd had a talk like this. If back then she'd followed the steps she now laid out for Eve. If she'd had any support whatsoever.

"Thank you for sharing, Gretch. You give me hope I can get over this too."

See? Mission accomplished. "The hardest part is over. You did it, Eve." Gretch spontaneously tossed the shredded tissue like confetti. "It's downhill from here."

The Wednesday dinner volunteer shuffled through the door with a large bowl of spaghetti, her face rosy and smiling. "Do you mind rounding up the troops?"

"I'm ravenous," Eve declared as they walked back to

the TV room. Her posture was straight, her head high. "Will you stay and eat with us?"

Gretch hesitated. Sean was out there, probably cold and hungry. And the residual horror of her stepfathers' cruelty induced a roiling in her stomach that served as a warning. She had a history of stress-induced vomiting; she should really be on her way. But after clamoring to be at Eve's side all day, surely she could sit next to the woman and her girls, and play with her food.

"Sure." She'd definitely buy Sean dinner, and double her efforts to remain kind and patient with him, no matter what.

19

"I'm taking you to dinner," Gretch announced. "The biggest steak in Chicago." Her smile was so open and friendly, Sean ached at shutting it down.

"I'm vegan, but thank you."

"Well, you have to be starving. Where can I take you?"

He picked up the duffel bag Dwayne had dropped off for her almost two hours ago, and eased the strap over his shoulder. "I bought a tofu bowl a couple of blocks over before Dwayne arrived. Oh, and he said you should read his text. He was pretty disappointed you wouldn't be home tonight. He had a surprise for you."

She nodded but didn't dig for her phone. "Let's stop for a drink, then. My treat."

"No thanks," he said lightly. No way could he follow vegan with: "I don't drink, either." His body was his temple, but explaining that sure made him sound like a sissy. "I'd just as soon drop you at your hotel and call it a night." He nodded stiffly in the direction they needed to head, and yep, he'd wiped the smile right off her face. But he was beat from last night's insomnia, and they were still in South Shore. It'd take an hour to get home even if he were to leave right now.

"You know what?" Gretch flipped a hand. "Just go. I'll be fine." She reached for her duffel, but he blocked her with his body. He never wanted a repeat of this morning, thinking she'd been kidnapped because he'd let her leave the dojo by herself.

She huffed out a breath, tucked her purse under her armpit, and walked rapidly up the street. In deference to her snit, he stayed half a step behind, but when they crossed South Colfax, he pulled abreast. He'd been curious about her volunteer work since Dwayne had mentioned it yesterday morning. "How'd it go?"

She shrugged. "Like always. You try to instill a sense of normalcy into lives that are far off the normal bell curve."

"What do you do there?"

"Mostly talk to the residents. Sometimes I give training lessons and nutritional advice."

"That's really cool, Gretch."

She shrugged. The pedestrian light turned red, and Sean automatically slowed even though the street was empty. Gretch jaywalked diagonally across the intersection, and he hurried to catch up. *Break rules. Bad boy. Got it.* "So how did you get involved with the shelter?"

Her brisk pace and hunched shoulders clearly signaled his lame attempts to engage her were getting on her nerves instead. "I champion the helpless. Women, children, old people..."

I'll say. "You had quite a reaction to Adyton in his shop after only meeting him once."

The *clip-clip* of her heels grew more energetic. Any faster and they'd break into a jog. Her feet had to be killing her. "You know, as hot as your brother is," she said curtly, "he's wrong about Adyton."

The words had the impact of a javelin, penetrating Sean's chest. Pain propelled him to chuckle without mirth. "I bet there's no provenance on that Quran."

"I'm not talking about smuggling art. I'm saying his money isn't going to that fundamentalist religion. He's Shi'ite. ISIS would kill him if they could."

"I didn't know you were familiar with politics in the Middle East." He meant it as a compliment, but by the rigid set of her shoulders, the comment had torpedoed whatever good spirits had existed between them tonight.

"This'll probably come as a great shock, Sean, but I'm not stupid."

"I never implied you were."

She glanced over, her curled lip resembling Elvis Presley at his finest. "But you think I'm naïve. Going out on blind dates. Walking home alone. Flirting with a terrorist so old he needs a cane."

He exhaled. Another conversation gone to hell in a handbasket because of his dumb mouth and her prickly exterior. "I think you're fearless," he said carefully, shifting her duffel bag to his other shoulder. "And some-times it skirts a line that seems unnecessary. Almost like you're daring yourself. Bottom line, if the FBI connects Adyton to ISIS, that's good enough for me." Levity popped into his brain, and he grasped it like a lifeline. "You won't catch *me* kissing the old man's cheek."

Nothing. She marched to the curb of a busier street and jabbed the pedestrian button a few times. He stood behind her, close enough to capture her body heat and breathe her fragrance. The walk signal blinked on. She crossed without a word or a glance back.

They climbed the station platform in a silence that was fast becoming uncomfortable. The lights were bright up here, and men's glances zeroed in on Gretch like heat-seeking missiles. Sean met every astonished look that slid his way with false confidence. *Yeah, she's mine.* Which didn't convince anyone, because she was behaving like he was gum on her shoe.

"What are the chances we can forget this conversation and start over?" he said. "Hi, how was the shelter?"

She jammed a hand on her hip and lifted her chin, looking exactly like a haughty supermodel at the end of a runway. "Who I flirt with is none of your damn business."

Fine. Why should he put up with the bitchy, self-righteous act when he was this tired? When this many men waited like wolves in a forest for him to leave her side. "Then why am I here?" he growled.

The *clickity-clack* of the train in the distance caught her attention, and she walked a few paces to the right. Others shuffled forward, drawn like magnets in an invisible gamble of where the doors would open. The engineer's face flashed past, the brakes squealed, and the train slowed. No doubt that guy had gotten a good look at Gretch too, because a set of automatic doors aligned flush with her stance. Just to prove he was right, Sean squinted at the engineer's face in the side mirror. The man's nose was bulbous and red, his eyes too narrow and deep-set. But his gaze was fixed and unblinking on Gretch. *You can't have her either.*

Sean shook his head and followed her onto the train. Hanging around her these last two days had given him a glimpse of how effortless life was for the beautiful people. Was that why she played so fast and loose with her personal safety—bad things never happened to her? Or she somehow felt invincible in the face of a stalker and a terrorist?

He sat gingerly next to her. The hotel was one stop away, so he was fine with the freeze-out. After he dropped her off, he'd do his best to get over her. There was no way a loser like him had a shot, and it was time he stopped the pathetic mooning. Christ, he was Alfredo in Act One of *La Traviata.*

They walked to the hotel entrance in silence. He checked out the bright lobby through the large windows and eyed the still-busy street around them. No preppie blond dude—

"I may not be smart like you," she said so quietly he didn't catch the warning until his surveillance was complete. He stared into her rosy face and furious eyes. "But I know how to handle my social life. I'm fully aware of how natural it is for men to prey on women. Whether it's me at a bar or battered women at the shelter. You're all the same. It's in your fucking Neanderthal DNA." She gripped his shirt in both fists. Her clenched teeth flashed white. "I also know you want me, Sean Quinn. Just like all the others. My staying away is for your own good."

His instant hard-on was the shameful exclamation point to the words she'd just spewed. But the passion shooting from her eyes, the feel of her pointy knuckles brushing his chest... He ached for her. "For my own *good*?" he sputtered. "How so?"

Her mouth screwed into a sneer. "I'd eat you alive." She spun on her heel and marched through the whooshing automatic doors.

The primal impulse surging through him fed on his anger, the days of sleeplessness, tonight's epic battle to be good enough for her. *Women like bad boys.* He lunged across the threshold, grabbed her arm, and spun her around. She collided into him, gasping. Her breasts bounced like plump pillows against his chest. He ignored his body's heightened response and steered her backward through the lobby, where Muzak played and a ponytailed clerk answered a phone in an overly cheerful voice.

The automatic doors eased shut. Warmth surrounded

them. His heart hammered. What was he doing? Her wide, chocolate eyes asked the same thing.

"Are you sure it isn't the other way around?" Sean blurted. "Maybe you're afraid you won't survive *me*."

Her disdain turned to surprised vulnerability. Her mouth dropped open, and he didn't hesitate. Cupping her head, he kissed her like he did in his dreams—powerfully, passionately, conveying all his raw need. For a second she remained stiff and unyielding, and his pulse spiked in panic. Just as suddenly, she melted into him, darting out her tongue.

The feel of her, the spicy scent in his nostrils, her raw, responsive kiss, triggered a massive blood dump, and he groaned. Slanting his head, he swept into her mouth, lingering to memorize her taste. He slid his hands down the silky blouse, caressing the sleek muscles bracketing her spine, tracing the seam of her bra. She kept her palms on his pecs, like she might push him away at any moment. It was sobering enough that he broke the kiss, breathless and burning for her. Her heavy-lidded gaze focused on his mouth, her expression—if he had to guess—was stunned.

"You have an unusual way of kissing," she murmured.

Well, shit. One more thing to add to his growing list of oddities.

But wait. She'd said it differently. Like *good* unusual. Or had she? There was no blood reaching his brain. "I have no response to that."

Gretch studied his face for a moment, then grabbed his hand and twirled toward the front desk. "Come on," she said, tugging. "Bodyguard me to my room."

He stumbled after her. "Wait," his mouth said before his brain could clue in.

She turned, eyebrow arched.

"What will happen at work tomorrow?"

"Are you an adult?" she snapped.

"Last time I checked."

"Do you want this?" She waved a hand down her body, like a magician's assistant.

He swallowed. "Hell yes."

"Then stop thinking with *this* head and let your other one take over."

His mouth finally complied with his screaming brain, and he shut up. She towed him to the desk and checked herself in. The clerk went through the motions on automatic, swiping Gretch's card and announcing the complimentary breakfast buffet in that gratingly cheery voice, not bothered in the slightest by their silence. Sean couldn't have engaged in meaningless conversation anyway; his thoughts were like hummingbirds on crack.

The clerk handed Sean the sleeve with two keys, and Gretch bristled. Thanking the young woman, he thrust the packet at Gretch and propelled her to the elevator. She stabbed the button several times. The softly pliant body he'd held moments ago was as stiff as a steel beam. She stabbed again.

"It's not going to come any faster," he murmured, studying the lit numbers above the threshold descending with the speed of a glacier.

She glared at his reflection in the metal doors. "I'm trying to get to the room before my microscopic attraction for you fades any further."

Instantly his hands grew damp. Maybe he wasn't an adult after all, because he had an incredible urge to bang the elevator button with his fist.

What was he doing? He'd never been with a woman as formidable as Gretch. He didn't have the suave moves or the self-confidence she was used to. Why humiliate himself any further? He turned to her profile. "Do you want me to leave?"

She swallowed, her mouth a grim line. The doors slid open.

"No," she said in a tired voice, stepping forward. "I want that unusual kiss again."

The second the doors closed, he dropped her duffel, pulled her in his arms, and put his all into the kiss. This time she moaned and clasped him, one hand sweeping up his back, the other messing up the hair on the entire right side of his head. It was a testament to his frenzy that he didn't smooth it back down once they stumbled off.

Gretch found her room with single-minded determination. It took her several tries to unlock the door. He almost snatched her card key in his impatience. The green light finally blinked, and he shouldered the door open and ushered her in. The reading light on the nightstand showered the room in a romantic glow.

The second the door shut, she shoved him against it. His head conked wood hard enough to jolt his brain. "Ow!"

She pressed into him, gluing him to the hard panel, and thrust her tongue in his mouth. Sean inhaled raggedly through his nose, absorbing this wild, wanton fantasy come to life. Like she was devouring him with the same passion he'd held inside for her.

He followed the curve from her hips to her waist, the silk blouse cool and slippery in his hot palms. Just shy of the undersides of her breasts, she smacked his hands away and broke the kiss.

"Strap in," she muttered. "You're going for a ride." Her eyelids were at half-mast; her focus was on his chest. Although his eyesight was hazy with lust, her face appeared grim.

Before he uttered a word, her fingernails raked down his front, just short of painful. She curled her grip in the waistband of his jeans and made short work of the button and zipper, then knelt, dragging his jeans and underwear with her.

He was about to tell her to wait. About to suggest they take it slow, maybe stretch out on the bed—

She took him into her mouth, more and more until the head of his cock touched the back of her throat.

Ho-ly shit. Currents of electricity ripped through him, short-circuiting his brain. She sucked him masterfully, aggressively. His hips surged, and his mouth sagged open as every nerve in his body funneled its way to his dick. *Freaking heaven!*

She pulled and sucked and milked him, her lusty technique wrenching guttural groans deep from his belly. Her clever fingers added swift caresses and soft scratches, working in perfect choreography with her mouth. His balls tightened in ecstatic anticipation. His gasps became pants. He muttered her name and feathered his fingers around her skull, trying to keep his grip loose while guiding her to the rhythm he needed. She began a quiet humming, which vibrated the back of her throat and sent mini shocks through his cock and up his spine. Her teeth dragged the length of him, evoking a full-body shiver. As she repeated the sequence, her pace increased and the humming vibrations grew.

He was lost. His orgasm shot through him like jagged lightning. He cried out hoarsely, holding her head immobile as he dumped himself into her in shuddering spasms. Her cheeks sucked, moist and warm, draining every drop until he palmed the wall to keep from pitching on top of her. Still she continued, as if she could make him hard again. The deep ecstasy turned painful and abhorrent.

"Stop!" He forcibly extracted himself, gulping oxygen like a drowning victim. "Jesus, Gretch," he said, panting. "What the hell…" The most earth-shattering orgasm of his life, and he'd never felt so disconnected. Even counting the wall sex last Saturday.

He gazed down at her as she primly wiped the corners of her mouth with her index finger.

"Just making sure it took." Her voice was a cold rasp.

He slid weakly down the door, his folding body forcing hers back. She looked like she was about to cry. His heart lodged in his throat. "What the hell, Gretch," he repeated. She kept her gaze averted, head lowered, so the only thing he caught was the tremble of her swollen lips. He reached out and stroked her cheekbone with his thumb. No response.

"Shhhh." He leaned in and embraced her rigid body. "Shhh." He ran his palms down her spine. The muscles of her back twitched where he caressed, almost like he was causing her pain. He paused. She'd wanted to do this, right? She'd invited him up here. The kissing on the way had been fantastic. She'd initiated the blow job. The mind-blowing, straight-into-orbit, best blow job of his life...

"Hey," he said softly. "Did I hurt you somehow?"

She slipped out of his arms and sat on her haunches. Vulnerability was a good look on her. The smudged mascara and puffy lips were a master artist's rendering of eroticism.

"It's been a long day," she answered. That raspy voice wasn't right.

Sean smoothed the soft, spiky hair he'd mussed like he was stroking a skittish kitten. She did look tired. Wrecked. And as human as this made her compared to the ice-princess act, it also shredded his heart.

"Let's get you to bed." He reached for her hands, but she simultaneously twisted away, and his palms brushed her breasts.

She jerked back, slapping air, partially connecting with his bicep. "You don't get to touch me!"

The shriek froze him. So did her glare. What kind of an emotional roller coaster were they on here? He tried to swallow, but his mouth was dust dry. "I was helping you up."

She studied the carpet, smoothing her skirt in a repetitive way. Awareness emerged like prickles along his skin. He almost shuddered at the horror of his realization. Ever so slowly, he rested his hands on his knees where she could see them. His half-undressed state still hanging out right in her line of vision should've embarrassed him, but he couldn't get past his suspicion. "Sex isn't dirty, Gretch."

Her smile could've won her the next Joker role. It was ghastly in the stillness of her pale face. "Get out."

He sucked in a breath. He had to say something. This was Gretch, his dream girl. How could it have started out so great and ended like this? How could they go on from here? At work tomorrow? He had to reassure her. But words didn't come, and he sat like a bump on a log. The longer he stayed motionless, the tighter the line of her pressed lips became.

"I said get out."

Sean tucked himself into his pants, his fingers spastic. Her phone vibrated. She scrambled inside her purse like she was searching for an EpiPen. He zipped up, ordering his body to stand, turn around, give her some privacy, but protectiveness held him in a crouch, adjusting a shirt that needed no adjusting as he peeked at her screen. The phone number and message were upside down but legible.

Why aren't you home? I want back in your mouth, bitch.

The final light bulb went off. "So this is what you do." He promptly wanted to choke on the words. Her eyes flared. He almost shivered at the hatred and bleakness in them.

"Get. The fuck. Out!" She twisted, throwing the phone across the room. It bounced off the side of the bed and landed harmlessly on the carpet, message side up. "Just *go*, Sean."

He couldn't leave her like this, but by the tension coiled in her torso, she was this close to a screaming fit. Mindful of her proximity, he slid up the door and stood without touching her. He couldn't open the door without thwacking the side of her face, though. Nothing about the distraught woman half curled on the floor resembled Gretch. His decision came easy.

"I'm not leaving." He tensed, but she remained deathly still, her gaze far away. After a long beat, he exhaled. "Not while you're like this. Not until I know you're okay."

Her shoulders slumped. She eased off those killer heels. Her feet were mutilated from the torture—blisters on her heels, red welts along the sides, and her toes were crushed and pointy, forming the shoe's wedged shape. Why would a woman who hated sex suffer through the torture of dressing to kill and suck men off like her life depended on it? Why *attract* the gender she clearly reviled?

"Go sit in that chair," he ordered. Ignoring the visceral need to help her up, he grabbed the stilettos, stepped over her hunched form, and placed the shoes side by side in the mirrored closet to her right. "I'll give you a foot massage. That's *all* I'll do." He adjusted a few hangers so the row was evenly spaced. "No talking, no singing. And absolutely *no* reciting Lord Byron. Even though I know that's what you secretly want me to do."

He glanced down. A faint smile appeared on her face, and for the first time in his life, he thanked God he was a nerd. Someone like his brother would've been halfway across the city by now, thinking he was respecting her wishes. Sean had to play this up. She had to know it was *him*, not just another guy. Not the guy who'd just texted that shit.

Gretch still hadn't moved, and it shattered him to see her so broken. Still, he kept his voice brisk and emotionless. "Do you need help to the chair? 'Cause those feet look like a FEMA disaster."

She held up a hand, and he supported her weight as she rose and walked to the teal armchair. She sat gracelessly, dropping her head back with a whimper. He'd bet his salary nobody saw this side of her, not even Hannah. Or her housemate. It was crystal clear why she wasn't in a committed relationship. It was brave as hell of her to keep volunteering at the shelter, revisiting whatever nightmare she'd gone through.

Sean went to the bathroom, washed his hands, and filled a glass of water. After pocketing the body lotion amenity, he returned to the bedroom. She was in the same position, staring at the ceiling. On the way over, he picked up her phone, pressed the bottom button, and noted the last text's number again. He tossed the cell facedown on the bed and held out the glass. "Here."

As she drank, he sat cross-legged at her feet. Rubbing the lotion briskly to warm it, he cupped his hands on his thigh and waited for a foot. Like a shy geisha, she raised her right leg and slid an ice-cold foot into his palms. Gently he compressed the mangled flesh and massaged blood back into it. He kneaded her high, narrow arch with long, repetitive strokes. Her intermittent sighs and warming skin gratified him as much as when he'd emptied himself into her.

Tenderly he separated her squashed neon-purple-painted toes, unable to stop his avalanching thoughts.

Who'd ruined her? When? For how long? How could he get his hands on the motherfucker? He'd gladly owe Jace favors for the rest of his life to gain intel.

At the digital clock's fifteen-minute mark, she snored softly. He released her foot, but since she was asleep and he could give his OCD free rein, he picked up her left foot and treated it to the same thorough care. The deeper she snored, the greater his satisfaction.

After another fifteen minutes, he stood and watched the steady rise and fall of her chest. Her face in sleep was angelic and untroubled. As horrible as this night had been and as embarrassing as work would be tomorrow, he was glad it had happened. He'd cracked through her iron shell. She could never again act like the queen around him and achieve the same effect.

Sean slipped the phone into her purse, then placed the bag and her duffel inside the open closet. Returning to the armchair, he reached for her, but hesitated. The chances of her waking to a man hoisting her into bed were too great. Leaving her in the chair sucked, but it was the less sucky option. He stripped off the coverlet and draped it around her, fighting the urge to kiss her cheek. Also not worth waking her. Besides, when was the last time she'd met a guy decent enough to leave her alone?

He straightened the coverlet until it was perfectly even. Grabbing the hotel pad and pen by the telephone, he jotted a note and left it on the floor. He flicked off the bedside lamp, and with the stealth of Cary Grant in *To Catch a Thief*, he let himself out.

20

———

Gretch startled awake to a crescent moon glowing in through the window of a strange room. The hotel...Sean... *Oh God.*

She took in the coverlet tucked around her, the neatly turned-down bedsheets, but most of all, the absence of a geeky fairytale prince. She'd ruined everything. All because his amazing kisses had swept right under her guard. "Oh, Christ in poopy diapers."

What had possessed her to *do* him? They'd have to see each other in a few hours! And every day after. They'd have to *talk.* This wasn't like the others, whom she never saw again unless it was on her terms. Where she specifically went to their place so she could leave afterward, on *her* time, instead of begging them to go like she had with Sean.

Gretch glanced at the neon numbers on the clock. Four twenty-two. There was no way she'd be falling back asleep.

She leaned forward. Her lats immediately cramped from the curved armchair. Groaning and gently stretching, she massaged the kink in her neck then wriggled her toes, which for once felt great. Sean's fingers had been magical. Not only did she not remember him working on her left foot, but she *never* fell asleep with a man still in her presence. Especially after she finished them off. She couldn't get them out of her sight fast enough. Why on earth had he stayed after witnessing her full-blown crazy?

Gretch rubbed her temples, groaning once more. She was going to have to quit her job; there was no way around it.

"So this is what you do."

He knew her secret. The disgusting part of herself she'd finally revealed to Eve last night. Not even an hour later, Sean had picked up on it like it was still floating out in the universe to snatch up, look at, judge. She bit her lip at the threatening sting of tears. She'd miss Moore and Morrow. Mourn not seeing Hannah each day. But no way could she face Sean ever again.

Gretch stumbled toward the bathroom, spotting a white pad on the carpet. *Please God, no.* What could he possibly say after all this? She picked it up and turned on the overhead light, blinking and squinting at his neatly slanted words.

Pick you up at 8am. We'll buy you a pair of sneakers for commuting. My treat!

A smiley face? After she'd disintegrated in front of him like that? Did he actually think life could go on as usual? "Like hell I'll be here at eight," she muttered, sweeping up her duffel. Her knockoff Jimmy Choos stood neatly in the open closet. Sneakers! *My treat.*

She lived and died by one rule: control men. That meant maintaining a great body, and showing that body off. Squeezing into sexy outfits and suffering in stilettos were mandatory to her image. She may despise men in general, but she needed them to ogle her like she needed oxygen. Her self-esteem and self-respect had been sucked into the void of self-hatred long ago.

Now Sean had toured the behemoth black hole. Did he run in terror? No. He skillfully massaged her feet and wanted to buy her sneakers. The guy was off his rocker.

In the shower, Gretch scrubbed herself viciously, as if she could wash away last night's massive mistake. She made quick work of dressing in Dwayne's selection of a black spandex-poly-blend dress and a thick red patent-leather belt. She zipped through styling her hair and applying makeup as if she were late for a world premiere. After donning chunky, look-at-me costume jewelry, she stood back and examined her reflection. There. Back to the Gretch who took on the world. She slipped on Michael Kors black patent-leather heels shot through with red slashes. *Fucking ouch.*

Scooping up her belongings, she found her phone in her purse. Brandon's text from the night before popped up the second she pressed the home button. *Why aren't you home? I want back in your mouth, bitch.*

Home? What the fuck? He couldn't possibly have tracked her—she'd given him a false last name. She scanned through her other texts, heart beating rapidly. Two from Dwayne. The first answered her text requesting he bring a change of clothes for her to the shelter.

Bummer. HUGE surprise for you. How do I know he's huge? I saw before. May not tell him you aren't coming home, so he hangs around a bit longer.

Forty-eight minutes later. *Told him to leave. He has a serious personality disorder!*

"Ya think?" Chills chased down her spine. Brandon had her address now. Thank God she hadn't gone home and walked in on him waiting. Although, to be honest, she'd replaced that disaster of an evening with one much worse in the long run. So, so much worse.

Gretch squinted at the digital clock: five fifteen. She slipped out into the hall. Her past was riddled with walking away and starting over. It was actually refreshing. Freeing. She could reinvent herself, her career, make a whole new set of friends... Granted, she'd never started over again this quickly, but it couldn't be helped. Sean had found out her secret. She was a frigid freak. There would be no looking back.

The elevator dinged. New life beginning in three, two, one... She stepped in, hit the lobby button, and calmly prioritized the morning. Head straight to work, type up a resignation letter, drop it on Walter's desk, clean out her desk, and text Hannah to meet for lunch so she could apologize in person. Without giving the real reason. Ever.

Gretch strode out into the quiet lobby, shoulders back, head high. *Showtime.* She flashed her composed smile at the night clerk behind the desk, a heavyset man with a shock of white hair a la Einstein. As expected, he blinked wide-eyed before muttering, "Good morning, ma'am."

She greeted him sweetly and checked out of the hotel. No way would she need the room again tonight. In an hour she'd no longer be employed with Moore and Morrow, so that vague threat was gone. She'd call Brandon and have the stone-cold heart-to-heart she should have had before leaving his bed on Saturday night. So much for hoping he'd get the gentler message of her radio silence.

"We hope you enjoyed your stay," the clerk said, handing her the receipt. Thanking him and smiling widely, Gretch swept up her duffel and strutted for the door.

Her heart seized. Her steps faltered. Across the lobby, Sean lounged on a pinstriped sofa, alert and expressionless. *No, no, no!*

"Not sure you should be checking out of here without clearing it with Margo." His voice was gruff, the shadows under his eyes more like indentations of exhaustion.

"Not sure it's any of your business." Her answer was high-pitched and tentative. Her cheeks burned. Her new life fizzled.

He stood stiffly and rolled his shoulders, waiting for her, but her feet wouldn't move. After a pause, he jerked his head toward the street. "Ready to tackle the day?"

"You've been here all night?" she asked, frowning. She would *not* feel bad. She'd told him she didn't need him guarding her. Told him to get the hell out.

"I went home. Showered, changed, ate." He spread his arms and looked down at himself. "Thanks for noticing."

Well, yes, he didn't have stubble, but he wore jeans and a blue button-down—how would she know that wasn't yesterday's? She held back a snarky response, because her confident-Gretch mask had cracked at the sight of him.

He was here. They were talking.

She waved her hand in a shooing motion. "I'm done with the babysitting routine. Go home."

"So you can skulk into work and resign before anyone arrives?"

She blinked, slack-jawed. His accurate guess didn't give her time to paste on outrage. "I...I don't..."

He strolled over and reached for her duffel, his expression carved into that typical introverted bad mood. Until she focused on his eyes. They blazed an ice-cold challenge. Her breath stilled.

"I'm escorting you to work today as if it were any other day, Gretch. And when we get there, you're going to resume being the Queen of Fucking Everything." He jerked his head again. "Move it. There's a Walmart on

South Cicero that opens at six. We can get there just as the doors open and buy you a pair of sneakers."

How dare he order her around! "Fuck you, Sean."

His luscious mouth curved. "That's my girl."

SEAN GLANCED at the reception desk. Gretch sat motionless, head firmly planted in her arms. *Perfect.* He had a solid hour before work began. It would only take a few minutes to find out what was hidden underneath the ugly charity painting. His heart pounded in anticipation. He laid the canvas on the empty worktable in what had been Robbie the intern's cubicle last fall, then swiftly unscrewed the offset clips and pulled out the industrial staples.

"Damn." Some idiot had pasted strips of double-sided adhesive tape around the edges of the two canvases. The oxidation factor of the tape alone made the need for restoration a probability. Sean slowed his work, separating in millimeter segments to make sure he didn't damage the painting underneath. It was killing him not to tear the top canvas off like wrapping paper, but his methodical nature forced him not to peek until he'd extricated all four sides.

Dane and Anna arrived, greeting a cranky Gretch. They knew better than to disturb him on their way to their workstations. A few minutes later, the smell of percolating coffee wafted in the air. Then Hannah's cheerful voice as she arrived. The day had officially begun. Sean rolled his shoulders and picked up his pace. He had three weeks to miraculously restore the Quran; this was so not a pressing matter in comparison.

The final edge peeled free. His pulse spiked. "Here we go," he muttered, standing and carefully lifting the ugly canvas. The other painting emerged, magnificent and unharmed except for the strips of adhesive tape bordering the canvas.

Chills pricked his limbs. Normal lab sounds condensed down to the thick *whoosh-whoosh* of his heart. He sat clumsily. "Holy. Shit."

Underneath his gloved fingertips lay Johannes Vermeer's masterpiece *The Concert*, stolen from Boston's Isabella Stewart Gardner Museum in 1990. The most expensive art heist ever. *Oh my fucking God.*

Flop sweat drenched him, as if he'd gone through an entire combat karate competition with no break. "Oh my God," he repeated, inhaling unevenly. His legs were too numb to stand. He scanned the fluidity of the scene inch by inch, jaw agape.

Vermeer had slanted in warm sunlight, bathing the dark hues of the musical-themed composition. The shafts of light masterfully led the viewers' eyes to the bright outfit on the girl playing the harpsicord center-left, then lit a path along the black and white floor tiles directly to the man playing the lute, his back to the viewer. An older woman, presumably the man's wife, stood to his right, hands raised and mouth open in song. A viola on the shadowed floor was visible. So was the intricately detailed Acadian landscape painted on the open lid of the harpsichord.

It was spectacular. Perfection. The work was three hundred years old and considered Vermeer's best. Of the five hundred million dollars' worth of artifacts stolen that night, the estimated value of this canvas was two hundred million. Minimum. It had been a while since Sean had read updates on the investigation, the various suspects, the dead ends, but without a doubt the FBI still actively hunted down clues to solve the enigmatic heist. And here was the most valuable piece of them all, hidden beneath one of the ugliest paintings he'd ever seen. A painting Harrison Wickham had banned from his house. One that should have been cleaned and donated to a senior center.

Laughter and the sounds of running water and clinking tools snapped Sean back to the here and now. Dane and Anna were fully into their restoration day, and Gretch was on the phone.

He hastily covered *The Concert* with the outer canvas, filled with unease, like he was part of the cover-up—literally. What should he do first? Telling Hannah would be smart. Telling Harrison Wickham would guarantee the painting would be snatched back, hung up in one of his private art galleries for years while the old man engaged in warfare litigation with the Gardner Museum. He'd probably end up winning, too, what with possession being nine-tenths...

Sean left the ugly canvas on the desk and returned to his cubicle. He should call Jace. But then presto-change-o, his brother would whisk the painting out of the lab and take all the credit. Did it matter? Sure, Sean could use whatever reward money was still being offered, but not the frenzied media attention. And if he told Jace, his brother's fame—and promotions—would know no bounds. He'd owe it all to Sean. Maybe Jace would finally respect him, owe him for life, treat him like a brother he was proud of—all miracles Sean had ceased to hope for long ago. Besides, the text from Gretch's stalker still burned in his mind. Jace would be able to trace the number in thirty seconds. A priceless painting in exchange for the bastard's address.

Sean dialed his brother's cell and rubbed his gritty eyes. The adrenalin of the last hour was leaching out, replaced by a treading-water-in-lead-boots exhaustion.

"Busy," his brother answered.

"Jesus, Jace. This could have been Hannah or Walter."

"They'd have called Margo." His brother sounded winded, and rapid footsteps echoed hollowly, like in a stairwell. "I don't have time, kid. I'm late for a crucial meeting."

Already the shiny dream of a beholden Jace withered. Sean rattled off the cell phone number anyway, peering over his cubicle in case anyone walked within hearing distance. "I need the address."

His brother sighed. "It's against policy to use our database to help you score women."

"First, when have you ever followed policy, and second, it's not a woman's number."

"It's against policy to help you score men, too."

"Come on, Jace." Sean kept his tone light, but it consumed all his energy. His muscles were so tight from the art discovery, the disastrous night, the lack of sleep... If someone engaged him in a judo takedown right now, he'd snap in two. "This is the stalker who's been sending hostile texts to Gretch. I caught the phone number last night."

"Last night?" A pause. "Something going on between you and Gretch I should know about?"

"I walked her to her hotel. You *do* know that." The scalding memory of his orgasm choked off any other reassurances.

Jace stayed silent. Of all four brothers, he'd always had the greatest acuity for ferreting out Sean's lies.

"Just trace the number, Jace. Please. I have crucial information to trade."

Sean held his breath. There were two ways this would end. Jace would give him the address, and Sean would unleash hell on the shithead, or Jace would visit the guy, flash his credentials, and give him a little Quinn love. Naturally, his brother would report back to Gretch, accepting all credit. Either would produce the same end result: Brandon would stop harassing her, so technically it was all good. But just once, Sean would love to be the hero in her eyes.

The clang of a heavy door sounded over the line, then background noises of a bustling office and ringing phones. "Okay," Jace said in a low voice. "I'll take it from here."

The banding up Sean's neck eased. "Thank you. Oh, and Gretch mentioned that Adyton is Shiʿite. The funds from blood artifacts aren't going to ISIS."

"He's actually Alawite, the same religion *and* a distant relative of Bashar al-Assad."

Sean shook his head; the cobwebs inside made it hard to process. "You're saying the funds from blood artifacts support the Syrian regime?"

"The very same regime we're backing rebel groups to overthrow, yes. Why don't you and Gretch stick to dusting art and leave the investigation to us."

Sean gritted his teeth to halt the obscenity. He had a two-hundred-million-dollar painting mere feet away that was about to rock the media worldwide. *You are so going to owe me for this.* "Also, I uncov—"

"Gotta go."

"Wait—"

Jace hung up.

Sean squeezed the phone. "Are you fucking kidding me?" Of all the buttons his brothers knew how to push, this was the big one. Not listening. Not taking him seriously. Dismissing his puny existence to go on about their exciting lives.

It took every ounce of composure not to slam the receiver back onto the console a few times, symbolically battering his brother's head. "Oh well," he muttered. "Sucks to be you, Jace." *Divine fucking intervention.*

The oil painting would remain Sean's secret a little

longer. Besides, maybe it worked out better this way. He'd spent three years consulting with the FBI; he knew the basics of an investigation. It wouldn't hurt to speak to the Wickham son who'd gifted the ugly art to his father last October. Find out where he'd purchased it. Get some intel to impress the FBI when he *did* hand over the world's most hunted painting.

And having more facts would make him look and sound more like the consultant the FBI had hired before Jace switched careers and wrecked Sean's reputation with his baby brother stories.

21

"It'll take years to trace everything Adyton's done," Jace said to the men and women around the conference table, "but based on the Lincoln Bank SARs, he's cleaning vast amounts of money."

"Preferred method?" Margo asked, furiously typing notes into her laptop.

"Two. Layering, meaning multiple deposits to offshore banks, then using those funds to invest back into small businesses around Chicago—a bakery next door, local art galleries—all in family members' names; and second, he uses smurfs: people who take his dirty cash, buy gambling chips or gift cards, and redeem for clean money. This bank's due diligence manager has loosely tied in the Chicago mob as the operational go-between that handles the enormous cash flow generated by the artifact sales."

Margo's fingers stilled. "The mob? Why would they help a lone wolf?

"No doubt they're receiving a massive commission, or maybe extorted Adyton to launder through them."

"How long has Lincoln Bank kept track?" Dirk asked.

"Reports go back to two thousand eleven, which is when the Syrian uprising began. Deposits are all under ten grand, but the sudden and excessive transfers offshore are what triggered the banker's suspicion."

"Sean said the warehouse he was brought to was stacked with crates. He took a photo." Margo's gaze flicked to the Chicago police representative. "Place isn't owned or leased by Adyton, though."

"No, ma'am," the cop said. "So far we haven't found any in his name. This particular warehouse is owned by a Tomas Hussain. We'll begin surveillance and send anyone entering or exiting through the facial recognition database. We'll contact ComEd and AT&T and have them pull their records."

Margo nodded her approval. Jace watched her enter the facts, but underneath the table he flipped his phone frontward and backward like a casino dealer. He could so multitask this better and get the task force back out on the street with their next assignments. She was taking too long to absorb all the intel.

"What about the rest of the eBay items?" she asked.

"His company account is listed as WindyCityAntiques," Dirk began.

Jace bowed his head, listening to his buddy's dry report as he plugged Gretch's stalker's phone number into the DAVID system.

Brandon Myers, thirty-three, divorced five years ago, with a restraining order shortly thereafter that was still in effect. Lived at a high-end address in Wilmette. Hedge fund manager at Hennings, a small but aggressive company twenty minutes from here. A quick swing by there before lunch and problem solved. *This is not your lucky day, Brandon Myers.*

"...we're filtering his listings through the International Foundation for Art Research," Dirk concluded, "and four cultural watchdog sites sponsored by INTERPOL and UNESCO."

Margo nodded. "That about wraps it up."

As the task force closed files and stood, Jace caught Margo's eye. "Is Gretch good to go back to her apartment?" *Or mine?*

"From our end, yes." The unspoken message hung in the air. Whoever was stalking her could still be a risk.

Jace nodded. "The other issue is taken care of too." He looked forward to confronting the fucker, reassuring Gretch, absorbing her gratitude. Although there'd been that odd tone in Sean's voice when he'd mentioned walking Gretch to the hotel. Jace flipped his phone back and forth faster to distract from the growing guilt. God knew he'd done enough poaching of his other brothers' women. He didn't need to steal from the one guy who was probably still a virgin.

———

AS HIGH COMMANDER of gutless wonders, Sean waited until Gretch disappeared into Walter's office to go refill his coffee. *Finally.* The morning had been a tense standoff beginning with no new sneakers and no syllable uttered about last night. Given the Vermeer and the damn Quran that took all his focus, his impasse with Gretch was beyond his energy at the moment. Thus not getting coffee until just now, so they didn't run into each other in the break room.

Sean reclaimed his stool, looked up the Wickham home number in the database, and dialed. It had been seven months since he'd worked in the mansion. What was the son's name again?

"Wickham residence," a woman answered. "May I help you?"

"Sean Quinn from Moore and Morrow art restoration—"

"I'll get Mr. Wickham for you, sir."

"Actually, I'd like to speak to his son." Devon—Hannah's sweetheart—was definitely not there, which left the son who'd bought the painting.

"Rick?"

That was it! "Rick, yes."

A pause. "You said Moore and Morrow?"

Sean grinned at the suspicious tone. Based on the hideous painting, Rick knew nothing about art or the priceless masterpieces his father collected. "This is in regard to the painting he gave Mr. Wickham last October."

"One moment."

Sean paced his tiny cubicle, ignoring the urge to hang up and hand the problem over to the FBI. Finding the criminal was such a long shot, and his brain was eking out final synapses after zero sleep. But the mystery of how the stolen art came to be in Rick Wickham's hands compelled him to hold.

"Hello?" Rick's voice was groggy from sleep.

Sean checked his watch. After ten. "Yeah, hi." He introduced himself and explained his role in restoring the gift. "May I ask where you bought that painting?"

"Some place on West Milwaukee. I forgot the name."

"It would be on the receipt."

"I left without one. I was in a hurry." The irritated tone nudged a vague memory of the man, whose natural expression even in unguarded moments screamed *entitled.*

"May I ask how much you paid?" Sean asked.

"Seventy-five bucks."

Gretch breezed out of Walter's office with a stack of folders, glancing Sean's way before he could hunker down in his cubicle. She stilled, expressionless, long enough for the moment to take an even more awkward turn.

"Hello?" Rick said loudly.

"Yeah." Sean nodded to her and slowly sank onto the stool. "Did the clerk know this was a present for Harrison Wickham? Or that you were his son?"

"No." A pause. "Why?"

This wasn't useful. "It's a question of the pigment the artist used," Sean lied. "We were wondering whether the store had other pieces by this artist so we can research further. Maybe they've sold to your family before."

"Sorry. All I remember is it was next to a Chinese restaurant."

Sean bit back a laugh. "And the name of the restaurant?"

"Dunno. It had a red-and-black awning and a Yelp poster for the best Peking duck in Chicago. I'd gone for lunch and realized it was my dad's birthday, so I stopped by the art store after."

It should not be this difficult. "Nearest cross street?"

"Kimball?" The questioning tone didn't instill confidence, but it was a start. Sean thanked him and hung up. He pulled up three Chinese restaurants on West Milwaukee and Google Earthed the location closest to the Kimball intersection. Bingo. ShenYen Restaurant had a red-and-black striped awning. The pink brick shop to the right had a giant paintbrush above the door. *Donatello's Art and Supplies* was painted in gold, although the font was chipped to the point of tacky. He Googled the store, but their website was minimal and unenlightening.

Sean sighed. Chinese food was near the bottom of the food chain, but if he went there for lunch, he could inquire next door. Actually, he could kill three birds with one stone—neither he nor Gretch had brought in a bagged lunch. Time to stop being a coward.

He buzzed Gretch's interoffice line, palms damp. His name would be blazoned across her console.

"Yes?" Her tone was guarded. He stared at his ash-gray partition because he had absolutely no comeback. She'd never answered the phone without insulting him before. Not even his first day, when any normal person would treat the new guy with kid gloves and overly bright smiles.

Then again, he'd seen for himself last night just how abnormal she was underneath the sassy personality and killer body. He ached for an insult. Ached to go back to the way things were before his stupid idea to hang at Teenie's last Saturday night.

"Got lunch plans?" He winced at his high voice.

The silence over the line went on long enough for a drop of sweat to trickle down his temple.

"Are you asking me out?" The incredulity was more like her, and his shoulders relaxed a fraction.

"More like inviting myself along." He kept his tone light. "Wherever you plan to go. Personally, I'm in the mood for Chinese. There's a place on Milwaukee I'm dying to try."

A muffled oath. He rose slowly, eyeing her down the hall as she thunked an elbow on the desk and slapped her forehead into her palm. *Come on, Gretch. Let me have it with both barrels.*

"All right." She sighed. "But if you start with that weird chewing, I'm outta there."

22

The overpowering combination of Chinese food, kitchen grease, customer perfumes, and an imminent sewage problem in the restrooms almost gagged Sean as they stepped into ShenYen. As the waitress seated them, he breathed shallowly, adopting the unawareness of Gretch and the rest of the patrons, who clearly weren't affronted by the stench.

As soon as the waitress took their order, Gretch sipped her iced tea and scrolled through her phone. *Perfect.* Sean excused himself to go to the restroom and walked out, gulping breaths of fresh air before heading into Donatello's Art and Supplies.

A young guy with a scruffy beard sat behind the register, leafing through a comic book and nodding in time to loud alternative rock coming from ceiling speakers. When he spotted Sean, he tipped his chair back, lowered the volume on the stereo, and slipped the comic book out of sight. "Can I help you?" His sullen tone implied the exact opposite.

"A friend showed me a painting he bought here in October. I was hoping to find more from this artist." As he spoke, Sean scanned the merchandise on the shelves. The brands were inferior, supplies Moore and Morrow would never use. The art on the walls was substandard. "It's a landscape of a wheat field in winter? Face of a bleak-looking farmer. The artist signed it Salvatore."

The slouching clerk popped off his chair. "You know where that painting is?"

The eagerness and recognition of such a shitty piece threw up a big, fat red alert. Sean shook his head and stuffed his hands in his pockets. "Naw. He showed me a picture on his phone. I think he took the art with him to Europe."

"*Who* showed you?"

Sean paused. This was so not the way he'd expected the conversation to go. "A college friend," he answered, even though Rick was eight or nine years younger. "It sounds like you recognize the piece."

"I sold it by accident." The clerk rounded the counter and strode forward so rapidly that Sean instinctively eased into a subtle martial arts stance. "I can't believe you found it." The clerk stopped in front of Sean, face flushed. He reeked of onions and BO. His nametag, *Johnny*, rose and fell rapidly on his chest. "I need to get it back," he said in a higher octave. "It's, like, crazy important I find it."

Sean lifted his palms and shrugged. "I can ask," he said. "Is it valuable or something?"

"My father painted it. He owns this place." Johnny waved around the store. "It was part of his personal collection."

Sean looked around the walls again. If this place was part of a black market art ring, it was in sad shape. "Why would he put his collection on display with the rest of these?" he asked, fishing for anything.

"It was hanging behind the register. Only two days,

man." Johnny thumbed the vacant place he'd just left. "Some guy came in and needed a gift, like, ASAP. When he pointed at it, I just made up a ridiculous price and out came this wad of cash. I never got his name or nothin'. I had no idea it was so important."

Sean's skin prickled. *It's two hundred million dollars important.* He had enough information to give the FBI. He needed to get back to the restaurant. Gretch had the patience of a gnat. "I'll tell my friend to call you. You got a business card?"

Johnny nodded eagerly and bounded to the counter, swiping one off a stack. He returned, beaming. "Thank God you came in. I need your friend to call me, today, bro. My old man's still yellin' at me."

"Sure." Sean pocketed the card. "I'll tell him it's critical." He turned on his heel while the kid still yammered over the importance of the painting. Dumbass hadn't bothered to get Sean's name, either. Johnny's father was going to hit the ceiling.

When Sean opened the restaurant door, the combination of odors hit him full in the face again. Stress or exhaustion always heightened his olfactory sensitivity, and he was a ball of both. How would he last through lunch? He swallowed his nausea and claimed his seat across from Gretch.

She lifted a shapely eyebrow without looking up from her phone. Their steaming entrees were on the scalloped paper placemats. Despite the reek, his stomach grumbled.

"Sorry," he muttered, "long line in there."

She flipped her phone over and pursed her lips. "Why are we here?"

"Sustenance. Also known as lunch, although the British call it dinner—"

"Why so far from the office?" she snapped. Despite

her expert makeup, dark crescents puffed under her eyes like smudged mascara.

"I heard they have the best Peking duck in the city."

"You're a vegan."

Sean modified the precise angle between his stinky plate and his iced tea. "I meant for you." This shallow breathing was making him lightheaded. His comebacks weren't up to par.

Gretch leaned forward, pointing her finger. "Don't bullshit me. We've never even eaten in the break room at the same time. What do you want?"

The brittleness in her eyes looked like treacherous black ice. He stilled. He didn't have the wit today. Honesty was the only option. "I want to talk about last night."

"It's over. If we're going to continue working together, you need to forget it happened."

A waitress holding an iced-tea pitcher approached. Sean shook his head in warning, but she smiled and bowed her head shyly, still on course. When she reached their table, Gretch waved her away with a formidable scowl. The poor woman scuttled off, shoulders hunched. It was uncalled for, and Sean sat up straighter.

"There's no need to bite everyone's head off, Gretch."

She sighed like the weight of the world just set up camp on her shoulders. "Look, Sean, you're a nice guy—"

He braced for impact.

"—and I realize you probably don't date, so let me clue you in. It's an unspoken rule that you move on from a one-night stand. You don't ask the girl out for Chinese; you don't discuss it. It's done."

She toyed with her food, expressions flitting across her face like she was arguing with herself. Finally, she lowered her fork and rubbed her lips together. "You *did* like it, right?"

Her vulnerable expression wiped the floor with his

heart. So they were going to discuss it after all. Sean paused. How to put this precisely? "I floated up to the pearly gates and high-fived all the angels."

She pricked her forefinger on the prongs of the fork, still lying on her placemat. "Then why aren't you acting like all the others do afterward?"

Christ, how do normal guys act? He'd massaged her feet, escorted her to work, taken her to lunch... "Give me a hint," he said, hating the helpless tone. What had he done wrong all these years with other women?

"I don't know." She waved her hand. "Grovel? Gush? Propose marriage to get me to do it again?"

He stared at her, and she stared back, chin up, lips firm. Given her reaction when he'd brushed her breast, those choices sounded abhorrent. How insensitive were these guys? Surely some, if not all, had tried to touch her before, during, or afterward. They hadn't picked up on the damage? "I may not date a lot," he said hesitantly, "but it seemed like you weren't having as good a time. At all. When I accidentally touched—"

"Check, please!"

"Gretch."

She grabbed her purse and began sliding out of the booth.

The terrified waitress appeared instantly. "You no like?"

"We're fine." Sean clamped Gretch's wrist across the table. "I'll shut up."

She hesitated, head down. His breath sawed so inefficiently he grew dizzy. Before this week, their relationship had been tenuous at best: a few insults, a lot of ignoring, occasionally agreeing to do a favor if it benefitted someone else. But all that time he'd hungered for her. The larger-than-life personality, her wit, the killer body she clearly had issues with.

The problem with last night was now he craved the real woman underneath that sparkly, prickly package. He wanted to shoulder the burden of her inner scars, wanted to heal her wounded heart. He was a certifiable doormat, which was tragic, because her attraction leaned toward the exact opposite. Shakespeare would've had a field day with this.

Gretch shifted back to the middle of the booth, and he released her wrist. With a nod of assurance to the waitress, he picked up his fork. The distraught Chinese woman slipped the little tray with the check and fortune cookies by his glass and hurried off. Patrons throughout the restaurant gawked at them. A few whispered.

What a freaking debacle. Sean dug into his steamed rice and vegetables, ignoring the way Gretch picked at her food. How easily this tactic came back to him. Eat fast, hold as still as possible, retreat into his head so deeply that he was only physically present. This whole fiasco was a replica of restaurant meals as a kid. His older brothers and their rowdy antics used to shrivel him in his seat. Countless times he'd shoveled in food, wishing he could disappear. Eventually the horrific meal would be over, his mother apologizing to the waitress, his father cuffing the boys or adding extra to the bill to pay for broken items.

"Do you always eat clockwise?" Gretch asked in a tone like, "Have you always had four nostrils?"

Sean blinked down at his plate. Dread slithered along his spine. When he ate in public, he was cognizant to pick from different areas of his plate even though it gave him the heebie-jeebies. She'd wound him up so tightly he hadn't paid attention. The precise wedge of food remaining resembled eleven to twelve on a clock.

He laid down his fork. "I can't believe you of all people didn't know it's International Eat Clockwise Day."

"I'm not an idiot, Sean."

"Google it."

Her unamused glare slathered on another layer to the already backbreaking tension. The contents he'd gobbled dumped into his stomach all at once. He almost moaned.

She placed her fork on her plate and patted her mouth. "Finished?" She'd had six pieces of chicken and thirteen broccolini spears when the plate had been placed in front of her, and that was what remained.

"Yeah. Thanks for coming all this way to sit with me." He dug for his wallet, counting out cash when she snatched the bill.

"I'll get this. I owe you."

He almost said *for what*? He'd caused her nothing but problems this week. And every time he'd tried to make it up to her, he just made things worse. If only he knew how to be normal. "Thanks," he said—and meant it, but it came out clipped and sullen.

She shook her head with an I-give-up expression and dropped a credit card on the bill. In seconds, the fidgety waitress rang it up and returned. Gretch signed, and Sean's heart thawed at the extravagant tip she left. Once again her prickly exterior hid a softer, decent side. Naturally, she noticed him peering at the bill and slid out of the booth with frosty displeasure. "I need to stop at the ladies' room."

"I'll wait outside." He shouldered the door open and sucked in air like he'd been exhumed from a caved-in coalmine. He shoved his fists in his pockets and stared at the curb. If it hadn't been clear enough last night that they didn't belong together, this meal was the fat lady singing. He shouldn't have asked her to lunch, hadn't meant to stare at the tip she left. It *was* socially unacceptable. Why did he do shit like this? *And now, ladies and gentlemen on the El, I give you another silent freeze-out back to work...*

A door chimed, the recognition of it like a two-by-four to the head. "That's him."

Sean pivoted, teeth clenched at his idiocy. Johnny stood just outside the art store with a morbidly obese, gray-haired man in a brown pinstriped suit. The man's beady black eyes held no humor. No humanity. *Oh shit.*

As sensei, he hammered home mindfulness to his students. Awareness of their surroundings, the threat level. What a fucking bonehead to have been so distracted by Gretch that he'd overlooked the obvious. Johnny hadn't gotten any contact information, so he'd be damn frantic to find Sean again. And here Sean stood, waiting to be found. His heart beat erratically.

"Sal Donatello," the older man said, unfastening the button of his suit. "My son tells me you know where my painting is."

Damn, damn, damn. "No, sir. I can't get hold of my friend."

There was no question the obese man was mob. High up in the hierarchy, too. Small potatoes didn't hang the world's most famous stolen painting behind the register disguised as crap. They stored it in a locked vault with high-tech sensors.

Without breaking eye contact, Sal jerked his head, and Johnny scrambled to open the door. The chimes jingled merrily again. Sal gestured magnanimously. "Come tell me all about your friend. You see, I'm very eager for that painting to be returned."

Sean shifted his weight. *Please don't come out right now, Gretch.* "I can't help you, sir. I only saw a cell phone picture of it. Months ago. I stopped by to see if there were other paintings by that artist—you, I mean. It was exquisite." He raised his palms. "I don't want any problems."

Sal smiled, a lizard-like flash. With a sleight-of-hand motion, he opened the right side of his blazer, where the handle of a menacing Sig Sauer glinted. He nodded to the door. "Inside."

Sean's combat composure emerged like the flipside of a coin. He could take these guys. Could definitely unarm Sal before the man blinked. The sequence whirled through Sean's head: pivot left, roundhouse kick to Johnny's skull, reverse pivot, uppercut to Sal's chin, unarm him as the man went down. "Sorry," he said, breathing in a feral sense of serenity. "I'm late for work."

The door behind him whooshed open; Chinese odors wafted out. "Thanks for waiting," Gretch said. "Sorry I ruined lunch."

Sal's tiny eyes widened, eating up her beauty head to toe. His smile broadened to a real one, which, ironically, was way more intimidating and deadly. Shifting his gaze to Sean, he placed a hand lightly near his unbuttoned blazer, message crystal clear. On some level, he must've known Sean wouldn't give in without a fight, but he was also confident Sean wouldn't dare risk anything now, with Gretch mere inches from a stray bullet.

Sal nodded to where his son still held the door open. "It's your boyfriend who ruined lunch, miss. Please step inside."

23

———

Gretch glanced from Sean to the obese man in the expensive but hideous suit. Tension crackled between them, while the hipster holding the shop door open gaped at all three of them. All she'd done was freshen her lipstick. What the hell had happened out here?

"She's not going anywhere." Sean's calm voice was the emphatic tenor from the dojo. The slouch who'd hopscotched through her brutally unforgiveable behavior at lunch was nowhere to be seen. His profile was chiseled steel, his posture formidable. The smoldering alpha metamorphosis sent a deep shudder through her.

He reached over and clasped her hand. His long, artistic fingers were warm, his grip firm, but after her conduct, this was the last thing she deserved. With a mild tug he eased her behind him. *What the hell?*

"We're leaving," he said to the two men.

Shaking his head, the older man reached into his suit jacket.

"Don't. You *will* get hurt." Sean's gaze stayed locked on the fat man, although he nudged her further away.

A few yards behind the fat man, a young power-walking woman wheeled a baby stroller toward them. She slowed, shooting an annoyed expression at the cluster of people blocking the sidewalk. Gretch glanced at the three men, who were in a glaring standoff. Here was her chance.

"Let me help you," she called to the woman in her trainer's bark. Both the man and hipster turned on instinct.

Sean dropped her hand. "Run."

He lunged forward, striking the older man's chin with an upward sweep of his palm. The blow slammed the man against the glass door.

Sean grabbed something from the man's jacket and whirled in reverse, kicking the hipster in the head. Gretch gaped at the graceful blur of fury. The boy sank to his knees, bleeding from the nose and mouth.

"I said *run!*" Sean snarled without looking at her, bouncing slightly on the balls of his feet in front of the dazed and wobbly fat man. The woman wheeled the stroller in a tight one-eighty and careened away. The baby began to wail.

"Jesus," Gretch muttered. "What in the hell is going on?"

"Goddamn it, Gretch!"

There was no way she was leaving Sean behind. No way in hell she was running in heels. She spun around, scanning the four streets of the intersection for a cop car or—

"*Taxi!*"

The cab pulled up, and she darted for the door. Before she got one foot in, Sean shoved her from behind, hard. She flew across the seat and banged her temple on the window. "Ouch!"

He slid in, slammed the door, and shouted, "Go," to the startled driver.

Wheels screeched as the sedan peeled out. Sean gave Moore and Morrow's address in his sensei tone. Gretch righted herself and yanked down her hem. She was oddly out of breath. Blocks whirled past.

She glanced right, immediately clamping her lips to hold back the shriek. Sean held a gun in his lap, loosely, like it was a toy. Except for a muscle working along his jaw, and a thin sheen of perspiration coating his temple, he was typical, laidback Sean, watching the scenery out the front window. His breathing was even, while here she was, fighting not to hyperventilate.

"Where did that come from?" Her voice sounded thick, like she was thirsty.

Although he didn't look over, a ghost of a grin appeared. "Abracadabra."

"What the hell, Sean," she whispered. "What just happened?"

He leaned forward and stuck the gun into the back of his jeans. After he flipped the shirt over the bulk, he studied her. His usual sad-puppy brown eyes were dark espresso and deadly. It was incredibly compelling—hotter than anything she'd ever seen. "Attempted robbery."

Gretch opened her mouth, but nothing came out. Her fingers trembled, and she wiped her palms on her dress. Everything was okay. He'd saved their asses, asses she didn't even know needed saving. Her warrior. "You did good," she said lightly.

"Thanks. And just for future reference, besides yelling 'run,' is there a magic word that'll get you to actually move?"

She crossed her left leg and tapped the toe of her Michael Kors on his sturdy knee. "No sneakers." She shrugged in fake helplessness.

He grinned in that lopsided way, his eyes twinkling crescents. Such a darling look. The surge of attraction knocked the breath back out of her. She reached for his hand, still welcoming and protective, and squeezed it. "Thank you."

His grin faded. He shook his head. "Don't. I did something so brain-dead stupid you almost got hurt."

Why he called exploding into a ninja and disarming a man *stupid* was beyond her, but she sat back and reveled in their safety, cherished the security his clasped hand brought her.

This was the palm that had brushed her breasts last night. She stroked it tentatively with the pad of her thumb. Callused and capable. Maybe the usual abhorrence wouldn't rear up if she knew it was coming. If she knew it came from *him*.

Maybe she could figure out a way to get him to kiss her in that all-consuming way again, until she was reeling with lust like last night. Only this time she wouldn't do her dog-and-pony show, tied to all the sick memories of powerlessness and horror. Just kissing until she was giddy, then try something new. Strictly over her clothes.

Hope radiated through her. God, to be normal! To enjoy sex and feel cherished by a man's touch... Butterflies pirouetted around her belly.

The taxi pulled to a stop outside of Moore and Morrow.

"What are you doing tonight?" Gretch asked, unable to hide the huskiness, the optimism.

"Karate class." The promptness of his answer was a guy on autopilot. He hadn't caught the innuendo, the dolt. He paid the driver, got out, and helped her to the sidewalk.

"What I meant was—"she raised her voice because he was already closing in on the door, "—can I treat you to dinner afterward, since I ruined lunch?"

"You paid for lunch, Gretch. We're square."

She slapped her hands on her hips. *For Pete's sake.* "I'm asking you out."

He swung around and gaped at her as if she'd confessed to being a two-headed alien.

She blushed, her defenses ramming a rod up her spine. "Please tell me you've been asked out by a woman before."

He blinked a couple of times and seemed to gather himself. "Yeah," he said, walking backward to the door and opening it for her. "But they weren't you."

His words sent her butterflies into a tizzy. She breezed by him and quickly sat behind her desk. The physical barrier brought a semblance of relief. "Okay." *Get it together!* "Stop by my place at eight."

"Eight thirty." He cocked his head. "Maybe you should go with me—"

She held up a hand. "No need. Hip-width stance, grab their arm, shift, pull. Got it."

"Come demonstrate." He gestured, sensei demeanor intact.

She snorted, remembering the downward dog fiasco. "I've maxed my quota of humiliating myself in front of you." *Especially last night.* The office suddenly felt stifling and airless. She flicked her pen in the direction of the lab. "Go on."

"I'll ask Dane to accompany you after work. You shouldn't be walking anywhere alone."

"Enough with treating me like a princess."

His face broke into that lopsided grin, and the butterflies revved up to Mach 2. "Confess," he said in a low voice. "Your birthday-candle wish is to be a princess for real, right?"

Responding intelligibly was beyond her. This guy was white hot when he put effort into being outgoing. Even those quirky, sloping eyebrows, like he questioned everything, were becoming endearing.

Then he ruined it with that weird knock-twice thing and strode off.

"Freak," she said softly, unable to hold back the smile. She brought up her email with surprisingly shaky fingers. The third email down was a response to her request for the Quran provenance. She downloaded the attachment and studied the timeline. Way too tidy. Absolutely a fake. If she hadn't known anything about researching an artifact's history, this would pass as legitimate, but provenances were rarely able to prove ownership without decades or centuries of gaps. She forwarded it on to Margo, her email brisk and professional. If this was the stuff the FBI did, she could so hold her own.

24

———

Sean grinned all the way down the hall. Sure, his face was on a bunch of security cameras in and outside of Sal Donatello's store. Sure, Gretch still needed a bodyguard because of his errors, but she'd asked him out. He barely felt the tile beneath his feet.

Stopping by Dane's desk, he asked the favor, and the man's eyes brightened; whose wouldn't at spending that much time with Gretch? Sean swallowed the surge of jealousy and walked to his cubicle, burying the Sig Sauer in his book bag. He reached for the phone, the thrill of finding the painting resurfacing. Time to update Jace about the Vermeer, and how it was connected to the mob. His brother's curt voicemail message started, and Sean blew out an impatient breath.

"Yeah. It's me," he said. "I've found a painting that'll make you look *real* good. It comes with a Sig Sauer and a story you'll be telling for years. You'll probably want to stop by instead of just calling back." He hung up, grinning. This was it. All he'd ever wanted from his earliest memories. The respect of an older brother.

He drummed his palms on the desk, too adrenalized

to get back to the intricate restoration. He should probably tell Hannah and Walter too. They would shit knowing the Vermeer had been stored here since October.

Both calls went unanswered. Seriously. The news of the century. Sean shook his head and phoned Gretch. Once again she answered like a normal person, which was mildly disappointing. Her snark kept him on his toes.

"Where are the bosses?" he asked.

"Out on a sales call. Why?"

"Need to show them something." If he stood up, they'd be talking face to face. A hall length away, but still. Their relationship was on the brink of something new. She'd asked him to dinner; he should stand up and smile as he spoke, right? Would that be flirting? Cloying? Creepy?

"They'll be back at three thirty," Gretch said in a perfunctory voice.

He rose to a crouch before he heard the distinct hang-up. "So. That happened," he muttered, face in flames, slumping on his stool. No big deal. A heroic afternoon loomed once Jace, Walter, and Hannah shared in his find.

Sean stuck in earbuds, chose Yo-Yo Ma's interpretation of Bach's *Six Unaccompanied Suites*, and picked up his tools, humming. Life sure had a way of turning around on a guy.

Hours later, while focusing on the exacting intricacies required to repair the Quran, his inherent pessimism crept back like an insidious fog. Jace hadn't stopped by— so much for the epic unveiling. And every moment that passed brought another explanation for Gretch's oddly affectionate behavior in the taxi. The joke about the sneakers. The slender fingers wound in his. Their repartee had felt so natural at the time, but now it was filtered through years of insecurity. Hell, she'd hung up when he'd been about to stand up and smile; that wasn't the action of a woman attracted to him.

That stuff in the taxi had to have been his imagination, because Jace was her type. And tonight... He'd read too much into her invitation. Obviously misunderstood the beguiling vulnerability in her eyes. Women who breezed through life with looks and personalities like hers didn't gravitate to OCD introverts who preferred the arts to human interaction. Last night was a fluke. Besides, as much as Sean wanted her, he didn't want to be responsible for her meltdown again. He'd eat the meal, picking from areas around his plate in no particular pattern, and call it a night. The perceived magical moments in the taxi would have to suffice.

He adjusted his earbuds and gently picked up a sheet of gold leaf with wide, padded tweezers. Should he have told her about Donatello and the significant threat they'd faced? No. Why worry her? Sure, the mob probably had security photos of them by now, and were undoubtedly scouring the city for any information on them or the stolen painting, but this was Chicago. The third-largest city in the nation. Neither he nor Gretch lived or worked anywhere near West Milwaukee. He'd only touched the outside door handle—no way could they lift his finger-prints from others. Hadn't given his name or business card. Even if the mobster had gone next door and—

Oh shit!

Sean jerked spastically, lurching the tweezers. The gold leaf fluttered to the floor. *Gretch paid for lunch with a credit card.* He'd spent hours mooning over the taxi ride instead of the single, minuscule detail that had probably outed them within minutes.

Sean wiped a hand over his mouth, heart hammering. All Sal Donatello had to do was describe her and get her name off the receipt. It would take seconds to trace her social media accounts, where she'd probably listed Moore and Morrow under *occupation*. No one in this office was safe. What a fuck-head move to attempt this quasi-FBI role this morning. He should've redialed Jace over and over until the butthead answered.

Sean jumped up and squinted down the hall. Dane chatted animatedly to Gretch as she gathered her things. Her imperial displeasure at the escort was written all over her face, which the man failed to notice.

"Hold up," Sean called. "Don't leave yet."

Sucking in a terrified breath, he pressed Jace's number. The life-and-death call landed once again in his brother's voicemail. Muttering an oath, he texted *sos* and shared his location. Again. Twice in three days. Couldn't get wimpier than that.

He gestured again for Gretch and Dane to wait, then scurried around cleaning up his cubicle. Sure, the secure world they all took for granted was about to fall down in an Armageddon blaze at their feet, but that was no excuse to leave his workstation in disarray. He'd obsess over it all evening. Hate for it to be his dying thought.

Sean hurried down the hall and sidled up to Dane. "On second thought, I've got time before my class to escort her."

"You never leave this early," he protested.

"I'm at a stopping point. Thanks for agreeing to walk with her, though." He ignored Dane's crestfallen expression. If the guy held a black belt, it would be a different story.

Sean peered into Walter's office. Dark and empty. Hannah's laugh trickled down the hall. She'd have to do. He turned to Gretch. "I need to speak to you and Hannah for a sec." He waited impatiently while Dane said goodbye to Gretch, which consisted of stuttering, scuffing his feet like he was in junior high, hitching his book bag, and all but bowing out the door.

"Jeez." Sean walked over and flipped the interior bolt. "Do I act like that around you, your highness?"

"Worse. You'd have double-knocked that threshold on your way out."

Sean cringed. The shit she noticed. Did he still do that? It was a holdover scar from childhood. "Come on," he said, heading to Hannah's office. "This isn't going to be pretty."

"Why?" She sounded tired, but he didn't turn around. "What's going on now?"

No time to explain twice. "Just brainstorming new and improved ways to annoy the hell out of you."

Behind him, she executed the perfect regal *tsk*. "If it's about the attempted robbery and your super-ninja moves, she already knows."

Sean swung around, jaw clenching, and waited for Gretch to catch up. "I don't think that was necessary," he murmured.

She patted his chest with a condescending smile. "It's what besties *do*. They share what happens in their day, especially if it involves guns and a dropkick to somebody's head."

Well, he was about to add a whole lot to that story. He eased away, but Gretch pushed him against the wall. Granted, it wasn't remotely like the head injury he'd almost sustained last night against her hotel door, but the similarity of her dominance tightened his groin. He opened his mouth. Maybe to ask her what the hell she was doing. Maybe to kiss her. She placed a manicured finger to his lips. "Shh."

Through a haze of horniness, he heard a man answer Hannah.

"Devon's back," Gretch whispered. "He must have gotten here while I was in Walter's office."

Sean shrugged. Hours had gone by where he'd been so fixated on being a hero that he hadn't pre-empted this crisis. *The Concert* painting, the mob, and whatever personal information Gretch had posted on her social media were a hell of a lot more important than Hannah's childhood sweetheart returning from a half-week trip to Manhattan. Sean straightened from the wall, but Gretch pushed him back, holding him there with a braced forearm and a dirty look. *What the fuck?*

Again she held a finger to her lips and mouthed, "Listen."

"...so given the judge's ruling, it looks like I'm in the clear," Devon said, followed by a little squeal from Hannah. "I'm relieved it's finally over. I can start giving my new company my undivided attention."

"Your company?" Hannah cooed.

"Oh, I have all sorts of plans for you, Han." The sound of kissing.

Ugh. Sean had barely spoken to the man, but it didn't take a whole lot of imagination to see him for what he was: an arrogant rich boy who'd never suffered heartache like Sean and Dane and the rest of the world's nerds. Sean twisted easily out of Gretch's hold, gripped her biceps, and drew her so close their lips almost touched. "I am not going to eavesdrop on them," he whispered, absorbing the tiny shiver that ran through her. "She's your bestie. This is her dropkick to the head to tell you about later."

He rounded the corner into Hannah's office and stopped short, fighting the urge to slip out as soundlessly as he'd arrived.

Devon sat in the office chair with Hannah on his lap —straight on, her legs straddling his spread thighs. He'd wrapped his hands around her ass, and his toes manipulated the swivel chair with a technique right out of a porn movie. From here, it looked like he wasn't kissing her as much as working her over in an obscene, no-holds-barred parody of a kiss. Maybe if Devon wasn't such an overconfident dick or Hannah wasn't like a sister, Sean could've tolerated this, but... *Gross!* He'd return to the hall and cough to warn them.

He pivoted and smacked into Gretch. Her *woof* was followed by two pairs of sucking lips hastily parting.

"Ohmygosh," Hannah gasped. Sean reluctantly turned back, fighting for a neutral expression. Hannah now sat primly across her boyfriend's lap, wiping her swollen lips. "Sorry. We didn't hear you."

"That," Gretch said emphatically, "was quite clear. Too bad Sean ruined the show." Her smirk and raised eyebrow set off a crimson blush on her friend's face.

"What's up?" Devon asked, looking completely unfazed and unapologetic. He trailed fingers through Hannah's ponytail, his gaze warm on Gretch and cooling when it met Sean's. Sean oozed his opinion right back. October had been nothing but turmoil for Hannah, all because of this good-looking, soulless guy who excelled at breaking hearts.

"Um..." Gretch turned to Sean, her hand out like she was about to introduce him. "I don't know. What's up?"

Crap. There was no way Sean was talking about any of this in front of a Wickham. "It's an office situation I wanted to discuss with you and Gretch," he said, eyeing Hannah unwaveringly, "in private." The swivel chair twitched, but that was all the reaction Devon gave.

Hannah patted her boyfriend's knee and stood, smoothing her wrinkled pants. "It's all right to talk in front of Devon. He's part owner in Moore and Morrow now, and a killer at problem solving."

"Okay," he said in a don't-say-I-didn't-warn-you tone. Haltingly, partially stuttering, and aware that his shirt plastered his back, Sean told them about stripping off the ugly painting.

"And?" Hannah breathed, her eyes wide.

"It's Vermeer's *The Concert*."

Her body sagged enough for Devon to effortlessly draw her back onto his lap. She leaned forward and folded her arms like she was cold. "Sweet baby Jesus."

"So?" Gretch asked in an unimpressed voice. "It's what—famous? Priceless? Stolen? No need to make Devon and me feel any stupider."

"It's stolen," Sean answered quietly. "It's famous. Not priceless. It's probably worth two hundred mil. And it's one of the FBI's highest-profile open cases, coming up on thirty years."

Gretch gasped. Devon's jaw dropped. Sean sped through the remainder of the day. "So Donatello's only lead is me," he concluded, "and there's no doubt in my mind he's mob. And Gretch paid for lunch next door with a credit card."

"Shit." Devon instantly got the connection. "No one is safe here."

Gretch socked Sean's arm hard. "Why didn't you tell me in the taxi?"

"I don't know." *Because you held my hand and joked with me, and that fucked with my mind all afternoon.*

"What are we going to do?" Hannah asked, her voice high with hysteria.

"I've texted Jace," Sean said hastily. "But I don't think that painting should stay in the office. And maybe we should keep the outer office door locked during the day except for well-vetted appointments."

"We'll need security cameras outside the building." Devon reached for the phone. "And a description of what the Donatellos look like."

"I'll Google them." Gretch marched over to Hannah's computer, her fingers flying across the keyboard. "Ta-da."

Sean checked the dark screen of his phone, his teeth clenching. Evidently the second *sos* was going to be ignored.

Hannah touched his arm. "Can I see the painting?" she said softly.

He led her back to the lab and unscrewed the offset clips. Slowly and without flourish, he peeled back the outer canvas.

Hannah gasped. "Oh, Sean, it's breathtaking. Can you believe we found it?"

Gretch and Devon were coming down the hall toward them. Sean tore his gaze from them to her. "Devon is right. None of us are safe. They'll find Gretch in a heartbeat. I'm surprised they didn't surprise *us* this afternoon."

"Sean, even the mob can't march into a business and shoot it up when they have no idea what you know about Rick's painting."

Sean's shoulders relaxed a fraction. "I told them the owner was overseas." Not that they'd believe him, but Hannah had a point. Sean had taken a ride on the paranoid merry-go-round all afternoon. Moore and Morrow probably wasn't in the imminent danger his imagination had created.

He was halfway through a calming inhale when his phone dinged. A message from Jace: *Open up.*

25

———

It was crazy weird how Sean's stature shrank around Jace. Gretch studied the pair walking side by side toward where she, Hannah, and Devon were clustered around the painting.

Except for being the same height, the brothers' personalities and body language were night and day. Jace, with his short black hair and crystal-blue eyes, strode like a Marvel Comics superhero, his eyebrows knit, his square jaw thrust in pursuit of justice. Beside him, Sean's long-legged form was all lanky angles. Even his mouth stretched into a sullen line. He'd found a two-hundred-million-dollar painting, dropkicked someone's ass this afternoon, and still walked like the dopey kid in trouble. As the brothers neared, it became evident that he was, and Jace's larger-than-life presence was due to fury. "...sending goddamn SOS messages like the sky is falling!"

"At the time I thought it was. It still could be."

"You need to see a doctor about that toxic level of estrogen."

"Jace, listen. We found—"

"Hello, Gretch." Jace smiled, the wattage and beauty

of it sizzling her like an egg on a scorching sidewalk. "Hannah." He halted near Devon, and the two alphas sized each other up. "Jason Quinn, FBI." He held out his hand, and Devon gripped it, supplying his name. The level of testosterone lowered slightly, and Jace turned back to Gretch. "I trust the texts stopped."

She blinked. "What?"

"I uncovered this," Sean blurted, pointing over the cubical wall.

Jace glanced down, looking unimpressed. Then his eyes bugged out. "One of the Gardner Museum's?"

"Yes."

"Excuse me," he murmured, and brushed around her to the desk. "Give me the facts." He took out his phone and snapped pictures, eyes shining like sapphires.

Hannah and Sean crowded in, explaining when and where and how. Devon rested an arm atop the cubicle, slightly bored, slightly amused, and more than marginally absorbed in Hannah.

Jace nodded and snapped. The more ecstatic he became, the more morose Sean looked. Gretch didn't get it. The FBI would protect them, the painting would go back to the museum, and Sean would be a hero—why the gloomy puss?

"Where's the Sig?" Jace asked, when Sean got to the part about the gun Donatello had pulled.

Sean retrieved it from his book bag and handed it over clumsily. See? He'd handled the gun like a pro in the taxi. *Weird.*

"You knew this was loaded, right? And a Sig doesn't have a safety?"

"Yes, Jace. I knew that," Sean retorted.

Jace shook his head, released the magazine, racked the slide back, and removed the round from the chamber.

He slipped the components in separate pockets. "The shit you get yourself into."

Gretch rolled her eyes at their dynamic and headed down the hall. Their volatile relationship was exhausting. And what the hell had Jace meant by that cryptic text remark? He'd asked for her phone number Monday. Tuesday he found out she was being harassed by Brandon. Had he pulled her phone records? Hacked into her texts? *Found* Brandon? She hadn't thought to check messages all day. If there were none from Brandon... Well, on the one hand, the freak would finally move on. On the other, she was pretty sure her civil rights had been grossly violated. Not to mention Sean had barely let her pee in private these last two days.

The overbearing assumptions of both Quinn brothers were too much. Gretch grabbed her phone and tapped the text icon. Two new dates from the LVR hookup site, both suggesting a meetup for drinks. None from Brandon. The last obscene text had been the one Sean saw last night.

So this is what you do. Her teeth clenched. She scanned recent calls. *Oh no.* One from the shelter an hour ago, no message left. "Please God, let everything be all right." If only she'd had the ringer on! She returned the call and asked to speak to Eve.

"Hello?" At Eve's timid voice Gretch caught her breath. She'd spoken to the poor woman enough times, trying to cajole her to safety, that she knew Eve's differing degrees of courage and determination. And she knew this tone.

"It's Gretch," she said briskly. "Just checking in."

"It's been...a rough day." The last word was said on a sob. "My parents said he went over there and got physical with my dad—knocked him to the ground. Threatened them unless they told him where I was. My mother's in hysterics. I'm afraid, Gretch. I need to go comfort my parents."

"Don't leave yet. I'm heading to the shelter right now. It'll take twenty minutes." She shoved her purse strap over her shoulder. "We can talk as long as you want, Eve. Promise me you won't leave before I get there." Silence on the other end.

She squeezed her eyes shut. "Please, Eve. He's probably parked out front of their house waiting for you. He knows what buttons to push. Think of your girls!"

"Okay," Eve said so softly it was a strain to hear over the celebratory exclamations in the lab. "I'll wait."

"Twenty minutes. Clock me." Gretch hung up. One last glimpse down the hall—Jace spoke animatedly into his phone, and Hannah pointed something out to Sean, their heads lowered in that worshipful art-geek manner.

Good. They wouldn't notice her slip away. She was sick of being escorted around like some fragile fairy princess when women like Eve were in very serious danger.

———

By the time Sean stopped ogling *The Concert*, not only had Gretch left, but he also had to book it to the dojo—as in sprint the entire nine blocks instead of waiting for the El and suffering through the station stops in between.

Where the hell had Gretch gone? She'd been available for an earlier dinner only hours ago and hadn't mentioned being in a hurry when Dane hovered at her desk, so her disappearance had to be spontaneous. When would she clue in to the danger she faced?

Sean hit the street and pumped his annoyance and worry into his stride. How had she gotten this far in life with all the risky pickups? As soon as the boys were squared away practicing their Katas, he'd try her cell phone, and by God, if she answered, he wasn't going to be pleasant, geeky Sean. Those days were gone.

Ten minutes later he pushed through the dojo door, sweaty and gulping oxygen.

"Sensei," the boys chorused, and bowed.

Randy, who owned the place and leased it Tuesday and Thursday evenings to Sean, threw him a dirty look.

"Sorry," Sean gasped, unzipping his gym bag, "held up at work." Which never happened. He was devoted to his teaching evenings. Just one more testament to how adventures with the FBI and Gretch had sent his serene life through a spin cycle. Randy grumbled unintelligibly and stood up from behind the desk, grabbing his keys and phone.

"Stretch out," Sean called to the boys, and spun back. "Can you stay one more minute while I change?" He whipped his *gi* out of his book bag and headed for the bathroom without waiting for an answer. He'd covered for Randy several times when the guy was too hungover to even bow. As much as the owner was probably jonesing for a beer, Randy wouldn't leave a bunch of eight-year-olds unsupervised.

Sean glanced around him at the filth of the bathroom, his skin crawling at having to change in here. Urine droplets on the floor, paper towels instead of toilet paper, a corner of the mirror cracked off. The dojo probably wouldn't stay open much longer, which was too bad. The place had gone from pristine to shabby in only a few years. Any cleaning of the workout mats and bathroom seemed to occur only on Tuesday and Thursday nights by Sean, after his students left. Tonight *should* be an exception—he had a dinner date—but he physically couldn't leave it like this. His OCD wouldn't allow it.

"Fuck," he muttered, wrenching the door open and

waving his thanks at Randy, who was tapping his foot by the door. Maybe he'd end class five minutes early, give each boy an area to wipe down. Sean would deal with the disgusting bathroom.

He stepped onto the mat, and as usual, the serenity and dignity of the art form flowed into him. Here, he wasn't geeky Sean, bullied since grade school, odd one out in his own family. He was Yondan, a fourth-degree black belt, a sensei who commanded respect and generated awe.

"*Fujikata Dai Ichi*," he ordered, and walked down the line, adjusting the boys' stances of the first and most basic kata. He spent extra time with Phillip Mayfair, who not only suffered from variations of that name (Fillie Fairy), but was also an asthmatic and too small and uncoordinated for his age. Empathy seeped from Sean as he patiently demonstrated the form again. His own childhood had smacked of similar torture until his mom had stuck him in karate class after he'd come home with a fat lip. It was the only day his father, grinning and puffing on his cigar, had shaken his hand.

"Hope the other guy looks worse," he'd stated, slapping Sean on the back. Sean hadn't the courage to tell him *she* had walked away completely unmarked and laughing with her girlfriends.

"That's it, Phillip. Great job." Sean headed back to the center of the mat. "*Fujikata Dai Ni.*"

The soft snick of the door and the boys' attention snapping that way broke into Sean's thoughts. He turned, expecting Randy to have forgotten something. Three men filed in. Their sheer bulk and gruesome tats radiated a menacing signal as loud as an air horn. Randy, in his haste to get out of here, hadn't locked the door behind him.

Although his heart seized to a stop, Sean schooled his

expression into the watchful calm of a predator. "Gentlemen. May I help you?" he asked pleasantly for the benefit of the boys behind him. He kept his hands loosely at his sides, his bare feet hip distance apart, weight shifted to the balls of his feet.

"You run fast. Manny, here, thinks you should try out for the Olympics." The man closest to the door had a voice like scraped gravel. He held the door handle shut. "Mr. D. would like his painting returned."

Sweat broke out on Sean's forehead. *Not here. Not with my boys here.* Why didn't they grab him back at Moore and Morrow?

He kept his gaze on the man who'd spoken, studied the flattened nose, the scar separating his right eyebrow, the incredible steroid bulk of him. He had size and power, but Sean had agility and speed—no problem there. The guy in the middle was the tallest and shaped like a mountain, his bald head absurdly small in proportion to the rest of him. Taking him on individually would've been an even fight.

The third was skinny and wiry, and breathed through his mouth. There was no question he was on rage-inducing uppers. His pupils were pinpricks, and his gaze shifted like a pinball from the boys, to Sean, around the room, back to the boys. He'd be a problem, strictly because of the unpredictable superhuman strength he might possess due to the drugs.

"I've already told him all I know," Sean said. But clearly that hadn't been enough to convince Donatello, so he added, "I'd be happy to discuss this another time. My cell number is on those business cards." He nodded at the stack on the desk. "As you can see, I'm in the middle of class."

"You can speak to him yourself." Mountain Man jerked his head left. "He's in the Lincoln right outside."

Sean flicked a glance through broad windows covered by large red words advertising the dojo's services. Had the list not clogged the view, a passing cop might have noticed the oddity in here. In the dusk, the headlights of a classic, dark Continental stood out among the parked vehicles lining the quiet block. Panic began to edge out his sensei bravado. "I'm in the middle of class," he repeated. "We finish at eight."

"Of course," Flat Nose said, "which is why we'll continue while you step outside." His grin was right out of a Freddy Krueger movie, and a gold-front tooth gleamed in the fluorescent light. He let go of the door and lumbered toward the mat. "How would you like that, boys?"

The dull thump of Sean's heart in his ears drowned out any responses the boys may have uttered. He stared Flat Nose down and eased into *Fujikata Dai Ichi*.

"Don't," the man said, flashing the chilling smile again. "My friends shoot to kill."

Sean couldn't endanger the boys any further. They were too young to see guns pulled. He held up a hand. "Wait."

Surprisingly, the man complied.

Sean exhaled. *Shit.* What was he going to do? "Call your boss. I can speak to him from here. I refuse to leave my students."

"Mac, we gotta hurry," Mountain Man said. "Too many people can see in here."

Actually, they couldn't. That was the problem. Although if the mobsters thought they could, they'd be less likely to do anything stupider than this.

"Manny, round up the boys and put them in there," Mac said, pointing to a closed door. The twitchy freak bounded across the room. Sean said nothing. It was a tiny closet for cleaning supplies and extra dojo equipment.

Even Phillip wouldn't fit in there. Manny flung open the door, shoulders slumping almost immediately. He looked at Mac for guidance.

"In there." Mac pointed to the other closed door, the wretched bathroom.

The thought of five boys smashed into that foul-smelling, germ-infested toilet turned Sean's stomach. "We walk out as one unit," he blurted. "I go talk to your boss, and the boys go next door to the deli. Wait for their mothers."

Mac exchanged a look with Mountain Man, who shook his head. Mac turned back and repeated the gesture, glancing at Sean's bare feet. "Put your sneakers on. You take Mr. D. to the painting, and we babysit. The faster you cooperate, the faster these boys get home for dinner. How 'bout it, boys? Let's see some moves." He rotated his hands stiffly in the clichéd gesture of karate chops. Jumpy Manny snickered and imitated him.

"I'm not leaving them with you." Sean kept his voice deadly soft. "And if you take them out that door without me, you're committing five felony kidnappings."

A few gasps behind him squeezed his heart. What a shitty lesson they were learning about the world tonight. Way too young. And this was all his fault. And fucking Randy for not locking the door. Sean glanced at his book bag behind the desk. On top of his folded jeans and shirt was his phone. But he'd texted *sos* enough times that even if by some miracle he could reach the phone, his lifeline was gone. Jace wouldn't pay attention.

"Manny," Mac said, reaching behind him in a not-so-subtle warning of the gun he possessed. "Stick the boys in there and guard the door."

The meth-head waved the boys toward the bathroom, his muscles twitchy, his wild eyes almost rotating. "Come on, you little shits. Move out!"

Sean stared Mac down, but it was no use. The ghastly smile returned; the gold tooth glinted. "See? We're keeping them as a unit and not taking them out of here. Please—" he nodded toward Mountain Man, "—he'll go with you. The boys will be perfectly safe."

26

This was the best fucking night of his life! Halting at the final traffic light, Jace glanced in his rearview mirror. The headlights of the Moore and Morrow van were right behind him, the journey to FBI headquarters on West Roosevelt blessedly uneventful.

In minutes he'd present *The Concert* to the hastily summoned heavy hitters: Margo's boss, Supervisory Special Agent Felix Garcia, and his boss, Special Agent in Charge of the entire Chicago field office, Jonathan Webb. Sure, the painting wasn't a blood artifact, nor did it have any bearing on all the different terrorist factions profiting off conflict antiquities that they were investigating. This was more like Tim Jennings intercepting those two passes last fall to lead the Bears to a 7–0 victory. An unexpected, miracle-out-of-nowhere bonus.

Jace exhaled impatiently as the light finally turned green. He led the van the remaining half-block to their destination, the intense pride swelling in his chest almost painful. He fucking deserved this.

Given the late evening hour, he was able to find two

parking spots close to the entrance. He cut the engine, jumped out, and waved Hannah Moore aside so he could assist Devon Ashby with the crated painting. "They're expecting me," he said to the security guard, flashing his credentials. The man nodded, and the trio rode up to the third floor. In the conference room, seven seats were occupied, and wide-eyed expectation shone on every face. As Hannah carefully uncrated the masterpiece, Jace stood next to her at the head of the table and filled the team in on the find. He nodded to Margo, who'd pulled intel on the Donatello family.

"Sal Donatello is head of the Genoa Family, mostly gambling, prostitution, and money laundering. Sixty-two. Married to wife, Sylvia, for forty-one years. Son, Johnny, is twenty, and the two much older, married daughters live in San Marino, California and Westport, Connecticut. Neither husband is associated with the family."

Hannah removed the top of the crate, and Margo ceased talking. Everyone leaned forward in their chairs and craned their necks. Almost immediately a collective exhale went through the room.

"Out*standing*." SAC Webb smiled up at Jace. "Excellent work, Jason."

"Actually," Hannah said, "his bro—"

"This was underneath a painting given to Harrison Wickham," Jace said quickly. "Even though he requested that other art be donated to charity, we should probably notify him of the find."

Webb glanced over at Devon, lounging by the door. "Isn't he your father?"

Devon nodded, expressionless. "I'm sure he'll want to see this returned to the Isabella Gardner," he said. "The positive publicity alone will make up for the loss of ownership."

"That doesn't sound like the Harrison Wickham I

know," someone muttered, and Devon searched the table for the speaker.

"You'll find he's a different man," he said slowly to the agents. "But if he does take issue, let me know and I'll step in."

Hannah's tender smile at her boyfriend was so filled with meaning that Jace shifted uncomfortably. He ran from intimacy. Smiles like hers scared him more than an ISIS ambush.

He turned back to the team. "We have an APB out on Donatello and are acquiring a search warrant for his residence. Hopefully we can capture the rest of the looted art."

The SAC held up a hand. "We've already notified the Boston team in charge of the nineteen-ninety heist. They're flying their agents out tonight."

Jace clenched his teeth and managed a nod. The Boston team had found squat for almost thirty years. "Margo and I request clearance to assist them while they're here." He ignored Margo's startled head jerk. There was no way he was walking away from this find, and all the glory that came with it.

SAC Webb folded his hands and said quietly, "Denied. You're too valuable on the Blood Antiquity Task Force, and we're too close to uncovering the snake head behind the smuggling."

Margo visibly relaxed, and Jace struggled to remain expressionless as he stared at the painting by his side. *So goddamn close...*

A rap on the door captured everyone else's attention.

SSA Garcia's assistant stuck her head in. "A Mrs. Sandra Mayfair is on the phone. Her son wears a GPS watch capable of sending emergency signals and two-way communication. She received an alert from him at

Randy's Dojo. The class is being kidnapped. Instructor was just led out the door."

Jace stiffened, blood draining from his head. He gripped the table for balance as agents rose around him to get organized. "It's Sean," he mumbled. The late lunch he'd eaten pitched upward, and he swallowed hard.

"What's that, Jason?" the SAC asked.

"The instructor. It's my brother." His lips felt numb. "This is Donatello's work. He's not giving up the painting without a fight." He fumbled for his phone and looked at the screen. No SOS this time. *Figures.*

THE PLASTIC ZIP tie that bound Sean's wrists behind him was much tighter than the one circling his ankles. Or maybe it was because he instinctively kept trying to get his hands free. The plastic cut deep. The pain kept him sane and focused. The rancid garlic and body odors permeating the car did not. "Let the boys go," he said for the millionth time. "They have nothing to do with this."

The ancient leather on the front seat crackled under Donatello's weight as he peered out his window. A wasted move. Even from the back seat, the mass of swirling police lights illuminated the night like a tropical blue paradise. Donatello sure had balls, parking a block from his own felony in progress.

"I would dearly like to call it a night," the mobster replied. "I'm missing the Cubs." He turned to his driver. "What's your take on Martinez?"

Sean gritted his teeth. "Mr. Donatello—"

"Mr. Quinn." His beady eyes focused on Sean in the rearview mirror, the gaze so deadly that Sean shuddered. "I've gathered quite a few facts about you since this after-noon. I know where you work. My colleagues visited your firm an hour ago. Evidently my canvas is still in your company's possession, but the painting underneath is not. *Where* is it?"

"I would guess FBI headquarters, since, as you know, it was stolen."

Donatello sighed. "Those small boys must be very hungry."

Sean squeezed his eyes shut. He couldn't think about the guys smashed into that tiny bathroom. Their fear and confusion. Their parents' terror. And if Donatello's men had rummaged through Moore and Morrow already, God knew how much theft and damage the company would find tomorrow. Surely the place was under FBI surveillance. How had the mob slipped through? Where had Gretch gone, and was *she* safe?

Sean opened his eyes to the neon-blue lights and the claustrophobia of two very large, stinking men stuffed in the front seat of a luxury car.

"You're not a stupid man, Mr. Donatello." Sean waited for the death glare in the mirror again. He met it without flinching. "There's no way your men are getting out of that dojo. You have me. Call them off, and let the boys go home."

Donatello crooked a brow. "You're not a valuable asset to trade for the painting. Five small boys? Now I have bargaining power."

Sean felt the flicker of victory. Or bottomless fear. "I *am* an asset. The agent who's no doubt taking credit for finding your painting is my brother. Call the FBI and ask for him. His name is Jason Quinn."

"You're family; you're off this case." Supervisory Special Agent Garcia swiveled from where he sat in the SWAT van, surrounded by other agents all active in the hostage crisis. Everyone had a role in saving Sean and the kids. Everyone except Jace.

"All I'm asking is to remain on the *scene*, sir." Sweat soaked his suit, as if the rage and helplessness had nowhere to go except through every pore. He met his commander's glower with the intensity of a twice-decorated former SEAL. He wasn't fucking slinking home and popping a beer while this went down. The glory of the painting find had been snatched from his grasp, which was why Garcia's boss, SAC Webb, wasn't on this scene. Handing over the credit to the top brass had been a professional blow, but not like this—not knowing how to save Sean's life and lay waste to whoever was responsible.

The moment crystalized to just the two of them: the clash of wills between a red-tape policy-and-procedure wonk and a former SEAL who knew how to get things done. Around them, the glow of the monitors and the squawk of walkie-talkies lent a surreal quality, like the kidnapping was just a Hollywood bit. Pass the popcorn.

The SSA jabbed his finger at a chair in the corner. "Don't make me regret this. No interference, no heroics. You know the drill."

Jace swallowed a caustic reply and sat at the edge of the hard vinyl. Immediately his right knee pistoned, another body part protesting the inaction. He clamped a palm on his quad muscle and squeezed. Out the tinted windows, Randy's Dojo was deceptively empty and lit in welcome. The lone person by the door was the hostage negotiator, a bald guy who could've been a Bears linebacker. At the moment, he tapped the bullhorn against his thigh. No one within had responded to his requests to set up communication. Crowds of lookie-loos strained against the secured perimeter of waist-high metal gates. A sea of media spotlights blended with the cruiser blues. No doubt all five sets of parents were gathered somewhere nearby. A chopper circled overhead, blinding everyone with its beam and scattering litter in the downdraft.

Jace's phone rang. Caller ID: *Private.* "Quinn," he barked.

"You have my painting," a man calmly said. "And I have your brother. May I suggest a trade?"

Heat flash-banged through him. It had been over an hour of trying to communicate with whoever was behind this, determine what they wanted. Mission accomplished. It was their worst-nightmare scenario: Donatello, notorious for his lack of human compassion, had Sean. Jace stared blankly at the negotiator pacing in front of the dojo like a caged tiger. No one had answered; no one had even appeared. Where were Donatello and Sean?

"Proof of life," he said, thankful his voice didn't tremble. Garcia whipped around from his command post four feet away.

"Jace?" Sean's voice sounded strained. "Is Gretch all right?"

The last word was barely audible, the phone snatched away. Garcia was shaking his head and holding out his hand. *You know the drill.* Like hell Jace was going to hand over his own phone and have Garcia negotiate. He held up a finger, defying his boss. He could do this. "Let all the boys walk out safely right now, and we'll talk."

Donatello hung up. Horror punctured Jace's lungs. His body misread his racing heart and pumped out more sweat. He lowered the phone in the thick silence and met his SSA's eyes.

"There's a reason you're not in hostage negotiations, Jace," Garcia said quietly. "It's an art, and it takes unfathomable patience and fortitude under pressure. I get that, as a SEAL, you think that's an innate talent, but not in this case. Especially when it's your brother you're negotiating for. You *are* the special program to show Webb we can hire vets working on degrees. Don't blow it."

Jace nodded once. Garcia held out his hand a second time, and Jace handed over his phone. "It was Donatello."

Garcia nodded. A few seconds later, the phone rang. Garcia pressed the speakerphone icon and answered with his full credentials.

"Felix," Donatello drawled. "It's been a long time. How's Mary?"

"The twins keep her busy." Garcia's tone was light and friendly, although the strain showed in his tight jaw. "And Sylvia?"

Jace rubbed his mouth. Seriously? An SSA and mob boss were chitchatting over the laundry line? He couldn't register the words as Donatello answered. He didn't care about Sylvia and Mary. He had to get to Sean! And Gretch. Wherever she was, she was a sitting duck.

"So. How can we put an end to this and get back to our wives?" Garcia said calmly as he stared at the dojo.

"A painting was taken from me."

"Is this the same painting that was taken from the Isabella Gardner museum?"

Donatello laughed. "I didn't steal it, although I know who did. I bought it last year, and it cost me plenty. I'd like it returned."

Jace closed his eyes and listened to any noise over the line that would give away their location. An ambulance siren several blocks south of the SWAT van screamed down Cicero, but it didn't come through the phone line. He heard a faint sniff. Then another. He frowned.

Back when he was a teen—probably fourteen or fifteen—he'd had to babysit his four brothers. He'd been studying Morse code for Scouts, and to keep his rough-and-tumble brothers from burning the house down, he'd made a game of seeing which one could learn it the fastest and find the most creative way to use it.

The winner? Sean. Age four. He'd sniffed the entire alphabet. He was already reading and writing by then, a child prodigy, but shit, had the other three been pissed. And Sean's method was authentic enough that the next day in the kitchen, when he sniffed Jace a message —*cookie please*—their mom had promptly stuck a ther-mometer in Sean's mouth.

Jace grabbed a pen. A longer sniff, so real it sent chills down Jace's spine. Silence. So that was short–short–long. U.

"You know we can't give you the painting back, Sal." *Sniff sniiff.* "How do we get the boys home to their moth-ers?" *Sniiff sniff.*

P.

"We're at an impasse, then, my friend. I can have a boy's body brought out."

"That's not necessary. But how about we bring in a couple of pizzas for them while you and I keep talking?"

Jace focused every ounce of energy on sniffs that anyone else would take for allergies.

UPST. Upstairs? Jace grabbed binoculars and scanned the one-story dojo. Was there an attic space? A way out up there? Heart drumming a hollow beat, he showed the pad with the letters to his boss and gestured for Garcia to draw the conversation out. His SSA gazed at him in concern.

"I think the press needs a little feeding, Felix," Donatello said.

The SSA turned his attention back to the dojo. "I'm not sending pizzas to those vultures."

"More like the press should film someone. Set an example. I'll have the little boys count off, and you pick a number from one to five."

Garcia chuckled, although perspiration beaded his forehead and the pen in his hand trembled. Jace gestured again. *Keep him talking!* Garcia didn't blink his attention away from the red mats.

Jace studied his pad. UPSTLCNTL. *What the fuck?*

"Pick me," Sean piped up in the background. This time Sal chuckled.

"You wouldn't make the ten o'clock news, son. Murdered children make headlines."

"I'm a fourth-degree *black* belt. Only sixty-five people in the world have achieved that."

Jace jerked from studying the nonsensical words. Sixty-five? What kind of an asinine lie... *Sixty-five.*

He wrote the number on the pad and *black*, because Sean emphasized the color again. Sean *never* talked about being a black belt. It was his hidden superpower—

like he enjoyed people underestimating him. OCD nerd, no special talent here, folks.

"I don't care if you have every color belt under the rainbow," Donatello said.

Come on, Sean. What are you trying to tell me? Jace scratched his ear violently, parsing out the letters and numbers again. He was running out of time. A boy's death would be on his hands...

UPSTLCNTL65black. *Think like Sean.* The light bulb went off. His jaw sagged. Garcia squinted at the jumbled letters and shook his head. Jace scribbled:

Up the street. Lincoln Continental '65, black.

He dropped the pen and shouldered his way out of the van. One thing about Sean: his need to be precise drove people out of their minds. But this time it was a freaking asset. If Sean and Donatello were *up the street,* then they were a block north. Not two blocks or three, and not in any other direction. That was how Sean's disorder worked.

But it meant Donatello was close enough to see the whole circus. Jace would head south, immerse into the crowd of gawkers behind the police lines, then cross two intersections over and come at the '65 black Lincoln Continental from behind.

Catching them off guard required stealth. He was a SEAL. *This* he could do.

28

———

Gretch sipped the enormous iced tea she'd bought on the way over. She'd give her right arm for a glass of wine instead. For the second time she'd shared her most gut-wrenching childhood scars so Eve would realize how returning to her husband would affect her girls. Close to an hour had passed, comforting Eve, listening to her fears, trying to reason with her, and it had only left them at an impasse.

"I can't have him hurting my parents. Next he'll go after my friends." Eve paced, fists clenched, red blotches staining her cheeks. "He can do so much damage when he wants."

"Then we apply for a restraining order." *Or get Jace Quinn to pay him a visit.*

"He won't quit, don't you see? He can't live without us..." She slumped back in her chair, her face puffy from crying and sleeplessness, her voice hoarse. Gretch ached for her.

"I know he won't do it again," Eve said. "This time it'll be different. I have to go back, Gretch."

"That's not the solution. For any of you. *Please,* listen."

"I read some books in there." She jerked her head to where the study was. "One was on forgiveness. I can learn to forgive what he did to us."

Reading volumes of books had not, in any way, helped Gretch. In fact, she'd dented quite a few walls in her apartment throwing hardbacks that encouraged self-love and letting go. "He's not going to stop, Eve," she said quietly, with her trainer intensity.

The woman squeezed her hand. "My daughters won't suffer like you did. I'm sorry for all you went through, but in the end, you're the most put-together woman I know."

Gretch pressed her lips against the scream. How ironic that the outer shell she worked so hard to maintain was the reason behind her failure to help Eve. If only she could confess to this woman that put-together was acting the opposite of how she felt—a freak who found physical contact with men repulsive. The same future Eve's daughters faced. She opened her mouth to spill her final secret, but self-preservation kept the words buried deep inside. "I don't know what else to say," she whispered instead. Here was her chance to save two girls from the same fate. If only Eve would *listen*!

Tears welled, and Gretch kneaded her temples. *Jesus.* She never cried. Had never leaked a single tear throughout her stepfathers' abuses and protests of innocence. Had stared down her mother's expressions of distaste and disbelief, her accusations that it was merely Gretch's attention-seeking behavior.

Amy raced in, her pounding steps startling them. The girl paused just inside the room, staring at Gretch's weenie crying-fest.

"It's okay, sweetie," Eve said. "We're telling sad stories. What is it?"

"My friend Phillip got kidnapped! It's on TV." She pointed toward the living room, her eyes wide with fear.

Gretch hurried after Eve and Amy. The room teemed with residents and their kids, all glued to the breaking news segment.

"...naturally, we cannot show pictures or list the names of the five young boys," the newscaster said to the camera. "But earlier this evening Sandra Mayfair Face-Timed us with how she heard about the kidnapping." A video followed of a frantic woman with frizzy blond hair explaining the two-way communication with her son via his high-tech watch.

"How do you know this is Phillip's mom, honey?" Eve asked after a minute.

"I've seen her at school. Phillip says she talks to Principal Walker a lot about the bullies."

The video of the mother cut to a live shot of swirling blue police lights, and a swarm of uniformed officers outside a brightly lit storefront with large red letters. *Individual Lessons. Group Lessons. 555-6928. All Martial Arts Available: Karate, Judo, Hapkido.*

Gretch's legs numbed. Beyond the words cluttering the window, red mats lined the dojo floor. Nausea churned. "My God..."

This couldn't be real. Sean was supposed to be at her place in an hour. Dinner. Trading barbs. Kissing. At some point Gretch would dredge up the courage to invite his hands to roam her body, and she'd explore whether a sexy misfit could help her feel normal.

The camera panned the empty storefront again. "Why are they filming there?" she said, her voice shrill. "The place is empty."

As if hearing her, the newscaster said, "According to Sandra Mayfair, the instructor was forced into a car while the children were led into the gym bathroom. This is where they're being held against their will right now, and it's when her son activated his high-tech watch to alert his mother. For more on this special watch and its sophisticated technology, Paul Hightower joins us—"

"I'll call you tomorrow, Eve," Gretch blurted, and raced toward the foyer. Hank was streaming the scene on his iPad.

"Your phone's been ringing and ringing," he said, nodding to where she'd stashed her purse behind his desk. Lady Gaga's "Poker Face" jingled within merrily.

She swallowed convulsively and dug out the phone. Jace's name was emblazoned on her screen. "Jace?"

"Where are you?" His voice was low and curt.

"At a women's shelter. Sean—"

"We're on it, but you're not safe."

"Me?" Her heart stuttered to a stop. "Does this have to do with—" she glanced at Hank, "—the painting?"

"I'm not at liberty to discuss. Do not go home."

"I—I have a housemate. Are we in danger?"

Hank glanced up.

"We'll send someone for her."

Gretch turned her back, lowering her shaking voice. "He's a him. He's usually out on Thursday, but I'll call. What should I say? Where should he go? Where should *I* go? Seriously. Does this have to do with the—"

"Pull it together, Gretch."

She gulped a lungful of air. Vomit was imminent; it was only a matter of when. How could she be in danger? "Okay," she breathed out in a huff. It did nothing for the jittery shakes. "Officially pulled together. Now what?"

"Give me your address. I'll send an agent."

"I'm not waiting around." This had to be the mob, right? "I don't want to lead them here." Hank stopped pretending he wasn't eavesdropping and stood up.

"I'm in the middle of an op, Gretch," Jace barked. "What's the nearest El station?"

"Um..." Gretch walked in a tight circle. Her brain wasn't functioning right. "Windsor Park."

"There's a fire department a few blocks north," Jace said rapidly. "Station one twenty-six on South Kingston. Turn off your phone and head straight over. I'll text my brother. Stay with him until I can get to you."

Gretch frowned. "Wait." None of this made sense. "You're texting Sean?"

"My brother Patrick. He's the lieutenant there. *Go!*"

She hung up and looked blankly into Hank's concerned face.

"Everything all right, Gretch?"

"No." She walked to the window and peered out. The soft light from the street lamp displayed a typical quiet evening in a suburban neighborhood. "Keep a close eye out," she warned him. "And can you order me an Uber? I don't want anyone to find the location I'm headed."

Hank nodded and walked back to the desk. She slipped into the bathroom and immediately called home, fingers shaking spastically. Got her own voicemail message. She pressed end and called Dwayne's cell. His outgoing message played, and she listened, because it was new. He changed his greeting weekly, usually something witty and outrageous. This one rhymed. Had Sean and the boys not been facing a life-and-death situation, she would have howled. At the beep, she blurted, "The second you get this, turn on the TV. Sean and some little boys have been kidnapped. There's a huge chance it's the head of the Chicago mafia, Somebody Donatello. You need to split, Dwayne. They probably know where I live. I'll be at Fire Station one twenty-six in the South Shore. Call there, because I have to turn my cell off."

She texted a briefer version, then turned off the phone.

GRETCH WANDERED into the open garage where a lone fire truck gleamed under the fluorescent lights. No one was about, but the homey smell of pot roast permeated the air, and a side door stood propped open with a folded chair. Beyond, a Cubs announcer on TV declared a "foul ball" to the groan of the stadium crowd and several men nearby.

"Hello?" she called.

A chair scraped, and seconds later a young man with auburn hair and a goatee jogged out. After a blink of male awareness, his face settled into concern. "May I help you?"

"I'm looking for Patrick Quinn."

He motioned to the night beyond. "He's out on a call. It was a false alarm; they're about to head back."

Gretch stayed where she was, just inside the garage, and linked her fingers together. What now? Where was Sean? Had the boys been released? A scream of frustration lodged in her throat.

"I'm Chase Whitley." The young man thumbed the room he'd just come from. "Would you like to wait in here? We're about to serve dinner, and the game's on."

"Is it possible we can turn to a local channel and get an update on the kidnapping?"

He blinked. "The what?"

"It's on the other side of the city." She walked rapidly past him into a large kitchen with older appliances and a long Formica table set for eight. Two blond firefighters slouching on the rear legs of their chairs were riveted to the television. "Stee-rike," the younger one called simultaneously with the announcer, and pantomimed shooting the pitcher.

"Hey, guys," Chase interrupted. "This is..." The three men looked at her.

"Gretch." She twisted her fingers tighter. "Gretchen Allen."

"Who's here to see Trick."

The one who'd called the strike muttered, "Of course she is." Gretch frowned.

"Shut it, Danny." Chase motioned to an empty chair. "Ignore him; he's a probie whose mouth is going to get him into trouble one of these days. And that's Pete." He reached for the remote. "She said there's been a kidnapping."

The men thumped down their chairs. "What?" Pete sputtered.

"Five boys," Gretch explained. "At a karate gym on West Chicago Avenue. The instructor is Patrick's brother."

"Shit," Chase muttered. He rubbed his goatee with one hand as he flipped channels. "Water? Soda? Dinner?"

She sank gracelessly onto a wooden chair. She was famished, but anything that went down wouldn't stay. How her pre-anorexic status as a tween hadn't clued her mother in... "Some ginger ale?"

Pete stood. He had to be well over six five, and thin as a whip. In two strides he was across the kitchen, pulling a glass out of the cabinet.

Onscreen, a different local newscaster was summing up the same information Gretch had heard at the shelter. A very unattractive photo of Sean's puzzled face covered the upper right corner of the screen. Her breath seized. *Sean. Are you all right?* The reporter's tone was gravely concerned, but the excitement in his eyes triggered her panic anew. Just another victim. Just another half-hour of local news to fill. Who in the media was looking out for the boys instead of the ratings? Pete handed over the glass and reclaimed the chair he'd just vacated.

"Does Trick know?" Chase asked.

Trick? What a stupid nickname. "I don't know." The combination of anxiety, mental exhaustion, and low blood sugar overrode the innate need to keep her blond-bombshell mask in place. She couldn't bring herself to straighten her shoulders or keep her chin up. Couldn't look the firefighters in the eye. It had to be the mob, right? Were those darling little boys okay? Would they get out of this safely?

The rumble of an engine down the block grew steadily louder until it roared directly outside. Sharp beeps followed as it reversed into the garage. She almost gagged at the thick exhaust floating into the kitchen. Slipping a napkin from underneath a place setting, she held it over her mouth, breathing shallowly.

"Here's Trick now," one of the guys said above the din.

Would he look like Jace or Sean or a combination of the two? Christ, she was delirious, focusing on shit like this when the lives of Sean and five boys were in danger.

The engine died, and several boots hit the concrete along with men's voices—and one woman's.

"Where is she?" someone called, and Chase, maybe Pete, answered. Gretch laid the napkin on the table and rose. Already oxygen wasn't pumping to her brain, and a dull buzzing sounded in her ears. She knew this signal.

A striking man turned into the kitchen. No resemblance to Sean, more like Jace's great looks and heroic presence, frosted with a dark, Zen-like sensuality. Glossy black hair curled in haphazard layers, and the uniform both deepened his warm cobalt eyes and showcased well-defined muscle. Thick evening stubble gave him a rogue-pirate look.

Trick sized her up with genuine friendliness. Not a

flicker of the attracted-male awareness emanated, and she was an authority on spotting that. His grin deepened, carving hollows into lean cheeks.

"You must be my damsel in distress."

Danny snorted. More boot steps and more faces clustered in the doorway.

The ringing in Gretch's ears grew sharp and piercing. Through the haze of her tunnel vision and irregular thumping heart, she stretched out a trembling hand to stop Patrick from getting any closer. He misinterpreted the gesture and stepped right up, shaking it. "Lieutenant Patrick Quinn, at your service."

She projectile-vomited all down his torso.

"Dang," Danny chirped over her heaving. "That's a refreshing change from all the chicks who faint when they see you."

29

"Don't do this, Sal," came the stern voice over Donatello's phone speaker. "You're not this rash. You'll spend the rest of your days as a hunted man. Sylvia couldn't live like that. Let the boys go home."

Sean froze in place. Silence seemed to envelop the world. He'd stopped the Morse code a while ago; Jace either got it or he didn't. Scratching the zip tie on the seat would've been more distinct, but Donatello would also have picked up on the damage to his leather, rather than thinking Sean was a dweeb with allergies.

"We're at a stalemate, my friend." The sadness in Donatello's voice was genuine, which ripped into Sean's gut.

"Leave the boys alone and take me," he pleaded, straining against the tie again. His wrists had chafed to the point where they were slick with his blood.

Donatello ignored him. "This is on you, Felix. I'll keep the line open in case you want to change your mind." He placed the phone on the dashboard and held out his hand. After a slight hesitation, Mountain Man slapped another phone into his palm. A look passed between the two, then Mountain Man looked away, jaw wired tight and eyes troubled.

Sean slumped back, which pulled his aching shoulder blades. Maybe Jace hadn't picked up on the Morse code. Maybe he wasn't even in the van. It seemed inconceivable, given Jace's need to be the center of attention, the nucleus of action. It was what had made his SEAL career so difficult—no credit, no recognition, and definitely no fame for the real-life superhero work.

"Mac," Donatello said into the second phone. "Show them a boy."

Sean squinted at the dojo, focusing on the corner section of the bathroom's faux-wood door visible from here. Muttered swear words and a complaint about squeezed sardines were clear over the line. Seconds later, the door swung outward. Phillip Mayfair both stumbled and was thrust out. Only the hands of the mafioso were visible, the right fist gripping the back of Phillip's *gi*, the left planting a gun into the boy's temple. Based on the way the gun shook and jerked, it was the meth-head —Manny.

A frenzy of activity renewed on the streets, like a surging wave, held back at the last second by the police blockade.

"Give him the fucking painting," Sean screamed from the back seat, his voice cracking. No answer from the cell phone on the dashboard. Tension crackled all around him, over the phone lines, out in the blue, swirling lights that burned his retinas. Every molecule in Sean's body willed him to close his eyes and turn away, but he owed Phillip to have this atrocity seared into his mind for the rest of his days.

He stared at the Phillip's stoic expression, his overly large watch, his stance in the first kata, *Fujikata Dai Ichi*. The little guy was going down as a warrior. Sean held his breath, straining against the tie, wrists dripping blood now. He welcomed the slicing pain. Tears welled freely in his eyes.

"For the love of God," he croaked, "take me." Again he was ignored.

Donatello sighed. "Last chance, Felix. You and I both know I don't want to do this. His blood is on your hands."

A deep breath came from the speakerphone. Sean kept his eyes glued to Phillip's face. Peripherally on the right, a blur came from nowhere. The back door to the Continental opened, cool air rushing in. Jace body-slammed Sean aside, claimed the space, and pressed the Glock .22 into the thick gray hair in front of him. "Bitchin' ride," he said through his teeth. "Except that antique cars don't sport power locks, and you fat fucks were too arrogant to reach back and take the simple precaution of locking the damn door."

"Quinn?" The stern voice sounded tinny on the dashboard.

"Yes, sir," Jace called, slicing through Sean's zip ties like butter. He snapped the Swiss Army knife shut on his knee. "Go," he muttered, shoving Sean with his shoulder.

"Gretch…"

"With Trick. Find Margo, near SWAT. She'll take you both someplace safe."

Sean stumbled from the vehicle, sucking in the fresh night air. He flicked life back into his wrists and stamped his feet. He should head down to the SWAT van. Be there for the release of the boys, hug Phillip, speak to the parents, even find a freaking lawyer for all the lawsuits he'd face tomorrow.

Instead he sprinted in the opposite direction, away from the lights and the noise and the nightmare. Racing down city streets in full karate gear and sneakers, prepared to run the whole fucking way to Gretch.

This whole week, his brother had mocked him for his dire warnings. Margo had remained indecisive, wanting more concrete proof of every microscopic thing they investigated. Sean was done with the FBI. Donatello might be in custody, but he was head of a large family who'd be out for revenge. No way was Sean hanging around a SWAT van waiting for the Bureau to secure the scene. It was time to grow a pair and deal with a situation he'd single-handedly manufactured. He'd get Gretch, all right, but he'd take her somewhere no one would find them. Once they were safe, he'd figure out what to do next.

GRETCH JERKED upright at the sound of a footfall. Trick stood in the threshold of the room designated for women firefighters, basically the size of a prison cell. Should she tell him her suspicion that the mob was behind the kidnapping? Was it fair to scare him senseless with only a gut supposition? But why else would Jace have her hide here? And why not tell her outright?

"You up for some company?" Trick asked.

She nodded wearily and huddled on the cot. Even though she'd showered and dressed in firefighter Cheryl Limon's spare uniform, her stomach roiled ominously, and she couldn't stop her teeth from chattering. If her hands would stop shaking like she had palsy, she'd retrieve her gum from the purse at the foot of the cot. The taste in her mouth was awful.

Trick glanced over his shoulder, where Danny shadowed him like an overgrown puppy. "Blanket and bag."

The probie dashed off, and Trick carried in a metal chair, flipped it back to front, and straddled it with a grunt.

His hair was still damp from his shower, his face cleanly shaven. He smelled divine, resembled a movie star, and could host a *100% Testosterone* YouTube channel. Yet all she could think about was his younger brother holding her hand in the taxi.

"Any news about Sean?" she whispered through dry lips.

He shook his head and leaned his forearms on the back of the chair. "I texted Jace for news when you arrived," he said to the floor, then rubbed his eyelids with his thumb and forefinger. "Guess he's too busy to respond." He looked up with a tired grin. "Sean has a knack for taking care of himself, though. Always has."

Danny raced in and dropped an old-fashioned black doctor's bag at Trick's feet, then unfolded a thick blanket over Gretch's shoulders. "I also brought you a water." He pulled a bottle from the back pocket of his uniform, almost dropping it in his haste to hand it to her.

Gretch murmured her thanks and placed the ice-cold bottle by her purse. No way could she stomach that. Trick nodded a gentle dismissal, and when they were alone again, he righted the chair and reached for the bag. "Mind if I check your vitals?"

"No need. I'll live."

Trick cocked his head. His kind eyes called her bluff. "Somehow I doubt you're usually this pale. And your breathing is pretty shallow."

She flushed. No way would she admit it was because her boobs were smashed into this tight top. She didn't dare take a deep breath. "Honestly, I'm fine. I'm sorry again about the..." She regarded his clean uniform, and he waved it off.

"People react to stress in different ways."

And yet your brother's been kidnapped, and you look like you just finished yogi meditation.

"Sean will be okay," he said again, as if he'd read her thoughts.

She ruminated on his calm reassurance. Here was a man who knew Sean way better than she did. Maybe Trick was right. So much had happened in these few short hours, like Sean walking away from a mafia gunfight without breaking a sweat. But what *if*? And Dwayne?

"I'm also worried about my housemate," she admitted. "I never had a chance to warn him we pissed off the mob and they might be able to identify us."

"Where do you live?" Trick plucked the station's neon-yellow, industrial-sized cell phone from his breast pocket. "I'll have the squad closest to your neighborhood check it out." His voice was deeper than both his brothers', and so peaceful he'd make a great living recording bedtime stories.

Gretch rattled off her address, and a few minutes later a text dinged, confirming a squad was on its way.

"Now." He rummaged in his doctor's bag. "When's the last time you ate?" He pulled out a blood pressure cuff.

"Um..." She almost said lunch, because that was when they'd run into Donatello—and started this massive shitstorm—but she hadn't eaten. And this morning she'd woken at four twenty-two and basically fled the hotel. "I may have forgotten to eat today." *Stupid.* She preached six small meals to anyone who'd listen.

Trick didn't comment as he Velcro-ed the cuff around her arm and reached for his stethoscope. When he placed the button inside her elbow, his grip was firm and capable. He pumped the rubber ball, then concentrated on whatever he was hearing. She couldn't reconcile this man. His youngest brother was someone's hostage. His older brother was trying to negotiate for six lives. Trick's unflappable manner was either a testament to his firefighter nature, or he could compartmentalize like someone with a split personality.

"Your BP is phenomenal," he said, unplugging his ears and ripping off the Velcro.

"I used to be a personal trainer."

He nodded his approval. Vanity aside, it was remarkable to have been in his presence this long and not have any indication he was attracted to her. Of course, his first impression was her vomiting up a twenty-four-ounce iced tea, but still.

After he took her temperature, felt her pulse, and shone a penlight in her eyes, he pronounced her well. "I'll send in some chicken noodle soup. Try to eat all of it."

She held up a hand, which still quivered like a junkie's. "And maybe a wide straw—I'd hate to ruin Cheryl's uniform too."

His slow grin showcased flawless white teeth. "I'll ask her to bring the soup. If you're still in bad shape, she can always feed you."

See? The perfect opening to offer to feed her himself or make some innuendo about warming her up enough to stop the shaking. "Are you gay?" She cringed the second the words were out of her mouth. This was what low blood sugar did to you! "I'm sorry," she muttered, red-faced.

He chuckled. "No need to apologize. And no. Married my soul mate right outta high school." An expression flashed across his face that her weary mind couldn't catch. He wasn't the poker-face champ his brothers were, though. "Try to rest until the soup arrives."

Danny raced in. "Kids just got released. Media is saying the kidnapping was mob related."

"And Sean?" Gretch blurted.

Danny shook his head. "No sign of him."

"Did you say the mob?" The confusion on Trick's face would've been priceless if her skin hadn't begun crawling like scuttling caterpillars. She knew it!

"It's the painting Sean uncovered," she said faintly. "They found him at the dojo." This *was* the worst-case scenario. Where was he now?

Trick dismissed Danny and settled in his chair. "I think I better hear all of it."

Heart in her throat, Gretch explained the lunchtime violence and the stolen painting Sean had shown them just before she'd left for the shelter, walking out as if her world would be untouched. So stupid. "They must have traced my credit card to me, found out where I worked, and followed Sean when he left." How else would they know he taught at the dojo? And he'd left *after* her. She may have passed right by them in her haste to get to the shelter.

Trick looked grave and said nothing. Both reactions were blaring alarms, given his Zen approach to life. Gretch twisted her fingers. "You said he'd be okay." Her tone came out petulant. Like Trick had promised something and wasn't delivering.

"So I did." He leaned forward and stuffed his instruments back in the bag. "And so he will." His confidence was awesome. She almost believed him.

"What do you think is happening?" she whispered.

He readjusted her blanket. "If there were any updates, Jace would call. It'll turn out fine."

How could he be so calm and certain of everything? "The painting was just good, you know?" she said, and to her horror, tears pricked her eyes. "Not great. Not 'two hundred million, kidnap Sean and five boys' great."

Trick reached over and squeezed her hand. For a second she couldn't bear to let go. Not because he was a man or Sean's brother or she wanted to indulge in her sexual-control game playing. Simply because Trick was human, and compassionate on a level she'd never experienced. A lifetime of depending only on herself suddenly weighed too much. She clung to the rough palm searching for a subject. "How did you get your dumb nickname?" she whispered, the only inane thought that came to her head.

He broke into that tranquil grin. He must think she was a lunatic by now, zigzagging through topics like this. "It's a secret," he said. "But there's a big, juicy, *unbelievably* convoluted story behind it."

She smiled back. Smart man. Trying to refocus her anxiety to what could possibly be juicy and convoluted about the name Trick instead of Pat or Rick. Too bad all she could think about was his brother, still somewhere out there with the mob.

"What was Sean like as a boy?"

"Odd."

She rolled her eyes. "Tell me something I don't know." When he didn't volunteer anything, she asked, "Why do you and Jace look like you came out of the same pod and Sean looks like a different species?"

He sat back in the chair, shaking his head. "Recessive gene, I guess. He's definitely ours. When he was a little kid, Gage goofed on him and convinced him he was adopted. That he'd been found at a highway rest stop and brought to one of the fire stations where my dad was district chief."

"Did Sean believe it?"

Trick nodded. "Evidently for years."

"You're kidding! What a horrible joke."

He kept nodding, his lips pressed into a straight line. "First of all, he was an impressionable kid. Secondly, he's always been cerebral, and the story made perfect sense to him. There's a seven-year gap between the four of us and him. It explains how Sean's interests and skills land on the other side of the spectrum than all of ours, and—" he shrugged powerful shoulders. "—our dad couldn't really bond with him. Didn't know what to do with this little guy who wasn't tough as nails. He still doesn't."

Gretch hugged her knees under the blanket, picturing the little boy who couldn't fit into his own boisterous family. They had something in common after all. A torturous family life and a coping strategy to shut out the world.

Trick stretched out his legs, looking remorseful. Women must be all over this guy when he flashed that vulnerability. "I'll always feel bad for going along with the joke," he murmured. "It never occurred to me Gage hadn't recanted it. Or that Sean would believe it for years."

"How did you all find out?"

"When he was fourteen, he wrote a report on how it felt not to know who your real mother was." Trick's laugh was partly a snort of disbelief. "Holy shit, did Mom thrash us. Verbally," he added quickly. "We were all grown and out of the house by then. Jace was stationed in Kabul. I was a probie about to take my exams, and the other two were at boot camp in Fort Jackson.

"She called each one of us. You should know she's second-generation Irish. After a blistering lecture, she put Sean on the line." Trick's eyebrows knit, and his eyes focused on something far away. "Try apologizing to a socially awkward teen for a joke you barely remember participating in." He rubbed his palms over his face and sighed. "Sean's always been way too serious. Book smart but *so* bad at relating to people."

A moment of silence passed, him deep in some recall and Gretch visualizing the teen Sean would have been.

She hurt for him. Was he safe, or had he traded himself for the release of the five boys?

Trick snapped out of his reverie and slapped his knees. "You need rest."

He crossed the tiny bedroom in two strides, halting in the doorway when the phone dinged. For a moment all she saw was a powerful guy backlit in an alpha stance: legs hip distance apart, broad shoulders bowed over the phone in his hand. Then he slipped the phone in his breast pocket and turned in what seemed like slow motion. The sympathy on his face gripped her around the throat.

"I'm sorry, Gretch. Your housemate didn't make it."

Her lungs seized. She opened her mouth, but no words came out, no air went in.

"Gretch?"

Dots swam before her eyes and panic built. Just as he took a step toward her, her chest loosened. She heaved oxygen noisily.

"Put your head between your knees." The authoritative command overrode the soothing yoga master voice. She shook her head and held onto her knees for dear life. She was fine. She was in control. Slowly her body stabilized.

"What do you mean he didn't make it?" she whispered, even though she knew what he meant. But how? When? Had Dwayne suffered? The poor guy had never been good at suffering in any form. Teasing, bullying, a sunburn...even his tummy aches as a little kid were considered an epic crisis requiring bedside vigils by Gretch or his mom.

Trick shoved a hand through his hair. "The squad called Chicago's Crime Scene Unit. No doubt the FBI will get involved." His face was pale, which screamed so much more than his quiet voice. "It...looks like the act of a lone wolf."

Honestly, she'd never skip a whole day of meals again. Clearly she was hallucinating. "It's the mob," she corrected.

He shook his head. "Doesn't fit their MO. I'd—rather not give out any more details."

"I've watched all three *Godfather* movies. I get it. Dwayne died horribly. Just spit it out."

The lieutenant looked away, his firm chin at a stubborn angle. They could sit here all night as far, as she was concerned. Dwayne was her best friend. His death was on her hands. "Tell me."

Trick sighed, his gaze returning to hers almost apologetically. "He was beheaded."

30

———

A noise burrowed into Gretch's brain, disturbing her dreams and wrenching her from safety. Whispering. Two men. Consciousness dragged her reluctantly to a surface heavy with exhaustion and emotions too deep to bear.

"I'm sure the FBI is at her apartment by now." Trick.

Dwayne!

"How is she?"

She knew that voice. Gretch bolted into a sitting position, squeaking the cot. She was still at Station One Twenty-six. The only light in the room came from the fluorescents out in the main garage. "Sean?" Her voice was rusty from shrieks of grief, thighs bruised from her fist pounding.

A shuffle, a slap on the back. Suddenly the light in the doorway was haloed around a tall, slim man, still in his karate uniform. A build she'd recognize anywhere. "You're all right!" A lightness like helium filled her chest.

Sean strode to her bedside and leaned into her outstretched arms. He smelled like lemons and sweat. His *gi* was damp, but beneath her grasping hands, his body was warm and strong and very much alive. "Thank God," she said, sobbing.

"I'm so sorry," he murmured into her hair, hugging her hard. "About Dwayne. About everything."

"How are the boys?"

"I don't know. Couldn't stay. I'm sure they're safe," he assured her. "Jace saved the day."

She clung to Sean, a sense of security budding. He'd made it through, exactly as his brother had predicted. Sean. This capable, sensible warrior hiding inside a snarky introvert. How had she been so blind to the real him?

He broke the embrace and brushed the hair from her face. The taped gauze on his wrists scraped against her cheek.

"What happened?" Gretch asked, fingering a bandage.

"Zip tie was a little tight."

See? The king of understatements. With bandages that thick, the tie had probably been a tourniquet. "Thank God you all made it through," she blurted. "I've been worried sick." She flushed and fluttered a hand at the clear dent in the pillow. "I mean, I was. I'm embarrassed I even had the audacity to sleep—"

"Trick said you passed out more than fell asleep. And I don't mean to alarm you further, but we've gotta go." He clasped her biceps and gave them a reassuring squeeze. "He's gathering some supplies for us. I'm taking you somewhere safe."

"Where?"

"I haven't gotten that far in my plan yet. Everywhere I come up with, I know they'll find us."

"Who?"

"Donatello's men."

"Why us? I'm assuming Jace took the painting."

Sean spread his hands. "I don't know, Gretch. Revenge? I'm not willing to sit around debating this. I saw how ruthless these men are—the lengths they'll go through to get what they want." He wiped the sweat still trickling from his temple. "If they want us dead for going to the FBI, then we need to split. And I mean like five minutes ago."

Gretch clawed the blanket off her. "What time is it?"

"Almost ten thirty. Nice shirt."

She'd forgotten the constraining firefighter top. "I don't suppose your brother has an extra t-shirt hanging around. I can't leave the station like this."

He kissed her forehead. "There's my queen. Making sure she's dressed for the occasion."

The observation stung. Dwayne had been killed in the most barbaric manner imaginable. Little boys had been held hostage, which would keep them in therapy for years. Sean was taking her *somewhere* to escape mob *retaliation.* "Forget it, this is fine," she said quickly, in lieu of the shamed apology.

"I meant that as a compliment. Believe me, I need a wee bit of normal right now." As he left his footsteps were as silent as if he walked on air.

"Normal," she whispered to the empty room. *That* had always been her birthday-candle wish. How funny Sean thought she already was.

31

I*s this a practical joke?* Jace stared at Trick in the twin glows of the streetlight and the fluorescent lights within Station One Twenty-six. The evening was chilly. The thumping bass of rap music a few blocks west echoed in his pulse. Screeching tires and raucous laughter just to the south made it difficult to think straight after the adrenalin dump from Donatello's capture.

"Sorry, man," Trick said. "Sean said those were your orders."

"Why would I order you to pack supplies and have them run off into the night?"

His brother spread his palms. "When has Sean ever lied? I knew you were cleaning up the dojo scene, and Sean said your partner was meeting them outside the Windsor Park El station."

No. Margo had been hanging by the SWAT vehicle waiting for Sean. Until she finally figured out something was wrong. "When did they leave?"

Trick glanced at his watch. "Fifteen minutes ago."

"Shit!" Jace walked in a circle, hands clasped above

his head. He'd just gotten through handing Donatello over to SSA Garcia, and humbly accepting SAC Webb's effusive compliments, only to have to go back to headquarters with *this* news!

Trick scrolled through his phone. "I'll call in backup and help you find them."

"*Where*? What were they even wearing?"

"My clothes. They basically stripped me of everything I had in my locker. Sean has on black jeans and a White Sox tee. Gretch is in a blue tee with the station logo, and earlier she'd borrowed tan cargo shorts and kicks from a woman on my crew. Both have Station One Twenty-six sweatshirts and windbreakers. I packed two knapsacks with blankets, aluminum wraps, ponchos, flashlights, water, and protein bars. And hand sanitizer. Sean wouldn't leave without a full bottle."

"You didn't happen to give him your cell phone, and I could call this a night?" Jace said wearily.

Trick spread his hands again, his face a mixture of worry and frustration. "He never lies, Jace."

"The good thing is one bottle of sanitizer isn't near enough for him to camp outside. Did you give them any money?"

A muscle flexed along Trick's jaw. "Gang emptied their wallets and took up a collection. Sean said the FBI would reimburse. Over two-fifty."

Jace scratched the bristles on his jaw. He could fix this. He *would*. God forbid Mom found out her baby boy was back in danger.

Trick shifted his weight. "You should also know Gretch's housemate was executed."

Prickles crawled up Jace's neck. Even as he asked for the name, his phone buzzed Margo's text with the news and answer. Dwayne Collins. The banker had flirted with someone on the phone the other day, mentioned a female housemate, and texts not returned. Of *course* he was Gretch's housemate. Had Dwayne let something slip last night that forced Brandon to kill him?

Jace shook the supposition from his head. He was clearly losing it. Beheading meant ISIS or a Middle Eastern connection. The FBI was dealing with a two-headed snake tonight: the mob kidnapping boys for a stolen painting, and Adyton or an unrelated terrorist cell doling out a brutal form of revenge. Why? Had Collins' years of paper trails found massive money laundering that required silencing? If Adyton was behind this, how would he even know who Dwayne was or where he lived? Or that there were files proving money laundering that Jace had reported on this afternoon?

Tumblers clicked into place. A mole in the task force. Jace's heart beat off rhythm. And if *that* were so, then taking Sean and Gretch to a safe house would have signed their death warrants.

"Okay." Jace forced his brain to calm down and lock onto the problem at hand. They were potential vics, not his brother and his brother's hot coworker. There was no way they'd be successful at staying off the grid on their own. He had to find them first and protect them from multiple factions, including the FBI. *Concentrate!*

"Sean doesn't have his wallet, license, or phone." Jace ticked them off his fingers. "They were in the book bag in the dojo. Presumably Gretch does have those items, but I told her to keep her phone off, so there's no way to trace GPS. Neither has a car." He paced the wide driveway.

A firefighter walked out with two steaming mugs of strong-smelling coffee, exactly how Jace liked it. He nodded his acknowledgement as he took one, still brainstorming possibilities. "They can't take the El anywhere because they'll want to stay away from as many security cameras as possible unless it's an emergency. Emergencies include emptying as much of her bank account as an ATM allows and buying a burner phone."

"And he's a fanatic about bottled water," Trick pointed out. "I packed enough for an hour, the way he drinks it."

Jace nodded. "So that's potentially a hundred convenience stores in the surrounding blocks." His spirits flagged. "Where would they go? We need to think like Sean."

His brother snorted. "That's the problem."

"Not necessarily. We know his quirks, so we have the advantage over whoever is after them."

A shriek in the distance and glass smashing on cement sent chills racing up Jace's spine. This wide-open, teeming city at night was no place for his little brother. Sean belonged in his quiet little art world with his paintbrushes... Or in his sterile-looking apartment and mind-numbing social life.

Trick's phone dinged. He breathed a sigh. "My guy can replace me. I'm good to go as soon as he gets here."

Jace waved him off. "Don't bother. Two brothers driving around the streets of Chicago? This is going to take manpower and technology. I'll call a task force together."

"You just said you need people who know Sean."

Jace gulped the coffee. Too hot, but even the burn gave him a much-needed kick. Endorphins jolted, and he breathed the rush in. "Call or text if you get any ideas where he might be." Trick rubbed a palm over his mouth, an old childhood signal that he was straining to hold back a verbal assault. Jace handed him the empty mug. "Just say it."

"If one thought in my head helps find them, can't you put aside your need to be the sole hero just this once and let me tag along?"

The sarcasm pushed the right fraternal buttons. A

stubborn band constricted Jace's chest. "Maybe if you had an ounce of distrust you'd have asked yourself why I would order you to pack camping gear. I'm the FBI. We have comfortable lodging at our disposal."

A sneer hovered at the edges of Trick's mouth. "You're sure wasting a lot of time assigning blame and deflecting accountability."

"Thanks for nothing, Trick. Glad I asked you to come to the rescue so you could fuck things up a million times worse." Jace spun on his heel and stalked toward the Suburban.

Everything came so easy for the asshole. Trick led a charmed life: had found his soul mate in high school; won a lottery four years ago and didn't even *need* to work; had known he wanted to be a firefighter like Pop by the time he was old enough to hold a hose... which, naturally, had vaulted him first in line for Pop's affection. Jace yanked open the car door so hard it bounced back and slammed his shoulder.

"I'll comb the streets anyway," Trick called. "If I find anything, I'll send out the bat signal."

Ha ha. "Go home to your wife and kids, Trick." *Go home to your fucking happily ever after.*

32

Sean had no close friends, an insignificance he'd worn like a badge of honor till tonight. Even more revealing, though, the Queen of Fucking Everything only had two friends. And one had been beheaded.

Understandably, Gretch wasn't remotely interested in risking the safety of Hannah, or an acquaintance named Zamira. It had taken them an hour to come up with this option, and who knew if it'd work?

Sean hunkered on the doorstep of the women's shelter, which had been Gretch's brainstorm and was brilliant, because it covered all the bases. It was located on a dark residential street, nowhere near security cameras; no one would think to look for a man shacked up in a shelter for abused women; and it provided safe lodging for the night while they tried to figure out what to do next.

She'd gone in to convince the night manager to bend the rules. Sean shivered in the borrowed windbreaker, too exhausted to even pace or windmill his arms for warmth.

The door clicked open, and he gazed over his shoulder. Gretch beckoned him and put a finger to her lips. "We can sleep on air mattresses in the director's office, but we totally have to be out before she gets here in the morning."

He nodded and stepped into the foyer. The warm earth tones and plush upholstered furniture would've given off a homey feel but for the formidable security guard parked behind a massive desk that blocked the rest of the house. On either side of the desk were two closed doors, no doubt locked.

The guard gave Sean a hard once-over before turning back to Gretch. She unlocked the door on the left and handed him the key. "Thanks, Hank. I owe you big."

Hank grunted "goodnight," and Sean followed Gretch into a spacious office overlooking part of the side lawn. She flicked on the light and went straight to the wall-length closet, randomly opening doors. The deep shelves resembled a convenience store stocked with hotel-sized amenities, dry goods, bottled water, toys, burner phones, and stacks of DVDs and tablet devices. Garments for women and children were piled neatly by size. Gretch tugged out a deflated mattress and an electric air pump from the bottom shelf.

Sean dropped the two knapsacks Trick had given them by the door. "I'll do it." As he knelt and attached the nozzle, Gretch rummaged through the food shelves.

"I wish they stored little liquor bottles," she said, fatigue and grief threading her voice.

He scrutinized the mattress unfurling an inch at a time. "Do you want to talk about him?"

"No. I don't think so." A pause. A small sigh. "He was such a fussbudget," she blurted, spinning around. "I'm no slob, but he couldn't stand it if *one* thing was out of place. A dirty dish in the sink, a glass not on a coaster, a dent in the middle of the toothpaste tube. Used to drive me nuts, you know?"

Sean nodded, because he did know. Quite well.

"I'll miss him so much..." Her voice was barely audible over the hiss of air. "The way we'd hang out. How he didn't care what the world thought of him. How I never had to *be* someone around him." The last few words wobbled, and she inhaled sharply. "I just don't understand—*why*. It was Dwayne. He never harmed a flea."

The same thoughts had haunted Sean. He reached for the only answer that seemed plausible. "Dwayne told me he was a whistleblower for his bank. Maybe that was the motivation for..."

"He did piss people off. And I mean rich people with powerful connections." Gretch hopped over the mattress and transferred the lunchbox-sized snacks to the desk. "He went after them like a pit bull. Prosecutors loved his fastidious recordkeeping. And you should've seen him celebrate a white-collar conviction." That was her first smile since the taxi ride after lunch.

"Sounds like he harmed more than fleas, then," Sean remarked. "I highly doubt it was a random lone-wolf attack on an innocent. He was the target."

Her smile disintegrated. She returned to the closets and grabbed an extra-large t-shirt and a package of cotton underwear. Sean tightened his grip on the air pump seal and focused on the expanding mattress.

"What if he wasn't the target?" she mumbled without turning around.

"What do you mean?"

"A beheading could mean a Middle Eastern tie. Maybe to an organization like Adyton's. What if this was about our company getting tangled up with him?"

Sean half snorted a chuckle. "Then I'm pretty

comfortable calling you delirious. We're in danger from Donatello's men, not Adyton."

She slumped against one of the doors, head bowed. "Gretch?"

"I may have given Adyton a motive to visit my apartment," she said. Her shoulders lifted and settled as she breathed a sigh. She turned back. Her eyes glimmered with tears. "I placed a bid on the Quran and requested the certificate of authenticity on Tuesday. I used a dummy contact name. They sent back a COA that was clearly bogus, but I doubt anyone who isn't in our industry would've known that. Maybe Adyton found out it went to me."

"Did you tell Margo?"

"I forwarded the email with my suspicions after we got home from lunch today."

"Still seems a stretch to kill your housemate." There was a tad too much condescension in his tone, and he winced.

"There's a connection somewhere, Sean," she snapped. "I may not be as smart as you, but I live and die by gut instinct." She stopped short on a harsh exhale. "Poor choice of words," she muttered, and her shoulders hitched.

Her supposition wasn't worth arguing about. They were both strung out and filled with recriminations. For Sean it went all the way back to accepting his brother's request for help last Saturday. He wasn't cut out to be a hero, and his pathetic lifelong quest had led them down a sewage hole to this moment: Him blowing up a mattress and Gretch selecting food better suited for a vending machine.

"The FBI will uncover who did this," he said at last. "You have to know my brother. He doesn't give up until everything's fixed and the good guys win."

She shrugged and swiveled around. "I guess so." Her tone said otherwise, but she was already fluttering her arm like Vanna White. "Do you want anything from here?"

He eyed the unopened array of burner phones. "I better check in with Jace."

She snatched one from an upper self, her sleek muscles flexing against the lines of the t-shirt as she reached. God, she was stunning. His cock agreed, and he swiftly lowered his gaze.

The mattress was almost inflated, and he dragged his attention to the next fiasco: it looked to be a full-size. For sure not a queen. He glanced around the rest of the office, because there was no way the two of them would fit on this without spooning. The director's chair looked deep and comfortable, but it clearly didn't recline. The twin chairs on the other side of the desk were too sturdy to be an option. In fact, he'd have to move them over by the closet so if Gretch flung an arm out in sleep she wouldn't smack into them.

He'd just have to stretch out behind the executive desk and sleep on the floor, that's all there was to it. Immediately the tension in his shoulders eased a fraction.

After disconnecting the air pump and fastening the plug, he straightened the mattress at exact angles to the room, selected clean, folded sheets that nevertheless smelled a little stale, and made up the bed with a single pillow.

"What's going on?"

Sean looked up from tucking a blanket corner with military precision. Gretch was seated in one of the twin chairs, with packages of food and water bottles open on the desk like a little picnic. Her brows were knit in displeasure as she sipped a lemon-lime power drink.

"I don't understand the question," he said bluntly.

"You don't sleep with a pillow?" She gestured at the lone one centered precisely in the middle.

"I'll sleep over there."

Silence descended. He was through making the bed but couldn't seem to stand and join her. The topic wasn't over for her, he could feel it in his bones, but he was done. With everything. He'd sell his soul for a few hours of sleep.

"Come eat," she said.

"After I touch base with my brother."

"Come on. You look like you're about to drop. Call him in five minutes."

He stood stiffly and claimed the other chair. His stomach grumbled fiercely, and he counted the hours since the Chinese lunch. Over nine. He shoveled in a handful of potato chips, so many he could barely close his lips. Aware of her scrutiny, he concentrated on chewing like a normal person. Ended up biting his cheek. *Fuck it.*

"Ever seen one of these?" She pointed to the virtual-assistant cylinder by her elbow. He shook his head and shoved more chips in. She leaned toward the device and spoke its name. Neon lights raced around the top. "Play 'Irreplaceable' by Beyoncé."

A female voice repeated Gretch's wish, and just like that, music filled the room. The lyrics were brash, confident, and oh so Gretch. She bobbed her head to the upbeat tempo and nibbled a pretzel, chewing in a pleasant, symmetrical way. A wavering smile stayed on her lips long after the song ended, and her eyes grew misty.

"That was Dwayne's favorite song," she said finally, flicking Sean a glance. "If he were here, he'd make us listen to it another twenty times."

Her face crumpled. Without a second thought, Sean

leaned in and embraced her, stroking her back and cupping her head as he murmured through her heart-wrenching sobs. Ever since Trick had broken the news, Sean's imagination kept playing out the horrific stages of the execution. Dwayne taking forever to open that outer door, seeing a stranger and halfheartedly accusing him of being religious fanatic with pamphlets. What had gone through his mind when the sword flashed through the air? How could an entire neighborhood not have one witness? Who could have done this and why?

A disquiet settled over him. Was there any merit to Gretch tying Adyton and his cohorts into it? That seemed a huge stretch by any imagination.

Sean held Gretch long after she stilled. Eventually she eased from his arms, wiped her eyes, and sighed the remnants of her grief. He crunched on another handful of chips as if it was natural for her to fall apart and require his embrace. Thank God she had no clue how much her need for his comfort and the feel of her body were balms to his soul.

"Doesn't it seem like last night was a million years ago?" she asked quietly.

The events flashed back—being pinned to the hotel door, clutching her scalp, thrusting into her mouth. Yes. A lifetime ago.

He remembered every second of that nirvana. And the colossal aftermath. He struggled to keep expressions off his face. Managed a shrug as he reached for the last of the chips. "Guess so."

A moment went by. It was clear she was building up to something by the way her fingers knotted in her lap. She took a deep breath. "Sleep on the mattress with me, Sean."

There was suddenly no saliva in his mouth to mingle with the chips. All his bodily fluids dumped into his hardening cock. The erotic way she'd said that created an urgent response in every part of his body for a repeat of... well, most of her skills. He wanted her so goddamn badly.

He sipped water, but his fist clenched the bottle too hard. Water flowed down his chin and onto his shirt. *For fuck's sake!* He thunked the bottle down. "I can't. I don't have it in me to comfort you when you freak out."

"I won't freak out. I need your arms around me tonight. I need to feel safe."

He twisted the bottle so the label faced him. "There's nothing safe about us being smashed together on that tiny thing." Just saying it opened the floodgates, and filthy scenarios cascaded into his mind.

"We're adults, Sean."

"Exactly." He poured all the pent-up desire into his gaze. Her eyes widened, and her lips formed a beautifully shaped O.

"Let me draw you a picture," he said succinctly. "My erection will press into you all night. It'll be thick and urgent and won't allow me to fall sleep. Every time I move or breathe, no matter how much I try not to, I'll brush against your...um...lady lumps."

Her brows rose. A smile slowly spread across her face. She snorted softly. "Hell, you can't even say what they are."

He grinned, half sheepishly, half warning her not to go there.

"Come on." She crossed her long, shapely legs that looked dynamite in those casual cargo shorts. "Say it. Any of the synonyms." Her mood lightened, the silliness due to intense grief and utter exhaustion, but he went with it.

"Girly bits," he said solemnly, and she burst into giggles.

"Raunchier," she commanded.

His groin ached. "They're attached to your body, Gretch. You should know what they're called."

Her smile died like it had been dipped in sulfuric acid. What had he said? He searched her face for a clue, and she stared back with an intensity that was unsettling. He eyed her half full bag of pretzels. Should he keep eating as if there hadn't been a lighter mood to ruin? Why couldn't he learn the pragmatic parts of joking around with another person?

Gretch leaned forward and covered his hand with trembling fingers. He fought the instinct to freeze. Slowly she transferred his palm to her right breast and pressed his fingers into plump warmth. Any remnant of exhaustion left his body as his senses pulsated to life. He gulped in air.

"Say it," she whispered.

Heat suffused his face, like he was prepubescent. "Breasts." When her gaze held his unwaveringly, he swallowed convulsively. "Boobs, tits, tatas, jugs."

"Squeeze it."

That didn't sound like such a hot idea. Any second now she'd fling his hand away. Her posture was ballerina-straight. Her breath came rapid and shallow, which heaved the breast in his palm.

He swept aside the chip bag with his free hand and cradled his head, watching her languidly, like this was no big deal. When she didn't flip out, he tightened his fingers imperceptibly, amazed as ever at the dichotomy of firm, yielding flesh. Women's bodies were freaking miracles of beauty and function. The exquisite nudes in paintings he'd cleaned over the years had given him a healthy sense of worship, and now, feeling *this* particular breast sent goosebumps skittering over him.

Gretch yanked up the hem of her t-shirt, revealing mega-toned abs and a half-inch of a black tattoo low on her right pelvic bone that disappeared into her shorts. His gaze snapped up as she briskly transferred his palm beneath the shirt. His heartbeat stalled. Just like that, he clasped prickly lace. The outline of a taut nipple prodded his palm. Her fingers urged his again, and he whispered her name, caressing her more confidently.

A look of wonder widened her eyes. Like this was the first time she'd experienced a man feeling her up. Clearly he was losing his mind.

He circled the areola through the lace, watching her with such intensity he caught every flicker of her eyelashes. Gretch stared right back, clamping her bottom lip between her even white teeth. He thumbed her nipple once, twice. She inhaled a shuddering breath. "That feels...wonderful," she whispered.

Slowly, trying not to startle her, he caressed his way to her left breast and repeated the tender ministrations. Her eyelids drooped, and a small smile appeared. "Kiss me."

Sean straightened from his self-imposed slouch. Tracing her jaw line, he tilted her chin and settled into a slow, deliberate kiss. He waited for her to slide her tongue in first, then gently imitated her lick-and-curl technique, concentrating on his exploration. She tasted of lemon-lime and something darkly sweet, like currants or raisins. Her fingers tangled in his hair, and as the kiss deepened, she raked his skull.

Their breathing quickened, but he was in no hurry to move this along. No doubt he'd broken through a massive barrier just now, but there had to be other triggers for her. Something he would do in the course of loving her that would turn this dreamlike moment into something horrific and dirty for her. Although his cock strained, greedy and insistent, he was content with the simple purity of kissing her supple lips and caressing her pliant body.

He traced the elegant curve of her waist, reveling in the juxtaposition of her silky skin and formidably toned muscle, before sliding up to fondle her breasts again. She moaned softly, leaning into his palms this time. Over and over he thrust his tongue or traced her mouth, learning what tricks would quicken her breath. He followed the seam of her bra to the clasp in back and fingered it, so she'd know his interest in proceeding, then stroked down her long, taut lats until he got a clear signal.

She pushed his shoulders and slid from her chair to straddle him. Her pelvis was a hair's-breadth from his throbbing hard-on. It was sobering enough that he broke the kiss and leaned his head against the wooden chair. He stroked the tops of her thighs with his fingertips, drugged by the vision of perfection. This was Gretch on top of him!

"I love the way you kiss," she said, trailing her hands across his shoulders and down his chest. "I like how you make me feel." Her chocolate irises had darkened to coal, her lips were swollen and poppy-colored.

"How do I make you feel?" he croaked. What was he finally doing right?

She lifted a shoulder. Her t-shirt was askew, and as erotic as the sight of a partially bare shoulder and bra strap was, he straightened her clothing.

"Cherished, I guess," she said in a low voice. "The others just want to get to the end goal."

"My end goal is whatever yours is."

A shadow crossed her face, and he swallowed hard. Sure, he could kiss her all night, but they were at the edge of something here. "What is your goal, Gretch?"

Her lashes lowered. "To feel *normal*. To...um...like it."

"All right." He worked in miniscule increments daily. Patience was his most honed skill. "Let's break it down."

His fingertips feathered a trail up her thighs again—just to the edge of the shorts' seam. "Do you like this?"

She nodded, eyes still downcast.

Ever so slowly, he slid his palms around her perky ass. "What about now?"

She rubbed her lips together, peering at him almost curiously. "Not so much."

"Okay. Good to know." He groped for the bra hook and flicked it open. A flush covered her cheeks, but her eyes stayed curious. Taking as much time as he would to unwrap a priceless statue, Sean neatly rolled the shirt and eased up her bra until plump breasts with dusty-pink areolae lay inches from his lips. "Can I taste?"

She bit her bottom lip. Her fingers played with strands of his hair. Finally, she nodded shyly, encircling his skull and guiding his head. His heart thrummed. His cock strained. He lapped in wonder. Her satiny skin tasted salty and still smelled of pepper spices.

She moaned softly, and the sound of it, the vibrations under his tongue, cracked the last of his self-control. He broke away. "God, I want you, Gretch."

"Yes!" She laved his mouth with her tongue, thrusting and curling wickedly, sighing with glee. He shook with need, and urgency replaced gentleness. He pulled her fully onto his hard-on. She stiffened instantly, wrenching her lips from his.

Shit! Profuse apologies formed as he tried to push her back, but she fought it, and an instant later her mouth slammed onto his. He grunted in surprise at the violent pressure. Her tongue drilled so deep he fought the gag. Her hands snaked to his jeans, fingers gripping his waistband. He'd been here before. This wouldn't end well. Twisting his head, he broke off the kiss.

"No," he growled, snagging her wrists. The glittering gaze staring back at him held no warmth or desire now, only empty, black revulsion. It sealed his determination. "Get your hands off me, Gretch."

She froze, wide-eyed, like he'd doused her with ice water. "Excuse me?"

He panted, guilt and respect for her battling his mindless lust. She eased back onto his knees still gaping at him.

"I don't know what happened in your past, Gretch," he said between gulps. "But it seems to start with your need to suck a man off as fast as possible, and get him the hell out of your sight."

"How dare you—"

"We're stuck here together," he plowed on. "We don't need this complication." He loosened his grip on her wrists, and she yanked down the hem of her shirt.

Sean mustered his gentlest tone. "How about we lie down on the mattress and call it a day."

She staggered into the director's bathroom. He stiffened in anticipation of the door slam and the household of women who would awaken. Of Hank's sharp knock on the door. The biggest surprise of the day was the soft click instead.

He groaned and adjusted himself painfully. What a long, tense night they had ahead. He eyed the burner phone. May as well call Jace and get the "you're such a fuck-up" lecture over with too.

33

———

Crime scene tape roped off a generous area around the open door to the Allen/Collins apartment complex. The outer door stood open, and bright police lights spilled out into the night. Even from half a block away, the massive puddle of blood in the foyer hall and along the top step was gruesomely apparent. Jace glanced around the cozy neighborhood, lined with terrified faces and a frenzy of reporters. How, in the age of smartphone cameras and live streaming videos, had no one caught the beheading?

Jace shouldered his way into the crowded crime scene just as the body bag was being wheeled out. He stood back respectfully, a tightness gripping his throat. For as many terrorists as he'd killed in the line of duty, and friends who'd been killed, he still reacted to the instant permanence of death like a sissy. *One second you're here, the next you're gone.* Dwayne Collins had annoyed the hell out of him yesterday, so very much alive, but the man hadn't deserved this.

Jace sent up a quick prayer as he scooted by the

photographer, and halted by Dirk. "Bring me up to speed."

Dirk jerked his chin by way of greeting. "Complex doesn't have security cameras, but the neighbor directly upstairs heard a high-pitched scream just after eight. Vic had defensive wounds like he tried to block the blow. Half his forearm was severed too."

Jace nodded, shutting down any physical reaction. He was a former SEAL, for fuck's sake. When would he get used to the horror of people's last suffering moments on this earth? "Any evidence left behind?"

Dirk scowled toward the uniforms grimly combing the scene. "They don't think they're getting much. It's SOP with fingerprints and trace right now."

Jace muttered his thanks and crossed to the far end of the complex foyer where Margo spoke on her cell phone, finger plugging her free ear. Beside her was a wizened man, whose white hair had to be a true bowl cut. His face was sorrowful, eyes rimmed in red. Jace introduced himself.

"Dennis Rutledge. I manage the place." They shook hands, and Jace offered his heartfelt condolences.

"I'm assuming you gave Special Agent Hathaway your statement?" Jace nodded to his boss, who sounded like she was wrapping up with, "Yes, sir. Will do, sir."

Rutledge nodded. "I wasn't here when it happened. I wish I had been. I would've given my life for that boy. Heart of gold, that one."

"I met him yesterday. It didn't strike me he ran with a dangerous crowd."

"No, sir. Most of them boyfriends he brought home were quiet and upstanding."

Margo was off the phone and excused herself to Rutledge. She pulled Jace a small distance away. "That was Garcia; he's heading to the police station. Evidently

Donatello has information he thinks he can bargain with. Did you find your brother?"

Jace nodded. "They're bunking the night at a women's shelter. I'll pick them up at seven tomorrow morning."

"The same place Gretch went when we all thought she was kidnapped?"

"Yeah. South Saginaw and Seventy-fourth." He glanced around the busy foyer where his task force team mingled with the local PD. Was there a mole here who had pointed out Collin's investigative work to Adyton? Jace didn't have enough proof to voice his concerns. "I'd just as soon the location remain between us for now," he ended cryptically.

Although she threw him a questioning glance, Margo nodded. "Did you know Gretchen Allen from Moore and Morrow was the vic's housemate?"

"I didn't make the connection until you called me with this news. But at his office yesterday, Collins spoke to someone on the phone and mentioned his housemate. I believe the person on the phone was Brandon Meyers, the stalker I paid a visit to yesterday on Gretch's behalf."

Margo studied him like he'd fucked up good. "And then this stalker shows up at her *home*?"

Seriously? Now she was jumping to conclusions without gathering all the facts? "Meyers is a high-profile hedge fund manager, and the vic worked exclusively to out wealthy clients for money laundering schemes. In fact, Collins mentioned he was days away from busting some big names in Chicago. There could be a connection that resulted in Meyers coming here to see Dwayne, not Gretch."

Margo's eyebrows knit as she typed the name into the database on her phone. Seconds later, she flashed the screen at him. "Him?" Meyer's cocky mug smiled up at him.

"Yep."

She motioned Rutledge back over and showed him. "Was this the man Mr. Collins argued with?"

"He was here, all right."

Margo's fingers flew on her phone as she typed the information in. "Mr. Rutledge here told me this gentleman visited Dwayne last evening and a loud argument ensued about an hour later. We're combing the apartment for forensic evidence."

Jace turned to him. "Did you hear anything specific?"

"No, sir." Rutledge folded and refolded his hands in a wringing gesture. "Dwayne, he didn't know what an indoor voice was, though. That boy was so loud. An' when he was angry, the whole building knowed."

"What did they argue about?"

"I could hear 'em fine, but I couldn't follow the words they shouted."

Jace interrupted. This was about either Gretch or the opposite sides of the financial spectrum they represented. "Did you hear them mention Gretch's name?"

"No, sir."

"What about the words: smurf, layering, placement, or white collar?"

Rutledge stared at the wall beyond Margo. "Can't say as I heard those exact words, but it was words like that. Words that don't make no sense."

Excitement stirred, and Jace glanced at Margo. "Meyers trades mortgage-backed securities at Hennings. Wonder if there's any connection with the money-launder watchdogging Collins did?"

Margo broke into her sunny smile. "It's enough of a lead to visit him first thing tomorrow. Great work, Jace."

It was a far-reaching lead and one that shouldn't be their priority. The second Margo had thanked Rutledge and they'd both said goodnight to the old man, Jace drilled her with an annoyed stare. "It's a stretch to think Brandon came back here tonight with a sword and a Middle Eastern vendetta. Collins had evidence of massive shady transactions for Adyton. What if the old man found that out?" *Like from a mole in the task force.* "It's Adyton we should interview tomorrow morning."

Margo's amused expression brought him up short. "That's one of the good things about a task force," she said lightly. "We have the manpower to go several places at once and follow multiple leads."

"Of course." Jace forced a tight smile. It was his exhaustion. He hadn't had back-to-back mission-critical assignments in so long that his body and mind were sluggish on the uptake now. "How about if Dirk and I go interview Adyton?"

She patted his bicep. "How about you get a good night's sleep and pick up your brother and Gretch in the morning. We'll make sure they're off Donatello's radar going forward. I doubt the mob wants anything to do with them now that the painting is headed back to Boston."

He was assigned chauffer duties again. Super. Jace pivoted before his face outed him. Dirk stood close enough to have heard the order as he signed a chain-of-custody form a cop held out. He glanced over at Jace. "Go on, man. This is grunt work that'll take until the wee hours. You may as well crash. You've been the superhero long enough." Crooked teeth flashed a teasing grin.

"Right." Like hell he was going back to his place to sleep. "Goodnight."

34

"Christ in a splintered cradle." Gretch hugged her knees on the lid of the director's toilet. Humiliation curled hot flames through her. Sean had pinpointed her deepest flaw. Destroyed her lifelong compensatory strategy with the precision of a heat-seeking missile. Hadn't she predicted this? He'd always been too observant.

She sat up and pressed icy hands to flaming cheeks. Really, who was she to sit here feeling sorry for herself? Someone had killed an innocent man who'd simply answered the doorbell.

The fresh horror catapulted her off the toilet seat. She washed her face and rinsed out her mouth, each step strengthening her sense of control. Sean was right: they had too much to figure out to waste time dealing with the repercussions of whatever it was that overtook her when sex entered the picture. She eased the door open. Sean had cleaned up the food and moved the side chairs and knapsacks. He lay on the edge of the mattress closest to the door, facing away from her, still in his brother's t-shirt.

She'd bet her paycheck he still wore jeans under the blanket, too.

She flicked off the bathroom light. The sound tightened his shoulder blades. "I—I'm sorry I freaked out," she said.

"I'm sorry I freaked you out." No movement, and nothing more.

Gretch stripped off the cargo shorts and slipped out of the loose bra without removing her shirt. In a heartfelt nod to Dwayne's fastidiousness, she folded the items and laid them on the corner of the desk. Stepping over a corner of the mattress, she flicked off the overhead light. A crescent moon shone through the window, illuminating the room in a romantic glow.

She edged onto the mattress and air displaced immediately, lightly bouncing her and probably Sean. He was right: they'd be all over each other on this dinky thing. *My erection will press into you all night. It'll be thick and urgent and won't allow me to fall sleep.*

She cleared her throat, the sound overly loud and awkward in the brittle silence. "I can lay behind the desk if you want."

"Just lie down and go to sleep, Gretch. My brother is picking us up out front at seven sharp."

"No worries. I wake up way before that."

Sean folded his pillow and shifted further from her. "I doubt I'll fall asleep."

She sighed quietly and eased between the tightly tucked blanket like a cat burglar. "Goodnight, then," she whispered.

He grunted.

She lay on her right side and, yep, her lower half pressed right up against rugged jeans, hard limbs, and the solid curves of his ass. Neither of them would be sleeping.

She tucked a hand between her cheek and the pillow. *Think of something calm.* Instantly Dwayne's last seconds on earth launched into her imagination in vivid detail. She squeezed her eyes shut. *Don't!* She forced the image to change to Sean's magical hands raking her thighs, the feel of his soft lips on her breast. How he'd effortlessly coaxed the very first flame of need to life. Desire felt lovely. Scorching. She palmed her breast and squeezed gently like he'd done, then twitched restlessly. Her ass bumped his hard. She stilled. "Oops. Sorry."

He grunted again.

Closing her eyes, she tried to visualize sheep jumping a fence. Replayed the kickass dance moves on Beyoncé's newest music video. Brainstormed how to find the Parisian shop inventory all the way back to 1965. None of it worked. She stared into the darkness, stiff and alert, straining to hear a snore or deep breathing, anything to signal that Sean was asleep so she could relax. Moments passed. Nothing. In fact, no sound of breathing at all.

His body was a freaking furnace. Gretch waited in paralysis as long as she could, until her borrowed t-shirt was as damp as if she'd sat in a sauna all this time. Lord have mercy, she was in hell!

Ever so slowly, she peeled the blanket off, a task doubly difficult because he'd tucked every centimeter of it so tightly under them and now even her slightest twitch jiggled the damn mattress. She made incremental progress, reveling in the inch-by-inch coolness of office air. A fraction at a time, she raised her left arm and leg into the clear. *Almost free.* The blanket snagged at the bottom corner, the snuggest place he'd tucked, and her ankle tangled in a pocket of cloth. *Damn it.* She rotated her foot. Nothing. She tried to flick the blanket with her fingers. The mattress jostled, and she froze. After infinity and a year passed, she micro-kicked her leg. The blanket dropped with ease, and she connected with his shin instead. "Oops," she whispered, cringing. "Sorry."

"Gretch?"

"Mmm?"

"Do you think Hank would grant me shelter in one of the rooms beyond his desk? 'Cause on some scale, this qualifies as abuse."

She *tsk*ed in disgust and shifted onto her back, which naturally molded the entire left side of her down the incinerator of his backside. The folded sheet beneath her was sopping. "*I'm* the one suffering here, Sean. Jesus! You're so fucking *hot*."

The mattress bounced violently as he turned on his other side and rose up on an elbow. In the pale moonlight, his eyes glittered icy and alpha-like. "I know I'm hot," he snarled. "But you're just going to have to restrain yourself, madam."

His unexpected response dissolved the fatigue and frustration. Gretch burst into giggles, helpless to stop when it turned into snuffling snorts. "Madam," she wheezed, tears running down her face. "*Restrain myself...*"

She clasped her aching stomach and flutter-kicked her legs. Tears streamed freely down her face.

"Shhh..." His lips rested on her forehead, the smile evident. "How can I get you to go to sleep? A massage? A pillow over your face?"

Her giggles ramped back up, her fresh hysteria no doubt making a racket. She covered her mouth with both hands, to no avail. Hank was probably going to knock any second. Sean jostled and bounced the mattress further, but she was too helpless to care. As her mirth subsided, though, she grew aware of the new sleeping arrangement. His pillow was lodged between his groin and her hip. The blanket was on the floor. His right hand cradled his head and his left roamed in a feather-whisper over her bare, damp stomach. The guy had taken the liberty to ease her shirt up, almost to her breasts.

"What are you doing?" she whispered.

"Cooling you down, for starters." He leaned in and blew a steady stream of air on her midriff, raking the tips of his fingers in a slow circle. Goosebumps coated her skin. Her nipples strained to attention.

"What's your tattoo?" His thumb traced the ink in the dim light, and because the design disappeared into her panties, his fingers slid the elastic down. Her breath caught. He dipped his head until his face was an inch from her pelvis as he tried to make it out. On instinct, she combed fingers through his hair. The intimacy of the moment spread so much joy through her that her chest hurt.

"It's a black chess queen," she whispered.

"How *perfect*."

Yes, Sean was definitely different. Usually she got a confused "Why?" But a tattoo of the most powerful piece in the game of chess *was* perfect for her. And black because...well, there wasn't anything lily-white pure about her.

He kissed it reverently, then licked the entire outline. In the moonlight his ministrations looked sexy, like he was deeply enjoying making out with her pelvis. His dark hair tickled her midriff, his hot and delicious tongue branded her tat, and his warm breath kept the shivers rippling on the surface of her skin. It was a sensual assault, and everything between her legs sparked and tingled. She tried to catalogue all these new sensations. Erotic languidness, desire, excitement. But there were darker things—urgency. Impatience. An instinct to spread her thighs, so she did. His fingers slowed.

"What are *you* doing?" he whispered.

"I don't know," she admitted. The intensity from earlier flickered to life, along with an agitated need to relieve it, like an itch needing scratching. She pushed the hand now resting on her abs until his palm cupped the panties at the juncture of her thighs. Instantly her body rewarded her with more tingles. She arched and moaned her pleasure.

"Have you ever come, Gretch?"

She paused, the exquisite sensations taking a back seat to the glaring awareness of her wanton position and Sean's humiliating question. "Yes, of course."

"I mean with a guy. Not you or a dildo."

She shoved his hand away and snapped her legs tight. Mustering her frostiest tone, she said, "Roll over and go to sleep, Sean."

He had the audacity to chuckle. "Like we have a prayer of that happening." His palm glided over her hipbone and nestled right back between her thighs. Her eyelids fluttered shut, and when she exhaled through her mouth, a deeper sound came out. She sank into the sensations of his gentle hand, the brush of his lips on her temple, the warm male scent of him.

"It's like a bonfire down here," he muttered. "No wonder you're flopping around like a hooked fish."

He brushed the length of her and she arched, opening wider. A childlike voice inside began as a whisper but spread with chilling intensity. *Please don't touch me.*

She turned her face toward the window, biting her lip and squeezing her eyes closed. This wasn't the same. It was Sean. She was safe. She could do this.

He trailed kisses along her cheekbone and caught her earlobe between his teeth. "You're so beautiful," he whispered.

Ugh. They all said that. Stopit, stopit, stopit!

She panted anguished breaths, her focus slipping.

"Shhh." His hand stilled. Seconds passed. He raised up on an elbow and called to the virtual-assistant cylinder. The neon light awoke. "Play the *Intermezzo* in *Cavalleria rusticana* by Muscagni."

Soft strains of violins floated in the air. Gretch gulped a breath, her muscles so tight they were seconds from spasming.

Sean gathered her close and settled on his back. "Just listen for a while. *Feel* it."

The melody built, and the ethereal longing from the other day swirled in her soul. She swallowed hard before tears filled her eyes. "Tell me about this song," she whispered, twining her fingers in his.

"I already did."

"Tell me some more."

His chest rose and fell. "The composer heard about a competition and wrote this opera in, like, two months flat." His breath stirred her hair. The whole orchestra played, building the sweetness, and with each note the tension in her muscles melted. She focused on the music and his calm voice.

"Did he win?"

"Yes. One of three winners, but it launched his career. Shh. You're missing the good part."

As the music climaxed, Gretch uncurled her fingers from his and lay back on the mattress. She eased his palm over her once again and closed her eyes. He let it rest there, almost as if getting physical wasn't as important as the *Intermezzo*. So Sean. She smiled and let the last strains of the violins wash away her fear. When it was over, she opened her eyes. An edge of the moon was still visible in the window, pale and glowing. She sighed, groggy and relaxed.

"'I met a lady in the meads,'" Sean whispered, "'full

beautiful, a fairy's child.'" His hand pressed her gently, as if seeking permission to move. "Her hair was long,'" he continued, his tone gentle. "'Her foot was light, and her eyes were wild.'"

"What are you doing?" she grumbled.

"Reciting John Keats."

"Why?"

"So you'll know, without a doubt, it's *me* here with you." He kissed her temple and ear. "Try not to interrupt." He kissed her nose and the corner of her mouth.

"'I made a garland for her head.'" He slowly stroked her again. "'And bracelets too, and fragrant zone.'" He kissed her for a long time, abundantly tender and giving. When he withdrew, his inhale quivered. "'She looked at me as she did love, and made sweet moan.'"

His timbre held her spellbound. Her muscles remained relaxed. There was only the moon and his voice and his deft fingers waking the fragile sensations again: the damp heat, the ache. She closed her eyes and guided his palm faster. *It'sSeanit'sSeanit'sSean.* Her core caught fire, and she gasped and writhed beneath his touch.

"This next part's pretty dirty." The preciseness of his words, their meaning reached her, like a match to gasoline. She strained into his hand.

"'I set her on my pacing stead...'"

"Oh my God," she muttered, visualizing riding Sean, long and deep. She was so close! Wrenching her panties down, she pressed his fingers to her, flesh on flesh. He roamed freely, igniting fires like a maniacal arsonist.

"'And nothing else saw all day long.'" His voice deepened. His nose nudged her shirt and his tongue snaked out, lashing her nipple, suckling, biting.

She panted and bucked wildly. *Almost...*

"'For sidelong would she bend, and sing.'" He caught

her earlobe between his teeth at the precise moment his finger eased into her swollen depths.

"Oh... Sean..."

"'A faery's song.'" His thumb flickered her rapidly again and again. "Come for me, Gretch."

Her nerve endings seized, shivered, and exploded into cosmic smithereens. She arced in a quaking mass. His mouth descended onto hers, swallowing her scream, absorbing her bliss. She twisted the pillow from between them, knocked his hand aside, and rolled his jean-clad body on top of her. Twining her legs around his ass, she rode the end of her climax on his erection. "Oh, Sean, oh, God..."

He grunted, initially trying to hold himself still, but suddenly he thrust his hips sharply, the rough zipper seam chafing her from her orgasm. Seconds later he stiffened, and moonlight sparkled off his clenched teeth. A long groan came from deep within and then he slumped on top of her.

Gretch grinned and palmed his ass. She'd done it! She'd had an orgasm with a man. And not just any man—Sean and his odd, darling, crazy-hot skills.

"Shit," he wheezed into her neck. "A guy's worst nightmare."

"What?" She giggled again. "Premature ejaculation? Coming to your own poetry recital? Soiling your brother's jeans?"

"Worse." He rolled off her, clearly not finding humor in her sass. "Having to raid that closet for clean underwear."

"But there are only women's in there."

"And you get my point."

35

Sean stored the deflated mattress and made a final slow inspection around the office.

"You've totally outed us," Gretch observed, standing between the knapsacks by the closed door. "Now it's way cleaner than when we arrived."

She munched a granola bar, looking freaking adorable in cargo shorts, no makeup, and a Cubs cap pulled low over her brow. Sure, she was a knockout in her skintight minis and stilettos, but this Gretch looked young, fresh...approachable.

"Why are you staring at me?" she demanded.

She'd never perceive his tomboy observation as a compliment, so he grasped for the usual insolence. "Because you're dropping crumbs where I just vacuumed." He pointed at her feet. "It's like you're a toddler."

"We're about to walk out the front door and potentially face a mafia hitman. I'd think you'd be less worried about cleaning."

Sean let the comment lie and returned the dust rag and hand vac to the bathroom storage shelf. There was no threat. Jace would be out front in minutes. He'd convinced Sean last night what a stupid and reckless maneuver running off into the night had been, and Sean had lain awake for hours battling all-consuming guilt. Jace was right—as usual—and Sean had fucked things up again trying to be the hero. His brother would stick them somewhere safe until the task force finished the investigation. At the very least, Sean would have a whole day of Gretch to himself, which was probably more dangerous than facing terrorists. He allowed himself a smug grin and stripped the gauze off his wrists. Tiny razor-type lines encircled both wrists, but the cuts had scabbed overnight and barely hurt. He stuck the bandages in the mini garbage near the toilet and twisted the bag closed. "Do you think Hank will take this garbage? I hate leaving it for your director."

"Focus, Sean. We're in escape mode."

Reluctantly, he left the bag where it was and flipped off the bathroom light. "Ready?"

She rolled her eyes and picked up her knapsack. They slipped into the foyer, and Gretch locked the office with the key Hank gave her, then handed it back with an envelope. "I don't know when I'll be back," she said to him. "This is a note for one of the residents—would you make sure she gets it?" Hank nodded, and she kissed the tired man's cheek. "Massive thanks, dreamboat."

The security guard flushed and beamed. "Enjoy the day, folks."

Sean held the front door for her, and they stepped out into the cloudless dawn. The residential street was empty and quiet. Traces of budding spring flowers and sweet, dewy grass permeated the morning air. Family SUVs and a few newspapers littered driveways as far as the eye could see. Far down the block, a man in a black Bulls sweatshirt jogged with a Great Dane.

"Think your brother can be talked into stopping by a

Starbucks?" Gretch muttered, sitting on the top steps and adjusting her cap.

Seriously. Too cute. "You have a lot more influence than I do. You ask." Sean draped his knapsack over his shoulder and walked to the curb, scanning the scene. Well-kept middle-class homes and low-rise condos stretched down the block, the lots uniform, the land-scaping tidy. It all lent a surreal quality this early. Like that Jim Carrey mov—

Two men, concealed in black hoodies, stepped around the high shrubbery next door. Sean recognized the pungent body wash a second before he pegged the face, but it was already too late. Victor raised a 9mm pistol. "Get in the car."

JACE PARKED the Suburban outside the shelter's address and plucked the phone from the beverage holder. The new phone number Sean gave him last night rang unanswered. Jace flicked a glance at his watch. Seven on the nose. He unhooked his seatbelt and flung open the door, frowning up at the house.

Oversleeping was not Sean's problem. As a kid he'd been a sleepwalker, causing Mom untold anxiety that he'd wander out into the city streets. Wasted energy in the end—all Sean ever did was clean the house, or gather anything on tables and counters and line them all up by size.

Jace grabbed the thick file off the passenger seat and opened the rear door. Three banker's boxes stuffed with more money-laundering evidence waited. He'd stayed at the office most of the night, combing through two of the boxes, and could probably recite the pages verbatim. Of great interest were several small businesses Adyton either bought or sold from Salvatore Donatello. Collins had dotted other substantial lines between Adyton's blood artifact smuggling and the mob cleaning the vast sums to smuggle offshore. Just wait until the task force heard about this. Jace jammed the file into its designated slot and slammed the door.

He vaulted up the front steps and pressed the buzzer next to the keypad. A male asked his business, and he answered with his credentials. The door clicked into unlock mode, and Jace strolled in. "Looking for Sean Quinn and Gretchen Allen," he said to the compact security guard.

"They walked outta here about ten minutes ago."

Shit. Adrenalin dumped into Jace's bloodstream. He glanced at the security screens on the desk. "Did you see anything?"

"Guy stood at the curb looking down the street then called to Gretch. They both walked off screen."

Before the guard was even through the explanation, Jace shook his head. Sean didn't just walk off. He obeyed like a puppy, always had. It was why Jace had sought him out last Saturday night. And, as expected, Sean's brilliance had delivered instantaneous results. Jace jerked his head at the monitors. "Let me see."

The video replay showed exactly what the guard had seen—if you didn't know Sean. His at-ease body language consisted of a slouchy looseness and an expression just shy of sullen. Both characteristics were prominently visible when Sean, knapsack slung over his shoulder, had reached the curb and glanced around. What the guard hadn't picked up on was the subtle slide into what Gage used to call Sean's Cornered Rat stance. The alert shifting of his posture, the way his expression shuttered. All precursors to usually impressive, whiplash-fast kicks and punches. This time, though, without looking at Gretch,

Sean said something, and seconds later she rose from the top step, picked up her knapsack, and followed him past the row of hedges, off screen. "Play it back."

No one was visible on the other side of the hedges, but seeing Sean morph into Cornered Rat a second time brought out the scorching flare of fear that Jace had battled all week. He should have never gotten his brother so deeply involved. The help at O'Hare had been enough. Now two more lives were in the hands of terrorists who had no qualms with savage executions. Jace sucked air in through his mouth, sweat streaming down his back.

Which faction of the underworld was responsible this time? Who else knew Sean and Gretch were sheltering here? On Sean's request, Jace had notified Hannah that they were safe but hadn't told her where. *Only Margo knew.*

Jace grew aware of the guard studying him curiously. Christ, how long had he stood there gaping indecisively? "Thanks," he said, pivoting for the door.

Outside, the street was waking up for the week's final workday. A screen door slammed; an SUV reversed out of the driveway catty-corner to the shelter; a woman in a housecoat a few doors down stooped to collect her newspaper. Jace rounded the thick hedges and stopped short. Footprints dented the dewy lawn leading from the driveway to the hedge. He crouched, combing the area for any other clues. Deep underneath the thick branches lay two black CFD Station One Twenty-six knapsacks.

He grabbed the bags and rifled through them. Sean's burner phone lay on top of one, and Gretch's phone was stuck inside a manila envelope in the other. No voicemail or texts on Sean's to explain the disappearance. Jace turned Gretch's phone on and paced while the device sought service. As expected, unread texts popped onscreen without needing her passcode. One from Dwayne Collins. Just before eight last night.

A deep chill shuddered through Jace as he read probably the last text that man had typed.

Donatello? Nasty!
Just connected him to a massive ML scheme involving
huge Chicago names. I'll be famous this time next
week!
Stay safe, buttercup.

"Hell, Collins," Jace muttered. "You were famous about fifteen minutes later." He grabbed his own phone and called his boss.

Margo chirped out her usual cheerleader greeting, which triggered fresh rage and screwed with his usual ice-cold command of a situation. "Donatello is rolling on Adyton," she crowed. "He's supplied the old man with multiple warehouse spaces, has steered him into local investments that are shams for hiding money, and Donatello will turn state's evidence. As soon as you collect Sean and Gretch, come right back to headquarters."

"They've been kidnapped," Jace snarled through his clenched jaw. "Who'd you leak the address to?"

36

———

A few blocks from the shelter, Victor swung into a gas station and parked around back. Even though Sean breathed through his mouth, light-headedness paralyzed him. The overpowering smell of sweet body wash stole all the fresh oxygen.

"What the fuck is going on?" Gretch, seated in the front passenger seat, demanded loudly for the third time.

"Would you shut up already?" Victor threw the car into park and motioned to Black Hoodie. The two men forced them from the Jetta and toward a white van with ELIAS BAKERY stenciled on the sides. Sean scanned the lot. There were no windows on this side of the gas station mart. One security camera hung off-kilter, connected by a lone screw.

"Get your hands off me," Gretch shrieked. Sean twisted from Black Hoodie and lunged toward the body-builder. Victor dragged Gretch in front of him, one hand splayed over her boob, the other aiming the 9mm at Sean's face. Sean halted feet from impact. A front snap would take care of the weapon, but not the other gun, now trained on him from the left side.

Sean exhaled harshly. "Get your hands off her." His voice held all the authority of the sensei, and Victor's brows rose.

"Or what, nerd?"

"Or I'll fucking kill you."

Victor snorted and jerked his head. "Get in the van." His left hand hadn't moved, and Gretch's expression mixed mutinous hate with panic. Sean backed away. It was the wisest move, but his martial arts side trembled with bloodlust.

She was shoved in first and cried out in pain. Sean leaped in unassisted and crouched beside her prone body.

"Come here," he murmured, hauling her upright. The windowless doors were slammed shut, enclosing them in darkness and the residual buttery scent of baked goods. He encircled her shivering body in a tight embrace.

"Who is that? Why is he doing this?" Gretch asked. In two years of dodging her regal insults and haughty retorts, he'd never glimpsed a softer side to her. A side that had turned out to have extensive tentacles of warmth, fear, and love tunneling under her prickly composure. Now the terror in her outraged tone was nakedly transparent.

"Adyton's great-nephew," Sean explained.

"*Adyton?*" She jolted against him, her breath puffing his cheek. "Oh yeah," she said. "He was one of the body-guards who came in last Monday."

"This van is from the bakery next door to Days of Olde, so I guess that's Adyton's too, and no doubt where we're headed."

The driver's-side door slammed, and the men spoke unintelligibly beyond the dividing panel.

"You said I was delusional," Gretch accused. "That only the mob was after us."

"If there's a connection between Donatello and Adyton, it has to be micro-thin."

"Well, here's your damn proof." She *tsk*ed her disgust. Beneath his palms, her muscles were both rigid and quaking. "If we get out of this, I am totally applying to the FBI."

"God help us all," he muttered, then grinned at the kick to his shin. The angrier she got, the less room there was to be afraid.

The van roared to life. "Listen," he said, stoking the fire. "When we get to wherever he's taking us, let me do all the talking."

"You are on my last nerve, Sean Quinn." Her voice floated viciously in the dark. Strange how if he couldn't see her wrath, it held less power over him.

"Good. Keep that thought." Tires screeched, and the van peeled out, tossing them to the floor. Immediately a wheel hit a pothole, which almost dislocated a vertebra in his neck. Gretch uttered profanities, and Sean continued bracing her against him through the aggressive speed and sharp turns, while visually mapping their route. About five minutes later, he was certain they'd entered the I-90 freeway.

"What do you think's going to happen?" she asked in a small voice.

Damn. The fear had returned. He tightened his arms. "If there's a God, the police will see this wildly erratic driving and engage in a high-speed pursuit."

She shrugged out of his grip. "We're in trouble, Sean. Snap out of the smarty-pants responses."

Sean kept silent. Social niceties were beyond him on a good day. Spouting false comfort completely eluded him. They were screwed, full stop. He sucked in air to dissipate the despair. "I don't know what's going to happen, Gretch," he said. "I don't know why Adyton would want us. If only I hadn't chosen to get off at that fucking El stop."

A pause. She gripped his hand in hers. "If only I wasn't such a whack job you had to bodyguard from stalker dates."

He could barely make out her features in the dark. "You trying to own my guilt?"

"Just sharing the burden. You tend to be very grabby with the martyr role."

He grinned and squeezed her hand. Yeah. He'd needed her snark as much as she needed to be angry. His thoughts shifted to action. These van doors latched in the middle. At the destination, one of the men would be standing right in the center, well within ambush kicking distance.

Gretch snuggled back in Sean's arms and sighed. "We need to think. Preplan. I say Adyton is aware I'm behind the eBay bid."

"Or he caught you in one of those lies Tuesday. But that would mean he never bought my Bixby role or the conduit service between art buyers and sellers. So why keep the Quran at Moore and Morrow for restoration? Why waste my time the next day at that warehouse on Knox?"

"Knox?"

"Mmhmm. Hundreds of crates. You can't believe how much black-market smuggling is going on right beneath Chicago's noses."

The van exited the freeway. Their bodies swayed together with each acceleration and brake just like Tuesday on the train. Sean let his head loll on the metal siding, picturing the van parking, doors opening, him crouched to kick the gun out of Victor's hand.

"There may be another connection," Gretch said softly.

"What?"

"I saw an inventory list on Walter's desk last Monday from Adyton, listing a Knox address. Twenty items totaling a hundred thousand dollars. But after he met with Adyton, he gave me the list to type up and the price had been whited out and changed to sixty million."

"*Sixty?*" A chill spread goosebumps along Sean's arms. "What kind of items?"

"Pottery, statues, reliefs... that sort of thing. And a few words were handwritten in Arabic. I meant to go back in and use the translating app on my cell, but forgot."

"Did you tell anyone?"

She snorted. "The week got a little crazy after that."

Sean processed the information and shook his head. "There's no way Walter is involved."

"You'd think, right? What with the whole churchgoing, 'our company's reputation is critical' thing he's got going on?"

"Do you remember the buyer?"

She whistled out a breath. "Umm... Tomas Hussain. Not a name I recognized. Not one of our regulars."

The van braked hard again, and they fought for balance. After righting herself and swearing revenge, Gretch said, "Walter's definitely been in a crappy mood lately, though. I just figured it was issues at home. I know his daughter goes off to college this fall. What if he needs more money? What if he thought connecting up with Adyton's crates of artifacts would help expand the business? The week goes on, your brother and Margo storm the office..." Her shoulders rose and fell. "Suddenly there's suspicion the Quran may be connected to terrorism. Walter's bad mood could be his guilty conscience."

Sean shook his head again. "It's not Walter. We need to find out who this Hussain is. A hundred thousand changed to sixty mil sounds like massive bribery to me. Or hiding money."

"Hiding money?"

"Massively overpaying for goods or real estate, like in messy divorce proceedings, for example. The husband might divest as many assets as possible before the wife's lawyer finds them."

"How is that hiding? Now the husband is out sixty million."

"Because in return, the other guy, the buyer, will sell something back at a later date for the same figure minus a generous fee." So the question was: had Dwayne found out about this list? And what did this have to do with them being dragged here at gunpoint?

The van whipped in a tight circle, throwing them to the cold metal floor again. A grind of gears, and the van lurched in reverse. They righted themselves once more, and Gretch's string of profanities grew.

"Listen," Sean said, leaning so close his nose bumped her neck. "The second Victor stops this van, I'll be looking for a chance to kick his ass. If there's even a remote opportunity, you need to run, okay?"

"Wait—"

"Run, Gretch. Doesn't matter where. Don't look back."

The motor died. Two doors slammed, rocking the van. Sean scooted to the middle and lay on his coccyx with his knees raised, feet aimed at the latches.

"Sean, wait," she whispered urgently.

"Shh!"

The doors whipped open. Light blinded him, but not enough that he couldn't see. No Victor. Instead Black Hoodie and another young man stood on either side of the open doors, .45s pressed low to their sides. Because the open doors blocked them, no one outside the van would see the guns. *Shit.*

"Hop along," Victor said, rounding from the driver's side. Sean studied the three men—two on the right, one on the left. All holding guns. Behind them was the open back entrance to the bakery. The freshly baked aromas were tantalizing and completely at odds with the threat they faced.

Sean was manhandled out and shoved through the door. "Tie him," Victor called, and in seconds, more slim plastic encircled his wrists. Behind him, a scuffle ensued and Gretch swore loudly. Sean spun and plowed into the other two men. Black Hoodie fell with the loud thump, but the other guy jabbed his gun in Sean's side. He froze as the hammer was cocked.

Two feet away, Victor and Gretch were in an all-out struggle, him trying to take liberties and her attempting castration by kicking. "You and me," Victor muttered with a leer, "we're going to have some fun."

Sean yanked at the zip tie, and last night's scabs split open. "Leave her alone," he snarled. Black Hoodie staggered to his feet and jammed his gun against Sean's forehead.

"I will kill you," Gretch shrieked. She let fly another off-balanced kick that Victor easily sidestepped.

"Vic, she's making too much noise."

"Fuck it. My great-uncle hates delays." Victor spun her around and pushed hard. Teeth gritted in fury, eyes glassy with hate, she plowed into Sean's chest and bounced off with a *whoof*.

"Move out," Victor barked. They trooped single file through a large storage room, weaving between boxed items stacked on carts, ready to be loaded onto the van. The two men dropped back, and Victor led them to a door. He knocked a rapid beat and, at a muffled sound, threw it open. Adyton's moldy-smelling office lay beyond. Victor shoved Sean over the threshold first. The old man sat at his desk, black-framed glasses on the tip of his nose, scribbling something in Arabic.

Gretch halted next to Sean, her eyes searching his. He shook his head. He had no hope to give. Her brow furrowed as she looked away, and before she clamped her jaw, her chin trembled.

Victor closed the door on the other two men and stood in front of it, gun aimed casually at the floor. Adyton signed his name with a flourish and glanced up.

"Ah, Miss Allen." Adyton smiled thinly. "You look a bit...different. And Mr. Quinn."

Sean blinked at the correct use of his name. "When did you know I wasn't Bixby?"

"When a Suburban very clearly belonging to the Feds screeched to a halt outside my door."

About a second after they met on Tuesday. "Then why the ruse of returning the next day to discuss our services? Why did I hoof it all the way to Knox for the statuette?"

"That's information you don't need to know."

"My brother is FBI. He was in that Suburban."

"I knew that within a few hours on Tuesday as well." Adyton removed his glasses and folded them. The merry old man was long gone. A ruthlessness carved his features. "You see, I know Walter Morrow quite well."

Sean swallowed his panic. Walter's pristine reputation had cloaked a massive operation of blood artifacts right underneath his employees' noses. Surely if he was in bed with Adyton, it gave them purchase. "Gretch is innocent in all this, and Walter knows it. Let her go."

Adyton laughed. "She lied from the moment she opened her mouth in here. It was you we had questions about. The blank look on your face when you came in to collect Miss Allen on Tuesday made me think you might be innocent, in which case I was willing to let you continue with the restoration. Instead you signed your death warrant by spewing more lies the next day. Quite unfortunate that a federal agent tailed you and Victor to the warehouse."

"They probably still are," Sean replied, scrounging for anything that would slow this train wreck. "They know all about the document charging sixty million for artifacts worth a hundred thousand, so they've got you on money laundering. I doubt you want kidnapping charges on top of that."

Gretch stepped closer to Adyton. Victor watched her lazily. "Did you kill Dwayne?" she asked in a steely voice.

Adyton shrugged and steepled his fingers. His lack of surprise and silence were clear admissions.

"Just tell me why," she whispered, her chin quivering again. "He was my oldest friend. You aren't going to let us live, so why not tell us?"

"And why use an ISIS method?" Sean asked. "We know you're not. You're the Syrian president's cousin. Your black market profits support his chemical warfare against innocent people."

Gretch gasped. In the chaos of the week, Sean had forgotten to share Jace's revelation about Adyton's connection to Bashar al-Assad. Unfortunately, with her arms behind her back, the gasp showed off her assets, and Victor stared with open lust. This was going to be a huge problem. Sean ground his teeth and tried to flex his wrists another millimeter apart.

"You're a heinous beast," Gretch shouted, which startled the old man into a series of rapid blinks. "How do you sleep at night?"

"Quite easily, Miss Allen." Adyton's features sharpened into suppressed anger as he primly folded the document he'd just been signing. "I am a proud nationalist living in a country I hate, to support one I love." He began stuffing the letter into an addressed envelope, but a quiver in his hand made it a clumsy task. He slapped the items aside. "Your presidents have systematically supported the overthrow of Middle Eastern rulers since Victor here was a babe. One by one the countries have fallen like dominos, citizens initially rejoicing, believing that they too will have cars for each family member, televisions in every room, liberation for all." A muscle in his cheek twitched. "Alas, we are a different kind of people. Every single nation is much worse off because of U.S. policy and the destruction you left in your wake."

"And destroying your own ancient culture restores order?" Sean blurted.

"You need not preach my culture's history to me!" the old man roared. His rheumy eyes grew bright. "If I have to sell ancient baubles to your greedy society to fight all the factions that have been freed like rats, so be it. I think my ancestors would approve—even offer up their tablets and vases and jewelry. Syria was an ally of the United States. We are founding members of the United Nations. You turned your back on a regime that saw peace for years."

"But Dwayne," Gretch insisted. "He was harmless."

"There is nothing harmless about a gatekeeper interfering with fund transfers from American-Syrians *for* Syrians." Adyton's voice lowered to a growl. "He had no business freezing our accounts. Do you realize how many thousands of people would die on the other side of the world at the stroke of this one man's pen? His death was *celebrated.*"

Gretch stepped back, her face draining of color. She clamped her lips shut as her chest rose and fell. Was she going to vomit? Sean dragged his gaze away and steeled himself against the need to comfort her. Here was his opportunity. He gauged everyone's positions again. Adyton seated to the right and feeble; even with their hands tied, he couldn't physically stop them from walking out of here. Sean required only one shot at Victor, who conveniently gripped his gun way too loosely, but inconveniently, he was on the other side of Gretch in the tiny office. If Gretch distracted these two by throwing up, Sean would lunge left, execute a front sweep behind Victor's knees, and head-butt the old man. Then what?

"Accounts don't unfreeze just because you butchered Dwayne," Sean said, eyeing Gretch again. The sickly pallor was receding, damn it. "Another banker will step right into his position, probably already has."

The old man shrugged. "We were able to eliminate Mr. Collins before the freeze went into effect, and I'm happy to report we withdrew our funds from that particular bank with a lesson learned. We'll be much more diligent in our methods of transferring money in the future."

"It's too late. The FBI is closing in." Sean dredged deep for a casual tone to hide the lie. "Your operation is finished."

"If the FBI intervenes, it will be extremely detrimental to the city of Chicago. We are prepared to behave like ISIS, as you have already noticed with the unfortunate demise of Mr. Collins. He isn't the first. We watch in amusement as ISIS gleefully accepts credit for stabbings and bombings in these American cities that they had no hand in."

Sweat broke out on Sean's brow. "Then let me make a call and warn them not to go near the warehouse."

"They'll know soon enough. And now we have the two of you. You could say we are in a position to finally step out of the shadows. We have all the negotiating power."

"Negotiate for what?"

Adyton glared at him like a stern schoolmaster. "For the U.S. to withdraw all military interest from Syria."

Sean laughed without humor. "Yeah, I don't think the two of us are that important."

"I agree, Mr. Quinn. You both are mere pawns."

Sean swallowed the absurd urge to correct him. Gretch was no one's *pawn*.

The old man motioned in the direction of the street. "We've spent all night placing pipe bombs in public containers around downtown. The more your government chooses not to engage in negotiations, the more trouble we are caused by police or agencies looking for my artifacts or for you, the more bombs we detonate." Adyton spread his hands. "Naturally, the death of many Chicagoans will be on your heads if you two attempt to escape or alert the authorities."

The old man stood slowly and stuffed his spectacles in his breast pocket. "That being said, untie them when they get to the attic, Victor. I am confident they won't try to escape. We'll finish this at dark." He white-knuckled his cane and gestured to the bakery. "This way."

"Finish what?" Gretch sputtered. "You just said you needed us for negotiations."

"If you knew anything about chess, you would know pawns are sacrificed for long-term strategy. Your officials will not take us seriously until many pawns are sacrificed." Adyton motioned wearily to his great-nephew. "Go with Victor."

"No," Gretch said through barely parted lips. "I'm not going anywhere with him."

Victor smirked, opening the door. "Like you have a choice, babe." The other two men filled the doorway. Sean scanned the new fight parameters. Three men, three guns, and an old man to dispatch—all without the use of his arms. Highly improbable. And now every attempt to save themselves would blow innocent people to smithereens.

37

Jace strode down the hall toward Conference Room Three.

"Don't interrupt their meeting," Margo called, hurrying from behind. "We can interview him when he comes out."

"Fuck that." He spun around so abruptly she halted an inch before smacking into him. He leaned into her personal space. "And fuck you too."

She stiffened under his aggressive stance. "Back off, Quinn. It's not what you think."

"Why would you tell *anyone* where Sean and Gretch were hiding?"

She blushed and waved her hands. "Joe Taylor isn't even on our team. Why would he have anything to do with their disappearance?"

"I don't know," he sneered. "Let's go ask the dweeb."

"We can't inter—"

Jace burst through the conference room door, ignoring the startled glances as he scanned the members of another joint task force. The contract anthropologist was down near the end, too far to lunge at or grab without interference. Jace pointed to him. "You. Where are Sean and Gretch?"

Taylor had enough survival skills to look terrified. "Why would I know?"

Wrong answer. The correct one would've been: *Who are Sean and Gretch?*

"What's this about?" SSA Garcia demanded from the head of the long table.

"Sorry for the disruption." Margo's gaze skipped to Joe, and she flashed him a warning plea. "If we could have a moment of Joe's time."

A moment. As if this interruption was frivolous. The rage boiling inside Jace made it difficult to breathe. Garcia frowned as he scanned all three faces. "What for?"

"Our contract anthropologist has gone missing—"

"My brother," Jace growled. "And his coworker. The security camera shows a probable abduction; their knapsacks were discarded in shrubbery." He had Garcia's undivided attention. "And only three people knew their location. Me, her, and him." He jabbed a finger at Taylor again.

Garcia's confusion grew; who could blame him? That someone with Margo's looks and poise would consider Joe Taylor a catch was unbelievable. That pillow talk with that balding, scrawny geek could lead to Sean's disappearance was fantastical. But Jace couldn't care less about the revolting secret love affair. He needed answers. He jerked his head at Joe. "Hallway. Now."

Garcia stood and motioned to Joe. "If you'd all excuse us for a moment." He eyed Jace and Margo sharply. "My office."

Once inside, Garcia assigned chairs with a sparing glance. Jace was placed on the opposite side of the room from Joe, who got the chair closest to the door. Margo sat primly in the middle, her face a study in dread. This was one hundred percent her fault, and she knew it.

"Go ahead," Garcia said quietly to her when he was seated.

"We're wrapping up our smuggling case; have the locations under surveillance, phones tapped, proof of money laundering, and a warehouse jammed with looted artifacts. Yesterday the suspect pulled his assets before we could freeze them, and the banker who'd blown the whistle was beheaded. Now two citizens who may have knowledge of this terrorist ring are missing."

Garcia directed his attention to Jace. "Is this the same brother from last night and the mob?"

Jace nodded a tight affirmative.

"He seems to get himself right into the thick of things," the SSA murmured.

No. He doesn't. He prefers his own company and should never have been brought back on board. Jace glared at Joe. "How do you know Adyton?"

Taylor rubbed his palms on his thighs. His face was shiny with sweat. "He's an acquaintance from the art world."

"He's more than an acquaintance if you're spilling FBI secrets. Why the hell would you tell him where to find Sean and Gretch?"

The bespectacled man gulped in a cartoonish way. His gaze flitted to each of them, unable to land and focus.

"Mr. Taylor?" Garcia prompted.

"I want immunity."

"Oh, Christ," Margo mumbled.

Garcia considered him for a long moment, his eyes glacier cold. "Depends on what you've got."

"I provide clean provenances for him once in a while."

Margo lurched in her seat with a gasp. Another look

flashed between them—his apologetic, hers murderous. She closed her eyes and hung her head. After Sean quit the FBI, it had been Margo who'd hired Taylor. Had they already been in a relationship? Had Taylor come aboard specifically to spy for Adyton, or to be closer to Margo?

"Where are Quinn's brother and the woman?" Garcia asked.

Taylor spread his hands. "There must be some mistake. Adyton is well respected in the art community and very generous with scholarships to budding artists—"

"His banker was beheaded," Jace ground out. *Fucking scholarships?* "Can we stay on point? When did you call him, and what did you say?"

Joe blew out an aggravated breath. "Last Saturday you picked up an artifact at O'Hare, and Adyton knew it was a matter of time before he landed on your radar. He asked for my help to redirect your attention elsewhere, but I wasn't assigned to the task force. All I've done is keep him informed on your progress."

"So he knows his warehouse is under surveillance, his phones are tapped, and we've taken the bank records?" Margo asked in disbelief.

"The old man has been playing us all week," Jace said. "Why? And why take Sean and Gretch?"

Taylor adjusted his glasses, warming to his role as informant. "Probably for leverage. Adyton knew too late that he'd handed over his Quran to a restoration firm that was suddenly helping the FBI. He also knew if he tried to pull the project, you'd confiscate it, so he shortened the time frame, hoping the firm would refuse his ridiculous request and hand the artifact back." He turned to Jace, lip curled in scorn. "Instead they assigned your perfect brother to perform a miracle."

Jace jerked to his feet. Sitting was no longer an option.

Talking was no longer on the table either. He faced Garcia. "Plan of action?" The man had one chance at this, and if he pulled a let's-gather-the-facts approach, then the FBI was not a career Jace could endure a second longer.

The SSA studied him for a long moment before turning his attention to Margo. "The locations that are under surveillance. Has anyone seen anything suspicious?"

"None at the warehouse. A van arrived at the bakery half an hour ago and is being loaded with goods. The Days of Olde shop should be opening just about now."

Garcia nodded. "Inga Harvey is fresh off an assignment. I'll send her to speak to Adyton."

Margo straightened. "I should go. Despite this setback, I'm head of the investigation."

"I could run circles around your leadership," Jace ground out. "All we've done is sit on our asses and collect data. *I'm* going."

Garcia opened his mouth, but Margo bolted out her chair. "This isn't a clandestine, no-personal-accountability adventure. We work as a team, gathering irrefutable evidence for federal prosecutors." She jabbed a finger into Jace's chest. "Your lack of impulse control and disregard for authority have been detrimental right from the start. You hired your brother without my knowledge or authority. That's what got us into this mess, Jace."

"I beg to differ, Special Agent Hathaway," he snarled. "Your inability to keep your legs and your mouth shut are entirely to blame."

Margo's eyes flared. Garcia gestured to the empty seats and yelled, "This isn't a goddamn reality show. Sit back down."

"Sitting is all we do on this task force," Jace said,

clenching his fists. "I request permission to go on the interview. Sir."

Garcia paused, and Jace held his breath. This whole career-after-the-career-of-his-dreams came down to this moment. He'd brought in a two-hundred-million-dollar painting the FBI had searched for these last thirty years. He'd saved five little boys' lives and his brother's too. He'd nabbed the head of the Chicago mafia. Garcia *owed* him this deviation from the knot of red tape.

"You may go as Special Agent Harvey's backup. You may not engage with Adyton in any way. Am I making myself perfectly clear?"

Jace nodded, jaw cramping from all the clenching. Christ, another woman. He appreciated everything about them from here until next Tuesday, until it came to taking orders. He hadn't found one yet who made the right decisions under pressure. He blew out a breath. Aw, hell. At least it was a clean slate. He'd flirt and cajole and mold this second chance into a decision-making role again, while he figured out where Sean and Gretch were and how to save the day.

"What about me?" Margo asked her boss tentatively.

"Until I investigate this breach further you're on the beach."

Administrative leave. An agent's worst nightmare. Jace almost fisted the air.

Garcia turned to Taylor. "I'll take your immunity plea up with the DA. If she declines, you realize you've implicated yourself as an accessory to smuggling, money laundering, and kidnapping?"

The pathetic dweeb stayed silent, his mouth a defiant line. Margo's hands were clenched in her lap. She glared at Taylor like she was ready to launch from her chair and rearrange his face. "Who else is on your fake provenance client list?" she asked.

Taylor shrugged without making eye contact. He'd probably lawyer up as soon as he stepped out of this office.

Garcia's grim expression indicated he knew that too. He picked up the phone. "We'll have the search warrants ready in a jiffy, Taylor."

38

———

Gretch peered through the fixed slats that afforded a microscopic view of the street below. Her hours of vigilance finally paid off. "There's Jace now! That doesn't look like Margo, though." The agents passed by her tiny field of vision before she finished the second sentence. "I wonder what took them so long?"

She stretched the kinks from her back and shoulders, hope rising. Sean continued his fastidious work without a grunt of acknowledgement that he'd heard her. The second the lock had clicked on the other side of the attic door, he'd begun inspecting every inch of the walls and floors like a blind man. Pressing, knocking, pulling at wooden panels, inspecting the light switch, twisting the lone light bulb hanging from a chain. She didn't have the heart to discourage him. This wasn't Hollywood. A magical escape route wouldn't appear. The FBI going next door was their only hope.

Gretch turned back to the slats and the sunny street. Within a few minutes, the agents reappeared, walking much slower. Instinct overcame caution and she banged on the wood, yelling Jace's name. It accomplished nothing, because they were three stories up and next door, and the sturdy wooden slats gave her no access to the little round window.

"Fuck!" she yelled as they disappeared from view. She spun around, emitting a bitchy sigh to cover the sense of doom. Her stomach churned in a frenzy. She bent over, hands to knees, breathing rapidly and swallowing hard. *Please, God, don't vomit.*

In an instant Sean was behind her, flipping off her cap and running fingers through her hair. He gently pressed different pressure points on her scalp, whispering shushing sounds. Slowly she straightened and drooped against him. Within minutes his calm spirit enveloped her in such tranquility the nausea receded and her energy rebounded. It was a freaking miracle.

"How'd you do that?" she murmured, turning and finding herself in his warm embrace.

"Ancient Chinese secret." Amusement lit his deep-brown eyes.

She squeezed his bicep, then gestured about the bare attic. "Is there a way to get us out of here?"

"No." His lips pressed together. "And based on the sun, it's about midafternoon. There's not much time left."

Fear sliced through her. She had so much left to do on this earth. She'd spent her life feeding her anger and bitterness instead of—

"Hey." Sean's arms banding tighter drew her attention. "I'm going to teach you self-defense until they come to get us, okay?" The quizzical eyebrows and fox-sharp angles of his face were suddenly breathtakingly handsome. So much time wasted when she'd had this all along.

"I love you—r face," she blurted.

His eyebrows rose further. "No you don't."

"What I meant was..." The three words welled again. "I love—how nothing freaks you out." God, she was such a coward. Her life was down to mere hours.

Sean chuckled. "Who are you and what have you done with Gretch?" He brushed her hair back. "Everything I do annoys you."

"I was terribly mistaken." God, to have a do-over with him. A wish as elusive as waltzing in a red gown. And so unimportant because the end of her life was directly in front of her. It was all about *now*. An intensity gripped her, and she clenched his t-shirt in her fists. "I'm sorry I've been such a prima donna all these months."

Another chuckle. "Months? Don't you remember how you greeted me on my first day?"

Hell, Hannah, call the headhunter back. This one won't even last until lunch. She cringed. "I was molested," she blurted, and paused, heart jumping to her throat. She hadn't even remotely meant to say that. He tensed and frowned, like he hadn't heard right.

Well, she couldn't take the words back. Besides, he deserved to know. "Repeatedly," she continued in a halting voice. "By two different stepfathers. It started when I was eight."

Her breathing wasn't right, like she was supposed to inhale and her lungs were breathing out by mistake. It was all mildly dizzying. "They taught me all those tricks."

Pain clouded his features. Not pity or caution or disgust. He seemed to be waiting for her to continue. What else was there to say? She finally dragged in oxygen, and the swirling dots receded. She let go of his shirt and smoothed it out. Her hands shook. "I thought you should know, since... you jumped through so many hoops the last couple of nights."

He skimmed her forearms in a feather-light caress. "I

wouldn't call living out my wildest dream jumping through hoops."

He still didn't get it. "I'm not normal."

"Neither am I." His expression softened. "I'm beginning to think normal is pretty overrated."

"Look…" What would it take for him to see she wasn't worth the pedestal he put her on? "I hate sex, but I crave a man's attention. I don't trust them, but I need them to feel attractive. Validated. Alive. That's not normal." *And now we're going to die. I spent so much time blaming and hating instead of fixing myself.*

"Granted, it may not be normal, but it makes you perfect." He said it like he'd been explaining it to her for hours. He cupped her shoulders, digging his thumbs into the cramped tension. "You're the bravest woman I know, Gretch. There's nothing wrong with you, and you know if there was, I'd be the first one to point it out."

She managed a smile. How typically pigheaded of him not to admit she was right. But maybe that's where healing began. In the patience of someone who refused to allow damage to wedge in between them.

Sean cupped her cheeks. "Thank you for trusting me enough to share all this."

"I figured you ought to know my secret, since…we'll probably share a grave." She gazed at his stoic face. This man she'd constantly made fun of. Who didn't fit in and didn't care. The generosity he showed her now humbled her. Tears filled her eyes as she clasped him in a full embrace. "You should also know," she said, voice wobbling. *I love you.* "I have strong feelings for you." *Oh, fuck!*

See, the thing about Sean was: he got her. It was a copout, and he should have called her on it immediately. Instead, joy spread across his lovely fox face. His arms tightened around her again. "I love you too," he said.

She needed a minute to catch her breath. If only she were a girlie-girl who could squee and dance about when she was this happy. "Kinda sucks we're about to die, huh?" Her voice hitched.

"Hell no. 'These are the times that try men's souls.' That's all this is."

She blinked a few times, waiting for his point to sink in. It didn't. "Are you spouting poetry hoping to get in my pants?"

"Is it working?"

"No. I'd like to find a way out of here. I want a future with you beyond sunset."

His gaze slid to the slats. The gentle humor in his face dissolved. "Let's shore up your fighting skills, okay?"

She nodded, but as his arms loosened hers tightened. She couldn't face jumping back into that gripping fear. *Pretend there's hope.* "When we do get out of this alive," she said haltingly, "and we will, you're...well...you're going to need a lot of poetry."

He grinned mischievously. It was a great look on him. His fingers tangled in her hair again, and he bent closer. "I've memorized enough poetry to keep you in multiple orgasms for years, Gretch."

Thrills shot through her. "Huh," she breathed, glancing at his curved lips in anticipation.

"Now toss me until it's second nature."

***

JACE THREW himself in the driver's side. If it hadn't been for the new agent beside him, he'd have pounded his fists on the steering wheel. Adyton had been nothing but charming and blasé. The interview a perfunctory waste of time. No, he hadn't seen Mr. Bixby and Miss Allen from Moore and Morrow. Appropriate murmurs of concern. A sigh of regret. *The fucker.*

Inga shut the passenger door. "Where to next?"

Perfect. Give me free rein. "El Bashtan at BAM is at the bottom of the totem pole, but more likely to want to keep it that way even if it means squealing on the higher-ups. I say we visit him at the market and shake him down."

Inga nodded and sent back a message to head-quarters.

Once at the large marketplace, Jace marched up to the bushy-browed, bearded man at his tiny corner desk. "William Bixby," he said, slapping a photograph of Sean on top of the paperwork El Bashtan was poring over. "Seen him lately?"

The man studied the photo without expression. He looked up. "He came to my booth on Monday, and I saw him again on Tuesday at a colleague's shop."

The man's calm-to-the-point-of-cocky demeanor was a flash trigger setting off Jace's rage again. He leaned over the table, almost gagging at El Bashtan's ripe garlic breath.

"We have you on smuggling charges, Mr. El Bashtan. You've been receiving blood artifacts that came in from Frankfurt for months. We'll overlook an occasional bauble, but kidnapping and murder? We'll come down on you like a ton of bricks. Do you understand?"

Inga cleared her throat, but Jace took no notice. "Where is this man?" he asked with as much menace as he could muster.

El Bashtan's eye contact never wavered. "I don't know."

"Does Adyton know?" The man shrugged. Jace replaced Sean's photo with one of Gretch. "What about her?"

El Bashtan's gaze lingered on Gretch a moment too

long. It was all Jace could do not to snatch the photo back. He was losing it. He knew it, and there was nothing he could do except plow on. He was out of options. Except beating El Bashtan to a fucking pulp until he talked. Inga's phone dinged with an incoming text.

"I have not seen Mrs. *Bixby* since Tuesday morning either," El Bashtan said, his emphasis on the false name no doubt a middle finger raised at the FBI and their bumbling attempt to crack the blood artifact ring. He glanced at his watch and a ghost of a smile appeared. "I've answered your questions. I hope everything works out for the couple."

"Yes, Mr. El Bashtan. Thank you for your time." Inga pushed Jace out of the booth.

He scrubbed a hand over his face. "Give me a few more minutes with him."

She all but shoved him into the elevator and punched the button for the garage. "God damn it, Quinn, what's your problem?"

This was it; he'd pushed too far. "I'm sorry," he muttered. "Don't take me off the case." He wouldn't survive life without Sean. Couldn't live with the knowledge that because of his own epic failure, Sean and Gretch might be beheaded. Come to think of it, El Bashtan had looked a little too self-satisfied. Horror clutched Jace's throat.

Inga's phone dinged again, and she glared at the screen instead of him. The elevator doors opened with a long screech.

"It's Garcia," she said, striding rapidly through the parking lot. Jace sent up a prayer of thanks it wasn't the words he'd expected. "Your task force just surrounded the warehouse on Knox. We'll head there as backup." She glanced over at him. "This is your last chance to pull it together. Garcia says to tell you the honeymoon from the Donatello arrest is over."

"I can—" An earth-shattering explosion erupted, and they instinctively ducked. The blast was far enough away it was obvious the market wasn't the target. Near enough that it rocked the massive structure like it was made of matchsticks. Screams and shattering glass filled the air.

"Let's go!" Inga shouted, racing for the SUV.

Functional adrenalin pumped through Jace as he vaulted into the driver's seat. He peeled through the sharp ramp turns like an Indie racer. By the time he pulled onto the jammed street, Inga had both her phone and his plastered to her ears. The scanner radio squawked an address on Knox. Jace frowned as he flipped on the grill lights and swerved in and out of blaring, grid-locked cars. "Call Garcia," he shouted over the din. "The address sounds like the warehouse we were heading to."

He blasted through a red light, barely missing an ambulance careening around the corner. He waved the vehicle ahead. Its siren would clear a path faster than his SUV.

Inga yelled the question several times before the caller heard her. She plugged her ear and lowered her head, listening. When she sat up, her face was pale and drawn. "It *is* the warehouse your task force seized."

Jace frowned. *Who would blow up millions of dollars of Adyton's black market artifacts?*

"Place was rigged with explosives," she continued in a tight voice. "Casualties reported."

Dirk! Shit. Jace clenched his teeth and focused on the ambulance fender ahead.

39

Things were looking up. Sean's wrists were once again tied behind his back, but with rope, which provided more pull. The lethal weapon presently at his disposal was his geekiness. Pair that with the element of surprise and it was lights out for the three men leading them down the narrow staircase. Underestimating him would be their demise.

A simple dropkick in this enclosed space and the two men in front of him would tumble like dominos. Unfortunately, Gretch was directly in front of them. She'd end up at the bottom of the broken-necked heap.

Sean's heart beat steadily despite the Dead Man Walking journey they were on. All he had to do was keep a sharp eye out for the next opportunity.

One by one, they rounded the tight landing leading to the ground floor where the bakery was located. Out the window the sun had set, and a lamppost shone weakly. Sean paused, searching for anyone out there, but the back alley was empty. Victor prodded him from behind, and Sean descended the last set of stairs. Enticing aromas of buttery cake, cinnamon, and nutmeg drifted up. He was thirsty and famished enough to sell his vegan soul for any of it. In the distance, a television played a news channel loudly.

"...updating our breaking story. A pipe bomb went off in the warehouse district. There are an unknown number of casualties at this time..."

The hair on Sean's neck prickled. They'd both heard and felt an explosion a few hours ago in the attic. Clearly the FBI had shaken trees, and Adyton was carrying out his threat. But a warehouse? Adyton had made it sound like the bombs would target areas with potential mass casualties, like a theater or a park.

Gretch reached the bottom and stumbled, hitting the wall with her shoulder. Sean turned his head to the side and spoke to the nephew. "She needs to eat and drink."

"She won't be hungry or thirsty for long. Don't be giving me no orders, homie."

Homie. Victor had grown up in the belly of America, yet taught to hate the customs and culture he took from willingly. It was all so fucking senseless.

They reached the bottom and clustered near the back entrance, where they'd come in this morning. Victor pointed to the doors. "When we open these, you'll walk directly to the minivan. If either of you draws any atten-tion, we'll kill you out there. Which would suck for my family's businesses, and I'll make sure you suffer. Got it?"

Gretch nodded. Sean stayed silent and alert. One of the men stupidly had his gun stashed in the back of his jeans. The other guy, Black Hoodie, held his too loosely. Victor, however, gripped his 9mm tight as he pushed on the door. Cool air blanketed the crowded space. A car horn blared in the distance, answered by a longer, high-pitched one.

"Move out."

The two men flanked him and Gretch closely, and

Victor brought up the rear. Anyone looking out the window wouldn't notice two of the cluster had their hands tied behind them.

A dark minivan's passenger doors stood open, displaying two rows of tan back seats. Victor guided Gretch up front and loomed in her doorway, buckling her so slowly Sean caught the clear stiffening in her shoulders.

"Don't you worry, sweetheart." Victor tugged on the seatbelt. "You're not dying anytime soon. We plan on having a whole lotta fun with you first."

"Fucker!" Gretch tried to head-butt him, but he lurched to the side. She got a fumbling kick off, which caught him in the thigh. Victor whispered an obscenity, and a resounding slap rent the air. Gretch cried out in fury. The two other men pushed Sean toward the side door.

He gritted his teeth. *Now!* He reverse-pivoted, sweeping the knees out from Black Hoodie, who went down with a surprised *oof* and a heavy thud.

Sean kneed the second man in the groin, then used the man's crouched-over position for more momentum to finish him with a front-snap kick to the chin. The man flew backward, bashing the back of his head into the side of the van. He went down in a heap.

Click. Cold steel pressed into Sean's temple. Victor gripped the back of his t-shirt and slammed him into the van, profanities streaming from him. "Get. The fuck. In!"

Sean stumbled into the van, only to be hauled out, repositioned, and shoved in the far back row. He fell sideways onto the seat. By the time he'd righted himself, Victor was helping Hoodie up. "Where's your gun?"

The guy wiped his bloody lip. "It slid under the van."

"Shit. We're wasting time!" Victor handed off his 9mm. "Sit in the middle," he spat. "If either of them move, blow their heads off!" He bent over the man retching on the ground. "Sayid! Let's go." Sayid waved him off.

Victor spun around, cocked a finger gun at Sean, and pulled the trigger. "You're so fucking dead."

Sean grinned, adrenalin pumping energy and focus. He was so ready for this to end. So ready to defend Gretch from gang rape until his dying breath. "Bring it," he said through his teeth. "Right now."

Instead, Victor yanked the door handle. As the side door automatically lumbered closed, he jogged around the van.

Black Hoodie gaped at Sean with wide eyes that held a healthy degree of fear. Blood still leaked from the right corner of his mouth. He leaned back against the driver's seat, the 9mm shakily aimed at Sean. When the driver's-side door slammed shut and the van light went out, he said in a trembling voice, "Victor, anyone could have seen or heard us."

"Shut up, Nizar." Victor peeled out, but when he reached the busier city streets, he drove cautiously, his gaze in the rearview mirror switching between Sean and Nizar.

Minutes passed into miles. At each traffic light, Gretch leaned against her door and stared out the window. Sean fought a smile. *Play to your strengths, babe.* Ever the magnet for men's attention, she was clearly trying to signal someone, anyone they passed. Very few pedestrians were out, and the ones who were looked shell-shocked. The bomb... How many people had died? Had the FBI backed off Adyton and the investigation to flock to the scene?

The van turned onto State and picked up speed. Victor blew through a yellow light, and Nizar gasped. "Do you want cops breathing down our necks?"

"We're on the other side of town now," Victor scoffed. "The cops are over by the bombing. I could kill these two on the sidewalk and not have a pig anywhere near here."

Sean's heart rate picked up. No lucky breaks tonight. The city had been terrorized by a no-name group, and Adyton was counting on ISIS to take the credit.

The van plowed down Milwaukee, only blocks away from the Chinese restaurant he'd brought Gretch to yesterday. God, *yesterday*!

Sean worked the wrist binds, which quickly broke through the scabs again. But this rope was looser and more pliable than the zip tie, and he was gaining momentum. Not enough for freedom. Enough to slip his arms under his tucked body and have the distinct advantage of being bound in the front. This would open up blocks, chops, and strangulation options.

Struggling into the tuck under watchful eyes and a pointed gun, however, wasn't optimal. The bench seat between him and Nizar was the only visual protection he was going to get, and Sean steadily slumped down, working his overly stretched arms around the soles of his sneakers. Where he got stuck. He hid the grimace of pain. If his arms gave another millimeter, his shoulders would pop out of their sockets. He broke out in a sweat and gasped air.

Under the streetlights streaming past, Nizar kept the gun trained on him, but the metal quivered, as did his voice. "You're doing it, right, Victor?"

No answer. Victor flashed his brights at someone and swerved into an empty lot filled with rows of dumpsters and surrounded by a chain-link fence. A dark form held the gate open and closed it after they'd passed through. Back to three men; two now knew Sean could fight.

The van screeched to a halt. In Sean's compromised tuck, he rolled off the seat. Using the momentum of his fall, he wrenched his arms the final bit, grunting from the shock of pain in his shoulders. His left knee smashed something metal on the floor, and stars burst before his eyes. He snaked his stiff arms up the front of his body.

"Where'd he go?" Victor's voice held deep suspicion.

Before Nizar could glance over the seatback, Sean hauled himself up enough to stick his chin between the headrests. "Learn how to drive, douche." His voice was weary with pain. The hunger and thirst made his muscles quivery and weak. He had no time for this!

Victor snapped his gaze to his friend, jaw twitching. "Yes. To answer your question. You better fucking believe I'm doing this."

The guy outside yanked the passenger-side handle, and the heavy door lumbered open. The interior light blinked on. The overpowering stench of refuse and mildew wafted in. Sean swallowed his revulsion and braced his aching shoulders. His glance skimmed the three terrorists and landed on Gretch, awkwardly turned in her seat to see if he was okay. He quirked a brow, something that usually annoyed the hell out of her, and her eyes filled with tears.

"Leave her here. She can watch." Victor unbelted himself and slammed out of the vehicle.

This was it. Adrenalin kicked in. Before two men became three, Sean dove forward, knocking the barrel of the gun with his bound wrists. It clattered to the floor. He encircled Nizar's head and yanked him into the headrest dividing them, then heard and felt the man's nose crack, followed by a shrieking howl. Using the momentum of his grip, he swung his right heel up, connecting to the new guy's Adam's apple as he leaned in the doorway. The guy flew out into the night.

"Squirm out of the seatbelt, Gretch," Sean said, panting. "We're about to book." He squeezed to the open door and launched himself at Victor, coming around the back-side. The surprise on the bodybuilder's face was price-less. Sean body-slammed him to the ground. Victor's breath *wooshed* out just as Sean's injured kneecap struck asphalt. He roared in pain and gasped breaths, trying to regroup from the white-hot agony. The stench of putre-fying refuse and Victor's body wash were all over him now too. Sean's stomach heaved. He squeezed his eyes shut, but the stink was overwhelming. His brain went on overload, dissecting the layers, strongest first. *Sour milk. Decomposing rodent. Mildew...*

"Sean!" Gretch screamed. "Sean, get up!"

He rolled off Victor and opened his eyes. Stars twin-kled. *Feces. Hopefully dog.* He had precious seconds left to get up. *Rotting fish.* Standing meant he could strike, block, or kick. If he lay here obsessing about smells, he'd end up in a wrestling match with useless hands and a bum knee. *Victor's sweet-woodsy wash...no. More syrupy than sweet. And a hint of something dark, like tobacco. No. More like...*

"Sean!"

Shut. It. Down. Gretch's life is on the line!

Sean sat up and shook his head violently. Clarity prevailed. No way would he allow himself to die here in a lot filled with decaying garbage. He scrambled to his feet, and his leg buckled, knifing pain through him. "Shit." Shifting his weight onto his right leg, he limped toward the open passenger door. The 9mm lay on the floor.

Two feet away, Nizar sprawled across the middle row, wailing and wiping the gushing blood from his swollen nostrils. He silenced when he registered Sean's focus on the gun. Victor rolled onto his knees. The new guy remained on the ground, back heaving as he gasped for breath. A sedan slowly drove by, but turned the corner.

Fighting fair was out the window. Just as Nizar reached for the pistol Sean lunged and grabbed him off the seat, hurling him, WWE-style, into Victor. They both collapsed in a heap. Sean hobbled over and opened Gretch's door. Thankfully, she was out of the seatbelt as instructed, but her hands were still behind her; she wouldn't be able to defend herself or hold the gun if need be.

Sean whipped the 9mm off the floor and aimed it at the bodies on the asphalt. "Get up," he snarled. Victor climbed slowly to his feet. The other two remained conscious but were clearly down for the count.

Sean felt more than saw Gretch's presence by his left shoulder. "Untie her," he ordered, limping over to Victor and sticking the barrel to his temple.

Within seconds, Gretch's rope fell off, and she untied Sean.

"You think you'll get away with this?" Victor sneered. "My great-uncle will burn this city down."

"I'm betting his blood tie is stronger than his mission. Your life for millions of Chicagoans? He'll trade." Sean waved the gun at the three men. "Gretch, get one of their phones and call nine-one-one."

"Let me just do this one thing," Gretch answered, turning to Victor, lips curled into a snarl. "This is for Dwayne." She hauled off and slapped the bodybuilder so hard he staggered. Before he could recover, she grabbed his arm and snapped him over her shoulder. His body thudded onto the asphalt. He let out a long groan and lay still.

"That was beautiful," Sean said. Victor had over a hundred pounds of muscle on her, and she'd taken him down like a pro. "Great form."

She bowed with a smile. "Thank you, Sensei." A quiet confidence came to her eyes. A true sense of control. No man would ever successfully mess with her again.

40

———

S wirling azure lights of the CPD, garnet lights of the CFD, and numerous high-beams all mixed together, blinding Sean. He slouched in the open doorway of an ambulance, sipping water like an elixir while a tech swabbed alcohol on his bloody wrists and knuckles. An ice pack was firmly wrapped around his throbbing knee.

He glanced at Gretch, ten feet away. She sported a serious case of hat hair and a bruised cheek from Victor slapping her, and Trick's t-shirt covered her like a sloppy CFD tent. Sean couldn't remember her more beautiful. *Real.* Although uninjured, she was attended to by three strapping EMS guys, whom she completely ignored. She tilted her head and smiled at Sean like he was a hero.

Yeah. He officially was. The final Quinn to reach that status. But he shook his head gently, hoping his meaning was clear. Life would suck if Gretch lost her sass and started fawning over him.

"I'd like to check on her," he said to the tech ripping the backing off a bandage.

"Soon."

Jace hurried around the back of the vehicle, breaking into a relieved smile. "Hey." He hunkered down and embraced Sean, which seemed much more natural than the shoulder-clap attempt at O'Hare a week ago. "You look a hell of a lot better than those three."

Sean's lips twitched. "You should have seen Gretch go after them. Wasn't pretty. She totally saved the day."

"We know it was you, Nancy." Jace cuffed him gently and pulled out his phone. "Mom wants to FaceTime immediately."

"Not yet." Sean leaned forward. "Listen, that bomb—how many people died?"

"Three agents. Including Dirk."

The breath left Sean's body in a whoosh. "I'm sorry, Jace. You know it was Adyton, right?"

His brother nodded tightly.

"What did he blow up?"

"That warehouse you went to on Knox."

Sean jerked in surprise. "He blew up his *own* merchandise?"

"Turns out it wasn't his place."

"He had a key. He gave it to his great-nephew."

Jace shifted his weight and brushed a knuckle across his eyelid. "Then it must have been stolen. You were taken to his rival's warehouse. Adyton probably planned to kill you there and our focus would have reverted straight onto the rival. A Tomas Hussain."

Hussain… "That's the buyer's name on a bogus sixty-million-dollar inventory list. According to Gretch, Adyton's artifacts are only worth a hundred thousand. He's hiding money, or maybe some kind of sophisticated money-laundering scheme."

"I doubt the inventory list is legitimate. We've interviewed Hussain for hours. Those men have never done business together; they're on opposite sides of the Syrian civil war. Adyton's gone out of his way to set up Hussain these last few days."

"He's gone out of his way to set up Chicago and the government, Jace." Sean waved into the night. "Adyton planted many more bombs and will set them off every time the FBI interferes." He quickly told Jace all they'd learned about the small faction letting ISIS claim responsibility, the confession to Dwayne's death, and now wanting negotiating power for a U.S. exodus in Syria. Jace texted somebody like a demented man.

"So whatever your task force did today to interfere set off the first bomb," Sean said, smoothing a jagged tear in the label of his water bottle. "Maybe use his great-nephew's custody—he's the bodybuilder over there—to negotiate a ceasefire." Sean paused. "Also, Walter, our boss, may be involved. I really hope it's an ignorant business deal."

"It isn't," Jace said. "We've spent hours interrogating the anthropology consultant—"

"I know Joe."

Jace scowled. "Turns out he's been supplying false provenances for Adyton's artifacts. And guess what? He's Walter's cousin."

It still didn't add up. "I know it looks bad, but Walter doesn't even jaywalk. Besides, if the sixty-million-dollar list was bogus, then all Moore and Morrow did was accept a gold-leaf Quran from a then-legitimate antiques dealer."

Jace massaged his bristled jaw. His exhaustion and puffy features made him look ten years older than the self-assured renegade who'd taunted Sean on the way to the airport. His phone dinged, and tension ratcheted up his spine. "I gotta go." He clapped Sean's shoulder. "Listen. You did great work this week. I'm damn proud to call you my brother."

Sean blinked. The words and the sincerity resounded like an echo in his head. If only he had a recording device to hear it again just to be sure. To replay over and over when his brain wasn't this fatigued. To overlay onto a Mozart sonata... His brother stared at him expectantly.

Sean shrugged and flushed. "You too."

"Say. There's an opening for a consultant." His brother broke into a sheepish grin as he stuck his phone back in his suit pocket. "I'd be happy to recommend you."

Sean dredged enough energy to return the grin. "I'm ready to go back to my unobtrusive life, thank you. Listen, have you heard anything about my students?"

"No one was harmed, and the little guy Phillip is being treated as a national champ. He was on the *Today* show this morning."

Good. Phillip deserved the kudos, and would no doubt stand up to any future bullies at school. "And the painting?"

"Boston already came and got it. Donatello made bail this morning." Jace looked a little green saying both sentences.

Sean couldn't resist poking him further. "And now this. Who'd have thought I'd save the day and get the girl?"

His brother frowned.

"Aw, come on, Jace." Sean broke into a grin. "You've gotta know by now that she likes me better."

They both glanced at Gretch, whose eyes were trained on them. When Jace saluted, she waved. Her gaze strayed back to Sean, and a small smile played on her lips. Jace *did* see this, right?

"Well, shit." His brother cleared his throat. "You know how hard this is for me?"

Sean nodded, warmth skidding through his veins.

Jace checked his watch and jerked his head. "Come

on. Looks like she needs rescuing from the throng." He assisted Sean up, and they pushed their way past the hovering technicians. Gretch seemed completely at ease with five men jostling before her. Her smile morphed into something more sassy and royal.

Jace reached for her hand. "We could have been something, you and me," he said solemnly, "but I'm going to have to uninvite you to my mom's birthday party."

"Okay," she answered, barely giving him a glance. That weird feeling settled over Sean again. He wasn't used to winning The Girl. Certainly not one who had the rapt attention of medical personnel and who barely registered his hero brother.

Sean stuffed his hands in his pockets at her expectant expression. Naturally, his brother, who'd been in a hurry moments ago, wouldn't move off, and the other men turned one by one, to eye Sean's lingering presence in puzzlement. "Would you...uh...like to...meet my family Sunday?" he stammered. He didn't mean for his eyebrows to tilt upward—she hated that.

She nodded, beaming. "Yeah. I'd like that a lot."

Euphoria spread like molten lava through his tired limbs. "Great." He smiled so hard his cheeks hurt. Score one for the geeks.

41

———

Gretch writhed beneath Sean's powerful thrusts. Quaking desire built to pulsing tingles and something else, just out of reach. The haunting notes of *Cavalleria rusticana* strained to a crescendo over stereo speakers.

"'And when convulsive throes denied my breath,'" Sean muttered, nipping her earlobe. She moaned and gripped his undulating ass, tilting her pelvis higher, searching...

"'The faintest utterance to my fading—'"

There! "Oh my God," she shrieked, as lightning arced through her, sizzling every nerve. She squirmed wildly as he plunged again and again, drawing out her throbbing orgasm. Suddenly his eyelids squeezed shut and his muscles seized. A harsh groan escaped his clenched teeth. Gretch gaped at the passionate intensity on his face. A new emotion rushed hotly through her—one that was clean and loving. It wasn't about control at all; it was about giving. *She'd* put that joy on his face. She'd made him pant like this.

He sagged onto her, the pulse in his neck hammering rapidly. Sweat trickled from his temples. He opened those deep brown eyes and broke into a smoldering grin. "Jeez, Gretch, I think they heard you down the block."

No way was she taking that as a jibe. She'd done it! She'd come with a man inside her. Who knew it could be this wonderful? She exhaled a luxurious sigh. "Wow. This was just... Wow."

"Sooo, that's interesting." He quirked a brow. "Sex makes you pleasant—"

Guess so, because instead of snark, gushy words of love hovered on the tip of her tongue. In movies the characters immediately shared gooey feelings, but real life? This was all brand new. She'd have to take her cue from Sean. He rose on an elbow and fumbled for the remote, lowering the volume. The strong lines of his traps and delts undulated with the task. She sighed deeply. Yeah, maybe she'd have to take the lead in this area. "I...love you."

The corners of his eyes crinkled as he glanced down at her. "And I have strong feelings for you too, Gretch."

They burst into silly laughter, the movement ungluing their damp bodies. The subtle slide of him sparked tiny tremors back to life. On instinct, she cinched her legs around his ass and squeezed, extracting every last mini jolt. She reveled in his sharp inhale, the comfortable intimacy between them.

"When can we do it again?" Even the husky eagerness in her voice was a milestone.

He chuckled, the vibrations from his chest warming her blood. "When have you ever asked for something nicely?" He aimed the remote at her nose and pressed buttons. "The queen's gotta be in there somewhere."

He had a point. Her fawning was annoying her. She

snatched the device and shoved it under the pillow. "Next time I'm on top," she proclaimed regally.

"You'll love it up there." He grinned wryly and lowered his head, kissing her earlobe, her temple, her cheek, then finally trapping her mouth. His tongue milked more shivers. After a long while, he broke off with a contented grunt and pulled out of her. "No more lollygagging. We've got a big day ahead."

"Lollygagging?" she muttered. "Who even *says* that? Was it in the poem? It can't have been. That would've turned me right off."

"Thank *God* you've returned unharmed." His grin sculpted hollows in his cheeks. "I thought my extraordinary lovemaking skills conquered your rudeness for good."

She slapped his bicep, hard. In retaliation, he kissed her nipples reverently, then slid down her body and planted a lingering kiss on the chess queen, an area he seemed to be obsessed with, which was downright hilarious. Still, beneath the silky press of his tongue, she twitched impatiently as her new sensuality awoke. Of their own volition, her thighs parted further in invitation.

Sean paused over the juncture, his angular face taking on a hungry wolf look. "You're a siren," he muttered, his breath tickling her in exquisite torture. "We don't have time for this."

He sat up and stripped off the condom, folding it neatly inside a tissue like a miniature package. She rolled her eyes and trailed fingers along the etched lat muscles of his bowed back.

His phone buzzed on the bedside table. "Jace," he announced, and pushed speakerphone. "What's up?"

She loved the new confidence in his voice.

"I told Mom to cancel her party tomorrow," Jace said in his authoritative bark. "All law enforcement branches are still searching Chicago for the bombs. Trick's even gone straight from a forty-eight-hour shift to volunteer. We've successfully retrieved three so far. Who knows how many are left."

Sean shot her a grim look over his shoulder. He inched the phone closer as if she couldn't hear from this side of the bed. "Have you arrested Adyton," he asked, "or are you afraid to?"

His brother let out a weary sigh. "He's in custody. We're in very complicated negotiations, but he's on the losing end, and my gut says he's ready to finish this."

"He didn't strike me as a guy who thought he had much to lose."

"He does now. We have his great-nephew and all the merchandise he stored in Donatello's warehouses."

The sinewy muscles along Sean's torso contracted as he inhaled deeply. "What about Walter?"

"We've got him for altering a price point on the fake inventory list for Hussain, which is technically money laundering, but your boss has agreed to work with us to take down Joe Taylor's counterfeit provenance business and will also testify once we fold Adyton's op."

Gretch sat up and plastered herself along Sean's back. "Count us in too," she called toward the phone. "I'd be happy to help the prosecution, especially for that fuck-head Victor."

"Oh. Hi, Gretch." The tinny voice took on a strange tone, and Sean both blushed and beamed.

"Anything else?" he asked Jace, crisscrossing her arms over his chest like the sleeves of a sweater. "We've got a full day."

"I'll bet you do," his brother murmured, a clear sulk attached to the words. Gretch kissed Sean's ear and folded back on the bed like Cleopatra.

Sean ended the call and twisted, running his palm

along her hip. "You did that on purpose," he accused, although the reverence in his expression belied his tone.

"It strikes me your brother is never on the losing end with you. In anything. I figured a reminder once in a while might be healthy for his ego."

His gaze lingered on hers, the tenderness there stealing her oxygen. "Thanks."

It was suddenly too much, all this lovey-doveyness between them. "Do you think I'd make a good FBI agent?" she asked archly, so he wouldn't know how much his answer meant to her. Naturally, he saw right past her act and stroked her hip thoughtfully.

"You're efficient. Good at getting people to do things your way. And I'm in awe of your courage." He nodded. "Yeah, you'd make a great agent, Gretch. You've got all the characteristics of a hero. And being a Quinn, I'm a master expert on that subject."

Sean, Jace, and Trick. All superheroes in their own right. No doubt all hiding layers of conflict and damage. "You Quinn boys sure are a lot of trouble. I'm trying to make up my mind whether any of you are worth it."

He grinned, trailing his hand around back and smacking her rump hard enough to sting.

"Ow!"

"Get up, princess. As soon as I've scrubbed you in the shower, I have a tin of mints in my book bag I've been meaning to give you." He brushed a thumb along her chess queen tattoo.

She frowned. "Are you implying that I smell bad?"

"God, no. That pepper scent is exactly right for you."

He'd said that before. "A pepper? What the hell's wrong with your nose?"

"Nothing. You're hot and spicy." He snatched her borrowed shorts and t-shirt from the floor. "And a slob. Look at this place."

She scanned his neat room, making sure her pout looked bored. The sterile place didn't reveal the complex layers she was discovering by the minute. Like his outer façade, this functional space lacked personalization or warmth. It made her ache for the saggy purple sofa-and-chair combo, or Dwayne's outrageous collection of male nudes. Her place was still a crime scene, so the day ahead included retrieving some clothes there, then going to Dwayne's memorial service in the evening. Gretch sobered and sat up, hugging her knees.

"He would have liked you," she said, perusing Sean's lithe body and sensational ass as he crossed to the bathroom.

"He did like me," he called, turning on the shower. See? He automatically knew who she was talking about. "We chatted Tuesday morning while you prettied yourself up."

She rested her chin on her knees. "Chatted about what?"

"Stuff."

She smiled. Of course Sean wouldn't elaborate or gossip. Even two days ago, that would have annoyed the hell out of her. Now she liked the way he kept confidences. Warmed at how he had his own memory of Dwayne that he didn't feel was necessary to share. She held zero control or influence over him, and appreciated every challenging second.

Sean reappeared in the doorway, splendidly nude and all hers. Last week this would have shocked her stupid. Now her heart thudded a trembling rhythm. "By any chance do you ballroom dance?"

He folded his arms. "No. That would have been the last straw for my father. There's no doubt in my mind he'd have kicked me to the sidewalk." He grinned at whatever image went through his head. "Why?"

"I've always wanted to waltz."

He nodded. "Then I'll sign up for lessons on Monday." He swept an arm wide. "Any day now, your majesty."

She nodded. The sheer force of love swelling in her chest kept her in the tucked position. "In a sec."

Sean rapped twice on the threshold and disappeared inside. Okay, so *one* behavior had to stop. "Has anyone ever encouraged that?" she called.

"Encouraged what?" He popped his head back out, his quirky eyebrows tilting. It was a look she'd grown to adore, and it took a second to recover her snark.

"That." She waved her hands. "Knocking twice when you leave a room. What the hell does it mean? And don't say 'ancient Chinese secret.'"

A slow grin bloomed on his face. He braced a bicep on the threshold. "I swear I don't even realize I'm doing it."

"Is it a secret code?"

"Sort of." He shrugged, a flush creeping up his neck. "When I was a kid, my brothers instilled a healthy fear of ghosts in me." He patted the crown molding. "This is how I'd warn the spirits I was entering a room."

She sucked in a breath. See, just when you understood Sean, he'd say something to knock you for a loop. That annoying knock wasn't his introverted signal for goodbye. It was a hello to the spirit world. "Do you still believe in ghosts?"

"Sure," he said in a tone like she'd asked a ridiculous question. "Doesn't everybody?"

She also loved that he kept her in constant surprise—and yes, okay, slightly annoyed. But her adult self ached for the little boy who'd been so indoctrinated to alert ghosts of his silent presence that he carried the habit still.

She stood and swept across the room, giddy at the

way he ate up her nudity, purposely grinding out her haute runway walk. She had a freaking boyfriend! And it was *Sean Quinn*.

Gretch knocked the threshold twice as she sailed by him. "You coming or what?"

ACKNOWLEDGMENTS

Once again, my heartfelt, undying, gushing thanks to Anya Kagan of Touchstone Editing for the embarrassingly large number of hours you took shaping this story, patiently talking me off ledges, and always maintaining that wry sense of humor. Thanks, also, for helping me brainstorm *Damaged Heroes*: *Book Three*, a.k.a. "Best Book Ever."

Christa Holland, of Paper and Sage, for another amazing, compelling cover. This is sooo Sean!

Arran McNicol of Editing720 for providing copy edits with a super-sized side of humor. Note to self: don't look over the comments while drinking coffee.

John R. Stanton, a.k.a my Real Life Superhero for butching up my alpha-speak, correcting the details of JTTF, CBP, TSA, and all things weaponry.

Amazing author Elizabeth Heiter for her KOD FBI course. Any errors within are what I like to call: creative license.

Kelly Reid for capturing my heart sixteen years ago and, more recently, describing a precise gesture in Chapter Three. That being said, girlfriend, do *not* turn the page and start reading! Maybe in five years or so... Seriously. Close the book now. 😜

Mark Kraushaar for taking the time to provide kickass martial arts advice and lingo even though you're one of the busiest men I know.

Lark Howard and Judy Jaastad, my go-to CPs, for slogging through the dreck-filled drafts of this story. Only you two know just how badly I write. (Remember the pinkie-swear pact of never telling anyone else...) Thank you also, Lark, for the riveting back-cover blurb.

M.E. Stanton for shaping my lifelong love of operas and classical music. Also for the rich description of a Vermeer painting so I could cherry-pick jargon to sound like my artist character.

Kim Huther of wordsmithproofreading, many thanks for your eagle-eyed proofreading services.

My "It Takes a Village" people: Mary Lynn Ziemer, Collin Brown, Dee Harris, and Anna Toole. I'm so grateful for your cheerful optimism, high energy, and the lengths you've gone to these last month to keep me sane and svelte through my deadlines.

Lastly, to Scott. Thank you for putting up with the Other Me, that monster of cranky moods, questionable hygiene, and the demeanor of a daydreaming zombie. Nothing romantic about being married to a romance writer, huh? I love you. 🩶

We'll play golf soon. Real soon.

ABOUT THE AUTHOR

ROMANTIC SUSPENSE THAT KEEPS YOU UP ALL NIGHT

Sarah Andre is a RITA® finalist, which is Romance Writers of America highest award of distinction. She lives in serene Southwest FL with her husband and two naughty Pomeranians. When she's not writing, Sarah is either reading or coloring. Yes, you read that right. She's all over those coloring books for adults.

For more information please visit:
www.SarahAndre.com

facebook.com/SarahAndreNovels

twitter.com/SarahRSWriter

goodreads.com/Sarah_Andre

bookbub.com/authors/sarah-andre

ALSO BY SARAH ANDRE

Locked, Loaded and Lying

THE DAMAGED HEROES SERIES:

Tall, Dark and Damaged

Capturing the Queen

A Savage Trick

Incendiary Attraction

EXCERPT FROM A SAVAGE TRICK

DAMAGED HEROES, BOOK THREE

CHAPTER ONE

The ransacked living room spiked a fresh surge of panic. Trick Quinn paused in the threshold, forcing in a *pranayama* breath. Why the hell did this mayhem still catch him off guard? Sofa cushions and magazines were strewn across the carpet. Articles of clothing dangled from various chairs. Even the blinds hung at irregular angles... *Eve would have a heart attack if she walked in here.*

Trick shook his head. Who was he kidding? First, even without the restraining order, she wouldn't set foot in here. Second, it was way past time to stop seeing life through the lens of his wife's perceptions. This was Pete's house and Pete's mess. Trick's bedroom was spotless, as was his freshly ironed shirt with the CFD logo. That was good enough.

Trick crossed to the kitchen—another disaster zone. Today's *Chicago Tribune* lay among the debris littering the counter. From seven feet away, the photo of Trick's own face on the front page startled him a second time. *Firefighter Hero Accused of...*

"Damn it." He shut his eyes to the rest, a wave of

despair threatening to mow him down. All around the city, people—including his parents and brothers—were waking to new lies about Lieutenant Patrick Quinn's depravity. No amount of protesting his innocence, no stellar professional record, and definitely no cleansing yoga breath could combat the onslaught of accusations. "Damn it," he repeated, scrubbing his face.

He'd face the article soon enough—had to, so he'd know how to gear up for today's battle—but couldn't stomach it before coffee. He placed the CFD walkie-talkie on the counter beside the Keurig machine, which had a yellow sticky note taped to the handle. *Fed Blaze and put him out back. –6:30a. P.*

Trick crumpled the note, popped in a pod, then opened the back door and whistled. "Good boy," he called as his nine-year-old Irish setter loped happily across the fenced-in lawn. Trick smiled, embracing this one moment where his dog's joy superseded all the negativity in the wreckage of his life.

"Catch any squirrels, boy?" He scratched Blaze's head, then crouched down and accepted a couple of wet licks up his cheek. "You and me—we're gonna turn this crap around today, all right?"

The walkie-talkie toned out the alarm for Station 74. Not Trick's firehouse, and besides, his shift didn't begin for a couple hours, now that he was stuck on admin duties. "Engine Forty-Three, Ambulance Three," Dispatch began, "residential fire, two-twenty North Whipple Street…"

Trick's hand stalled in his dog's fur, a sense of déjà vu paralyzing him. That was his address… Eve and the girls! "Please, God," he whispered, bolting upright and snatching the radio. "Please be safe."

He sprinted out of the house and jumped into his pickup. His breath came in shallow gasps as he gunned the engine to life and slapped the portable strobe light on his dashboard. "Dear God, dear God, dear God," he chanted, but couldn't add to the prayer. Couldn't conceive of a life without Amy and Tina.

He flew down the residential streets, rolling through stop signs and roaring past slow drivers. "Come on, come on!" He should have been there to protect his babies... should have been a better dad...should have never let Eve push things this far in the first place.

Miles passed in agonizing slow motion until he finally squealed around the corner onto his street. His heart stalled. The entire house was engulfed. Flames leaped from the kitchen windows, and dark gray smoke billowed in viscous plumes from the back of the house, where their living room opened to a patch of backyard. The engine and truck were already curbside. The squad had charged the hoseline and stood poised for action behind the firefighter battering in the front door. Trick careened into the Farnsworth's driveway and scrambled out at a dead run.

"Trick," a high voice shouted, "Trick!" He craned his neck without slowing. Mrs. Collins stood near the engine, a garden spade in her right hand. "Your wife's inside!"

Next to her, the captain was waving him off. Trick wasn't on the crew. Wasn't in his turnout gear. Too emotionally attached for a rescue. Probably half a dozen other reasons. He didn't give a damn. "My kids," he yelled, racing up behind the men who'd breached the door.

The captain hollered his name as Trick grabbed the end of the hose.

"They went to practice," Mrs. Collins called. "Eve waved goodbye and went into the house."

Soccer. Jesus, it was Saturday. Trick nodded, his throat swelling with thanks for the grace of God. The scowling captain was striding up the path to stop him. Too bad. There was no way Eve would die by fire. The door gave way, and the men shuffled forward as the pressurized water strained to tear the hose up and out of their grips. Trick leaned into the powerful flow and nudged the man in front of him. "Haul some ass!"

"Goddam it, Quinn." The captain gripped the back of his shirt and dragged him out of the pitch-black inferno. "Are you out of your cotton-picking mind?" He thrust Trick several feet away.

"My wife's in there!"

"I was right beside your neighbor when she told you!" The captain waved irritably. "Go wait by the paramedics. Trust us to do our jobs, lieutenant. You know better than this. We'll get her out."

The paramedics stood beside their stretcher and gear, gaping at Trick. No doubt they'd seen his life free-fall these last couple of weeks. By their curious frowns, they probably figured he'd finally snapped. But who left their wife to die when they were trained to fight flames and rescue victims? He had the highest save record in the city, for cripes' sake, and here he stood, with his thumb up his ass!

Trick paced past EMS, too agitated to stand still. How on earth had it started? The flames predominantly centered in the living room. Had they found her yet? Visions of blackened corpses, curled in fetal positions, flooded his mind. A primal scream lodged in his throat.

"Heads up, lieutenant," one of the paramedics said, almost apologetically. He pointed over Trick's shoulder.

Trick glanced back, stifling a groan. Media vans were arriving. Lots of media vans, not just the three locals looking for an evening news snippet. Trick spun away, closing the distance to the front door again. Behind him, vehicle doors slammed and shouts of

"There he is," and "Lieutenant, did you set this fire?" rang out.

His new normal: life as a monster.

"Lieutenant! Are you trying to kill your wife and daughters?"

"Stay back," the captain thundered at them, waving his hands like an agitated referee. "Stay on the other side of the street!" The fire was mostly out, and light gray smoke poured from the windows. Inside the living room, the paneling would be charred, and rivulets of streaming water probably rained onto the matching armchairs Eve had recently recovered. Had the crew found her yet?

"Why aren't you in there helping?" a particularly aggressive man shouted, echoing Trick's thoughts. Trick gritted his teeth but didn't turn. "What are you trying to cover up, lieutenant?"

A firefighter burst from the house, a body in his arms. Trick raced forward, heart in his throat. He'd been with Eve when she'd bought that white-and-yellow striped shirt. "It's my wife," he rasped.

"Stay back, lieutenant," the captain warned again as the firefighter laid Eve on the stretcher, and the para-medics went to work. Trick stepped away and gulped the smoky air as her stats were shared. She was barely alive. One tech inserted a nasal cannula; the other prepped an IV epinephrine infusion.

Eve's entire right side up to her neck was blackened flesh, and burned fabric adhered in places to her skin. A swollen knot marred the left side of her forehead, which the paramedics made note of, too.

After carefully slicing open her t-shirt, the EMT stuck AED pads to her chest. The men worked quietly and effi-ciently as Trick paid humbled witness to their heroic attempts to save her life.

"Fire was deliberate," a firefighter muttered from

behind. Without taking his eyes from Eve, Trick strained to listen. "The sofa cushions were all piled together like a bonfire. The rest of the living room looked like it had been tossed beforehand."

"Yeah," another firefighter said. "Completely ransacked."

Chills coated Trick's arms at the word he'd used less than half an hour ago. *Ransacked* meant a prolonged visitor with time on his hands. A place got tossed when someone searched for something. *For what?* They had nothing of value. Had the perp already been inside while Eve waved goodbye to Amy and Tina, or had he slipped in later? Why try to kill her?

Her left index finger twitched. Trick inhaled sharply and stepped closer. "Eve?" he said softly, capturing the attention of the crew around him. Silence fell even from the media across the street. "Eve?"

Her left eye opened a slit, dull with pain, and focused on his face. Slowly, the corner of her mouth lifted. His heart stalled. In any other circumstances, he'd have interpreted it as an attempt to smile, sure it wasn't a grimace. But if he'd learned anything these last two weeks, it was to distrust his perception of reality. Especially with her orchestrating his reality. She hated him, and she was in horrific pain. There was no reason to smile. Unless... Unless *she* set the fire.

His mind recoiled immediately. He had to be wrong.

"Lieutenant," the paramedic said gently, "we need you to step back."

"Eve, did you..." The rest of the sentence died on Trick's lips. The question was too insane. He had to be misinterpreting. Look at the knot on her forehead! She wouldn't have knocked herself out.

She released a sigh, and her eye drifted shut. Her muscles slackened. "We need to transport now." This time the paramedic's directive was sterner, and Trick stumbled back. The stretcher rolled past, wheel indentations flattening the dewy grass. If she died... What? Opposing words and emotions swirled and clogged his stunned brain. *If she dies...what?*

"Lieutenant," that same aggressive reporter called, "who gets the millions if your wife dies?"

CHAPTER TWO

Two Weeks Earlier

"There's another lone wolf out there," one of the crew muttered as Engine 126 rocked to a halt at the curb. "Or else they arrested the wrong guy yesterday."

Trick secured his helmet, surveying the flames engulfing the west flank of a two-story warehouse. Pitch black smoke billowed from the structure, choking the Friday afternoon rush-hour traffic for miles. The darker the smoke, the more toxic the contents inside. Could be they'd luck out and this place stored ingredients for fertilizer. Or the other side of the coin: the dense smoke meant homemade explosives, like nitrourea.

Either way, this fire was too big for the first due. Truck 49 with Captain Lewis and the rest of the crew would arrive in minutes, and Cap would take scene command, but for now, Trick was the first-in officer. He'd better get his head in the game. "Lead with the deck gun," he hollered, climbing out behind his men. "Attack from the corner of D side. Backup can take A."

"Witness at two o'clock." Pete Dobson jogged toward a heavyset man with a receding hairline who was waving his White Sox cap. A couple of cops ushered phone-wielding bystanders behind yellow barriers as sirens screamed in the distance.

Trick snatched the CFD walkie-talkie from his utility belt as he strode toward the inferno for a three-sixty take on the building. "On scene, Cap. This is a two-eleven. We'll need more apparatus, for sure a rescue truck. Fire's compromised D side, smoke is black and turbulent, marginal conditions at this point, could be too volatile for an offensive strategy."

"Copy. I'll call for a second alarm. Assess and report."

Trick hopped over the snaking hose and cut left to B side, his steps heavy and sluggish. Not from the jostling weight of his gear in the late May heat. Or even from nearing the end of a grueling seventy-two-hour shift instead of the usual twenty-four. It was because during this extended shift the only peep out of Eve had been a few cryptic posts to her social media pages.

When Trick did something wrong, he heard about it —loudly and in excruciating detail. The one time he'd forgotten their anniversary, she'd stopped speaking to him for a day. A *day*. Not three, like this time. Meaning he'd messed up huge. And every call he made that went unanswered ate up another chunk of his stomach lining.

"Witness said he heard an explosion," Pete said through the voice-activated telecommunication system, "followed by a male screaming inside the warehouse."

A victim in this inferno? "Copy." Trick buried his marital woes back into the compartmentalized vault. "Do we know what it housed?"

"He thinks it's imported artifacts."

"Roger." *Shit*. Yesterday, a bomb inside an artifact-filled warehouse had taken the lives of four FBI agents, including his brother Jace's best friend. But they'd caught that lone wolf, so who was behind this?

Cap barked in his ear, "On scene, over."

Trick bullet-pointed his assessment, confirming the change of attack to search-and-rescue, then headed around back. Heavy smoke spiraled out of an open steel door. "C-side entrance is open. Entering structure to search for the vic."

Cap acknowledged, followed by Pete: "Got your six, Lieu, over."

Trick adjusted his air pack just as Pete jogged up from behind and planted a palm on his shoulder.

They crouched and duckwalked into an inferno blasting heat upward of seven hundred degrees. Attacking a smoke-filled structure was as insulating as being blind. Trick paused and took stock, his breathing Darth Vader–loud above the snap, crackle, and roar around him. The firestorm was straight from the mouth of hell. Flames boiled up the drywall on the left and danced low across the ceiling. Embers of skeletal crates glowed in the blaze.

A thunderous pop sounded, like a blown transformer, and the men instinctively hunkered in place. A row of interior shelves collapsed, showering sparks and streams of fire with the precision of a flamethrower. Had they not ducked, they'd be dead. Divine intervention, instinct, luck—Trick never questioned it, but there was nothing like battling a fire to kick-start a screaming will to live. Pete's cursing through the comm came across loud and clear.

Adrenalized and determined, Trick rose, activating his thermal-imaging camera. He slowly scanned the blaze for the vic. "I feel him." One cosmic soul blindly reaching through the universe for another. *Where are you?* He stepped forward, Pete's gloved hand still clamped to his shoulder. Trick took in slow, deep breaths. The cool air from the SCBA and even the sci-fi sound effect steadied his nerves. He swept the TIC in another slow arc. Red, yellow, and orange hotspots lit the screen, but it was blowback from the pulsing heat; no shape of a body. They crept forward. The certainty that always preceded Trick finding a victim grew stronger. "He's close."

"You got this, bro," Pete muttered.

Trick ignored the reassurance. The second you started believing your own hype was the second you grew arrogant, careless—and ended up dead. Period. Fires were living beasts that commanded respect. A track record for prior lives saved was for shit when this blaze held a human hostage.

Another Darth Vader breath, a few more hunkered steps into the furnace. Trick strained to hear a cough or call for help, as remote as it might be over the roar. The infrared screen showed squat. A sonic boom reverberated, and they spun right like choreographed partners. An enormous crate at the back had exploded, raining flames and debris in all directions. The fire-ground conditions were declining rapidly, turning the operation into a defensive strategy. They'd have to pull out. *Just a few more seconds...* Trick stepped right, studying the TIC while projecting his *Ajna*, the sixth chakra or source of intuition, to turn him in the right direction. *Where are you?*

A deafening crack from somewhere close. "Eleven o'clock," Pete yelled, yanking Trick backward. A load-bearing beam mere feet away split, shooting flames to the ceiling. They were out of time. "Come on, Lieu. It's coming down."

The next instant, the twenty-foot beam pitched slowly, defying gravity and time as it groaned and timbered in a blazing fall. The ground shuddered on impact, and a surge of heat blasted them back a few steps. The impact broke the beam into three bouncing, rolling sections, and a trio of glowing readouts blitzed Trick's screen.

"The roof's gonna cave," Pete said. "Let's pull back."

"Not yet." Trick arced the TIC around the raging warehouse again. Nothing. They were out of time—the structural integrity was declining too fast. Chunks of roof began disintegrating feet away. Streams from firehoses were visible now, attacking from the left.

Trick gave his Ajna free rein. The vic was in here—a scream had been heard. *Go with your gut.* The TIC hovered as Trick concentrated on the man's spirit. Within seconds, Trick's hand jerked right, as inexplicably as a Ouija board. A distinct glow emanated on the screen where no flames were.

"There!" The body lay curled near where the beam had just stood. Trick sent up a quick prayer of thanks. Had that post not fallen, they'd have never found him. *Be alive.* He surged forward, clipping the TIC to his utility belt.

"The roof's going," Pete warned, his voice tinged with panic.

"We have time." Trick willed whatever universal power was out there to give him that time.

Pete reported the find into his headset as they serpentined through the bonfire. Trick crouched in front of the vic, gripping the unconscious man's upper torso and sitting him upright with bent knees. Pete folded the vic across Trick's shoulders, and helped him stand.

"Go, go, go!" Pete called as they navigated flames and falling rubble toward the back door, where blessed daylight shone like a dull beacon. "Thank you, hocus-pocus."

They charged out into the considerably cooler

temperature and jogged around front, where EMS stood locked and loaded on the sidewalk. As soon as Trick lowered the vic onto the stretcher, the techs slapped an oxygen mask over the man's gray face. Flecks of ash covered his forest-green jumpsuit, which was being sliced open. *Buddy* was stitched on a patch above the left front pocket. Aside from burns to the backs of his hands and singed hair, his body seemed unharmed. It was a freaking miracle.

Screaming sirens and the roar of three more engines, two trucks, and a rescue truck sounded down the block as the second due arrived. The sirens died as teams of firefighters jumped out and went into fluid action, tugging hose off truck beds and laying lines.

Trick yanked up his face shield, sweat streaming from his temple to his neck. His clothes were soaked under the heavy gear. His pulse thundered from the rescue, and adrenalin ignited every cell. The previous exhaustion was a memory.

Beyond the police barricades, two black Suburbans, dash lights flashing, screeched to a halt. Had to be FBI. *Please don't let it be Jace.*

"Pulse ninety, BP one-forty over ninety. Looks like he'll live," one of the techs called out.

"Let's get him into the ambulance."

Trick closed his eyes and lifted his face to the hot, smoky sky and the universe beyond. *Good going, Buddy.* Another life saved, another fire on its way to being extinguished. Trick allowed himself a small grin, his soul nourished and brimming with gratitude. Each time a victim made it out alive was proof that desire manifested reality. What a perfect life.

"Lieutenant," a reporter shouted from behind the barricade. "Hey, Lieutenant Quinn! Did you save another one?"

As busy as Cap was directing the second due, he paused to glare at Trick like that question was his fault.

Trick ignored the cameras. Someone on his crew had outed his sixteen-year save record a few months back, and now the local media hounded Engine 126 calls to see if the "Quinn Phenomenon" still stood.

"Lieutenant," another reporter called, "is this the work of terrorists?"

"Lieutenant, do you know where your wife is?"

Trick spun toward the last voice, frowning. A familiar woman with short black curls leaned over the barricade, microphone to her lips. Why would a reporter even know who his wife was? Why would she ask *where* Eve was? She was home, like always. Angry, sure, but home.

He swiped a gloved hand over his perspiring face and stepped off the curb. It was worth breaking from the action to get answers.

"Lieutenant," Cap shouted, beckoning him with an impatient wave. Trick huffed out a frustrated exhale and changed direction. He jogged by the vic being hoisted into the back of the ambulance. Buddy's face now had color under the oxygen mask.

"Good work in there," Cap said without taking his eyes off the full-scale battle. He paused and barked further orders into his headset, then turned the full weight of his attention on Trick. "I've told you before not to engage with the media. Especially not in the middle of an active structural fire."

"Sorry, Cap." *Do you know where your wife is?* What the fuck?

"Go help Danny. That probie's going to be the death of me."

"Yes, sir." Trick spun away, almost colliding with his older brother. *Crap.* "Jace."

"Trick." The tone was dismissive as Jace nodded to

Captain Lewis, flipped open his oversized wallet, and flashed his shiny gold badge. "Jason Quinn, FBI, sir. I understand there's a witness to the explosion?"

Cap glanced at Trick, who pointed out the White Sox man being interviewed by a cop. "Said he heard the explosion and a scream," Trick said. "We got the vic out." He jerked a thumb at the paramedics slamming the doors of the ambulance.

"Oh, good," Jace murmured, brushing by Trick. "You're still the angel of life, then?"

A firefighter from the 65th walked up, and although Cap turned to greet him, based on his tightening jaw, he'd caught Jace's remark. Captain Lewis despised strife —didn't matter if he witnessed it between blood relatives or among his crew; it triggered his rare temper. Problem was for the five Quinn brothers—especially the first four, each born a year apart—rivalry was a way of life. And as eldest, Jace had always elevated that fraternal competition to a blood sport.

Angel of life. Trick wiped his mouth, swallowing the half-dozen caustic replies. Jace was so not worth turning this grateful energy into something negative. A deep breath reconnected his chi to the high-frequency magic of the universe, where miracles like Buddy surviving the explosion happened. Where Trick manifested love for everyone, even Jace. He walked backward, calling out amiably, "Have a good one. See you at Mom's birthday party tomorrow."

Jace pivoted. "It's been canceled."

Trick paused, frowning. The backyard barbecue for fifty of their friends and family had been planned for months. He closed the distance so they weren't shouting. "Why? What happened?"

Jace's expression turned scornful. "The lone wolf bombings? Agents dying yesterday?"

"Thanks for the news flash. Most first responders have pulled back-to-backs helping the Bureau search the city."

"There's no way it's appropriate for Mom to hold this mega party." Jace shrugged. "I told her to reschedule it in a week or two."

"You *told* her?" Trick shook his head and gazed off in the distance. Why was this even remotely surprising? All the positive vibes morphed into exasperation. "What did Pop say?"

"He wasn't on the call. I'm sure he'd have agreed with me, though."

Trick tapped his helmet on his thigh. "Well, Jace, it's her sixtieth birthday tomorrow. There's no reason her *family* can't take her out to dinner or something. I'm sure the Bureau will let you off for a couple of hours."

"But I already canceled Sean."

As if canceling their youngest brother sealed the deal. Too fucking much. "So call him back. Make a restaurant reservation. Then call Mom and Pop."

The aggravated suggestions hit their mark, and Jace scowled. "How about you pull some of the load?"

"You made the mess, bro, you fix it. I'll bring Eve and the girls by Mom and Pop's tomorrow, and we'll drive them to the restaurant. Just tell me the time and place." Trick turned away before his brother could get in the last word and rejoined his crew, taking the mentoring time to call out instructions to Danny on the angle of attack or pointing out the smoke's changing color and viscosity.

Less than an hour later, the fire was out. Trick trudged toward the crew milling by the engine. "Job well done," he said. "The faster we pack up, the longer we'll have to stop for groceries before the AAR."

"And meditation," Danny said.

The guys snickered, and Russ muttered, "Yeah, fill up Danny's chi, Lieutenant Yogi."

Pete clapped Danny on the shoulder, which he shrugged off red-faced. Trick stifled his grin. As much as the guys pooh-poohed Trick's implementation of group meditation following an After Action Review—and still goofed on Danny for voicing his enjoyment—the entire squad secretly looked forward to calming the adrenalin and refocusing their mindfulness after an active fire.

"Yep," Trick said. "We'll kick ass with an epic meditation. Hop to it."

His team scrambled to their individual tasks, and Trick helped Danny haul and refold the supply line, immersing himself in the physicality and redundancy of the task. This two-alarmer clearly resembled the recent lone-wolf warehouse fire. Which meant that despite public reassurances and massive citywide searches, the FBI had not found and defused all the bombs. How many more hidden explosives were still out there? How many more innocent citizens would be injured or killed before this was all finally over?

He paused and looked around for Jace, but the SUVs were gone. Most of the media were too, although the dark-haired reporter still stared at him like she held the world's biggest secret. "Finish up here, Dan," Trick said impulsively. "I'll be right back."

He strode across the street, raking back his sweaty hair with a quick swipe. The closer he got, the more the reporter came to attention, nudging the cameraman, grabbing her mic off the floorboard of the open van, and facing Trick with professional poise. If it wasn't for what she could tell him, he'd never engage. He'd seen too many butcher jobs done on his fellow firefighters from media looking for a sound bite. He pasted on a congenial grin and greeted her with an easygoing "Hot day to stand this close to a fire."

She didn't bat an eye. "Traci Tedesco, Channel Thirty News. Is this the work of terrorists?"

He glanced back at the destruction. "Too soon to tell."

"Will the victim live?"

"The hospital can give you that information." He gently batted her microphone down and asked in a quiet voice, "Why did you ask about my wife?"

"Because you're a local celebrity. Why wouldn't Chicago want the scoop on why your wife was at court this morning?"

Trick frowned. *Court?* "It was nothing," he said quickly. "Paying a parking ticket."

Secret knowledge flared in Traci's eyes as she swung the microphone back to her mouth. "Why was your wife exiting the Cook County *Family* Court this morning, Lieutenant Quinn?" Her tone held a singsong, baiting quality.

Family court? His pulse spiked like when the beam had timbered. What the hell was going on?

"Lieu!" one of his men called.

"You're mistaken," Trick said affably into the mic, plastering on an easy grin. "No news here. If you'll excuse me, I need to return to my crew."

"Of course," she said sweetly, then glanced at her cameraman and drew a line across her throat. The second he lowered the camera, her smile slipped. "You realize, lieutenant, that court records are accessible to the public."

"There's no story here," Trick repeated. He strode back to his crew as if wading through hip-deep mud. His synapses were misfiring, his muscle coordination not assimilating with his goal of putting one foot in front of the other. *What the hell?* It had to be exhaustion from the multiple overtime, because the reporter's insinuations were laughable.

Sure, Eve got mad a lot, and yeah, their last interaction had been pretty brutal, which had to be why she'd been radio silent every time he'd called or texted. Overall, though, they were the perfect couple. Everyone said so. *She* said so. This was just a colossal misunderstanding.

CHAPTER THREE

The goodbyes on the other side of the two-way mirror were stoic and subdued. Not surprising, since the entire supervised hour had been steeped in misery. Zamira Bey slipped out of the observation room and met Mrs. Mulroney and her three kids as their playroom door opened.

"That went well," Zamira said, channeling genuine warmth and compassion into her smile. Only the youngest, seven-year-old Bobby, seemed receptive to the positive emotions and grinned back.

"When will we see you again?" the middle child, Heather, asked her mom. Guilt shadowed Mrs. Mulroney's face. Before she could hang herself with a caustic retort, Zamira sent out more vibes. *Let your love pour out. Show your kids how much you need them.*

"I don't know, dear." Mrs. Mulroney managed a thin smile. "As soon as possible."

The oldest, twelve-year-old Karen, rolled her eyes. "That's grownup talk for weeks." She marched down the hall without a backward glance.

Zamira grabbed Bobby's hand and motioned for the others to follow. At the juncture between the two designated exits, the group—minus Karen—clustered once more.

"I'll be in touch to schedule your next visit," Zamira said to the emaciated Mrs. Mulroney, whose flickering emotions hovered between resignation and irritability. "You did great today."

"Bye, Mama," Bobby said in an overly loud voice. His mother winced. The wince of a recovering addict barely hanging on. Again, Zamira mentally urged the woman to respond kindly. Two weeks ago, the initial supervised visit had to be discontinued due to anger and tears on both sides. No amount of positive energy from Zamira had diluted that outpouring of negativity.

"Bye, baby." Mrs. Mulroney's tone was filled with remorse, but love shone in her eyes as she kissed both children. "Give Karen a kiss for me."

Zamira led the two kids toward the south exit, where Karen stood with their father, who glared at his watch. They weren't late. Punctuality wasn't just a virtue for Zamira, it was a neurosis. Matter of fact, the session would conclude two minutes early, since the goodbyes hadn't required the factored-in time. She maintained her walking-with-children stride and streamed compassion toward Mr. Mulroney and his sullen daughter.

As they passed by her boss's open door, Andy called out, "Zamira, please see me when you're through."

She nodded and finished transferring the three kids back into their father's custodial care. Although Mr. Mulroney drilled her with questions and his suspicious nature never let up, she maintained a cheerful smile and answered with patience. Some custodial parents acquired the herculean compassion to support court orders that benefited their kids. Others, like Mr. Mulroney, found appointments at a supervision center a punishment and wanted any evidence it wasn't working so their lawyers could pull the plug.

Zamira waited on the top step of the parking lot until his Lexus departed. She inhaled the fresh spring air. Life was about perceiving and acknowledging *this* precious moment, *Insha'Allah*. In this instance, the beauty of her surroundings. The dappling play of sun and shadows across the windows of the postwar industrial building. How the three pink tulips blooming in the cracked flowerpot were an inch taller today. And how the gently swaying branches of the oak across the street looked like they were waving at her. Zamira would've waved back except for the cluster of kids playing basketball nearby. It was one thing to honor Allah by creating a life of joy and helping others, and another to come off as crazy.

She raised her face to bask in the warm sunshine and sighed her thanks for such a lovely afternoon. A minute later, she knocked on Andy's open door. He motioned to the chair across the desk. "I had a call from Nate Henderson's lawyer."

Zamira interlocked her fingers tightly in her lap. Mr. Henderson was another parent who couldn't see past his own pain to help his children through the familial crisis. She'd had to call security yesterday to escort him out his designated entrance instead of following her and his kids out the south exit, where his wife waited. The Henderson case was still relatively new; he just needed time to adjust. "Yes?"

Andy took off his glasses and immediately squinted. That wasn't a good sign. He only voluntarily blinded himself when he had bad news to impart. "He wants a different supervisor."

"I'm not surprised," Zamira said. "But I don't think it's necessary. I followed company policy to the letter, and no one got hurt. Except perhaps his ego."

"It wasn't the escort back to his car he took issue with." His squint focused on her teal *hijab*, a soft, lightweight jersey cotton with beaded trim. It was new; the beauty of it had enhanced her inner joy all day. Wait, he was still looking at it... Had strands of hair escaped? She fingered her temple before the regret in his expression burrowed into her consciousness. *Oh.* Her heart sank.

He waved the hand that held his spectacles. "The whole bombing situation and those poor FBI men dying. And there was just a news alert about another warehouse explosion in South Shore. I know that terrorist has nothing to do with you, but...you know how some people are."

Making sure not one muscle on her face twitched, Zamira nodded. "Our community is expecting a backlash, even though we're Sunnis from Egypt. Different country, different sect than the bomber. In Christian terms, it's about as crazy as American Mormons being blamed for Irish IRA bombings." She lowered her head at her sharp tone. Anger never solved anything. Henderson's Islamophobia wasn't Andy's fault, nor his problem. "I'm sorry it's interfering with my work." *And my social life. And my courage to walk anywhere alone anymore.*

She breathed in slowly. To stop this swelling frustration at Henderson's small-mindedness, she had to view it from another angle. Like pity for his small-mindedness? Compassion for his children's hard road toward healing? Relief she wouldn't have any more run-ins with such a mean spirit? Gratitude that her overburdened schedule had just lessened by one? *See? Many angles.* Anger at his bigotry was wasted energy, and this disclosure was not going to deplete hers. "A couple more

Hendersons and I can cut out the overtime," she joked softly.

Andy's shoulders lowered. "Thank you for understanding. You're the most positive, forgiving person I've ever met." He plucked a bright yellow file from his full inbox. "But no, there's no rest for the weary. This just came in. I was going to assign it to Ann, but I have a feeling she'll be the one who gets Henderson."

Zamira reached for the folder. Before she could open it, Andy continued, "Mother obtained court-ordered supervision today on charges that the father is sexually abusing the six- and eight-year-old daughters."

Zamira's heart clenched. "Andy—"

"I shield you as much as I can when it comes to assigning these, Zamira, but everyone's overloaded. You're losing Henderson, and this just came in."

The positivity she'd worked so hard to cocoon herself in evaporated. On instinct, she sent up prayers, beseeching Allah to intercede. Of all the horrific abuses suffered by children, incest was the most heinous. She despised these cases and loathed the offending parent. After six years in this profession, it still took all her training to supervise the predator, write unbiased observation reports, or testify without prejudice in court.

Zamira dug the nails of her free hand into her palm. Losing Henderson was not the ray of sunshine she'd believed. It was the gates of *Jahannam* cracking open.

Two questions left on the After Action Report before Trick could wrap this up. The guys had to be exhausted with the bomb-related back-to-backs, whereas every cell in his body vibrated with impatience. His thoughts scurried from the reporter's family court revelation to searching his memory for anything he could have done to piss Eve off, to the two more calls that had landed in Eve's voicemail. It wasn't like her to avoid confrontation. *Enough!* In Buddhism, this scattered inability to focus was called Monkey Mind, and boy, these monkeys were panicked. Fourteen more hours until his shift was over and he could go home and finally face this. Trick cleared his throat and summoned his laidback side. "Any thoughts on how communication went during the call?"

Danny raised his hand. "Yeah, uh, my headset didn't work properly. I couldn't hear Sam's directive."

"Maybe clean the wax out of your ears," Sam retorted, and the crew broke into jovial laughter, once again at Danny's expense.

Trick waved the clipboard. It was easy to get off task or keep things light, but AARs were designed to build trust, develop skills, and root out potentially critical issues like this—whether it was equipment failure or more headset-intercom training was required. "Sam, after meditation, switch headsets with Danny and verify any malfunction." Right on cue, Sam scowled, which Trick ignored. Their communication devices were four years old. To the taxpaying public, that probably sounded new, but not in terms of the beating these things took on scene, or compared to the newer technology that far surpassed these workhorses and would alleviate a lot of this engine company's headset/intercom complaints.

"Last item," Trick said. The crew straightened in their chairs, anxious to move on with their day. "What's one thing you learned today?"

"That Lieu is still one lucky sonuvabitch," Russ said. "Way to keep the record alive." Amid the laughter, he fist-bumped Santiago to his left.

"Yo." Trick tapped the clipboard on his thigh. "Looking for something deep so we can wrap this up."

The chuckling subsided, and the men glanced around at any inanimate object. Drawing out emotions from battle-worn firefighters was always a challenge, but the stats on substance abuse, mental burnout, and destroyed marriages significantly decreased when stations implemented this military exercise. Trick loved these men and this life; he'd do anything to protect both. Sure, talking about feelings made him a nerd, the Lieutenant Yogi, but so what? He was all over maintaining the healthiest brotherhood in Chicago. "Santiago?" Trick turned to the quietest member of the squad. "Any takeaways?"

The young man hunched his shoulders, his gaze fixed on the linoleum. After a silence that was fast becoming awkward, he said, "That we should relook at multiple back-to-backs like this. I'm so tired I'm a risk to my team, man." Others nodded solemnly. "I mean, I know these bombings were unprecedented, but maybe have the governor call in the National Guard or something. We're being spread too thin."

Mutters of agreement. Trick noted and starred the comment. "Thanks for the honest insight. Anyone else?" When no one responded, he shoved his chair back. "Okay. A quick meditation, 'cause I don't want any of you falling asleep"—someone coughed Santiago's name, and the group broke into laughter again—"and then chow."

He followed the men toward the rec room, where sofa and chair cushions would be used to pad the floor. Cap poked his head out of his office. "Lieutenant Quinn?"

Trick swiveled in surprise. Cap was rarely formal inside the house. Behind him stood a police officer with an official expression. Trick's adrenalin shot to red-alert range. Had something happened to Eve? "Yes, sir?" He gestured at Pete to start the session and headed toward the office.

As Captain Lewis stepped back to let him pass, the

officer held up an envelope. "Are you Patrick Oliver Quinn?"

What the hell? "Yes." It came out like a question.

The officer handed over the envelope. "Mr. Quinn, you've been served."